THE BRONZE DOOR

THE CYRENIAN ✦ BOOK II

THE BRONZE DOOR

KARIN CIHOLAS

atmosphere press

"The tyrant is a child of Pride
Who drinks from his sickening cup
Recklessness and vanity,
Until from his high crest headlong
He plummets to the dust of hope."

— Sophocles, *Oedipus Rex*

"*The best revenge is to be unlike the person
who performed the injury.*"

—Marcus Aurelius, *Meditations*

✦

A GAME OF CHESS

BETWEEN MEETINGS, VALERIUS ENJOYED ESCAPING for a moment from the confines of the palace to wander through Ephesus. It was a thoroughly Greek city that favored beautiful architecture, revered the goddess Artemis, and rivaled Athens in encouraging philosophers to roam the streets. One of his favorite vistas was from a tiled terrace just below the governor's palace. He went there now to gaze out over the Aegean Sea.

When he felt something at his side, he looked down and saw a little girl touching his military cuirass. When he bent to see what she wanted, the child gasped and fell. Then she started to cry. He picked her up, wiped tears off her cheek, and tried to console her.

Just then, a young woman rushed up to him to apologize. "I am sorry my daughter bothered you." She turned to scold her child. "Why did you do that?"

"I thought he was a statue." The girl whimpered and held her arms out to her mother.

Valerius laughed and placed the frightened child into her mother's arms. "Your daughter is charming."

The woman suddenly realized who he was. Aghast, she stepped back, apologized again, and seemed as stricken as her daughter. She clutched her child tighter in her arms and hurried off the terrace steps.

Valerius watched the woman's progress down the street through the crowds as she headed through the Mazeus Gate to the agora, where she disappeared from view. It occurred to him that he had been standing there much like a statue. Stalwart, strong, stern, and useless. He smiled at his self-description.

Publius Petronius Valerius was loyal to the Roman cause and never wavered in his faithfulness to his duties as governor and proconsul of Asia, but he resented the constraints of bureaucracy; the fact that imperial ambitions often made little sense in the provinces far from Rome; that governance by force ultimately turned to rebellion or even war. The worst aspect of his job was that he worked for an emperor he resented and despised, an emperor who imagined usurpers in every corner and allowed unjust treason prosecutions to go forward without proof and proper trials.

Valerius's father died because of trumped-up charges that had no merit. Up in his opulent eagle's nest palace on Capri, Tiberius didn't seem to care. When Valerius rushed to Capri to protest his father's death, the emperor tested his resolve, reviewed his leadership in Gaul, and surprised him by offering him the governorship of Asia with senatorial status. Valerius knew it was an act of belated remorse. The imperial appointment had left a bitter taste in his mouth. He thanked the gods that he had escaped Tiberius's wrath and did not have to tangle with Caligula, who was famous for his tantrums. Caligula lived on Capri and doted on his great uncle Tiberius in the hope of being appointed his successor.

After a long afternoon of judicial hearings where two businessmen were fined for extortion and a slave boy named Farid was set free, Servius brought in a large table with a chess game set up with black marble pieces on one side and white ones on the other. Servius was his legate and trusted friend. They had known each other since their army days in Gaul. While Farid's shackles were cut off, Valerius asked the young boy if he had a place to stay. The boy stared at the chess table and remained silent. Valerius made the first move, and Servius placed a foot soldier out as well.

Valerius observed how Farid was working out the moves and countermoves in his head and remembered when he was that age and was equally absorbed by the games that fascinated him. For Valerius, it was wrestling. That time seemed far away now. And yet, it was not so long ago that he was a young boy going off to school and spending his afternoons with his best friend. Wrestling came first. But he and Simon also wrestled with ideas—deep discussions about government, justice, power, religion, war, and peace. It amused him to realize how many solutions he found then for all the problems of the world. He soon learned that youthful idealism was trampled by experience. Today he would hesitate to claim that he had any answers at all. Inevitably, his thoughts turned to Rachel, Simon's sister, the woman he had promised to love forever. That, too, had become a lesson learned. Nothing in life turns out the way we think it will.

A messenger knocked with some urgency and handed Valerius a note. After he read it, he frowned and pinched the dimpled bridge of his nose, a gesture his staff recognized that meant he was pensive, troubled, or tired. Servius guessed he was all three.

Servius Marcius Verus was not only his legate and chief officer and aide but was also a trusted friend and shared most of Valerius's views. Ten years older than Valerius, Servius's weathered face and bearing attested to years spent on horseback on battlefields far from Rome in service to the empire. Valerius liked the fact that he always claimed he served the empire, not the emperor.

Valerius crumpled the note and turned back to the chess table. The last thing on his mind was a chess game. Yet—valiantly—he played. He lost several foot soldiers, his queen, and a rhuk before he toppled his shah and gave up.

"Why?" Farid fell to his knees at the chess table and shook his head. "You still have enough foot soldiers to make it across the board to crown a vazir. The queen is the most powerful of all. You can win." Farid pointed toward the chess pieces and looked like he was about to set the shah upright again when Servius reached for his arm and pulled him back.

Valerius stopped him and turned to Farid. "Go ahead and play for me. If you win, I'll give you a treat."

The boy reached out his hand to set the shah upright, then stopped. "No, I need to know first what my reward will be."

Servius was about to scold the impudent boy, but Valerius intervened. "I see we have a young negotiator here. Maybe even a diplomat. How did you learn to play this old Persian game?"

"I watch the rich play. I made my own pieces out of wood. Sometimes there is a competition in the public square in Edessa."

"You are from Edessa? You speak the Parthian language?" The boy nodded.

"Well then. Win the game if you can, and I'll hire you to work with my translators."

Farid threatened with his horseman. Servius made a counterattack. In six more moves, Farid cried, "Shah Mat!"

Valerius acknowledged Farid's victory by congratulating him and summoned an orderly to take him to join the translators. When he noted Servius's raised brows, he said, "Unhappy about losing to a sixteen-year-old kid?"

"Do you trust him? Maybe you just added another spy to your staff."

Valerius shrugged. "Parthian spies are everywhere. True, some are right here at the palace. I don't agree with the military tactic of torture to ferret out the guilty. I think I know who most of them are. Sooner or later, they betray their allegiance. We'll find out about Farid soon enough. It's interesting that chess is an old Persian game. Somehow, I believe we have just embarked on a rather serious chess game with the King of Kings." Valerius answered the question in Servius's eyes by showing him the note.

The note said: 'Artabanus II, King of Kings of Parthia, declares war on Rome.'

✦

After sending messengers to Capri and to the Governor of Syria, Publius Petronius Valerius ordered a cohort of his best men to be armed and ready for a mission of peace.

The irony of arming almost five hundred men to keep peace caused him to grimace, and lately, the very thought of a military confrontation triggered staggering doubts about the ever-widening reach of the empire of which he was a part. Valerius worked hard to mediate conflicts, encourage trade, and legislate justice with a calm and steady hand. He considered himself a peacekeeper. But after six years of constant petty crimes and larger infractions against Rome, he felt tired and disillusioned about any prospects for peace. In a moment of bold recklessness, he wrote a letter to Tiberius and warned that the desire of Rome to conquer ever more territory would ultimately lead to weakness and endanger the grand vision of the *pax romana*. Roman peace! He knew it was a laughable oxymoron.

The Romans called the province that Valerius administered Asia because it meant land to the east in Greek. It had been the dream of Alexander the Great to extend his realm into India and beyond. Motivated by such lofty ambitions, the Roman Republic and later the Empire relentlessly moved eastward and swallowed up Bithynia, Galatia, Cappadocia, Cilicia, and Pontus and pushed the border of the Empire all the way to Armenia and Parthia.

After a long thirty-day trek over rugged mountains, through cold and barren plateaus, into dense forests and highlands, Valerius and his cohort pushed forward toward the Euphrates River. About a day's journey from the Euphrates, Valerius sent scouts south to check on the progress of Lucius Vitellius, the Governor of Syria, who was supposed to join him with his legions to help secure the border.

As they descended rocky hills along a stream, Valerius and his cohort of Roman soldiers suspected they might encounter incursions along their route or even isolated skirmishes, but they did not expect to emerge from sheltering woods to confront the Parthian army in full formation on the plains below. Valerius cursed the lack of competence of his scouts and sent word through his centurions that his troops should refrain from any action or movement that would indicate they were about to fight. Valerius realized that the Parthians had spotted and expected his cohort long before they reached the border. He had expected Vitellius to be here with his legions.

Even at a distance, Valerius could see cataphracts—fully armored horsemen—standing in even rows with their long swords at their sides. Behind them, Parthian archers held empty bows ready to arm. He feared the archers more than the swordsmen because they possessed unusual acrobatic prowess. Parthian archers could twist around and shoot backward with deadly precision as they galloped away from the enemy. Behind them, he noticed soldiers on smaller Anatolian horses who wielded Scythian scimitars. Valerius remembered his admonishment to the troops that very morning when he told them they should always expect the unexpected. He was the one who had been caught off guard.

When no spokesman came forward, Valerius signaled for the cohort to halt and guided his steed slowly toward the enemy until he could make out the features of the men in front. He was surprised that no satrap or general stepped forward to speak. He decided the least threatening gesture he could make would be to raise an open hand to the sky and call out that the Roman cohort came in peace. When Latin didn't seem to work, he tried Greek. No response.

At five horse lengths distance, Valerius stopped and held out both arms to show that his hands held no weapons. A pesky fly landed on his cheek, and Valerius refrained from swatting it away lest his gesture be misinterpreted. He tried to banish the fly by contracting his facial muscles, but the fly refused to leave.

A large Parthian directly in front of him stared at Valerius's cheek with a quirky twist on his lips that made him look like he might burst into laughter or yell for the slaughter of Romans to begin. After what seemed like a very long time, the fly neared Valerius's eye and he blinked furiously and finally smacked the fly away, missed his mark, and lowered his arm. The Parthian yelled an order Valerius didn't understand. Where were his translators when he needed them most? The faces of the threatening Parthians were unreadable. Their eyes remained focused on him. The insanely ludicrous thought occurred to him that he might die because of a fly.

When the middle phalanx of Parthian horsemen began to move forward, Valerius decided to remain in place to face the threat head-on. Three horsemen placed themselves to the left and three to the right of Valerius but did not encircle him as he feared. Instead, their unusual maneuver repeated itself down the line and opened a path in the middle to a seated beturbaned official who raised his arm. Valerius wasn't sure whether it was a signal to attack or a greeting and waited. The satrap made a gesture to approach. Behind the satrap stood two guards who looked like they were made of solid rock. Heavily bearded and naked above the belt, they were apparently unarmed.

Slowly, Valerius rode through the tunnel opened by the Parthian troops and tried to anticipate their intentions. He kept his eyes on the satrap and refused to show any sign of his fear while he made a quick calculation and decided that the Romans outnumbered the Parthians two to one. That fact made him wonder how many Parthian foot soldiers might be nearby. He knew his centurions would lead the charge if they saw the Parthians reach for their swords or raise their bows. His horse tensed beneath him, and he steeled himself.

He gazed down at the satrap and inclined his head slightly.

The satrap stood and spoke in heavily accented Greek. "The Queen awaits you at the fortress in Edessa at sunset. You must come alone and unarmed. Your troops can camp near the bend at the Daysan River." He pointed to the south.

Later, when Servius asked why Valerius let the Parthians dictate terms to Rome, he answered, "I'm trying to avoid a bloodbath. I'll go find out what the Queen wants."

"Alone? Unarmed? Have you lost your mind? They will kill you."

"In that case, you are in command, and I trust you to respond appropriately by moving your cohort west to meet up with our Syrian legions. Even though we outnumber the Parthians right now, they are fierce fighters, and it would not serve Rome to lose valuable men over border incursions. We are not at war. Yet. Even though Artabanus claims that we are."

Shortly before sunset, against the advice of his officers, Valerius mounted his horse and rode unarmed through the gate of Edessa.

✦

The Queen of Parthia, wife of Artabanus II, sat on an elaborate throne carved of pear wood and held out a beringed hand to be kissed. Valerius had learned that such obeisance cost him nothing and paved the way for diplomacy. Behind her piercing stare, he sensed a will of steel, a vicious determination to get what she wanted. He noted her intense scrutiny of his face, the kind of examination he would expect from an enemy who was about to gauge his weaknesses and strengths. He assumed she ruled when her husband was away. From her demeanor, he wondered if she ruled even when he was not away.

She made a statement he did not understand. It was greeted with applause and approving nods from her entourage, which was composed mostly of men in trousers with long, ornate tunics that fell to their knees.

Valerius brought greetings from the emperor and got straight to the point. "I am here to restore peace. Parthian invasions into Roman territory must stop immediately. You must remove your troops from Cappadocia, Cilicia, Pontus, and Syria. You must restore peace with Armenia. The killing, looting, and burning beyond your borders must stop. Your army has violated the peace treaty the King of Kings signed with Rome."

The Queen's stern expression did not change while she listened to the translations of what he said.

The Queen held up her hand to speak. "We do not want war." This time her words were translated. "We seek long-lasting peace with Rome that will link Parthia and Rome together in a much stronger bond than victory on the battlefield can provide." She gestured toward the satrap Valerius had met on the battlefield and gave an order Valerius didn't understand. The satrap came forward with a young girl at his side and placed her beside the Queen in front of Valerius.

Surprised and curious, Valerius waited for the Queen to explain. The Queen clasped the girl's hand and said, "This is my daughter Musalina. The King of Kings is her father. We give her to you as your bride to seal the peace between Parthia and Rome." She smiled then. It was not a smile of friendship, but of triumph.

Valerius gazed into the eyes of the young girl the satrap proudly presented to him and realized she was troubled, perhaps almost as troubled as he was. He had no idea how to react to this shocking gift he did not want. If she was truly the daughter of King Artabanus, then the Parthians were suspiciously eager to placate Rome. He looked from the daughter to the mother and tried to determine what had motivated such an unexpected proposal.

The satrap spoke pompously. "The great Queen of Parthia and the King of Kings welcome you into their illustrious family. The daughter of our King will be your bride, and your marriage will ensure lasting friendship with Rome." He gestured for Valerius to take the bride's hand.

Valerius knew that even touching the girl's hand could be interpreted as a symbolic act of commitment. What protocol would be demanded of him that would not insult all the Parthians and create another cause for war? He had walked right into a trap and hardly heard what the satrap was saying. This proposal was probably just as awkward for the girl, yet she had surely been told what to expect and had likely been reared with this kind of political marriage in mind. He glanced at the girl and sensed anguish in her bearing as she stared down at her feet. She was covered from head to toe by a brightly colored chador and wore a veil that fluttered with her breath and only revealed her averted eyes.

Valerius said, "You will have to make any such proposal to the emperor."

The Queen glared at him and lifted her shoulders in a gesture that conveyed the message that she was in charge and not he. She apparently was not backing down from her proposition. She insisted that the proper message and formalities had been sent to Tiberius. To prove the allurement of her side of the bargain, she yanked off the veil that hid her daughter's face and caused the chador to slip from her shoulders, revealing a slender girl who was probably not yet fifteen. Valerius felt sorry for her. He thought if he could speak to her alone, he could explain the impossibility of such a treaty and smooth ruffled feathers, but he doubted he could do the same with her mother.

The girl was trying to retrieve her robe to cover herself up again. Her black hair fell in long braids to her waist, the ends curling upward, clasped in gold. He thought he could detect a trace of tears along one dimpled cheek, and there was no indication of a smile on her reddened lips. A wide silver belt cinched a narrow waist, and heavy jewelry circled her neck. Just as she was pushed toward him, he caught a glimpse of her eyes. Shy, beautiful eyes. A lustrous and vivid blue like sapphires. He sensed her fear but there was curiosity there too.

Valerius did not need to ask if she was a willing participant in this deal. He would have to insist on a delay, and that alone would trigger a negative reaction and could be interpreted as insulting. He knew he would have to find a way out of this dilemma without aggravating the hostilities he had come to stop. In a firm and commanding voice, he said, "We cannot go forward without the emperor's response. In the meantime, your troops must stop all incursions on Roman territory. My cohort will guard the border."

This statement was met with a flurry of translations back and forth and didn't go over well. But oddly enough, the Queen seemed to take his response as an acceptance and issued the order for wedding preparations to begin. Stunned, Valerius wondered what had been lost in translation.

That evening, Valerius ordered Farid to wander among the Parthian soldiers and mingle with the people of Edessa to discover any news. Servius thought Farid would be an unreliable spy.

Valerius shrugged. "What can he reveal about us that they don't already know? And what might he discover of interest? This marriage proposal strikes me as strange. Where is Artabanus? Where is the rest of his army? Where are his foot soldiers? I fear this wedding is a diversion to keep us in Edessa while he creates havoc elsewhere. I suspect Artabanus is out to conquer Armenia again."

✦

The very next day, two scouts returned with news that Roman legions had been seen near Samosata. There was no news about Artabanus. After conferring with his guides and cartographers, Valerius realized that the shortest route for the Syrian legions from Antioch to Armenia led east to Aleppo and then north along the Euphrates. He guessed the Syrian legions would probably ford the river near Samosata and then make their way through less mountainous territory toward the walled city of Artaxata, the capital of Armenia.

After meeting with his tribunes, centurions, and the head of his cavalry squadron, Valerius sent orders for his troops to be ready for a quiet departure during the night and sent a messenger to the governor of Syria to report that he would join him close to the Armenian border. It took longer than expected to overcome the Parthian guards and drag them bound and gagged into the woods and get the camp ready for departure.

Before dawn, Valerius led his cohort out of Edessa toward the Euphrates River and then headed north along the river. When morning light filtered through the trees, they searched for evidence that Roman soldiers had traveled the same route. Two legions of more than twenty thousand troops could not march through the countryside without leaving traces of their presence behind. Valerius also had his scouts look for Parthian weapons—pieces of scimitars, arrowheads and shafts, hoofprints from smaller Anatolian horses, and fragments of mail armor from the cataphracts. There was no sign that either army had recently been on the same route. Valerius started to worry that Artabanus might not be heading toward Armenia at all.

Halfway through the day's march, a rider came charging up and threaded his way through to Valerius. It was Farid, out of breath and agitated.

"They're coming after you."

"How much of a lead do we have?"

"Not much."

Valerius sent scouts forward to discover suitable battle terrain and sites where the river could be forded and conferred with Servius and his top centurions. Servius and Valerius agreed that the cavalry squadron was more vulnerable to archer attacks than foot soldiers who carried shields for protection.

Valerius didn't like to break up the cohort but ordered the cavalry to ride ahead and ford the river so they could catch up with the Syrian legions. He asked Servius to lead the infantry, and Valerius would bring up the rear. Servius pleaded with him to join the cavalry and warned that, at the rear on horseback, he would be a sitting target.

Valerius addressed his troops. "When you hear my signal from the rear, set up the testudo formation—curved shields on the sides and front and straight shields in the middle overhead for full protection from the archers. They will likely send their archers first. The heavy armor of the cataphracts will slow them down, and we might not have to deal with them at all. Let's pick up our marching speed before nightfall."

The next day, thundering Parthian hooves approached the Roman cohort with an explosion of bloodcurdling cries. Valerius gave the signal for defense against the Parthian archers, who were already rushing toward them. The archers stopped abruptly, then released their arrows backward as they rode away. The clatter of arrows hitting the Roman shields made startling metallic pings punctuated by the sound of hoofbeats surging forward and retreating. After three rounds of archers, the next onslaught came from the cataphracts. Underneath the linked shields, the troops held firm and waited until the last moment to hold out their swords like spits to impale the charging horses. Horses and riders fell to create a tangled barrier for the riders behind them. More Parthian arrows bounced off the Roman shields. Then the Roman cohort lost several soldiers when Anatolian riders galloped upstream to reach their left flank with scimitars. After the initial shock, the Romans regrouped and held steady against thrusts with their shields and immediately jumped forward to wound with their broadswords. Men fell on both sides and turned the riverbank red.

When a foot soldier was shot in the back by an arrow that found its way through a gap in their defense, Valerius jumped from his horse to tend to him. Valerius was too preoccupied with the wounded soldier to realize that the next arrows might have bored into him had he not jumped down. He called for Lepidus, their only medic. Lepidus ordered two soldiers to carry the wounded to safety. The raucous, guttural yelling slowed down. Then the clatter of arrows against metal stopped altogether. After a while, the Parthians drove their horses back south, but their next charge was ineffectual. The clanging of swords and scimitars continued sporadically amid anguished cries of the wounded and terrible screams and groans from horses left behind to die.

As the sun set over the battlefield, there were isolated sword fights against scimitars. Then the clatter of retreating hooves faded into the distance, and the Romans took care of their wounded and made camp farther north. Valerius discovered a small scrape on his horse's neck and quietly tended to it. As night fell, he thought he heard activity in the Parthian camp and decided to hold vigil with two guards while his cohort slept.

At dawn, the Romans quietly armed themselves without stopping to eat and approached the battlefield to discover the Parthians were nowhere in sight. Valerius sent horsemen off with a cart of wounded to the closest Syrian village. After burying their dead, they picked up useful weapons left behind and stowed them in a camp cart. Camp followers arrived quickly, ready to loot fallen soldiers and carve up dead horses for meat. Valerius hated the blood and gore of battle, and the aftermath made his stomach churn. He ordered his troops to regroup upstream near fresh water.

When the cohort from Ephesus met up with the Syrian

legions near the border with Armenia, there was no time for celebration. Artabanus and his army had already invaded Armenia in a battle with the Roman-appointed king Mithridates and were preparing to place Artabanus's son on the Armenian throne. Mithridates had escaped to seek safety with the Roman legions. Lucius Vitellius, the Governor of Syria, ordered his legions to prepare for battle just as Valerius arrived to ask him to shock the Parthians into submission without fighting.

Mounted on his steed, Lucius Vitellius cut a striking figure in his gleaming armor and helmet, his features etched with the signs of a lifetime spent commanding Roman troops.

Valerius urged him not to charge into battle.

Vitellius raised his eyebrows, obviously stunned by the audacity of Valerius's request, and studied him with skepticism, impatience, and irritation.

Valerius looked Vitellius straight in the eye. "Even Julius Caesar preferred peace talks to battle."

"Do you know Artabanus?"

"No, Sir."

"This is not the first time I have had to rush to the border to stop Artabanus, who calls himself the King of Kings. He is amazingly stubborn. When he got his way two years ago and I allowed him to place his son Arsaces on the throne, peace didn't hold for a year. We had to make a firm treaty to place Mithridates on the throne and nullify Parthian claims to Armenia. And you think we can just scare Artabanus away? He won't budge."

"We could try." In his torn and bloody military outfit, Valerius knew he must look like a berserk novice who didn't have a clue about military protocol. Yet he persisted. "Once Artabanus sees our strength, it would be suicidal for him to proceed. No one wants to fight unnecessary wars. And I believe he will agree to peace terms."

Vitellius scowled. "I don't share your view."

"Let's push closer with our full manpower and force him

to see what he's up against. Your troops are behind the trees. Have them come up to the clearing."

"Son, I've been winning battles since before you were born."

Valerius wouldn't back down. "How many men does he have?"

"My scout says eight thousand. Give or take a few hundred."

"And we have two legions and my cohort. We outman them three to one. And we haven't counted the Armenian troops with Mithridates nearby."

"My point exactly." Vitellius gave him a lopsided smile. "I'm glad you finally see that we will have a decisive victory."

"I'm not the one who must see that. Artabanus must. Ask your troops to come forward. Have your Syrian standard bearers march by in formation in front. And I will order my cavalry to show off their captured Parthian weapons."

"How many battles have you won?"

"I've just come from a battle I won against Parthian cataphracts and archers. I found it a waste of good blood on both sides. They attacked first. I had no choice. Here we have a choice."

Vitellius frowned and gazed over at his legate. He turned back to Valerius. His eyes narrowed. He looked grim. "We will proceed as the Governor of Asia suggests, leaving all options open." He nodded to his legate. "Order a big show of power with trumpets and be ready to send a messenger to Artabanus."

✦

In a luxurious tent flanked by Roman centurions holding the standards of Syria, two Roman governors met with the King of Kings over a finely prepared meal and expensive wine from Colchis. Vitellius had his legate check Artabanus for arms and remove a small dagger from his boot. Vitellius summoned his team of translators. Valerius chose Farid who had been nosing around the troops on both sides since an immediate confrontation had been called off. Valerius soon understood what Vitellius meant about Artabanus's intransigence because Artabanus balked at the terms Vitellius proposed that were reasonable and far from harsh.

In clear and precise language, Vitellius presented his requirements for peace: Artabanus must concede the throne of Armenia back to Mithridates, must sign a new peace treaty with Rome, must make obeisance to the standards of the Syrian legions, and must vacate the city and cross back into Parthia with his troops by nightfall the next day. Furthermore, the Parthians must stop all incursions on Pontus, Cappadocia, Syria, and Cilicia.

Artabanus refused and demanded safe conduct back to the fortified city of Artaxata.

Valerius suggested it might be wise to include Mithridates in the discussions. Vitellius raised a skeptical eyebrow but called for Mithridates to appear before them. At the entrance to the tent, Mithridates was thoroughly searched and let in. As soon as they saw each other, the two kings glared at each other like two roosters prepared to peck each other bloody.

It was suddenly clear to Valerius that the enmity between Armenia and Parthia had little to do with Rome. He decided there must be something deeper and more vicious between them.

Vitellius demanded that they talk to each other, and Artabanus let loose a torrent of Parthian. In turn, Mithridates did much the same thing, addressing his invectives to Vitellius.

Vitellius turned to his translators who shrugged.

Valerius turned to Farid, who said, "The two kings have reached a stalemate. Both kings are in a corner, and neither can move."

Artabanus sneered at Mithridates and spoke in Greek. "I refuse to talk to *him*." He jabbed his finger in Mithridates's direction. Then he got up and demanded safe conduct back to the city.

Vitellius rose as well and unsheathed his sword. He pointed it first at Artabanus who took a step back. Then he turned it on Mithridates, whose face contorted with fear. For a long moment, there was complete silence. No one dared move.

Vitellius kept his sword at chest level and spoke. "I place you both under arrest. Under lock and key. Together. By morning, you must reach an agreement. If, however, you choose to kill each other, you make it easy for Rome, for Rome will place a new king on the Parthian throne and a new king on the Armenian throne. If you come to no agreement by tomorrow morning, Rome will choose new kings. If only one of you is alive tomorrow, the surviving king will be charged with murder under Roman law, and Rome will choose new kings." He turned his sword on Artabanus. "Repeat exactly what the conditions are."

When Artabanus refused to speak, Vitellius asked his scriptor to read them and added one more. "If you have not killed each other by tomorrow morning, you, Artabanus, must sign all the conditions, evacuate Artaxata, and move your troops south over the border to Parthia. Any damage to this beautiful Armenian city will be paid for by Parthia."

After the guards took the two kings into custody and hauled them off, Vitellius sheathed his sword and sat down. There was complete silence in the tent. Valerius could hear an owl hoot in the distance and thought of his sister Aurelia who believed owls were good omens.

Vitellius called for wine.

Valerius watched the orderly drink eagerly. Finally, he could not refrain from asking, "So—do you think they will kill each other?"

Vitellius shrugged. "Maybe. We'll see."

"I sense visceral hatred between them. I could see right

away that Rome had little to do with it. This must be a long-standing feud that goes beyond the usual grab for power and land."

"Valerius, you are very perceptive. Artabanus and Mithridates are brothers."

✦

On the way back to Edessa, Vitellius and Valerius led their troops south at a leisurely pace. As they left the highlands near Armenia and could no longer see the snow-capped Mount Ararat to the east, the weather became warmer, and Vitellius suggested the troops rest during the heat of the day and proceed farther south during part of the night.

After several hours on the road, Valerius asked, "Do you think there will be peace now between Parthia and Armenia?"

"No, Son. It won't last any longer than last time. But thanks to you, no battle was fought, and no Roman lives were lost."

"I assume that was your plan all along. You do realize that Artabanus feels cheated out of his victory, and you gave him no choice."

"He won't accept it for long. Artabanus has always bullied his younger brother, and he won't stop now. I felt a little sorry for Mithridates. He's weak. He and his brother fought over the same princess and Artabanus won."

"Ah! The Queen!" Valerius gave the word such an odd emphasis that Vitellius laughed.

"You met the formidable woman? Now there's a woman who should rule Parthia."

"I think she already does." Valerius told him about his encounter with the Queen and her proposal that he marry her daughter.

When he finished the whole story, Vitellius whistled, then doubled over with laughter.

"It was not a laughing matter." Valerius was indignant.

"Any objection I made could have gotten me killed on the spot for insulting the royal family."

Vitellius was suddenly serious. "Well. I admit, it was an awkward situation. And dangerous. Very dangerous."

"What do you mean?"

"Her proposal for marriage could have been an act of revenge."

"Against me?"

"Against Rome. I gather you don't know the story of Musa, the most powerful Queen of Parthia. She was a Roman slave in the household of Augustus and very beautiful. About fifty years ago Augustus gave her to Phraates IV, the Parthian King, who made her his favorite among his wives. After her son Phraates V came of age, she poisoned her husband and ruled along with her son as Queen. Artabanus's mother was the daughter of the murdered Phraates IV. It sounds complicated and long ago, but seething revenge can fester for generations."

Valerius felt his mouth go dry and found it difficult to speak. "You think—you believe her daughter could—"

"Her mother would have no doubt helped her."

"And I just thought it was a calculated diversion so I wouldn't head off to Armenia." After a long silence, Valerius said, "I don't believe she knew your legions had already arrived there. But I'm sure you understand why I do not want to be present when you meet with her in Edessa to tell her the conditions Rome has imposed."

"I suspect she already knows. They have an amazing network of spies. We could learn from the way they organize it. Your Farid seems quite clever."

"He has been helpful. But I believe his allegiance lies with Parthia. His grandfather fought against Crassus when thirty thousand Roman troops died. But he did warn me about the approaching Parthian soldiers."

The next day, they stopped at the village where Valerius had quartered his wounded troops. Several had died, but Valerius greeted the others with such concern for their welfare that Vitellius gained a new respect for the way he treated his soldiers. When they came across two wounded Parthians, Farid translated and introduced him to a local man who was ministering to the wounded. He was using ice to soothe sprains and swollen limbs and still pain around wounds. Both Valerius and Vitellius asked where he found ice, and Farid showed him a large clay cone called a yakhchal that made ice in the winter through evaporative cooling and stored it through the summer. Valerius and Vitellius had never seen anything like this and learned that some domed cones had been in use for five hundred years and dated back to the Persian Empire.

Before they headed into Edessa, Valerius noted that they would soon part ways. He would be off to Ephesus, and Vitellius would return to Antioch.

Vitellius invited him to come to Antioch and let Servius lead his troops overland back to Ephesus. "By sailing up the coast from Antioch, you would be back in Ephesus long before your troops. Have you ever been to Antioch?"

Valerius's heart raced at the thought that he could see Rachel again, and he was tempted to accept his offer, but he knew he could not leave his troops.

Vitellius expressed his disappointment and insisted that an opportunity to see the way he organized his governorship could be educational. "Besides, I have an ulterior motive. I would like you to meet my daughter. Vitellia has been an amazing help to me in my duties as governor. She takes care of most of the finances and even oversaw the building of a new aqueduct. She interviewed the engineers. I think you would find her more appealing than a princess bride." There was a twinkle in his eyes as he studied Valerius's face for a reaction.

Valerius smiled as he politely and firmly said that he must stay with his troops. But behind his smile, he gritted his teeth. Two possible brides in one month and the one he really wanted was married to another.

✦

ANTIOCH

Rachel knew she should stop examining her son to see if he was beginning to look like the villain who had raped her. She gazed down at him and caressed his cheek. Matthaios was sleeping quietly with a smile on his face. She envied his innocence, his ignorance of evil, his uncomplicated view of the world, and hoped he could remain untouched by heartbreak as long as possible. Could Matthaios be so beautiful, so endearingly boyish, so full of life and affection if he were the offspring of violence and rape? At least Sedek fervently believed Matthaios was his own son and was already teaching him the family legacy and the long history of their people.

Matthaios's eyes fluttered open. "Mama!" He sat up and raised his arms to embrace her. He was getting too big to lift easily and Rachel hugged him close. Every day she studied him closely, looking for signs in his expression: the way the morning light reflected in his eyes, the shape of his mouth, and how he wrinkled his forehead when he was confused or upset. Could she detect the traits of the monster who had raped her? Her vision blurred so that she could no longer discern what she saw and what she imagined.

"Mama, you are crying."

"But you, Matthaios, always lift my spirits." She sat on the side of his bed, rocked him in her arms, and sang to him softly. It was the same song she had sung that had once inspired Sedek to buy her at the slave market in Alexandria.

"Beautiful." Sedek stood at the doorway.

Rachel started and gazed at Sedek through her tears. "I didn't know you were listening."

Sedek smiled. He was a kind man with curly grey hair and a white beard that framed his face and made him look distinguished, patriarchal, and wise. His deep-set brown eyes expressed tenderness and concern. He crossed the room to her and gathered her to his chest. "You must not weep, my dear. I know it is difficult for you to forget." He wiped her cheek with his hand and cradled her face. "Pain always leaves scars. And joy brings smiles. Surely you rejoice in our son."

She nodded and looked into his eyes and saw his devotion, his pride in his son, and his pleasure in greeting a new day, and wondered if she could ever feel for Sedek what a wife should feel for her husband.

Sedek raised her hand to his lips. "The Most High watches over us."

Rachel watched him leave to begin his morning prayers.

It was his ever-faithful belief in the goodness of God that most endeared Sedek to Rachel. Late at night, Sedek often rose from their bed and wandered out under the stars. When she asked him what he was doing, he would answer that he was talking to God. He reminded her of the sages of old she had read about who gazed deeply into the mysteries of the universe. Except for Sedek, no one she knew looked for God with such awe and reverence in the vast expanse of the heavens. Her own view of the world was simpler. She was deeply grateful that she could embrace her little boy with overflowing love in her heart. But she also shook her fist at the heavens and wondered why God allowed so much evil in the world. Her father thought God was a stern taskmaster—punitive, vengeful, and constantly demanding. Her brother had a very different view of the world. Simon wanted to penetrate creation's secrets to find new remedies to heal the sick. He wrote her letters about young Sosias, who was excited about how all the levers and screws and pulleys of nature worked together. Sosias believed the world was one big machine governed by the principles of science.

She remembered Sosias with fondness and with a catch in her throat. Simon had rescued Sosias when he was close to death, and she had helped nurse him back to health. Sosias had been a part of one of the most meaningful moments in her life. Eight years ago, in another life, in another city, Sosias had been watching when Valerius kissed her and made promises about their future together—promises he would not be able to keep. It was a moment from a lifetime ago, one that she had vowed to forget, but one that remained painfully vivid and still made her weep.

Matthaios sprang from the bed and pulled open the shutter at the window. "Today, you promised to take me to see the horses. I can't wait." He grinned at his mother.

Before leaving the house, Rachel asked Mara to dress Matthaios warmly because she could hear the palm fronds hitting against the peristyle and knew the north wind was churning down from the mountains. Sedek's villa stood high above Antioch in Epiphania and looked down on the city that was bordered on the west by the Mediterranean and protected on the east by the mountain ranges of Lebanon. Below, Rachel could see a checkered display of tile rooftops nestled against the breast of Mount Silpius, stacked one upon the other like the toy blocks Matthaios loved to play with. Here and there she could glimpse the silver thread of the Orontes that snaked through town and flowed north toward the harbor where it spilled into the sea. Below, the main boulevard cut a wide path through town. It was named the street of Herod and Tiberius.

She thought it odd that the dead Jewish king and the living Roman emperor shared a street. It curved gracefully from south to north and was bordered on both sides by a double row of covered columns. In the summer, the roofed colonnade provided protection from the burning sun and pleasant alcoves for merchants to display their wares. In the winter, beggars huddled underneath in small clumps, seeking shelter from gusting winds and rains. Fortunately, the spring rains had not yet started, and a cloudless sky already promised bright sunshine for their morning adventure.

As Rachel and Matthaios rode in Sedek's litter to the brand-new hippodrome, Matthaios told her about Nazir's father, who took care of the horses. "Nazir claims the horses at our hippodrome are the finest in the whole empire!"

"I'm sure they are. Does Nazir's father drive the chariots in the races?"

"I think he grooms the horses and trains them. I want to learn how to ride fast."

"You are still way too young. It's too dangerous, and you will have to ask your father for permission."

"Father doesn't like horses. He says they mess up the streets."

They passed neighborhood shops—a cluster of small brick houses with wide awnings over shelves of colorful fruits and vegetables that tempted buyers with enticing aromas. Next, the smelly laundry and more odiferous fish market made her place her kerchief over her nose and turn toward the larger shops facing the colonnades where fabric merchants displayed bright, shimmering silks from Palmyra, Parthia, and India. Even the richest shops had little statues of gods and goddesses hanging over their doors to protect them from thievery and vandalism. When they entered the Jewish sector, the doorposts were adorned with small mezuzahs that encased scriptural blessings. Rachel always enjoyed entering the goldsmith and silversmith shop Sedek owned and stopped to greet the artisans and study the new displays of artifacts and jewelry. Sedek's shop did not just rely on the mezuzahs for protection. There were also two guards on duty. One of them brought her the account books she checked and kept current for Sedek.

Beyond the more glamorous shops, the road curved downward and provided glimpses of the river to the west and vistas of the mountains in bright sunlight to the east. The haphazard nature of the shops and houses in the lower sector of town reminded her of the quaint streets of Cyrene. Red and purple flowers dripped down the walls in terra cotta pots with ropes of laundry crisscrossing between houses that arched over the street. Barefoot children were playing a ball game against the walls and pushed up against the litter, begging for alms. Rachel gave Matthaios some coins to place in their grimy outstretched hands, but he stopped the litter, climbed out, and deliberately chose those who had not been clamoring for coppers. Rachel warned him that his selection of the meek could make them victims of the bold. Before they turned the next corner, they looked back and saw bullies wrestling the coins away from the smaller kids. "That is so unfair," he said.

As they turned the next corner, a gruff beggar poked his hand in front of her face. Rachel jumped in horror, but Matthaios swatted him away.

The nightmares that made her dread sleep still haunted her by day. She always awoke at the moment Meidias's foul breath touched her face as he forced her legs apart and violated her body over and over again. His sadistic groans of pleasure, the stench of the dark hole, and the lurching, creaking roll of the ship provided a nauseous accompaniment to atrocity.

Would she ever be free of the terror that haunted her nights and still made her dread venturing through the streets of Antioch? Every stranger who resembled the height and build of Meidias caused nausea to mount in her throat. When Sedek tried to reassure her that he would never ask her to travel with him to Alexandria, where she would be reminded of the slave market, she turned away from his gaze so he would not see her anguish. He did not understand that the humiliations of the slave market remained vivid in every detail, no matter how distant or how long ago it happened. Before that horrible night in Cyrene when she was abducted, she had never given the plight of slavery much thought. Then the sudden, brutal reality crushed her: a slave was a mere object with no will and no soul who was not supposed to have feelings. Passively, she submitted to probing fingers. Her hips and thighs were examined as though she were a broodmare, and her teeth were counted, tapped, and inspected. Standing next to the horse market, she was shocked to realize that an ordinary horse was selling at ten times the amount that they charged for her.

It did not help that the latest letter from her brother described increased violence and vandalism against the Jews in Alexandria. Even though Simon did not mention Meidias by name, she read between the lines that her brother suspected him of being behind most of the unrest in Alexandria. She knew the Romans had ordered imperial troops to track Meidias down without success. Therefore, Meidias could be anywhere. How certain could they be that he was not here in Antioch?

At the hippodrome, Rachel sat back under the spectators' awning and studied the account books while Matthaios ran off with Nazir to play in the stables. She thought both boys were much too small to be able to climb on the horses and was surprised when she looked up from her work and noticed Nazir on horseback prancing around the racecourse. She ran down to the stables to stop Matthaios before he tried to emulate his friend, but Matthaios was already on horseback and trotting toward her. Terrified, she ran out onto the muddy track to stop him. Matthaios jerked on the reins and called out. His horse reared in front of her.

Rachel screamed.

Powerful arms snatched her away from descending hooves and plunked her down near the side of the racetrack. Then the stable hand went to calm Matthaios's horse and yelled at her, "Never go out in front of a running horse!"

She was splattered with mud and petrified.

Matthaios slid off his horse and quietly led it back into the stables.

On the way home, Matthaios sat silent and contrite. Rachel felt stupid, distraught, and shaken. She had been blind to everything but the imagined danger Matthaios was in and had rushed into harm's way without thinking. She had not even stopped to thank the muscular giant, who had rescued her from being trampled, before she hustled her son back into the litter.

Near home, she warned Matthaios that they would not go to the hippodrome again and told him he could no longer play with Nazir.

Matthaios protested. "But he's my best friend."

"For now, you will stay home."

"That's not fair."

✦

Two weeks later, Matthaios came running with the news that the governor of Syria was on his way to their house in his litter. Rachel quickly put away her sewing, straightened the room, asked Matthaios to wash up and gather up his toys on the atrium floor, and went to alert Sedek in his study.

Like a typical seven-year-old, Matthaios grumbled that he didn't need to wash up and remarked that the next time the governor was coming up the hill in his litter, he wouldn't tell her so he wouldn't have to pick up his toys.

"Off with you, young man! Go wash your face!"

At the door, Sedek and Lucius Vitellius embraced warmly. When Lucius Vitellius became governor of Syria, he formed a close friendship with Sedek, who knew all the magistrates and officials in Antioch and soon became his unofficial advisor about political issues in Syria and Judea.

Sedek said, "I thought you were in Judea."

Vitellius greeted Rachel and tousled Matthaios's dark curls. "I bring news that changed all my plans." When Sedek gestured toward the privacy of his study, Vitellius said, "I want all of you to know as quickly as possible. We have a new emperor."

It was Matthaios who dared say the name that was on everybody's tongue: "Caligula!"

Vitellius nodded. "His real name is Gaius Julius Caesar Augustus Germanicus. I was in Jerusalem when I heard Tiberius died a day after the Ides of March. All of Rome is celebrating, I hear. As word gets around Antioch, there will be wild celebrations here as well."

"What changes do you foresee?"

"The first thing I did was to stop the war. Tiberius ordered me to wage war on Aretas, the king of the Nabateans. My legions were ready to strike. That was Tiberius's war, not mine."

"And Aretas?"

"We made peace for now. He was relieved after seeing our legions all lined up on the border, a tactic I used in Parthia as well."

"And the trouble in Jerusalem?"

"I spoke with Theophilus ben Ananus, the new High Priest. He's on notice. If he doesn't keep the rebels down and the warring factions at peace, he knows I will depose him. They assured me things have been quieter since I sent Pilatus back to Rome. Tiberius was outraged that Pilatus had massacred so many in Samaria and had governed with cruelty and arrogance. We'll see what Caligula decides to do with him. The new prefect of Judea will be my friend Marcellus."

"I hope that's good news."

"We'll see. If Marcellus doesn't keep the peace, Caligula could appoint someone worse. There's new friction brewing in

Jerusalem. When you people are not fighting Rome, you fight each other."

Sedek sighed. "The Sanhedrin is too rigid. If someone doesn't share their point of view, they are quick to resort to persecution. They have imprisoned followers of Yeshua without trials."

Vitellius ran his hand through his white hair and grimaced. "These religious squabbles are getting too violent."

"Many of the followers of Yeshua have left Jerusalem and come here."

"I hope they don't bring trouble. Why did they choose Antioch?"

"For the same reasons my ancestors moved here generations ago. When the Seleucids founded this city, they urged many Jews to move here and granted them full rights of citizenship and religious freedom. For the last one hundred years, Rome has done the same. Let's hope that doesn't change."

Lucius Vitellius agreed. "Here Syrians, Lebanese, Seleucids, Jews, Greeks, and Romans worked together to transform Antioch into a grand city. Did you know that we are now the third-largest city in the empire? I want Antioch to remain an open and free city that respects all peoples, but if troublemakers keep coming from Jerusalem, we'll have to crack down." He took a sip of wine Rachel had placed before him and smiled. "As long as I can, I will protect all our people in Syria. To grant freedom of religion seems to me a wise policy that Rome has followed in our provinces. But—"

Sedek leaned forward. "But?"

"But the day might come when zealots and fanatics need to be reined in."

"By whose definition is someone a zealot or a fanatic?"

Vitellius looked at him sharply. "Excellent question. I would say by Roman definition."

Matthaios spoke up. "I'm glad I'm not a Roman."

Vitellius placed his hand on Matthaios's shoulder. "Why do you say that, young man?"

"The Romans rule the world. That's too much work!"

Vitellius bellowed a hearty laugh and agreed. "So, Matthaios, are you being a good boy?"

Matthaios looked over at his mother and took the question to heart. "My mother doesn't think so."

"And why is that?"

"We argue about horses. She says I'm too young to ride a horse. She fusses when I don't pick up my toys. And I really didn't wash my face properly."

Vitellius grinned at Rachel. His deep-set blue eyes twinkled in his broad face tanned by the sun. His prominent nose and blunt chin gave him an air of determination and power, but his ready smile set people at ease. He hugged Matthaios to his chest. "I miss my sons. They are grown now, but I remember when they were your age." He sighed. "They grow up way too fast." He looked over at Rachel. "I have greetings for you and Sedek from your brother-in-law, Publius Petronius."

"Valerius!" Rachel blushed and was immediately flustered, fearing she had betrayed her deep feelings for Valerius.

Vitellius sipped his wine and gazed at her over the lip of his goblet. "Not long ago, we were together in Parthia, and I got to know him very well. In part, thanks to him we were able to avoid war with Artabanus."

"How is Valerius?" Rachel cleared her throat nervously.

Vitellius thought for a moment. "Overworked. He tries to do the work of ten."

Rachel looped a stray curl around her ear, her face clouding with concern. "So, he doesn't take care of himself?"

"He looks thin and worn out. I told him he needs a wife." Vitellius laughed. "In fact, I'll let you in on a secret. I have arranged for him to meet my daughter. I couldn't ask for a better son-in-law."

Sedek wanted to know if he was a good governor.

"I confess I was skeptical when Tiberius appointed him governor of Asia. I thought he was too young and inexperienced, but I find his peacekeeping tactics with warring tribes quite bold. Admirable. Publius Petronius has the respect of his soldiers and of the peoples he governs—a remarkable achievement."

Rachel wanted to know more, but the conversation turned to the new emperor, and everyone agreed that it was hard to know what to expect from Caligula.

✦

Rachel had just placed her cup of herb tea on the table when she noticed the liquid tremble and spill over. At first, she thought she had set it down too forcefully. But then the crockery on the shelf rattled, and a plate fell to the floor. The air became oppressive, and she felt a vague shifting of tiles below her feet. Outside, dogs began to bark in a terrifying crescendo. Next door, the chickens raised a cacophony of squawks and suddenly fell silent. Then everything was eerily quiet, as though the world had stopped in its tracks before starting its daily rounds again.

All she could think of was her urgent need to find Matthaios and shelter him from harm, but she stood frozen to the floor. Below her feet, a strange vibration began that finally propelled her to run out to the peristyle to find Matthaios sliding down the hill in a cloud of dust kicked up by pebbles and stones tumbling toward the valley. She stumbled after him, clutched him in her arms, and watched in horror as the houses below looked like they were being tossed by a gigantic wave in the ocean. Then a deep rumble erupted from the earth and opened a chasm nearby that swallowed vines, trees, fences, and stone walls before billowing clouds of dust and smoke obscured everything.

Rachel and Matthaios huddled in fear against the heaving earth. An old cedar tree shivered near them and split open, dropping a canopy of leafy branches over them and scratching their faces as more stones rolled down the hill. Just when they thought it was over, a mighty thundering convulsion jolted them, and whole pieces of the mountain broke away above them to topple pell-mell down the hillside. Underneath the branches, Rachel started to claw out dirt with her fingers, trying desperately to find shelter from falling debris.

After a long rumble beneath them, followed by death-like silence, Matthaios emerged spitting from the rubble, lifted off their shelter of branches, and tried to clear the dirt from his mother, who lay pale and horrified beneath. She was too afraid to move for fear the treacherous earth would swallow them whole, but Matthaios pointed toward their house and said, "It's still standing!"

"Sedek!" Rachel cried out and grabbed Matthaios's hand to scramble up the hill toward the house. They kept falling and scraping their legs on uprooted bushes, chunks of cement, and mortar. Sharp stones and tree branches obliterated the footpath that used to lead down to the city. At the house, she saw that tiles had slipped off the roof and fallen onto the peristyle, where they had shattered into hundreds of pieces. The southern edge of the peristyle had disappeared along with a column into a deep hole. Cautiously, they made their way over shards of broken tiles into the house, calling for Sedek. They found him calmly sitting at his desk, writing his daily commentary on the Torah. At several points, his pen had slipped across the papyrus in jagged squiggles, but other than that, he seemed unperturbed and looked up in astonishment when they entered gasping for breath with scratched, grimy, and alarmed faces.

In the kitchen, Mara cowered in a corner, her face as white as the snow on Mount Casius. On the table, Rachel found her cup of herb tea—cold now—with a fine dusting of white plaster coating the liquid. Rachel worried that they were not safe in the house, but Sedek refused to move outside, claiming the Most High would protect them.

On that day, thousands died as roofs and walls fell on top

of them. The old temple to Artemis collapsed, the temple to Ares was damaged, and the pediment of Jupiter Capitolinus, financed by Julius Caesar, crumbled and fell. The section of town where two- and three-story apartments housed workers was leveled beyond recognition. Massive columns in the colonnade cracked like dry sticks, and sections of columns rolled into the Orontes as though the gods were tossing them like bowling balls. Lucius Vitellius used soldiers to bury the dead, ordered the population to sleep outside away from walls and roof structures, secured the gold that had fallen from the ceiling of Jupiter's temple, and set up watches to guard against looting. Caligula ordered Vitellius to make plans for rebuilding and sent two senators from Rome with emergency funds and asked them to report back.

Vitellius was pleased with the new emperor's response. "So far so good," he told Sedek when the blocked road was cleared enough so he could come check on his welfare.

Sedek said, "I understand Caligula sent money but not nearly enough."

"That's why I've decided to use the gold from the temple to help rebuild the city."

"And you don't fear the wrath of Jupiter?" Sedek smiled.

Vitellius grinned. "If you wander through the fallen columns near the forum, you hear most of the Antiochenes blaming Jupiter for the earthquake. If Jupiter knocked the gold off his own ceiling, he must be pleased that I am putting it to better use."

Sedek pointed a warning finger at Vitellius, but his eyes lit up with mischief. "Do you think it wise to try to outsmart your gods?"

Meanwhile, Matthaios was deeply troubled. At the tender age of seven, he clung to a benign view of the world that the Most High had everything properly ordered in the universe according to a six-day plan of creation that made eminently good sense to him. But when the earthquake destroyed whole sections of Antioch and toppled the house of his best friend Nazir, who was hit by a falling brick that killed him, Matthaios began to question the wisdom of the Most High.

Matthaios asked questions Rachel could not answer because her world had been equally and inexplicably shattered when Meidias abducted her and sold her into slavery. Where in God's creation is there room for the likes of Meidias? Why does God allow earthquakes to happen?

Matthaios tiptoed into the inner sanctum of Sedek's study and sat at his father's feet until Sedek finally turned to his son and wanted to know what was on his mind.

Matthaios said, "God is not fair."

Sedek asked, "Why do you say that, my son?"

Matthaios asked why God had created the serpent in the Garden of Eden in the first place. Then he wanted to know why the nicest tree in the garden was forbidden. And is knowledge not good rather than bad? So why shouldn't we eat of the tree of knowledge? And why would God make man and woman in his own image and then tell them that it is wrong to make an image of God? It was also incomprehensible to him that God spurned Cain's sacrifice for no good reason. But the question that troubled him most was why Nazir was killed when he had done nothing wrong.

Sedek gazed at his son in silence for a while. Finally, he said, "You are right to ask these questions, but the answers you seek are difficult to find. First, you must know that your friend did not deserve to die. Nor did all the people who perished. The earth moved and walls crumbled, and we want to blame someone, so most people blame the gods. Some say it was an accident of nature. Some will say the builders who built the buildings didn't make them strong enough. That is probably true. But you should know that bad things do happen to good people, and you should go to Nazir's family and tell them you will honor your friend's memory. When you come back, we will read a book together about a man named Job who suffered unjustly, and we will study these questions together."

Sedek bent down to his son and opened his arms to him in a warm embrace. Then he clasped his cheeks in his hands and looked deeply into his eyes. "I am proud of you for your concern for Nazir and his family. I am proud of you that you are asking these questions. Soon I want you to meet a group of new friends we have in Antioch. We gather at the synagogue. We believe that God is a God of infinite love and compassion, and that this truth was revealed to us by his son Yeshua. You will meet our new friends who were his students. We will start this journey together because I still have a lot to learn." He bent down and kissed his son's cheek.

Matthaios saw tears in his father's eyes and was awed by them. He thought only women and children cried and that men didn't know how.

As he turned to leave Sedek's study, he saw that his mother had been listening at the door. She smiled down at him and took his hand and told him how sorry she was that he had lost his best friend. Then she led him to the kitchen, where she had baked rosemary bread. She wrapped it in a linen cloth and told him he could take it to Nazir's family.

Daunted by the task ahead, he asked, "What am I supposed to say?"

"You will find the words. Just being there shows that you care. Sometimes you don't have to say anything." She kissed him on the forehead and watched him make his way down the road with sober determination.

✦

WHICH EMPIRE WILL PREVAIL?

LUCIUS VITELLIUS WORE THE MILITARY CUIRASS MORE often than the purple-striped toga, but tonight a simple white tunic covered his large frame. He clapped for wine and waited for the servants to leave. "So, my dear Sedek, how is the family?"

"In good health, I'm thankful to say. Like many, we still grieve for good friends. Matthaios keeps asking me deep questions I cannot answer. As always, the poor suffer the most."

Lucius Vitellius frowned. "It will take time."

"Too many still suffer. So many are still homeless."

"I keep asking for more funds, and Caligula ignores our requests."

"At least most of the shop owners have rebuilt. But Rome keeps taxing those who have nothing. That policy only makes matters worse."

Lucius Vitellius lifted his arms in a gesture of helplessness. "I have personally stopped tax collections in the most devastated areas. It's a risky business. Caligula is not pleased. At least, for the moment, things are fairly quiet in Parthia."

"Rachel's father is just back from the east with his carts

full of spices. I'm surprised you cannot smell them from here. He was shocked to see the damage to our beautiful city."

"That's a fascinating journey to the east. Did he run into trouble?"

"Fortunately, the roads through Parthia are well policed since Antioch depends on the spice and silk trade."

"Rome depends on that trade as well. And for the moment, Parthia is not waging war."

"The news I hear from Jerusalem is not good. Things have not improved since you sent Pontius Pilatus back to Rome."

"I assume you heard that Caligula had Pilatus executed after his arrival in Rome?"

Sedek looked at him in surprise. "No, I had not heard. When he left Jerusalem, he told his friends he was being called back to be promoted. Did Caligula state his reasons?"

"Insubordination."

"That's a blanket accusation that can cover many crimes."

"Or none." Vitellius turned the intricate silver goblet in his fingers and traced its pert figure of Dionysios absently with his fingernail. "Marullus, you think, will not be able to keep peace in Jerusalem?"

"I received petitions for more peace-keeping forces." Sedek handed over several documents.

Lucius Vitellius sighed. "Theophilus ben Ananus is a reasonable man and is using his powers as High Priest to subdue the zealots who are stirring up trouble against Rome. Still, I find what I hear about this new sect more disturbing."

Sedek did not reply.

Vitellius grimaced. "I do not believe in the gods, but I also do not believe in provoking those who do. As you know, I returned the High Priest's robe to the temple and refused to march through Judea when I was asked to go to war against Aretas. I led my army through the great plain instead because your people's delegation of priests said your religion forbade the emperor's likeness on any standards and banners."

"You have been good to us. Our God most surely will reward you."

Vitellius smiled wryly. "I do not seek reward. I merely want peace. Peace!" He rubbed his forehead and frowned. "At the beginning, Caligula was reasonable. He did all the right things: a solemn funeral oration for Tiberius, the first real budget for the provinces, a new judicial division to speed up court cases, recognition banquets for our generals and equestrian knights, funds to help after the earthquake. Now? Who knows?"

Sedek leaned forward in alarm. "Caligula has sent orders for war?"

"Not yet. I hear rumors."

"What rumors?"

Vitellius rose, walked softly to the door, and yanked it open. Two slaves fled down the hallway. He returned to his seat. "I cannot be too cautious. Friends in Rome tell me that Caligula has gone mad. I believe them. From what they tell me, Caligula has declared himself the supreme god, the only god, a god more powerful than Jupiter. Perverse thought! He wants all the diverse peoples of the empire to bow down before him and worship him."

Sedek gripped the arms of his chair. "Surely you opposed this madness."

"Had I suggested he would be opposed, it would become a challenge. He would insist on it out of sheer bravado and insolence. The only way to appease Caligula is through flattery. As it was, the only price that he exacted at the moment is my position."

"Your position?"

Vitellius examined the goblet he held with sudden interest, as though he had never seen it before. His voice trembled when he spoke. "He asked me to step down. In fact, his letter states that my impertinence and insubordination would normally require that I do the honorable thing for Rome—fall on my sword. It seems my letter was not properly respectful, nor did I salute him as a god."

The consternation on Sedek's face evoked a strong response in Vitellius. He clasped Sedek's knee. "You are a good friend, Sedek. I will miss you."

"What do you plan to do?"

"I don't know. I must wait for my successor. If Caligula doesn't order me to fall on my sword, I'll retire to the countryside, at least until there is sanity again in Rome."

"You may have to wait a long time then."

Vitellius chuckled. "Well said, my friend! Well said."

"Do you know who your successor will be?"

"Someone who is already on tour of duty in the provinces, I presume. Or one of Caligula's puppets."

Sedek shuddered. "Is he really mad?"

Vitellius shrugged. "How does one define mad these days?" He leaned forward. "May I ask you a personal question? Are you one of the followers of this new sect?"

"I am."

"I see." Vitellius frowned. "My daughter Vitellia says she believes Yeshua was the son of a god. I have no interest in the gods, especially those who are human." He snorted. "Caligula proclaims himself a god, and Yeshua did as well."

"You think it's the same thing?"

"Isn't it?"

"For centuries the Jews have awaited the coming of the Messiah. Some thought he would be a great king and subjugate all peoples to his rule. Instead, our prophets proclaimed he would take on the sufferings of the world. This he did."

Vitellius smiled. "Impractical Jews! What you need is a powerful king to wield earthly power. With such an emperor—"

"Not impractical. Empires come and go. Nations rise up against nations, and the leadership merely changes hands. Sometimes we are fortunate to have good rulers. More often they are wicked, power-hungry, and self-serving. In the long run, the teachings of Yeshua will prevail."

"You call that practical?"

"The legacies of Egyptians, of Persians, of Alexander, of the Ptolemies, of the Seleucids, of Caesar, of Augustus… Where are they today? They did not last. What is the lasting legacy of Tiberius? What will Caligula's be?"

"*Tempora mutantur*…times change."

"The legacy of Yeshua is that God loves us. Yeshua promises a new age of hope and peace."

Vitellius snorted. "If all these grand sentiments were true, Yeshua would be far more powerful than Caligula."

"Yeshua does not seek power over us but shows us the way to God."

Vitellius shook his head and sighed.

Sedek continued, "The legacy of Yeshua is based on the simple but powerful truth of a new kingdom of love, compassion, and peace. His empire will prevail."

"So great was his power that he got himself crucified! Granted, Pilatus played a despicable role in the whole affair, but—"

"That was part of God's plan."

"Then explain to me why he did not save himself. If indeed he was the son of a god, how could he die?"

"He rose again on the third day."

"And that, my dear Sedek, is absurd!"

"From your point of view, everything hinges on death. Death is the final act. There follows—nothing."

"We cannot go against the laws of nature."

"The creator made all things. He made the laws of nature."

Vitellius shook his head. "Your new sect is based on magic. Simon Magus claims he can transform death into life, but it's trickery, an insult to my intelligence. This, too, insults my reason."

"Surely, you can acknowledge that the creator of all can transform death into life. He did so in the act of creation."

"No."

"When we are confronted with great mysteries beyond our understanding, we must rely on smaller truths to suggest larger ones. Do you understand how the small seed can contain life, how it must die in the ground to bring forth new life, grow, blossom, and bear fruit? All around us are miracles."

Vitellius slumped back in his seat and gazed into the distance.

After a long silence, Sedek rose to leave. The hour was well past midnight.

"The real mystery—" Vitellius stopped.

"Yes?"

"The real mystery is life itself. We can explain nothing, not even the tiniest seed!"

Sedek smiled. "The seed, the intricate veins in a leaf, a tree, the very stars in the heavens! What kind of God could create such a wondrous world? Would we, his creatures, have the capacity to understand him?"

"A frightening god!"

"Many believe that. As surely as our creator has spoken through lightning and thunder and fire, in Yeshua he has spoken through the voice of a man, and we could understand."

"Ah, you—perhaps."

"No one understands fully. It would be arrogant to claim we could understand God."

"But less arrogant than a man who claims to be god? Who will bring on the greatest upheavals and disasters—our emperor or your Yeshua?"

"I don't know."

Sedek gathered his cloak around him and summoned his litter. At the door, he embraced Vitellius warmly. As he rode home under a brilliant, star-spangled sky, he felt a violent jolt of despair surge through him. Who could protect them from a madman?

When he arrived home, he dismissed the litter-bearers

and let himself in quietly so he would not wake Rachel, but the atrium was fully lit with torches, and Rachel was pacing and didn't even look up when he entered.

"What is it, Rachel? Why are you not in bed?"

She gestured toward a letter on the table, her eyes wide and serious. "I read it over and over again and still cannot take it all in."

He looked at the broken seal. "From Alexandria? Is your brother all right? What is it?"

She shook her head.

"Is it Aurelia? Their sons?"

He began to read, his hand shaking. After a moment, he slumped into a chair to steady himself.

"Thousands dead! A brutal, senseless massacre!" He shook his head in disbelief. "An all-out war against Jews. And in Alexandria, the most enlightened city in the empire. How could that be?" He wiped his hand across his face and shook his head in dismay. "If it could happen there, it could happen anywhere."

Sedek crossed the room to cradle Rachel in his arms and tried to soothe her. "At least your brother and his family are safe."

"For how long?"

"From what Aurelia writes, Simon saved many lives. The Most High be praised! And Aurelia says she was able to convince the Roman prefect to provide military tents and supplies for the homeless afterward."

"And did you see this?" She pointed to the last part of the letter. "Meidias is dead!"

"You don't seem relieved."

"Aurelia doesn't say how he died."

Sedek frowned.

Rachel shuddered in his arms.

✦

ALEXANDRIA

IN ALEXANDRIA, AURELIA WALKED THROUGH THE peristyle to check on her children and found them playing quietly in the garden. She wore a straight shift with slits below the knees that allowed freedom of movement and made the silk shimmer in swirls around her legs. The lustrous blue of the fabric enhanced the violet intensity of her eyes. She needed no dark lines of kohl in the Egyptian fashion to make her eyes the most arresting feature of her face. Her light brown hair, parted and braided around her head in the Roman style, made her look like a strict Roman matron. She paused at her reflection in the fountain and realized she was becoming more like her mother every day. She used to think her mother worried too much and didn't know how to keep the proper perspective, and now she was being just as anxious and had begun to imagine greater dangers than the ones they had just endured. How often had her mother warned her about the hardships she would face by marrying a Jew? She had brushed her mother's concerns aside, but nothing could have prepared her for the visceral hatred that exploded against the Jews in Alexandria. As the daughter of a Roman senator, she thought that power, prestige, and position would provide protection. She blinked at the blinding sunlight in the fountain and shook her head over her own inexperience and gullibility. She had counted on the mutual ardor of their love overcoming any obstacle to their happiness and was unprepared for the corrosion and destructiveness of hate.

Since the devastating massacre, things had settled back into the usual routines, but nothing would ever be the same. The simple whiff of smoke from a candle evoked images of fire-scarred children and blackened, parched faces of the dying. The screeching call of a hawk reminded her of their screams. When she burned something in the kitchen, the smell seared through her and caused her to escape to the garden and gag. Even the stillness of the night made her think of the eerie quiet that descended on Alexandria after the massacre. But worse was the haunted look in Simon's eyes. He labored now with more fervor than before like one possessed to save all the infirm and ailing of Alexandria.

Suddenly overcome with the desire to protect her sons, she ran to them and interrupted their play with smothering kisses. She stroked Rufus's light curls and kissed the crown of his head where tufts of hair stood stubbornly upright. Alexander crawled willingly into her arms and snuggled happily against her breast. There was a fierce gentleness about her when she cared for her children. Simon called her overprotective, but she was stubborn about her desire to keep them from harm. As long as possible, she hoped to spare them knowledge of the cruelties of the world. After several hugs, the boys protested, and she retreated to the peristyle.

For a long time, Aurelia felt that the shadow of Meidias hovered over their marriage and created a chasm between them that she could not bridge. She knew his dark preoccupations with slave traders and evildoers would remain an obsession, but Simon had changed. He had become more stubborn about his deep sense of right and wrong, and she realized his very stubbornness was one reason she loved him. In so many ways, her father had been equally obstinate about doing what he felt was right. He had paid for that stubbornness with his life. In a flash of recognition, she remembered her mother kneeling in front of the altar of Juno in Rome and understood how strong and courageous she was. Is still. She was amazed that it had taken her so long to appreciate her mother's fortitude, her quiet resolve, her true character.

She wondered how her mother was dealing with the terrible loss of Antonia, her close friend and confidante. And now Antonia was gone, killed by her own hand because she could no longer cope with what her grandson Caligula had become. Aurelia grieved for a world that might have been; a world where Antonia would have lived to be proud of her grandchildren instead of in despair; a world where sanity would govern rather than madness; a world where Jews and Greeks and Egyptians could live peacefully under the banner of Rome. How would their children fare in such turbulent times?

When Simon came home late again that night, long after the boys had been put to bed, she wanted to know what had detained him.

"There's unrest in the delta quarter. There's been more looting. A little boy was injured."

"Isn't that Tiberius Alexander's responsibility until there is a new Prefect of Egypt appointed by Rome?"

"You still expect him to care about his own people?"

"I expect you to care about your own family."

Simon looked at her sharply and started to eat his supper. After a long silence, he said, "You don't understand. Just as I was coming home, there was a little crippled boy outside the Museion, crying in pain. He was also full of lice and scabies. I had to take care of him."

"You care more for the lowest, ailing beggar than for your sons who never see you."

"Are they sick?"

"No. Must they be? Is that what it will take for you to pay attention to them?"

"Please, Aurelia."

"You are too preoccupied with your mission to save Jews from the vicious gangs of Jew-haters who prowl the streets of Alexandria. Do you stop and think that you make yourself a target for their hatred?" Her voice rose in anguish. "And what about your family? Do you think about your sons? Philo has been warning you. Even Tarik, our maid, is worried about you. As an Egyptian, she hears what they are saying on the streets."

Aurelia studied her husband's grim expression. His brown hair and closely trimmed beard formed a dark oval frame around his strong features. Lately, she had noticed new lines around his eyes, a new harshness in his face, a rigid set to his jaw that made him look angry and intense. His athletic ease and wrestler's agility had always impressed her, but he still favored his left arm, which Meidias had slashed in their brutal fight. She knew he was still in pain from the way he walked and moved. They never mentioned Meidias anymore. But maybe they should.

"You still haven't come to terms with Meidias."

"What do you mean?"

"Your arm. It still hurts?"

"Not much."

"But it's not about your arm. It's the deeper wound inside you."

"What do you mean?"

"Meidias is dead."

"We all know that."

"You need to let go. For so many years, you have been his avenger—his *goel*—and now you should free yourself from the burden of vengeance that distorts everything you do."

"You sound like Cydias."

"You've always said he is the most perceptive physician at the Museion. Had you ever thought he might be right?"

Simon took a sip of wine and shook his head.

"What is it about Meidias that won't let you find peace?"

"I don't know."

He pushed his plate away and started to get up, but she grabbed his wrist and held it. "Simon, please talk about it. Tell me how you feel. You carry so many burdens. Wouldn't it help to talk about it?"

"Talking about it will accomplish nothing."

"How did you feel when you discovered that the patient you were required to treat was the mortally wounded Meidias?"

"I wanted to kill him."

"But you didn't."

"I could kill someone to protect you if you were in danger, but I could never intentionally kill a patient. He was unconscious."

"I understand that your oath to Hippocrates is sacred to you. What I don't understand is why you don't feel good now since you never violated that oath."

"But I wanted to."

Aurelia sighed. "Meidias is dead. It's over."

"That's the problem. It's never over. A one-eyed, wiry fellow named Dio took his place. He's half the size of Meidias but just as vicious and evil. Like Meidias, he's on a mission to kill Jews and he is building up a following based on tactics he learned from Meidias. It will never end. Hallas, his old accomplice, is still sailing up and down the coast capturing innocent children to sell on distant slave markets. Last week when I came home late, I went to check on Chana. She is no longer there, and I heard she was whisked away by a slave trader."

"Who is Chana?"

"Don't you remember? The little orphan girl who tried to console me when I was upset after I saved the life of a Jew-hater. Also, I just heard that a synagogue in Buto was torched last week."

"But our sons need you. They need to see their father and

learn from you. I need you."

Simon sighed. "I'll try to do better."

"Start tomorrow. Your friend Guryon ben Ephraim is arriving tomorrow and is supposed to come dine with us. I've invited Philo. Promise me for once you won't be late."

✦

The next day, Aurelia was busy preparing dinner in the kitchen with Althea and Tarik when Alexander came running with the news that they had a visitor.

"Who is it, Alexander?"

"A tall Roman with a sword! He asked me to run and fetch my mother." He pulled her toward the door.

Aurelia hoped it was not another summons from the prefect's palace. At the door, she gasped and then rushed into the visitor's arms. "Valerius!"

He crushed her with such a fierce hug that she almost cried out. "My dear Aurelia, you are as beautiful as ever!"

"Flatterer!" She laughed.

He tweaked her cheek as he used to when she was little and gave her a wide, boyish grin that lit up his blue eyes.

Brother and sister had not seen each other in over seven years. Aurelia was struck by the changes she saw in him. In his military dress, he looked vigorous, impressive, even somewhat daunting. His auburn hair glowed like copper in the sunlight and was now cropped close as their father's had been. The angles of his tanned, clean-shaven face were sharper, more prominent, more rugged than before. His wide stance exuded power and self-confidence.

Rufus and Alexander were already clinging to him and asking a hundred questions about being a soldier. Before long, Valerius opened his bags and pulled out sheets of fine papyrus, new pens, and a set of five vials of ink of different colors. After showing the boys how to use the new pens that came from Ephesus, he began to design small Roman helmets for them with brightly colored crests and promised them greaves, leather gloves, and tunics decorated with the emblems of his legions. He noted that both boys were already big for their ages. He had trouble taking their measurements because they were jumping up and down with excitement. As he wrote them down, he saw Aurelia's frown and told her not to worry, that he would get the armory to make the swords out of wood. She was less worried about that than the reaction Simon would have to his sons playing at being Roman soldiers.

Aurelia clutched his shoulder. "Don't get *caligulae*—little boots."

Valerius looked at her sharply and nodded.

While the boys made drawings with their new inks and pens, Aurelia and Valerius tried to catch up on seven years of their lives. Aurelia wanted to know more about his health, his friends, his daily life in Ephesus, and mainly whether he had met his future wife.

Valerius told her about long months spent on border disputes, legal conflicts, peace negotiations between fighting tribes and clans, the staggering amount of time spent overseeing taxation, and the ever-present task of checking the books. He never mentioned the battle in Parthia and the proposal to marry a Parthian princess. "Mainly I try to keep peace. Diplomacy is hard work—nothing as exciting as my first impressions of Alexandria and the lighthouse."

Aurelia had to smile as he described his reaction to the lighthouse. "Everyone is overwhelmed."

"Do you realize how tall it is? If you put eight arches of Augustus on top of each other in the forum, the lighthouse would still be higher. And that's not counting the huge statue of Poseidon on top."

Aurelia laughed. "I think it's supposed to be Zeus. You always measured everything in feet, palms, cubits, and steps before you could decide whether you were impressed or not."

"I'm impressed. In fact, I was speechless for a long time. When Guryon's ship turned and headed straight for it, Guryon had to shake my arm to get me to turn and look at him. He didn't need to ask. He could see what I thought in my eyes. It took a while to get my neck straightened out." He rubbed his neck.

"How is Guryon?"

"He's a jolly fellow. He thinks Simon is a genius. He could not stop talking about him."

"Guryon is very fond of Simon. Every time Guryon is in Alexandria, he stops by to see us and brings us fresh fruit from Judea. We expect him here for dinner this evening. And Philo will want to meet you. I assume you've heard about what happened to Flaccus?"

Valerius grimaced. "The news has spread as far as Parthia. He was banished to an island in the Aegean."

"Worse. Caligula sent a ship to the island, and his soldiers hunted him down and killed him. Like a hunting party pursuing a bear. And you know about Pilatus?"

"He was called back to Rome some time ago."

Aurelia nodded. "We heard Caligula had him executed. Simon believes Agrippa had a lot to do with it. He has a lot of influence on Caligula. I saw some of that on Capri."

"You were happy to leave that island."

"I hope never to see it again. The Villa Jovis is a magnificent palace with a breathtaking view. But it's a very sad place. Speaking of sad. Do you know about Antonia?"

"What happened?"

"After Caligula made Tiberius Gemellus fall on his sword, she took her own life."

"Both of her grandsons were in a fight for the imperial throne."

"It's all so tragic. And, as you know, Caligula is—unpredictable. I'll get her farewell letter. You can read it for yourself."

The boys were getting restless and ran off to play.

He handed the letter back to her, shaking his head. "You wrote to her on Flaccus's behalf!"

"I did. Simon and Philo believe he got what he deserved. I'm not so sure."

"I knew Flaccus. We traveled together on the same merchant ship. He had just been appointed prefect of Egypt, and I was off to Ephesus to be governor of Asia. I thought he was a decent fellow, but totally lacking in appreciation of the rich Egyptian culture. I could foresee that he would have conflicts with the local population. He had even less understanding of the rich Jewish culture. I was not surprised when he didn't stop the massacre."

"Philo and Simon were elated when Caligula arrested Flaccus and hauled him back to Rome and later had him executed."

"Things are often more complicated than they seem. So, what is the story on Meidias? Guryon told me he's dead. Is that true?"

"True. Simon still stews about him."

Valerius gave his sister a puzzled look.

"You know how Meidias worked his evil behind the scenes and escaped capture. Then he sold himself to the Roman high command as a mercenary. Flaccus was impressed with him and hired him as his bodyguard. When Simon discovered that, it was only a matter of time before he was going to challenge him. The fight was horrible. I was there. Meidias was armed. Simon was not. Meidias slashed his left arm. But" she raised both fists in triumph, "Simon won." More softly she added, "He almost didn't."

"Then Simon got his revenge at last."

"No, Tiberius Alexander deprived Simon of his victory. He stopped the fight and had the dazed Meidias hauled off to the palace. Meidias died later from the wound he got trying to defend Flaccus from Caligula's soldiers when they came to arrest him. Simon couldn't—or wouldn't—kill a wounded patient."

Valerius pressed his lips together in anger. "I'm not as noble as your Simon." He held his hand up in a menacing gesture. "Meidias was a man most vile. I would have killed him, wounded or not. I will never forgive Meidias for what he did to Rachel."

"You still love her?"

Valerius didn't answer.

When Simon came home, both men studied each other with cautious gravity before they shared a heartfelt embrace, exclaiming their mutual pleasure. Laughing, they performed a mock wrestling match right in the middle of the atrium. The reunion triggered endless stories about their boyhood pranks while Aurelia escaped to the kitchen to help Althea and Tarik prepare dinner. Valerius and Simon were so caught up in their laughter over the mischievous deeds of their boyhood that Simon said it was a good thing his boys were not around to hear what they were saying.

Suddenly, Simon frowned and looked around. "Where are they anyway?"

A quick search through the house established that the boys were nowhere to be found. In a panic, Aurelia sent Simon to search the gardens while she went to Philo's villa and asked his servants to help search. When Valerius suggested they should look outside the walls of Philo's estate, Aurelia told everyone that the boys had strict orders never to go out the gate.

Simon and Valerius looked at each other and dashed for the gate. Simon called back over his shoulder that Aurelia should stay put in case they came back. Aurelia heard a note of panic in his voice as he divided the city into districts for the litter-bearers to search. Simon and Valerius ran off to the main streets of the city.

Frantic now, both Aurelia and Althea searched through the house and gardens again and kept running to the gate to look out on the street.

Althea said, "Surely, they're just playing a game of hide

and seek. They're probably right around here somewhere."

"They wouldn't hide this long. They would be hungry by now. And it's getting dark." She clutched Althea in her arms. "What am I going to do? I was not this frightened during the massacre."

Tiberius Alexander appeared at the gate and was about to speak when Aurelia turned on him and asked him to leave. "Don't you see we have a crisis here on our hands?"

"And you want me to get you military tents?" Tiberius Alexander grinned.

"I don't have time for jokes or for your—your arrogance." She started to close the heavy door, but he stopped her.

"I was just coming to help you."

"You?"

"I thought you might like to know that two little boys have shown up at our military barracks near the Canopic Gate."

"How is that possible?"

"I came on ahead on horseback, but your friend Sosias is escorting them home as I speak."

Althea said, "That's wonderful news."

But Aurelia refused to believe it until she saw Sosias coming down the street with each boy held firmly by the hand. She ran to meet them and embraced all three.

Sosias explained that he was walking down a street near the Canopic Gate when he happened to notice Rufus and Alexander in lockstep behind eight legionaries on their way to camp. The soldiers were laughing and teaching the boys how to march in formation and how to cuss in Latin. "I grabbed them by their tunics and steered them straight home. Tiberius Alexander promised to come on ahead and let you know so you wouldn't worry."

Aurelia hugged Sosias again to thank him and hailed him as her hero.

Althea hugged Sosias close as well. She still thought of herself as his mother, because she had taken him in years ago when he was an orphaned thirteen-year-old and proudly called him her son.

At that moment, Simon and Valerius appeared with Guryon ben Ephraim, and Aurelia greeted Guryon, while Simon frowned a warning at the boys, who were hiding behind her. As Aurelia turned around, she bumped into Tiberius Alexander, and there was an awkward moment of silence before she had the presence of mind to thank him. Flustered, Aurelia introduced him to Valerius and then felt obligated to invite him to dinner. After all, he was the acting prefect of Egypt, and she had often warned Simon not to cross him.

Tiberius Alexander bowed and said, "I would be honored to dine with you and the Governor of Asia." Aurelia found some satisfaction in the fact that Tiberius Alexander was obviously impressed by her brother's title. But Simon signaled a silent glare of dismay while she went to arrange a new place at the table.

Still giddy with the thrill of their adventure, the boys were all achatter about their new vocabulary, but as soon as they saw their father fetch the whip, they fell silent and clung to Aurelia.

Valerius quickly intervened and said it was his fault because he had promised them little soldier outfits. "Let me at least try a little diplomacy first."

Simon set the whip in the corner but did not put it away. Meek and crestfallen, the boys listened to everything Valerius had to say.

"Do you know what they do to soldiers who don't obey?"

The boys shook their heads in unison.

"They whip them. Then they tie their ankles together with chains and throw them in a deep, dark hole with no light and just water for days."

Alexander began to cry.

In the end, the boys took solemn oaths that they would follow all orders from their father and mother and would never

ever run off again.

When Aurelia thanked Sosias again, Valerius echoed the name. "Sosias? I remember you. How old were you when my father ran over you in Cyrene?"

"Twelve."

Valerius said, "We were afraid you were going to die. You must have hated my family."

Sosias shook his head. "You probably won't believe me, but I will tell you the truth. It was the best thing that ever happened to me. I'm now an assistant engineer at the Museion. I owe it to the fact that the propraetor of Cyrene ran over me and Simon rescued me." Sosias looked from Valerius to Aurelia and then to Simon. "Simon stayed by my side without sleeping until I recovered. And Rachel nursed me. I fell in love with Rachel." He winked at Valerius. "I was not the only one in love with her." Sosias grinned brightly and took Alexander's hand in his to comfort him.

Sosias was the kind of young man whose innate enthusiasm and exuberance could not be dampened. Boyish and always a little disheveled, Sosias was fascinated by pulleys and gears and by how everything worked and was already the inventor of new mechanical contraptions that Simon thought a waste of time. But Sosias claimed that he was creating working machines that could irrigate fields and lift heavy loads into waiting ships at the dock. In fact, Sosias argued with Simon that the way to fight the slave trade was to create labor-saving devices, but Simon just shook his head and called him a dreamer. When that happened, Sosias turned to Aurelia, who would take his side and offer encouragement.

Aurelia hugged him close. "Sosias, you never told me how you were wounded. I didn't know."

Valerius laughed. "I'll have to remember what you said. 'Sometimes the worst thing that happens to you can turn out to be the best thing.'"

"I would not count on that!" said Simon.

Sosias was more concerned about Alexander, who was hiding at his side, his face a miserable display of fear, disappointment, and repentance. His lower lip puckered out and trembled as Sosias wiped away the tears trickling down his cheeks.

Sosias picked him up and said, "Know what we will do? We will go and fix that gate. It was bad. It opened and let you out. So now we will change this bad gate and make it a good gate." Sosias went to work, made Alexander feel like his assistant, and fixed the locking mechanism for the iron gate before Tarik and Althea could get food on the table.

At dinner, Guryon entertained everyone with stories about his travels over the Erythraean Sea and his adventures in the Indo-Scythian kingdom. Aurelia was happy for the diversion from any discussion dealing with current events in Rome and fretted that Philo was again so late that they had to eat without him. She knew Philo had a lot of correspondence to tend to and many official duties to perform for the Jewish senate and for his brother, the alabarch of Alexandria. Philo had become the voice of more than a million Jews in the region, and lately, she felt that the burden on the old philosopher's shoulders had become too heavy. He had aged a lot in the last few years and looked frail and exhausted. Since Simon was Philo's personal physician, she kept reminding Simon to encourage Philo to step down from some of his duties.

Casually, Guryon asked Valerius when he would be heading back to Ephesus.

Valerius said, "I don't know. The emperor has summoned me back to Rome."

Everyone stopped eating, and an ominous hush fell over the room.

After a long silence, Simon asked, "Do you know why?"

Valerius shrugged. "An administrative decision, no doubt. I've been governor of Asia for seven years. It's probably time to replace me."

Simon and Aurelia looked at each other but said nothing.

A cold sense of doom made her shiver.

When Philo arrived, she had already put the boys to bed, and she could tell by Philo's face that he was not the bearer of good news. But Philo—ever gracious and attentive to guests on his estate—immediately greeted Valerius and proposed a toast in his honor before apologizing for being late. Then he said, "I was delayed by a group of Jewish scholars who have just arrived in Alexandria for the festivities that begin next week. The annual commemoration of the translation of our Jewish scriptures into Greek will gather at the lighthouse to celebrate. A toast to that great achievement of three hundred years ago!"

After the toast, Philo turned to his nephew, Tiberius Alexander, and asked to speak to him privately in the gardens. The expression on Philo's face conveyed a sense of urgency and alarm, so Aurelia feared the worst and tried to keep the conversation going, but she was no longer listening to Guryon's stories about India.

When they returned to the dining room, Tiberius Alexander looked pale but calm and composed. Uncharacteristically, Philo seemed agitated and anxious when he spoke. "I have news from Rome. Caligula appointed Naevius Sutorius Macro, the head of the Praetorian guard, to become the successor to Flaccus as prefect of Egypt, but as he boarded the ship in Ostia that was to bring him here to Alexandria, Caligula's men arrested him and summoned him back to Rome, where he was forced to fall on his sword."

This announcement was met with stunned silence.

Then Tiberius Alexander announced, "I had heard Macro was being considered for prefect. For now, we will have to await official word from Rome. This means I am still running the prefect's office and vice-prefect Lucius Rectus is still commanding the legions."

Philo said, "My guess is that Macro was too powerful, and Caligula felt he would become a rival. Perhaps he already was. He was, after all, the Praetorian who brought down Sejanus years ago. Unfortunately, there is more. King Ptolemaios of Mauretania has just recently been summoned back to Rome to receive high honors. Many fear for his life."

Aurelia gasped. "Caligula must also see him as a rival since he is distantly related to Julius Caesar. Ptolemaios is the grandson of Cleopatra and Marcus Antonius and grew up in Antonia's household. To be called back to Rome by Caligula is—" She looked over at her brother and could not finish her sentence.

Philo nodded. "Far worse is the fact that Caligula has now decreed he is a god. First, he asked to be addressed as Jupiter and commanded the heads of several gods in their temples be knocked off and replaced with his own likeness. But this was not enough. Now he has proclaimed himself the one true and living god. He calls himself Neos Helios, the new god of the sun, more powerful than Ra. He has already minted gold coins with that inscription and his image on them. He established a shrine to himself with a life-sized gilded statue that he orders clothed every day in whatever he happens to be wearing."

Philo choked and had to take a sip of wine before he could speak again. "Such insane blasphemy has never been seen before. Caligula is obsessed with his apotheosis. He speaks of it as a divine power contest he will win. His next step is predictable. He will not stop at Roman gods. Or Egyptian gods. Or Greek gods. We all know where this is going."

Aurelia could sense Simon's growing fury and tried to head off an explosion of outrage, but she was too late. Simon pounded the table and swore that all Jews had to bond together and oppose the emperor, whatever the cost.

Tiberius Alexander said, "If the Jews bond together to oppose the emperor, you know that I will have to oppose you in the name of my oath of loyalty to Rome."

Simon gazed at Philo, hoping for a rebuke from him, but Philo averted his eyes and stared down at his plate. Simon turned to Tiberius Alexander and said, "This means that your oath to Rome is more important than your allegiance to the faith of our fathers. Have you completely renounced your own heritage? The heritage of your father and your father's father? Of your uncle?" He gestured toward Philo.

Tiberius Alexander picked up a piece of bread and chewed slowly while watching Simon with a twisted smile on his face. "The emperor can play at being god if he wishes. He has the power to do whatever he wants. I, for one, have no use for the gods. I have said this before, and no lightning bolt came down from the heavens." He erupted in mocking laughter.

Just as Aurelia started to warn Simon to stop a useless argument, Guryon intervened to ask Philo about how the Jewish population of Alexandria was recovering from the massacre.

Philo took a deep breath and closed his eyes. "It is a painfully slow process. Those who were poor now have nothing. Those who had houses now are homeless or have no roofs. We help where we can, but we lost half of the Jewish senate when thirty-eight senators were slaughtered in a gruesome and vicious spectacle at the theater. They were helpless old men. And Flaccus did nothing to stop it." Philo opened his eyes, gazed sadly at his nephew, and said, "Nothing!"

Guryon looked puzzled. "Was Flaccus not called back to Rome to answer to Caligula for the massacre?"

Aurelia was serving the fruit pie for dessert and shook her head as she handed a piece to Guryon. "No, he was summoned back to Rome because he had backed Tiberius Gemellus, who was Caligula's rival for the imperial throne."

Philo turned to Valerius. "Tiberius Alexander told me that Caligula has summoned you back to Rome. These are ominous orders. You should be prepared for the worst. Never underestimate Caligula! You do so at your peril."

Simon spoke through clenched teeth. "And do not underestimate the Jewish people. This will not end well."

No one dared contradict him. Aurelia wanted to reassure Valerius but could not find the words. She looked at her brother, wondering if this brief reunion would be his last gift to her and if she would ever see him again. Was that why he had made the trip to Alexandria before going directly to Rome?

The silence was interrupted by a timid little voice. "I'm afraid." Alexander stood blinking on the threshold, his small body trembling with fear. "It's dark in my room."

Aurelia scooped him up, cradled him on her lap, and held his head against her breast.

Philo walked over to Alexander and gently placed his hand on his head and blessed him. "We need not fear the dark. The God who led Abraham out of Ur and showed Moses the way through the wilderness will lead us to the light."

✦

The next morning, Aurelia decided to accompany her brother to the harbor. Every moment they still had together was precious, for she feared he might soon be gone forever. Aurelia kept thinking about the large number of prefects, would-be prefects, kings, propraetors, and governors who were called back to Rome and were sent to their deaths by an irate or vindictive Caligula. She begged Valerius not to go. She urged him to escape to the north beyond Germania or east to India to be out of the reach of Caligula's power. "From one day to the next, we don't know what can suddenly befall us. When the massacre erupted in Alexandria, it was because people were celebrating the arrival of Agrippa. We never know which sparks can start a fire, or which events can turn a crowd toward looting, destruction, and murder. Crowds are unpredictable. But in this case, Caligula is predictable. He is predictably evil."

"You know very well that I cannot run from this. Neither could our father when he confronted the senate. The awful truth is that our emperors are tyrants."

"But Tiberius with all his faults had some decency, some sense of right and wrong, a certain loyalty to old Roman ideals. Caligula has none." She told him then how Caligula had tried to molest her and how he professed his love for Tiberius while begging Simon to kill him so he could become emperor. "Caligula made others pay the price. Every time he got away with his treachery, it reinforced his terrible behavior and gave him permission to indulge his every urge."

Valerius studied his sister's face with a perplexed frown. "Little did we know then, when Tiberius insisted on appointing Simon to be his physician, that you would be forced to stay on Capri in such danger. You seem to have a certain fondness for Tiberius. How can that be? He was responsible for our father's death. He could have stopped those trumped-up trials of treason, but he didn't."

"True." The blow of their father's death in front of the senate was still very painful and raw. She gazed over at the lighthouse and wondered if she had been too quick to excuse the old emperor simply because he was so much better than Caligula. "I saw Tiberius only rarely. But I was able to remind him of his better nature, of the time when he was a military commander and was respected by his troops, of a time when the weight of the imperium did not crush him. I reminded him of the old days when he and our father were comrades in arms. Thanks to his affectionate memory of Father, I was able to persuade him to let us leave the island. Caligula tried to stop us."

"You don't suppose Caligula still holds a grudge against you and Simon?"

"I know he does. When we were leaving, he yelled threats at us. I can still hear those threats as they echoed down the stairwell. But at that time, he did not have the power to stop us. Now—? He has absolute power. That is why I plead with you to disobey his orders and escape to India or deepest Africa where Roman power cannot reach you."

"You know as well as I that I could never do that."

Aurelia sighed. "At least appeal to Agrippa. He might be the only one who could help you."

"How could Agrippa be able to help? He's just a minor king appointed by Caligula and has no real power."

"You are probably right. On the other hand, Tiberius appointed him to be Caligula's tutor, and, according to Philo, Caligula still listens to Agrippa and follows his advice. Agrippa grew up in Rome and has unusual insights into the workings of the imperial family and has a sixth sense about politics. When things blew up between Tiberius and Caligula, Agrippa took the blame and saved Caligula's skin. So far, Caligula has not forgotten what he owes him. Even Tiberius Alexander consults with Agrippa every time Agrippa visits Alexandria. Both are extremely ambitious Jews who want to wield power—Roman power."

Valerius studied his sister's face. "Last night at dinner I felt the tension between him and Simon. And then I noticed how Tiberius Alexander looked at you. I assume you know he is in love with you."

"Don't be silly!" Aurelia shook her head in surprise. "It is true that I feel very uncomfortable around him. But it isn't love. It's because he thinks I come from a prestigious Roman family, and he hopes to gain some kind of advantage from me."

"There's more to it than that. He couldn't take his eyes off you. And when you clasped little Alexander to your breast, he smiled so wistfully that I thought he was imagining being the one you were caressing."

"You are the one with a vivid imagination."

"No, it was obvious. I think Simon saw the same thing."

"Oh, dear!" She took a deep breath and let it out slowly with a sigh. "I sensed he was somewhat infatuated, so I used that to get help for the victims of the massacre. I hope you're wrong."

"I'm afraid you will have to be very careful. Unless, of

course, you would welcome his attention."

"Valerius!"

"Well, then. It's best to be cautious. I know the type. Very ambitious men will trample others to get to the top. They have no scruples."

"You and Simon agree on that point. Simon doesn't trust him. Even Philo shakes his head about his nephew."

At that moment, Guryon joined them and told Valerius his ship was ready to sail. Valerius turned to his sister and clasped her in a strong embrace.

"You will visit Mother before you—"

"That is my plan."

"Try to delay your arrival in Rome as long as possible. Maybe he will forget why he summoned you."

"Not likely. Don't look so somber. It's not wise to assume the worst."

Fiercely, she pulled him close again and clasped him tight in desperation, afraid she would never see him again. She blinked back tears as he stepped back and gave her cheek a tender caress.

Aurelia watched him go up the gangplank and enter the ship. Before he was out of sight, he turned and waved. She waved back and felt a strong premonition that Caligula's summons would be worse than they could ever imagine. As crewmen untied the hawsers from the moorings, oarsmen took over, and the ship glided into open waters and started turning.

Reluctantly, she headed toward her litter and bumped into Tiberius Alexander. She frowned and demanded to know why he was there.

He bowed and said, "I came to say goodbye to your brother and wish him a safe journey. But when I saw you both in deep conversation, I did not want to interrupt."

Annoyed and flustered, she wondered how much he might have overheard.

"I'll escort you home."

"I can manage on my own."

"No doubt. But a lady of your distinction should not be alone on the streets."

"My litter is here. I am well protected."

He grabbed her arm and led her to the litter. "After all, Simon would not want you to be out on the streets in danger. Although sometimes I think he doesn't seem too concerned about your welfare. He leaves you alone a lot."

"That is none of your business."

"Everything in Egypt is my business. You heard what happened in Rome. For now, I am prefect. Simon's fate is in my hands."

Aurelia leaned away from his face that was now even with hers as he kept in step with the litter-carriers. She knew he had just chosen to remind her that all the games he played were to be played by his rules and his alone.

$$\maltese$$

THE ART OF HEALING

AS SOON AS AURELIA LOCKED THE GATE AND CLOSED the door, a feeling of loss and emptiness invaded her. She dreaded the next weeks of waiting, knowing that there was nothing she could do to protect her brother. She wished she had the same confidence her mother had in the power of prayers to the gods of Rome. She longed to pray to Simon's omnipotent God as she used to when she lived with Rabbi Ezekiel in Rome, but lately, she felt she dared not approach a god who seemed so majestic, aloof, and frightening. Althea encouraged her to pray anyway and told her the God who created butterflies and hummingbirds, who protected widows and orphans, and who saved Moses from the wrath of Pharaoh would welcome her pleas for help. Tarik, her Egyptian maid, invited her to attend simple religious services where a former student of Philo, who had recently returned from his studies in Jerusalem, preached a message of forgiveness and compassion. Tarik said, "It is a different kind of community that welcomes everybody." Aurelia was not interested in theological arguments and dogmatic distinctions but embraced the idea that a religious community should welcome Jews, Greeks, Egyptians, and Romans with friendship and compassion. Tarik explained, "Slave or master, rich or poor, we can all come together to pray to God in any language."

Aurelia found a lot of comfort in that thought.

Later that day, when Sosias appeared at the gate and asked to see her, he looked uncharacteristically dejected.

Sosias waited for a moment at the door. "I wanted to ask you. How is Alexander this morning?"

Aurelia smiled. "At that age, great fears are easily forgotten come daylight. I wish that were true for me."

Sosias nodded.

Aurelia studied his face. "What is it? Come and sit down and tell me. Yesterday, while we were all so preoccupied with our missing sons and fretting about Caligula, you were engrossed in your own troubles and yet alert enough to notice Rufus and Alexander among the soldiers and rescue them. I cannot thank you enough."

Sosias eased onto a chair and looked around, hesitant.

"Is it about Rhoda?"

Sosias nodded. "Since the massacre, Rhoda's family has moved to a small village called Amaria not far from here. Yesterday I went there to visit her. Rhoda met me with tears in her eyes. Her little niece is dying."

"Have you talked to Simon about her?"

"Simon told me to bring her to the sanatorium, and he will examine her, but when I described the growth on her face, he didn't think there was much he could do. The whole family has given up on her. In fact, it's worse than that. When people look at Anna, they make the sign of protection against the evil eye and think the powers of sin and evil have made her that way. It is beginning to affect the poor child because she doesn't understand why her whole family rejects her. All except Rhoda."

"And how are things between Rhoda and you?"

Sosias looked away and his voice was unsteady. "Her family has rejected my offer of marriage because I am not a Jew."

"And what does Rhoda say about that?"

"She refuses to talk about it."

"Oh, Sosias! We must do something."

Sosias sighed and started to get up. "There is nothing we can do."

Aurelia's eyes flashed with impatience. "Of course, there are things we can do. We need Althea's help." She called for Althea to come into the atrium. "Do you remember when you invited Sosias into your family?"

"It was the day Yosef died while saving the Torah from being burned in the synagogue."

"Didn't you and Shemuel adopt him?"

"We took him in because he was an orphan and needed a mother."

"What role did he play in your family?"

"As you well know, he is like a son to us. And he has been such a comfort since Shemuel's death in the massacre."

"How do you feel about him now?"

"He is still like a son to me. I am proud of him." She turned to him, and her eyes glowed with affection. "As proud as any mother can be of her very own son."

"Well, Sosias. That makes it very clear." Aurelia bounded to her feet. "Come, Sosias and Althea! We are going to pay a visit to Rhoda and her family. And you, Althea, are going to tell them exactly what you just told me."

Sosias and Althea looked at each other with arched eyebrows and a strange, awed expression in their eyes, and dared not object.

✦

When they arrived at Rhoda's house, Rhoda's mother welcomed them nervously and kept apologizing for their humble dwelling and the lack of baked goods in the house with which to properly entertain the daughter of a Roman senator. Aurelia tried to put everyone at ease, but the family clustered around her, and Aurelia realized that Sosias was embarrassed. With uncles, aunts, cousins, and other relatives in the tiny house, Aurelia realized it would be difficult for Sosias to present his case, so she asked to speak with Rhoda's mother alone and walked with her down a sandy path that looked like it led out to the desert. Aurelia began with her concern for little Anna but soon learned that Rhoda's mother thought her deformity was an act of punishment from God because her mother, Rhoda's sister, had not married a fellow Jew and had died giving birth. Aurelia did her best to persuade her that she didn't think God punished little children, but her arguments fell on deaf ears.

When she mentioned how much Sosias loved Rhoda and that he had been adopted by a Jewish couple, the mother asked, "Can you say with certainty they will not have children who will be deformed?"

Stunned, Aurelia said, "No one can promise you that no matter who the father is. But one thing I can predict with certainty is that Sosias is one of the finest young men I know. He is pious like his adoptive Jewish mother you just met. He is a brilliant man with many talents. And most importantly, he loves your daughter and will take care of her. If I had a daughter, I would be proud for him to be my son-in-law."

"We will find her a Jewish husband."

Aurelia summoned Althea to her side and asked her to vouch for Sosias as well. Althea spoke with fervor. "Your daughter has loved my son Sosias for years, and you know that he will offer her a bright future."

Rhoda's mother kept shaking her head, and there was no point in pursuing the discussion.

On their way back into town, Rhoda came with them with Anna in her arms and tears in her eyes. Aurelia said, "Maybe Simon can cure her, and your mother will change her mind."

Rhoda clutched the baby to her breast. "She won't," she said. "As soon as Anna is three years old and can legally be sold, she plans to sell her. She doesn't want to look at her in our house and be reminded of her daughter's sin. I don't think I will be able to stop her."

"Her own grandchild!" Aurelia looked over at Sosias and winced.

When Aurelia arrived at the Museion with Anna in her arms, Galina, Simon's assistant, took one look at Anna's disfigured face and ran to get Cydias.

Cydias shuffled into the room, washed his hands carefully, wiped them on a towel, and raised both arms to greet her. "What a pleasure to see you! You do not visit us enough, and lately, your Simon has been more gloomy than usual. You should come and bring cheer to us all more often."

"I'm afraid I do not bring cheer." She turned Anna so he could see her face.

He took one look at the child and grimaced. "The little girl Sosias was telling me about?"

Aurelia nodded. "Surely, something can be done. This growth is getting bigger every day. You see how it is pulling her cheek out and distorting her mouth so that it pulls to one side. We are afraid that it will soon cover her right eye, and she will not be able to see."

Cydias was too engrossed in examining her to reply. He ran his fingers along the bulging tumor, felt its density, and put his finger into Anna's mouth to check its size. "Her mouth will never be straight again."

"But you could remove it?"

"Too risky. She could bleed to death. And the wound that is left could still leave her disfigured. What do her parents want to do?"

"The mother died a few days after the birth. The father disappeared. The rest of her family rejects her. She has no one. Rhoda takes care of her. Her family believes this affliction is a punishment from God."

At the mention of her name, Rhoda stepped forward with Sosias at her side and took Anna in her arms. "Please! Is there something you could do?"

When Cydias shook his head, Sosias spoke up. "We were hoping Simon might be able to operate."

Cydias looked at Sosias and shook his head. "I would advise him not to. But he will have to make his own decision. Right now, he is teaching in the surgery theater you designed. He is in the middle of a class about wounds, lacerations, burns, scars, and treatments. You could go watch from the spectators' deck."

Aurelia spoke up, eyes flashing with excitement. "Let's go. I have never seen Simon teach."

Cydias held up his hand in warning. "It might be difficult to watch. Today's patient has an ugly knife wound from a street brawl. There will be a lot of blood."

Cydias led the way and explained to Aurelia how Sosias had designed the room for surgeries. The room was set up like a small amphitheater with two levels of seats halfway around a center table holding a patient where Simon stood and was demonstrating his techniques.

Cydias pointed to the domed ceiling where an oculus—a round hole open to the sky—let in daylight. "Above the table, Sosias placed two angled mirrors so students can see the surgeon's hands and the patient to get a better sense of what he is doing. Today several physicians from Rome are visiting. They are intrigued by Sosias's design. We can look down at the operation through this window." He gestured for them to enter. "Simon will not notice you are here. When he is in the middle of surgery, he sees only the patient."

Fascinated, they all gazed down at Simon working on an open wound with what looked like simple tweezers. He was explaining that it was important to remove all debris and dirt from the wound before closing it up. His hands were red with the patient's blood.

Sosias asked, "What about the pain?"

Cydias explained that most patients get blue lotus flower,

poppy tears, or ground-up mandrake root to make them calm and sleepy. "But they can feel it."

After peering down at the wound, Rhoda turned her head away and looked like she was about to be sick, so Sosias rushed her out of the room. Aurelia stayed back to watch Simon thread a needle and begin to sew the wound closed with silk thread.

He told the students about different kinds of stitches and demonstrated the ones he used most. "There's nothing new or magical about this. Three thousand years ago the Egyptian embalmers knew how to do all these same stitches. The only difference today is that we do this to save the living, not to preserve the dead. Well, there are two other differences. The dead don't feel pain. But the wounded person is in pain and there's a lot more bleeding, as you can see." Simon looked up at the students and asked if they had questions.

Aurelia turned to Cydias, wide-eyed with wonder. Cydias nodded and smiled. "Your husband is one of the most gifted surgeons in the empire."

"He learned it all from you."

Cydias shook his head. "Oh no, my dear. I knew from the beginning that he had gifts way beyond mine. I am too clumsy. He has the healing hands for it. It is not for nothing that the word for surgery is *cheirourgike*—the work of hands."

She gazed at Simon with new appreciation and marveled that he had so many skills about which she knew so little. At the end of the class, Simon reminded the students that Cydias, the most famous physician at the Museion, had taught him the most important lesson about being a good doctor. He started to wash up. "You must always approach each patient with compassion and with clean hands. Much comfort is transmitted by human touch. But much disease also."

When Simon appeared, Aurelia held the baby out to him and said, "Look at Anna's large, expressive eyes! Simon, you must try to save her."

Galina, Simon's assistant, placed Anna on the examination

table. Obviously disconcerted by the insistence of her petition, Simon started to examine Anna, palpitating, pushing, and pressing on different parts of her cheek and jaw until Anna started her own petition by whimpering, then howling in displeasure. Simon shook his head and frowned. "It's too risky."

They all looked at each other in consternation, and Aurelia asked, "Isn't it just as risky not to do anything? Soon she won't be able to see out of that eye. What kind of life will she have?"

"Maybe Cydias—"

Aurelia shook her head. "He said the same thing."

Simon lifted his shoulders with a slow, audible release of breath. "I'm sorry."

Rhoda picked up the crying Anna and cradled her against her breast, trying to comfort her. Anna settled down a bit and burped, sputtered, and glared at Simon.

Simon noticed her expression and smiled. "She has spirit. I'll grant you that."

Aurelia said, "You once told me the scholars at the Museion can look through medical writings by physicians like Hippocrates, Herophilos, and Erisistratos and point to procedures and remedies that have been successful. Couldn't you ask the researchers about this growth on Anna's face?"

Simon replied, "When someone asked Herophilos for a definition of the perfect doctor, Herophilos said, 'The perfect doctor is the one who is capable of distinguishing between what is possible and what is impossible.'" Simon gazed into their stricken faces and left to go wash his hands again.

At the door, Aurelia took Anna in her arms. "I will take her home with me and talk to him."

That evening, Aurelia cradled Anna in her arms and asked Simon why God would allow a beautiful child to be disfigured by such an atrocious growth.

Simon studied his wife—the way she held the baby close to her breast, the tender concern in her violet eyes, and the look on her face when she played with the little button of Anna's nose that made Anna attempt a lopsided smile. "If love and caresses could heal, she would be whole thanks to you."

"If she were our daughter, what would you do?"

"That's not a fair question. She is not our daughter. But even if she were, I would not be able to make her face look normal again."

"Normal is not what Rhoda hopes for. She is afraid Anna will die. Won't this continue to grow and eventually kill her?"

"Probably."

"If she were a crooked tree, I would put stakes around it and gradually make it grow tall and straight. If she were a beautiful shrub that had a mushrooming growth on one side, I would cut off the parts of the plant that are feeding the growth."

Simon did not respond. Instead, he walked to the window and gazed out into the evening shadows while Aurelia put Anna to bed in a crib beside her sleeping sons. He turned toward her when she came back. "Your talk about gardening gave me an idea."

"You will cut off the ugly growth?"

"No. But I could take silk thread and gradually tie off some of the vessels that cause the tumor to grow. I have never seen it done, but I may be able to stop it from getting worse." He started for the door. "I'm going to walk through the gardens for a moment to think about the best way to do this."

When he came in from the garden, he took Aurelia in his arms and kissed her with passion.

She looked at him curiously. "Is there something wrong?"

"No, why would you say that?"

"I don't know. The way you kissed me."

He pulled her close again. "Like this?" He pressed her against him and caressed her breast.

"Whatever happened out in the garden, I like it." She returned his kisses.

Simon laughed. "I ran into Tiberius Alexander."

"And?"

"We had an argument."

"Oh?" She pulled back to study his face.

"About you. I wanted to knock his teeth out when he said your name, but then he said that I neglect you and leave you alone too much and that I don't even appreciate the fact that the most amazing woman in the Roman Empire is my wife."

Aurelia laughed. "You agreed. Right?"

"I agreed you are amazing. Do you think I neglect you?"

"Kiss me again and prove to me that you don't."

"I wanted to challenge him to a wrestling match."

"Which you would win. Come to bed."

She realized immediately that his encounter in Philo's garden had kindled his ardor, and she was amused and surprised that they could still undress with the rapid eagerness they shared in the first months of their marriage and secretly thanked Tiberius Alexander for provoking his jealous possessiveness. As his fingers teased and fondled her body, she remembered his dexterity in the operating theater and was awed by hands that could love so well and work to heal so many. He whispered the words of the *Song of Songs* in her ear, and she responded to his passion with complete abandon.

Later, in the afterglow of shared fulfillment, she expressed her dream of having a third child. As she dozed off, she felt him smile against her breast.

THE PROMISE OF PERMANENCE

A WEEK LATER, PHILO LED A COLORFUL PROCESSION of scholars, theologians, and linguists up the winding ramp of the lighthouse in his elaborately fringed and decorated litter. Musicians playing trumpets, kitharas, and timbrels set the solemn pace of their ascent. At the top of the first level, they entered a large hall where three hundred years ago the translation of holy scripture from Hebrew to Greek was completed, blessed, and dedicated by King Ptolemaios II Philadelphos, who had generously financed the project that became known as the Septuagint—the work of the seventy. At the time of their inspired work, the lighthouse was only one-third of its finished height. Over the years, the annual commemoration of this holy work at the Pharos had become a major event when both Jews and many non-Jews from all over the empire gathered to celebrate. During the day, small groups of scholars spread out into the very study rooms used by the original translators three centuries ago. They analyzed key passages that were chanted by young students who had been selected for this honor by their home synagogues.

In the evening, the whole conference came together for an

elaborate festival on the rocky coast north of the lighthouse. Just after sundown, everyone fell silent and waited for the flame to emerge at the top of the lighthouse. The first flicker of fire was difficult to see because the sheer mass of the Pharos blocked the view of the flame, but a crier signaled the moment from the northernmost tip of the island, and the crowd raised arms in chants of thanksgiving, praising God's creation of first light—"*genetheto phos!*"—"let there be light!" Then, as the flame grew larger, the reflected light appeared upon the waves of the sea like a solemn promise from on high. A runner bearing a flame from the Pharos appeared at the far edge of the crowd and lit the lamps in the back row. They, in turn, lit the lamps in the next row until the whole island was ablaze with flickering flames that danced in the breeze from the sea.

When the cheering stopped, Philo rose to speak and held onto a massive outcropping of stone to steady himself. "Tonight, we remember the seventy-two scholars who worked tirelessly on this very site to convey our holy scriptures into Greek. We celebrate their work by coming together each year to find renewed strength and glory in the Lord's holy word. We need that strength now, for a year ago we witnessed terrible slaughter in this city, and we still mourn for the many who died. We have not recovered our rights to land ownership and our citizenship, and I shall soon lead a delegation to Rome to demand restitution directly from the emperor."

The audience cheered, but Philo held up his hand for silence.

"It is a sad day for all of us that we must resort to this *legatio* to demand our rights. But we will go forth emboldened by your support to make our case to the emperor. And now, let us hear from our honored delegate from Jerusalem, Rabbi Gamaliel, master teacher and grandson of Hillel the Elder."

Gamaliel rose slowly and looked out over the crowd. He raised both arms to the heavens and spoke in a deep, melodious voice that made everyone listen closely. "The Most High speaks to us through the very light of the heavens. The Most High speaks to us in the burning bush. But we must always remember that the Most High also speaks to us through the small voice of a child if we care to stop and listen. And on this site, we are reminded that the Most High continues to speak to us through his holy word."

At the end of his long speech, Gamaliel brought greetings from King Agrippa and described the progress being made on the renovation of the temple under Agrippa's leadership. He thanked all the Jews of the diaspora for their valiant support of the temple.

Philo then introduced his brother, the alabarch of Alexandria.

Alexander Lysimachos rose to his feet, walked to the front, and faced the crowd with his back to the sea. Three boys held lanterns aloft so the alabarch could be seen in his richly jeweled white robe. "My fellow citizens of Jerusalem—for all of us call the holy city our home—we have just heard that our temple is being restored to its former glory by Agrippa, King of the Jews. This day, I am sending out a proclamation to all artists and sculptors everywhere in the empire to announce a contest to create a bronze door for the temple in Jerusalem. The artist with the best and most beautiful design will win the task of creating the door. I will provide the funds for it. A beautiful door of bronze is practical, enduring, and symbolic. Through this new door, we will enter onto holy ground. The door for the temple in bronze will endure for ages to come and proclaim the glory of the Most High. It is a promise of permanence."

His announcement was met with enthusiastic applause.

When Sosias read the alabarch's proclamation that was sent out across the empire and posted at the emporium the next day, he ran to tell his close friend Nicanor, who was an assistant to Zenodoros, a renowned sculptor in Alexandria, and told him he should stop melting down the bronze from statues of Tiberius and forget about making casting molds for Heron's pumps and steam-powered contraptions and dream of winning the contest. "Here's a challenge for you! You can do this!"

But Nicanor shrugged it off and said, "I could never compete for something so grand or so holy. I am not worthy of such a task."

"Nonsense," said Sosias. "We will go to Jerusalem and see where this door should fit and take measurements and figure out ways to make it unique and special."

"We? Since when are you a sculptor of bronze?"

"We're talking about a door. A door is not just a big slab of bronze. A door needs to fit into walls; it has to be designed to be fastened to the wall; it has to open and close. It may have to have a lock. You must consider the sweep and range of the door and the need for astragals for two bronze slabs to meet at the center. How do you propose to do that without an engineer helping you like me? Come! I'll show you the doors at the temple of Isis, and you'll see what we need to plan for."

Nicanor put down the bellows he was using to make the foundry fire rage over the coals, wiped his hands on his leather apron, and ran with Sosias to the emporium to read the proclamation for himself. His eyes grew large and were strikingly white against his soot-blackened face as he contemplated the enormity of the challenge and exclaimed, he would never be able to do it.

Sosias decided to take him to see Rhoda, hoping that she would be able to change his mind. Because Sosias had described Rhoda in such glowing terms, Nicanor asked Sosias to wait while he went to wash and dress in his finest robe. Rhoda welcomed them into her mother's small kitchen, where Sosias introduced Nicanor as his best friend and explained how excited he was about the competition for the bronze door. Before long, Sosias had spread out a sheet of papyrus on the table to make drawings, and Nicanor looked on while Rhoda's mother served refreshments and asked Nicanor about his family. When Rhoda asked Nicanor how he would go about designing the door, he started bragging about his ability to make the finest door in the empire, pulled the papyrus away from Sosias, and started to make his own drawings. Sosias was thrilled that Rhoda's questions had kindled Nicanor's interest. Rhoda's mother seemed more welcoming than usual, and Sosias was pleased when she made a point of inviting them back and did not pay attention to the fact that she addressed her invitation primarily to Nicanor. Sosias was so eager to compete for the project that he was relieved to notice Nicanor's sudden enthusiasm.

✦

That night, Alexander Lysimachos held a reception in his grand villa for the dignitaries who had come for the festival. Simon didn't want to go. He had never felt comfortable in large gatherings and found most of the social chatter inane and boring, but Aurelia insisted that dignitaries who had just arrived from Rome would be there, and she wanted to learn the latest news.

Simon protested. "Gossip more likely than news. You won't learn anything about your brother. I'd rather go check on my patients at the sanatorium."

Aurelia smiled as she pulled a brand-new white robe with beautiful emerald trim over his head and steered him out the door. "Anna is in good hands. Galina has fallen in love with her, and she's recovering nicely. You said yourself that you thought the tumor might be shrinking."

"I have other patients."

"You'll see them tomorrow."

At the reception, guests milled about tables laden with delectable exotic fruits, pastries, poultry on kabobs, smoked fish, artichoke hearts in oil and vinegar, breads made with five different grains from Ethiopia, mussels and shellfish in piquant sauces, grilled vegetables, and roasted morsels of lamb—all exuding enticing aromas—while servants circulated through the room with wine, fruit brandies, beer, juices, and hot teas.

Near a huge silver platter of fresh fruit, Gamaliel was answering a question about the latest unrest in Jerusalem where a man was brought before the Sanhedrin for preaching a new Messiah. Gamaliel explained, "He was eloquent and explained his beliefs convincingly with fervor. He traced our history all the way back to Abraham, and I cautioned the Council to set him free, but many took offense and hauled him outside the city and stoned him to death."

Someone asked if the Messiah this man preached was the same man who was crucified several years ago. Aurelia looked over at Simon and tried to catch his eye, but Simon was frowning at Gamaliel. Afraid Simon would get involved in an argument, Aurelia tried to pull him away. It would not be the first time Simon had ruined a party, and she regretted now that she had urged him to come.

Gamaliel turned toward the speaker and answered, "The same. The man who was crucified has many loyal followers who grow in number and stir up trouble."

Simon asked, "Enough trouble to warrant being stoned?"

"He spoke against the temple."

"What did he say?"

"He said, 'The Most High does not dwell in a temple built by hands.'"

"And for that truth he was killed?" Simon's voice betrayed his outrage.

At that moment, Philo clapped his hands for silence. He stood beside Alexander Lysimachos and said, "My brother has a special announcement." Both moved to the side to let a beautiful girl step forward on the arm of a young man who gazed down at his feet and looked awkward and uncomfortable. The young lady, by contrast, made a stunning figure in the arched entrance. Poised, self-assured, regal—she stood tall in a purple silk gown decorated with gold embroidery with bright gems on her arms and at her neck. She smiled and seemed to favor each guest with her personal attention. Her black hair was swept up in a crown of springy curls that bounced across her forehead as she stooped gracefully to curtsy.

Alexander Lysimachos nodded to her and proclaimed, "My future daughter-in-law—Princess Berenice, daughter of Herod Agrippa, King of the Jews. She and my son Marcos will wed next year. King Agrippa was supposed to be here tonight to make this announcement, but the emperor has called him away to Rome on urgent business."

Aurelia wondered if any of that urgent business included decisions affecting Valerius as she studied Berenice with admiration and awe. The feisty little brat who had refused to share her dowry linens for bandages during the terrible massacre had matured into a beautiful and seductive young lady. On this festive night, Marcos looked ill-prepared for the role of royal consort. Marcos was shy and sickly, totally unlike his older brother Tiberius Alexander, and seldom voiced an opinion of his own.

Gamaliel lifted his wine in a toast to the bride and groom, and the guests followed suit.

After toasts all around, Simon continued his discussion with Gamaliel, who gently tugged on his white beard and looked tired and frail. Simon led him to some chairs where the master teacher sat down with a sigh. Aurelia brought them wine and sat down beside them, wondering if Simon was going to continue his argument, and was relieved when she heard Simon ask about his sister Rachel and her husband Sedek.

Gamaliel smiled and sipped the wine. "Speaking of weddings. I attended theirs. It was a most delightful occasion."

"What is your opinion of Sedek, her husband?"

"Ah, Sedek!" Gamaliel smiled. "He can gaze at the stars in

the firmament and see revelations from the Most High. He is the most pious man I know. An unusual man. Like so many who live far from Jerusalem, he needs neither the scriptures nor the temple to speak to God."

"The scriptures and the temple." Simon paused for a moment. "Which is more important?"

"Excellent question. Must I make a choice?" Gamaliel stroked his beard thoughtfully.

"Perhaps not."

"But I will." Gamaliel smiled. "The scriptures will not perish. The word is eternal. Philo agrees with me. He loves to speak of the Logos, the everlasting Word of God."

Simon sat forward on his chair. "But when our host Alexander Lysimachos proclaims that the bronze doors for the temple are a promise of permanence, do you not agree?"

Gamaliel's eyes twinkled, and he seemed amused by the question. "You are leading back to our earlier discussion. A bronze door is made by an artist. A temple built by hands is not permanent."

"The young fellow who was stoned...?"

"Stephanos."

"What he said was true. And for that, he was stoned?"

"An unfortunate incident indeed."

Simon's face tightened. The muscles in his cheek worked back and forth, and he brought his fist down into his open palm. "You said there are others like him who are causing trouble?"

Gamaliel nodded.

Simon's voice rose in vexation. "While we in Alexandria deal with criminals, thugs, and looters who would like to wipe Jews off the face of the earth, Jews are fighting against Jews in Jerusalem, the city of peace. What are you doing to stop it? Why this fighting among us? There are many who want to harm us without Jews killing Jews!"

"The Pharisees and the Sadducees and this latest group

who proclaim the Messiah disagree—"

"To the point of stoning?"

Gamaliel held up his hand and started to say something but stopped.

Simon took a sip of wine and rubbed his hand across his forehead. "What do *you* think of the rabbi they crucified? Do you think he was the Messiah?"

Aurelia suppressed a gasp with a cough, but Gamaliel seemed unruffled by the question even though he must have been part of the Sanhedrin that had called for the Galilean's crucifixion.

"I will give you the same answer I gave to the Sanhedrin when they wanted to condemn Stephanos and Yeshua's followers: 'Do not take action against them! If what they have done is of human origin, it will disappear, but if it comes from God, you cannot defeat them. You could find yourselves fighting against God!'"

Aurelia expected Simon to tell Gamaliel he had carried Yeshua's cross up to the place of execution, but he did not. She gazed at him with a question in her eyes, and Simon looked away, shaking his head.

Aurelia decided to slip away in search of the Roman guests at the festival, hoping for recent news about Caligula and his intentions. Near the platters of sweet pastries, she saw one of the dignitaries dressed in the scarlet tunic usually worn under the cuirass of the praetorians. The strong military stance, the close-cropped hair, and the somewhat haughty air prompted her to believe he was the Roman commander she was looking for. She made her way toward him and greeted him in Latin. He bowed gallantly and responded in kind.

When she asked about recent events in Rome, he responded with caution and little news of interest. After mentioning her concern for her brother who had been called back to Rome by the emperor, his demeanor changed, and he took her aside and recounted a long list of Caligula's misdeeds. "Caligula has lost the respect of the military. He is only interested in self-glorification. He requires his advisors to kiss his ring like an eastern potentate. He has taken the entire military budget and spent it frivolously on pleasure boats on a lake near Rome and dedicated the whole thing to the moon goddess Diana. He has squandered the twenty-seven million gold pieces Tiberius left at his death. His folly has drained the treasury, endangers the security of the empire, will cause higher taxes, and will ultimately bring chaos to Rome. Caligula seeks to outshine the gods of Rome and boasts that he and his ships are indestructible."

Later, as Aurelia and Simon walked through Philo's estate to their house, Aurelia held onto Simon's arm and said, "Did you tell Gamaliel you carried the cross and witnessed the crucifixion?"

"No."

"Why not?"

"I don't know. My role was not important. The mob was determined to kill him. I couldn't do anything about it."

"I think Gamaliel is troubled. I even wonder—"

"What?"

"I wonder if he believes Yeshua was the Messiah."

"I don't know."

"But didn't you say the religious authorities like Gamaliel accused him and wanted him crucified?"

"I believe so. I never understood why."

Aurelia squeezed his arm.

As they readied for bed, she mentioned what the Roman commander had said about Caligula's pleasure boats. "Caligula claims they are indestructible."

Simon gave a hollow laugh. "It's folly to speak of permanence in this world. Nothing is permanent, not bronze doors for the temple, not even the stars that flicker in the firmament. And as for Caligula—how long do you think his indestructible pleasure boats will last?"

✦

ON EDGE

IN THE MIDDLE OF THE NIGHT, CALIGULA SUMMONED Agrippa to his quarters.

Nocturnal like a scorpion, Caligula roamed through the cavernous rooms of the palace, mourning for his sister Drusilla, who had died of a fever. For weeks he wept and raged against death. And then he made her a goddess. She was moonlight. She was the moon. She embraced him. She flowed through the windows, enfolding him in celestial luminosity. He flung his arms around himself and embraced himself by caressing the silver glow that bathed his body.

Agrippa watched Caligula slither up a column encircled by a vine where he held out his arms heavenward.

"*Ave*, Agrippa! Do you see her? Here she is in my arms. See how I make love to her! Come and stand in her light and pray to her!"

Agrippa did not move.

"What's the matter? Don't you see? She is all around us."

"You called for me?"

"First you must make love to Drusilla. Like this."

"Only the emperor can do that."

"I'm showing you how."

"When you are sober, I'll come back." Agrippa turned to leave.

"Stay! I command you!" Caligula gored him with an angry stare.

Agrippa waited.

Caligula climbed halfway down and jumped the rest of the way with arms outstretched and clung to Agrippa.

"You asked me here on important business."

"I did. I did." Caligula picked up a goblet, took a swallow, and smacked his lips with pleasure. "Have some!" He thrust a goblet into Agrippa's hand. "I will have my revenge!" He burst into a giggle, high-pitched like a girl's. "You will be so proud of me. I'll catch two boars with one net. No, make that three! For years I tolerated that Jewish physician at the bedside of Tiberius. He kept Tiberius alive way beyond the limits of decency. I was glad to kick him out. He married a Roman noblewoman who thinks she is superior to me. She had the audacity to spurn me." He exploded with a wild burst of laughter.

Agrippa looked away.

Caligula grinned. "Ah! I see you remember how she insulted me in Capri. I never forget those who wrong me. You look perplexed."

"You mentioned three boars in your net. You name only two."

"Right you are. Now we come to the crux of the matter— her brother Publius Petronius Valerius. I have called him back to Rome. Now Petronius will have to carry out my orders. The Jews will worship me and no other. I so decree! Let's drink to my brilliance!"

Caligula emptied his goblet in one gulp. Agrippa took a sip.

Caligula looked at him sideways and grinned. "We will start with you! You are a Jew. Bow down and worship me!"

Agrippa almost spilled his wine when he made a half-hearted bow. He realized Caligula was creating his own reality about what had happened on Capri. He knew Aurelia had fled from Caligula's advances and Simon was a constant irritant to Caligula like a boil that never heals, but he couldn't see how Aurelia's brother could have angered him. He decided to humor him to find out what he planned to do.

Agrippa knew that he was always answerable to Caligula, but he refused to become his puppet. He had to walk a fine line between being an advocate for his fellow Jews and being subservient to Rome and imperial whims. Toward morning, Agrippa started a long letter to Philo to warn him of the coming calamity and sent it off to Alexandria by a fast merchant ship. Could Philo find a way to placate Caligula, who was obviously out of control? Could there be a way to stop this looming disaster? At the very least, Agrippa could warn his fellow Jews that Caligula had dreamed up a diabolical plot that could bring about the deaths of thousands. And part of this alarming insanity was that Caligula thought he was being brilliant.

✦

THE NEW GOVERNOR OF SYRIA

WHEN SEDEK WAS SUMMONED TO THE OLD SELEUCID palace to see Lucius Vitellius, he found slaves hard at work packing huge wooden crates of belongings. The palace, formerly richly carpeted, now echoed hollowly with his footsteps. Vitellius greeted him with his usual warmth and invited him to be seated in his sparsely furnished study. The scrolls were gone, and no drapes hung at the doors and windows.

Sedek found himself talking in a whisper. "Lucius, my friend, I've heard you received orders to report in person to the emperor!"

Lucius Vitellius nodded.

"Those who know him well think these are ominous summons."

Vitellius sighed. "Indeed."

"Is there anything I can do for you as you get ready to leave? I am at your service."

"First, you know how grateful I am for your assistance over the last five years—your knowledge of Syria, of Antioch, of Judea, your advice, and above all your friendship have been invaluable to me. I hope you will be able to be of equal service to the incoming governor."

"That depends on who it is and how open he would be to heeding my advice."

"I thought you knew. Publius Petronius has just been named the new governor of Syria."

"My brother-in-law!" Sedek sat back and let it sink in for a moment. "I confess I do not know him and have never met him. My wife's brother is married to his sister. In family circles, they call him Valerius to distinguish him from his uncle of the same name. But what I do know about him is quite impressive. He has a fine reputation for just and even-handed governance."

Vitellius nodded. "Indeed. I know him personally. I worked with him to bring peace to Parthia. It is an ingenious appointment. He is diplomatic, intelligent, an astute governor. But—"

"But?"

"I hope you are prepared for the worst. Publius Petronius will have to carry out Caligula's orders."

"That would be true for any governor."

"True. But perhaps you have not heard the latest news. Caligula has ordered his statue to be placed in the temple in Jerusalem and wants to be worshiped as a god. And—*horribile dictu*—Publius Petronius Valerius must carry out his command."

Sedek reared back in his chair. "Impossible. Outrageous." After a stunned silence, he said, "Valerius will refuse."

Lucius Vitellius shook his head. "He will have no choice."

"There will be war."

"If Valerius opposes Caligula, he will lose his life. Caligula's wrath could extend to you—your wife, your family, his sister, and her husband. On the other hand, if Valerius should try to erect a statue of Caligula in the temple in Jerusalem, there will be bloodshed. Thousands of Jews will die."

"I don't agree with you. Our emperor may be mad, but God has answered our prayers before we even knew to ask. I firmly believe Valerius will never harm my people."

And so Sedek believed when he said the Sabbath prayers that evening and called down God's blessings on the new governor of Syria. When Matthaios had gone to bed, Rachel asked Sedek about his prayer for the new governor. Sedek smiled and caressed her cheek. "The new governor, my dear, will be none other than Publius Petronius."

"Valerius!"

Sedek saw only surprise in her expression and not the sudden alarm that caused her to avert her eyes.

✦

Rachel's hand shook as she brushed her hair and stared critically into the polished mirror. What she saw were not the expressive dark eyes that stared back at her, but the outline of a face she had tried desperately to banish from memory. Plaster busts of the new governor of Syria had been erected all over Antioch, and it was hard to escape the reality of his presence. The welcoming ceremonies for Publius Petronius were almost over, and she refused to join the curious crowds at the gate and gape at his parade and his accompanying knights along the Via Colonna. When Matthaios wanted to run out and watch the horses, she forbade it with uncharacteristic sternness.

She worried now about when their paths would cross. Not to see Valerius was impossible. After all, her brother had married Valerius's sister, and he and his wife were part of the family. The thought of his wife aroused her curiosity. The fact that Valerius had been married for several months made the prospect of his arrival both easier and harder to deal with.

Rachel knew Lucius Vitellius had plotted for Valerius and his daughter to meet. Rachel smiled to herself when she pictured Valerius standing tall and handsome in front of Vitellia. She imagined five or six possible scenarios for their first encounter, each more seductive than the last, and finally gave her dark hair such a violent brush stroke that her curls crackled with a life all their own.

"Rachel?" Sedek stood behind her.

She held her breath and turned to face him.

He studied her face for a long time but said nothing.

Rachel held his gaze for a moment and then turned away. He put his hand on her shoulder and pulled her face back to meet his. Suddenly flustered, she pulled away and struggled to hold back tears.

Sedek let go and crossed to the other side of the room. "You are troubled, I see. I know you are still fretting about the news from Alexandria."

"Simon writes that Meidias's old gang has started up again. So far, Simon and his family have not been hurt, but my brother can be hotheaded and stubborn and is a target for these vicious gangs."

"Indeed. When we met in Jerusalem, I was impressed by his devotion to our people. But then I was surprised when he chose to marry a Roman girl, the daughter of a senator."

"You disapprove?"

"I question his allegiance to his own people. I question his motives."

Rachel started brushing her hair again in long, even strokes. "Had you thought about the simple motive that they might love each other?"

Sedek chuckled and gazed thoughtfully at her face in the mirror. "Love is never simple. You have a starry-eyed view of marriage. Theirs might have been purely political. You know your brother. What do you think?"

Rachel stopped brushing and searched for the right words. "Simon is a passionate man in all that he does. He is passionate about his loyalty to his family and to his people, but he is not political. I am sure that his marriage to Aurelia is based on passion, not politics."

"The important thing for us is to find out if his wife could be useful to us."

"You mean politically?"

"Of course. Does she have influence with her brother?"

"I don't know. I haven't met her. My brother and her brother are very close friends. They have been close friends since childhood. I am confident Valerius will listen to Simon and want to know what he thinks."

Sedek reached out and ran his fingers along a strand of her hair. "The family connection will be useful. Especially now that your brother's friend is to be our new governor. I think it would be a good time to invite your family to come here for a visit. What do you think?"

A surge of fear made Rachel feel cramps in her stomach, but she managed a smile and said, "That would be wonderful."

He nodded and started to leave. At the door, he turned and said, "You were obviously close enough to call him Valerius."

Rachel's resolve to dismiss Valerius from her mind was easily taken and easily broken. Perhaps a family reunion would bring things into perspective. Any objections she might make would be impossible to explain. She couldn't imagine what it would be like to see Valerius again. How would he greet her?

It was not long before she found out.

✦

The very next day, when late autumn winds blew dark rain clouds over Antioch, Rachel was stoking the brazier to throw more heat in the room when she looked up at the sound of Matthaios running excitedly toward her.

"There are horses coming through the gate! Big white ones. I just bet it is my uncle you've told me about!"

Rachel dabbed at her face self-consciously, then ran to the entrance.

Valerius had just dismounted and shook the rain from his cape. She caught her breath. This was not the boyish Valerius she had known so many years ago. Strong and determined features left no doubt as to who was in charge. He gave an order to Farid and stepped into the portico.

Rachel was glad for Matthaios's impetuosity as he ran to his uncle to embrace him. Valerius laughed and clasped him to his chest just as he turned to Rachel. Their eyes met. For a moment time stood still, and she remembered their last lingering kiss in Cyrene.

Laughing still, he opened his arms to her and crushed her to his chest and held her tight. Rachel pulled back from him, and he held her at arm's length, smiling.

As yet, neither had spoken. Rachel turned abruptly to lavish attention on Matthaios, afraid her spontaneous outpouring of affection had given away far more than she had wanted to admit, even to herself.

"I want to see the horses." Matthaios didn't wait for an answer, but ran to the portico and dashed out into the rain to stroke the dripping animals.

Rachel called him back. But it was too late. Matthaios was already splattered with mud. She ran to get towels and alert Sedek that the governor of Syria had arrived.

"You will join us?" Valerius called after her but received no reply. He was left for a moment to examine the geometric mosaics in the floor.

Sedek came forward. "Hail, Publius Petronius! I am honored to welcome you to Antioch. The city has changed its festive coat for a dreary one, and for that, I apologize."

Valerius laughed. "I didn't know that you control the weather. From what I've seen, the farmers need the rain."

Sedek led him to his study. "True. Please, be seated."

Valerius watched Mara pour wine into silver goblets. Then he turned his full attention to Sedek. He was surprised that he felt so calm, almost lighthearted. His mission in Syria would be grim. Vitellius had warned him about the emperor's madness, the ungovernable Jews, the carping Syrians, and the unjust taxation policies. Valerius already knew about the problems with Parthia.

Vitellius told him Sedek would be a most valuable advisor, and yet Sedek was Rachel's husband. He seemed kind and wise and very old. He had anticipated feeling pangs of jealousy. Instead, he had to check an overwhelming desire to pour out his heart and confide his feelings to him.

Sedek held up his goblet. "Your arrival is an answer to prayer. As much as I admired and respected Vitellius, I have even greater confidence in you. I hope you will never harm my people." Sedek's smile faded. "You do know that you will be asked to do just that?"

"It is as though Vitellius were pulled from the stage just as the final act was about to begin, and I've been pushed out in front of a gaping audience, and I don't have the script. It remains to be seen whether I am playing a comedy, a tragedy, or a farce."

"It has all the makings of a tragedy."

Valerius noted with a start that Sedek seemed certain of his prediction. "Is there a way to avoid tragedy?"

Sedek frowned. "Your choices will be between death for the Jews or death for you. Not just for you. For your family, for the officers in your legions. In other words, your attempt to save us from the emperor will mean your peril."

"I must outwit the emperor at his own game." He paused and looked expectantly at the door that remained shut and ran his fingers through his close-cropped hair. "Once I swore that I would never put myself in my father's position where he had to die because of the caprices of the imperial system. It is a system most unjust."

"You are answerable to Rome, not to my people. Your noble declaration of support of my people will fall by the wayside when you receive imperial orders."

Valerius shook his head. "The reason Tiberius appointed me to Asia many years ago was because I did not blindly bow to all imperial whims."

"Caligula is no Tiberius."

"Agreed. Still, that fact causes you anguish and gives me hope. What do you know about Caligula?"

"Only the prevalent rumors in the empire."

"Which are?"

Sedek shrugged. "You know that as well as I."

Suddenly aware of Sedek's caution, Valerius's eyes narrowed. "You are afraid to say what every child in the empire knows. Our emperor is mad. Now the question is: Do I follow the orders of a madman? I may not be in as much danger as you think."

"I hope you are right. What news do you have of the situation in Alexandria?"

This was the excuse Valerius had been waiting for. "Surely, Rachel would like to hear about her brother in Alexandria and his family." He jumped up to call Mara to fetch her mistress.

When Rachel entered the room, Valerius immediately launched into a detailed description of his visit to Alexandria. As he told them what he had learned from Simon about the brutal slaughter, he stopped mid-sentence when he saw the expression of alarm on Rachel's face.

Rachel said, "I guessed it was worse than what they told us in their letters."

"But your brother and his family are fine." After a moment of silence, he said, "In the end, it was quite gratifying to see justice done! Flaccus paid the ultimate price for allowing the massacre to go on unchecked." Valerius placed a reassuring hand on her knee. "We can rejoice that it's over."

Rachel nodded.

Sedek said, "We are indeed relieved Flaccus is gone. Philo wrote me a detailed account of what happened and claims that Flaccus used to be a good man, a man of honor. His main mistake is that he backed Tiberius's grandson, Gemellus, and tried desperately to remedy that unfortunate mistake by currying favor with Caligula through his policy of persecuting Jews. His own tactics were turned against him. Now he is no more. But what frightens me more is that the arm of the emperor can reach to the farthest corners of the empire and snuff out a life at the flick of a finger. A most sobering fact, Publius Petronius." Sedek looked at him sharply and conveyed an unmistakable message of warning.

Valerius looked toward Rachel and willed her to return his gaze, but she kept looking at the floor like a timid schoolgirl who was unable to recite her lessons. He tried to reassure. "I vow to do everything within my power to keep peace."

Sedek shook his head. "You must understand. You have no power. At least facing the emperor, you don't. He has the power of evil, and against that power, you cannot prevail. The fact that it is arbitrary evil makes any rational approach impossible."

"Sedek!" Rachel protested, but Sedek held up his hand to silence her.

Valerius pounded his fist into his palm and started to say something, but thought better of it. After an awkward silence, he decided to change the subject and launched into a slightly exaggerated but hilarious account of his nephews and their escapade as little Roman soldiers. He was rewarded with laughter from Sedek and smiles from Rachel. She said, "I can imagine that Rufus, Alexander, and Matthaios could get into a lot of mischief together."

Valerius said he had no doubt that was true and rose to leave, bowing respectfully to Sedek. Then he turned to Rachel. "You must bring Matthaios to our stables to see all the horses. He'll enjoy that!"

Later that evening, Sedek commented to Rachel that he had great admiration for Publius Petronius. Rachel put on her wool nightgown in the unheated bedroom and said nothing. Sedek repeated his praise and said, "I think he will be a wise governor. What do you think?"

Rachel sat for a moment on the edge of the bed. The memory of Valerius's embrace lingered like a precious gift in her heart. Then she studied Sedek's face and realized that she was being foolish not to cherish the solemn questioning in his eyes and every wrinkle in his sun-darkened face. She admired him. She was grateful to him. But he was not Valerius. Valerius was like an apparition from a dream—dashing and unattainable and mysterious. Forbidden. She could not deny what she felt when he pressed her close. Sedek, by comparison, was her constant friend, stable and kind and predictable. "I am afraid for him," she answered. She quenched the oil lamp and lay down beside Sedek. In the darkness, she added under her breath, "and for us all."

FAMILY REUNION

VITELLIA ENTERED THE ROOM WHERE VALERIUS normally held audiences with local magistrates and said, "You ordered the staff to prepare rooms for the visit of your family?" She held her neck straight and twisted stiffly toward him, causing the crown of tight curls layered in three tiers on her head to tilt forward at a precarious angle.

Valerius looked up from a pile of documents on his desk. "I told you my sister was coming with her family."

Vitellia frowned. "Why are they staying here and not with those Jews—you know—his sister's family? What's her name again?"

"Rachel."

"Rachel. Why here?"

"Aurelia is my sister. Besides, we have more room. The children will have more space to play, and they can roam around the large gardens."

Vitellia sighed dramatically. "That's right. Two little boys. Another reason for them to stay with Rachel and her husband. I've just redone the palace and redecorated. I don't want them tearing down my hard work."

Valerius defended the boys. "Rufus and Alexander are very well-behaved. I don't think you need to worry."

"Well, they won't be used to such rich surroundings and might destroy things just out of curiosity."

Valerius laughed. "I doubt that very much. In Alexandria, they live on Philo's estate, and Philo's estate is the finest in Alexandria." He looked around the room. "Much nicer than this drafty palace."

Vitellia made a face and glanced down at the drawings on his desk. "What are these?"

"Plans to widen the harbor of Antioch at Seleucia Pieria."

"At the mouth of the Orontes River. That was my father's ambition. It will be a big boost to commerce for the region."

"True. It's a good plan. I'll be riding out today to study the exact dimensions of the proposal. We may even be able to hire local engineers to do the job."

Vitellia studied the drawings for a moment. "You should hire Roman engineers. They are the best. I'll go with you to meet with the local magistrates."

Valerius looked up at his wife. "Why would you want to do that?"

Vitellia bent over him and gave him a determined look. "I've always advised my father on these things." She picked up the plans and waved them imperiously in the air. "He deferred to me for major decisions." She put the drawings back on his desk. "Speaking of hiring Romans. When are you going to get rid of the stable boy?"

"Are you speaking of Farid? He's not a stable boy. I have appointed him as a special aide to work with my couriers."

"The Parthian." She screwed up her nose with some disdain. "You realize no Parthian can be trusted?"

Valerius decided that there were more important things brewing than engaging in an argument with his wife. Any day now, he expected to get marching orders to take his troops south to Judea to erect the statue of the emperor in the temple at Jerusalem. At least there was no word yet that the statue itself was ready. He didn't even know if it was being prepared in Rome to be shipped or being fashioned in nearby Sidon, which boasted the largest foundry outside of Italy. All he knew from imperial orders was that he was to stand ready with his legions to march south and that a statue of colossal proportions was to be erected in the temple.

To be ready with his legions meant that Valerius spent a great deal of time getting to know his officers and soldiers. He held several meetings with Manius Cornelius, his appointed legate. Valerius liked to observe the soldiers at their training sessions— javelin throwing, wrestling matches, target practice, and sword fighting with wicker shields and wooden swords. The Roman bows and arrows looked clumsy in comparison to Parthian weapons. He initiated discussions with several tribunes and centurions who were good leaders and treated the soldiers with respect while expecting performance and discipline. He also made friends with several legionaries and talked to them about their families and where they were from. Many felt flattered that he often remembered their names when he came back to their practice sessions.

Among his officers was Quintus, a tall blond tribune who looked too young to be in the army. Valerius was impressed by the way he treated the soldiers under his command. He was encouraging and demanding at the same time; his laugh and energy were infectious. One day, Valerius noticed that a brawl had erupted near the latrines. Valerius watched from afar how Quintus quietly walked over, picked up a shovel, and started digging the necessary trench. Before long, embarrassed soldiers stopped their fighting and meekly picked up their shovels again.

The next day, Valerius called Quintus to his headquarters and asked him about his military career and ambitions. Without hesitation, Quintus proclaimed that he hoped to serve in the senate some day. When Valerius raised his eyebrows in an unspoken question, Quintus explained that he had earned his wide purple stripe as tribune serving under Appius Junius Silvanus in Hispania.

"Appius Silvanus." Valerius repeated the name with a grimace. "We have more in common than you know. Silvanus was falsely accused of treason by Tiberius the same year as my father. He was fortunate to survive that crisis. My father did not."

Quintus responded with immediate concern. "I am sorry, Sir. My father died in service to the empire under Germanicus. He met my mother in Germania, but she insisted on raising me as a Roman."

"Now I know where your Nordic complexion comes from." Valerius smiled. "I would like to appoint you to my staff as personal adjunct. Your duties will include oversight and organization. You will have chances for early promotion and better pay. I expect you to show considerable initiative in matters that don't require my attention."

Quintus bowed and accepted with an expression of excitement and pride on his face. Several days later, Quintus was placed in full charge of the camp while Valerius was absent from the field to welcome his sister and her family to Antioch for a visit. After showing their rooms to Simon and Aurelia, Valerius gave a grand tour of the palace, and suddenly the hallways and cavernous dining and meeting halls rang with the sounds of children playing and laughing. Valerius joined in the fun and played hide and seek with his nephews as Aurelia looked on and chided them all for being too noisy. He sent a carriage drawn by two horses to pick up Rachel, Sedek, and Matthaios for dinner at the palace.

Vitellia presided graciously over a procession of courses and sent two dishes back to the kitchen, claiming they were unsuitable. Aurelia had no idea what they were and sent a questioning glance to her brother, but Valerius chose that moment to make a toast. Aurelia was intrigued by Vitellia's patrician demeanor and realized she took her duties as mistress of the palace and as governor's wife very seriously. Across from her, Rachel ate daintily and seemed ill at ease. Aurelia was eager to get to know Rachel and was sure they had a lot in common, including fond memories of Cyrene. Simon and Valerius were already deep into a discussion about the need for better roads and more housing to be built for the recent arrival of many Jews from Jerusalem, and young Matthaios was listening to their conversation and asking questions. Rufus and Alexander were apparently awed by the solemnity of the dining ritual and behaved themselves.

Vitellia scrutinized them with interest and turned to Aurelia. "Of course, you are raising your sons to be proper Romans."

"What do you mean?"

Vitellia nodded toward Rachel and Matthaios, then squinted at Simon before turning back to Aurelia. Pointedly, she said, "You know what I mean." Aurelia saw a strange look come over Simon's face and felt a sharp sense of dismay. She steeled herself against an angry response from Simon.

At that moment, Matthaios put down his goblet and stood up to face Vitellia. "I am a Jew, and I am proud of it," he declared. There was such sincere pride in his voice that it was obvious he had understood what Vitellia meant.

While most were watching Matthaios, Aurelia looked over at Valerius, whose eyes were riveted on Rachel. Aurelia saw a moment of shared understanding that made Aurelia look away as though she had accidentally intruded on a private moment of intimacy between them. She wondered if Vitellia had noticed.

But Vitellia was glaring at Matthaios. "When you are invited to dine with adults, you are not to speak. Your Roman cousins have set the example for you."

Valerius took advantage of the sudden lull in the conversation to summon Farid and asked him to take the boys to help feed and brush down the horses. The three boys ran to the stables with such excited shrieks of glee that even Vitellia had to smile.

Vitellia turned to Sedek, who, to this point, had remained silent. She gave him greetings from her father and asked about his health.

Sedek responded, "We are all anxious about the ordeal your husband faces."

"Ordeal?" Vitellia lifted her shoulders with an expression of incredulity on her face. "As governor, Valerius follows imperial orders. He does not need to make it an ordeal. You and your people make too much fuss over this. There are many more important things to work on, like the new harbor, and I've told Valerius he should just do the emperor's bidding and get it over with. I mean, what's so important about a stupid statue? There are thousands all over the place. One more or one less—"

Sedek's voice was grave and solemn. "My dear lady, your interpretation of the word 'ordeal' as a trivial inconvenience is wrong and does not begin to plumb the depths of despair we all feel for your husband in these trying times. May the Lord keep him and all your family and may his grace surround you with a shield of safety." Sedek rose and bowed to say his farewells.

Awed by the sincerity of Sedek's prayer, Aurelia realized that Sedek was the only one who had acknowledged the fear she felt for her brother. Even Valerius himself seemed to brush it off. She wondered how anxious he truly was and whether his rather jovial manner at the dinner table was an act to spare her grief.

After Rachel and Sedek left with Matthaios, Simon and Valerius walked out to the garden to talk. From her bedroom window, Aurelia could see their faces in the moonlight. Simon was waving his arms in agitated discussion. When she caught a glimpse of Valerius's face, her heart lurched in her throat. Her husband and her brother—two men who were inseparable childhood friends—looked like they were furious with each other. She went down to the garden to see if she could keep peace between the two men she loved most.

For a while Simon and Valerius walked in silence, their feet marking an off-beat rhythm against the gravel that lined the walkways. Simon stopped abruptly in front of Valerius and said, "Once you start out with your legions, there will be no choice. You will provoke violence by the mere act of setting out. Not all Jews will hold steady as Sedek wants you to believe. Sedek is a visionary, an idealist. There will be incidents of rebellion and violence when your troops will say they had no choice but to respond. Bloodshed will follow. And once that happens—"

Valerius shook his head. "Your view is that it is better if I just fall on my sword here and now?"

"That is not what I said." Simon sighed. "Remember our school days together when we debated grand moral dilemmas faced by generals leading an army to war? Well, this is not a schoolboy's problem in arithmetic. There are lives at stake. Thousands of lives. What would our old schoolmaster suggest to you today? What grand moral example would Aristodorus lay before you to help you?"

Valerius answered, "Aristodorus would dredge up the example of Antigone. Antigone defies an immoral order from the king. I have an immoral order from the emperor. She defies him. I defy him. She dies. I die. Ergo—"

"Ergo, she takes the moral high ground. You must do the same. One death instead of thousands."

Valerius turned toward Simon and shook him by the shoulders. "You are very glib about my death." Then he pummeled his friend's chest with both fists while Simon stood limp and didn't move a muscle. Aurelia drew a trembling breath and wanted to beg Valerius to stop, but her voice stayed stuck in her throat.

When Valerius finally stopped, Simon cradled Valerius's head on his shoulder, and they stood mute in each other's arms. Aurelia thought they looked like a sculpture depicting two close friends mourning the death of a third. Or were they mourning the death of their friendship?

Valerius let go and walked back toward the house. Near the door, he turned. "Creon should have backed down."

"If you think Caligula will back down, you are as unrealistic as Sedek."

✦

When Aurelia paid a visit to Rachel the next day, she was unsure how she would be received. Rachel invited her to sit in the peristyle, where a soft breeze stirred the heliotropes that framed their view of the mountains. Rachel was reserved and cautious and deeply influenced by the respect she owed to the family members of the propraetor of Cyrene, but Aurelia started in on a subject she knew Rachel would care about—her childhood in Cyrene, her relationship with her brother, and what Simon was like as a young boy before Aurelia knew him.

Rachel delved into these topics with enthusiasm, quickly forgetting to be intimidated by Aurelia, and confided in Aurelia that their father had punished Simon excessively and was unjustly harsh. "Simon was sometimes punished for things I did." Rachel smiled. "He never told on me. But I knew and I let it happen. I realize that was not fair to him, but he is noble in that way. He is courageous. He is also very stubborn. When faced with challenges, he never backs down."

Aurelia nodded. "I see these traits in him every day." She was delighted to hear the stories of his childhood. "You describe him so well. In some ways, I think that Simon and Sedek are very much alike."

Rachel looked at her in surprise.

"Maybe I'm wrong about that, and they certainly have different goals and different interests, but I believe they are both driven by a strong sense of purpose. Simon takes on too many battles, but he cannot win them all. I have the impression that

Sedek can be the same way."

Rachel nodded. "I know what you mean."

"I see some of that in your Matthaios. He was brave to stand up to Vitellia. I was so proud of him. You are obviously a wonderful mother."

"I don't think so."

Aurelia frowned. "Why do you say that? We were all impressed with him last night. Surely you are proud of him?"

Rachel said nothing. Her face showed a deep sadness that puzzled Aurelia. She waited while Rachel looked off into the garden and seemed to compose her thoughts. Her dark brown eyes looked so sad that they reminded her of the pet dog she had nurtured and spoiled for years in Cyrene. As she studied Rachel's expression, she saw tears well and trickle down her cheeks.

Aurelia clasped her arm. "What is it, Rachel?"

Rachel shook her head and made a half-hearted attempt to apologize, but Aurelia rose and went to her, enfolded her in her arms, and held her close.

Rachel shuddered. "It was terrible. I cannot forget. It was—"

Aurelia nodded in sympathy. "Sh—" She stroked Rachel's hair, holding her as she would a wounded child, voicing soothing syllables near her ear. She didn't need to know all the things she had suffered through. A litany of details would merely bring back the past. Instead, she wanted her to feel the cleansing relief of tears and the consoling presence of someone who cared deeply.

After a moment, Rachel tried to wipe at her tears, but Aurelia stopped her. "Let them flow. It will be good for you."

Rachel looked at her and did not seem to agree, but the tears continued. Aurelia felt tears clog her own throat, and she, too, began to sob. They stood there in each other's arms and wept. After a while, Aurelia felt wetness penetrate through her stola down through her palla and trickle between her breasts. She continued to hold her tight as painful sobs shuddered through both of them.

Rachel started to sniffle and draw quick, stuttering breaths.

Slowly, Aurelia led her back to her seat and unwound the long stola that covered her head and wrapped around her waist and gathered the fine silk in her hands to wipe Rachel's face, a gesture Aurelia had used so many times with her children that it had become a natural part of her devoted motherhood.

Rachel looped a wayward curl over her ear and smiled when the absent stola revealed Aurelia's contours. She asked, "When is your baby due?"

Aurelia smoothed her palla over her stomach and smiled. "Four more months. Simon and I had a long discussion about the dangers of traveling here under the circumstances, but I persuaded him to come now because I'm so worried about Valerius. When he left for Rome, I thought I would never see him again. Then we found out what Caligula wanted, and— At first, I refused to believe it. But I told Simon if we didn't come now— Well, you know what we all fear."

"I know." Rachel stood and walked along the peristyle and looked down at the rooftops of Antioch.

Aurelia rose and stood beside her. "We both suffer and fear for his life. We both love him."

Rachel said, "Valerius told you?"

"A long time ago. In Cyrene. I knew before he told you."

Rachel nodded.

Aurelia took her hand and squeezed it. "Rachel, even then I wanted us to be friends. Every time Valerius came back from your house, I asked about you. I didn't know Simon then, but I felt like I knew you. Valerius would tell me what spices you were drying in the courtyard and bring me a sample you gave him. He would tell me what foods you were preparing, the color of your clothes, how you wore your hair. He would dream about defying our father to marry you."

Rachel spoke wistfully. "For a while, we had a beautiful dream."

"He wrote moving poems about you and called your dark eyes sparkling jewels. Many times, I asked if he would take me to meet you, but he never did. Then, after we lost you and thought you were dead, Valerius could not be consoled. My father allowed Roman troops to be used to find you. Did you know that?"

Rachel sighed. "I guess I caused a lot of trouble."

"You were never the cause. You were an innocent victim of the vicious criminal Meidias."

"Is he truly dead?"

"He is. You don't have to be afraid of him anymore."

"He still haunts me."

"That's another reason why we came to see you now. Simon wants to talk to you about what happened. How Meidias died. This morning he went with Valerius to visit the harbor project, but on his way back he will stop by to speak with you. You deserve to know."

Aurelia clasped Rachel in her arms and held her close. "You do realize that we have a lot in common? You and I?"

Rachel's face showed she was dubious.

"We are both mothers, and we will fight for what is best for our children. And you and I both love the same men—Valerius and Simon—and we fear for their safety."

At that moment, the three cousins ran up from the pirate games they were playing on top of ruined walls that had not been repaired after the earthquake. They were breathless and wanted snacks and water and couldn't stop arguing about who had won.

Later, when Aurelia asked Simon about his talk with his sister, Simon claimed he told her that Meidias could no longer harm her.

"It was good that we came so you could reassure her."

"What did you do? When I talked to her yesterday, she was distant and very upset. But today, after your talk with her, she seemed almost serene. What did you tell her?"

Aurelia smiled mysteriously. "Nothing. We held each other and cried together. As a physician, you should realize that sometimes tears are the best medicine."

"Agreed. I think she is still afraid for Matthaios."

"You mean Valerius."

"That, too"

"Why would she be afraid for Matthaios? I was so impressed with him the other night when he affirmed that he was proud to be a Jew. I think his bold affirmation showed character and strength."

Simon nodded and decided to drop the subject.

Later, in their bedroom, Simon was undressing when Aurelia turned to him and asked, "Are you and Valerius still friends?"

The muscles in Simon's face worked back and forth at his temples the way they always acted up when he was tense. "I hope so," he said.

"You still don't see a way out for Valerius?"

"No, Aurelia, I don't. The whole foundation of our faith is under attack by Caligula. The Jews must resist this evil."

Aurelia sighed against his cheek. "I hate statues."

CHARMED BY A SMILE

AFTER AURELIA AND SIMON LEFT ANTIOCH WITH
their sons to return to Alexandria, Valerius walked through
the palace and missed the sound of children playing and
laughing and running up and down the hallways. He was not
sure if he missed Simon. In fact, he was not sure how he felt
about Simon. In all the years they had been friends, he had
never felt this disaffected and bitter. He understood Simon's
zeal to save Jewish lives. He even agreed with Simon that outright war would be devastating and would accomplish nothing. He also realized he found himself in an impossible political and military position, but he could not accept that Simon
showed so little empathy for his dilemma; that he was so dis-
missive of the sacrifice demanded of him; that he was so cav-
alier about his death. When Simon argued that Valerius must
consider "the greater good," he showed little anguish over the
price Valerius would have to pay. In the short talk afterward
with Aurelia, he understood how distressed she was, and he
refused to add to her burden by accusing Simon of cruel dis-
regard for their friendship and family ties. He was gradually
becoming aware that there was an intransigent harshness to

Simon's character that he found disturbing and merciless.

He looked out the window and thought that a ride on his favorite horse might lighten his mood. Eager for attention, Rex threw his head back and nuzzled up to Valerius. Valerius smiled. Animals, he thought, are straightforward and loyal in their affection. Almost without realizing it, he guided Rex toward Epiphania in the hope of seeing Rachel. He wondered if she was feeling more lonely than usual after her brother's departure.

When he arrived on horseback, Matthaios ran to greet him and wanted to talk about his horse. Rachel watched them from a bench in the portico.

Valerius said, "Rex lets you know when he's happy."

"How?" Matthaios rubbed Rex's forelock, scratched him behind the ears, and ran his fingers down his glistening brown coat.

Valerius said, "He's smiling. Do you see it in his eyes? Like you, he likes to be loved. When he's happy, the muscles around his eyes are relaxed, but when he's afraid or tense, the muscles tighten here. A horse doesn't lie to you. Rex tells me when he is afraid, but he also tells me when I should be afraid."

"He can do that?"

"If someone comes up from behind, he will see him before I can. The way his eyes are placed on his head, he can see almost all the way around, and he warns me."

"That's amazing." Matthaios stroked the white stripe on his nose. "He has beautiful eyes. What do you do when he has a will of his own and refuses to obey?"

"A very good question. You tell me what you would do. Your answer will show me whether you are ready to be a good horseman and can be trusted with my horse. What do you think I should do when Rex refuses to obey?"

Matthaios stroked Rex's muzzle and whispered into his ear. "When you are unhappy, I would look at your hooves to see if you have a sore, or a rock or a spike or nail lodged in the hoof."

Valerius heaved Matthaios up into the saddle. "Excellent answer. Now ride him around and come back and tell me if he favors one leg over another."

Matthaios glanced over at his mother and back to Valerius. "You'll let me ride him? By myself?"

Valerius smiled and gave Rex's rump a little smack. "Go down to the far fence and circle back while I talk to your mother."

Valerius sat down beside Rachel and squeezed her hand. The slightest touch evoked a turmoil of emotions in him. He wanted to protect her and shield her from harm and sorrow. At the same time, he was determined to be honest with her. Most of all he wanted to slide his hand up to her shoulder and turn her face toward him so he could kiss her. For the moment, he was grateful that Rachel did not pull her hand away.

She was watching her son. "He is so excited to be on your horse. Do you think it is safe?"

Valerius smiled. "He's ready. It's important he learn from someone you trust. You do trust me?"

She squeezed his hand. "You will be a wonderful father when the time comes. I can see that in the way you teach Matthaios. You don't know how fervently I have wished that he were your son." She turned toward him. Her eyes told him more than she would ever say.

He brought her hand to his lips and kissed each finger before she retrieved her hand. "I would be very proud to be the father of your child. I am already proud of him."

"When do you leave?" she asked.

"Any day now. We have to wait for the final marching orders to load supplies."

"Do you think it will be as devastating as Sedek claims?" Her voice was barely above a whisper.

"It's hard to say. I don't know. But one thing I do know—I will try to avoid bloodshed. That is my solemn promise to you. As long as it is within my power, I will protect your people."

"At the cost of your life?"

"At the cost of my life if need be." He clasped her hand to his chest.

"I don't like that answer."

"Nor do I. But should the news arrive that I have died, you should know that when I draw my last breath, I will be thinking of you." He looked deeply into her eyes.

She held his gaze until her eyes teared up.

Valerius rose, pulled her to her feet and into his arms. He cradled her head against his chest and held her tight. "Since our childhood in Cyrene, I have loved you, and I always will." He kissed her gently on the lips. "And I remember the moment when I first discovered I loved you. Do you remember?"

"Mama, Mama, look how happy Rex is!" Matthaios was trotting back up the hill. Grinning, he slid down from the horse and handed the reins back to Valerius. "His legs are fine." Then he announced, "When I get my first horse, I will name him Rex!"

Valerius tousled his hair. "You did that very well. I have no doubt you will be a master horseman soon."

"But my mother doesn't want me to have a horse."

Valerius looked at Rachel. "Well, you should always listen to your mother. But you are gifted with horses and should learn. If your mother agrees, one of my stable hands could come once a week with the grey stallion and give you lessons. You will have to clean the stall for him before he can come."

"I will!" Matthaios looked toward his mother. "Please!"

Rachel said, "We'll see."

"It would be the safest way to learn. In the meantime, Matthaios, I have a big job for you to do."

"What is it?"

"You may have heard that I must leave with my legions soon, and I may be gone for a long time. Your job is to take care of your mother while I'm gone. Can you do that?"

Matthaios nodded soberly.

As Valerius mounted his horse, Matthaios gave a military salute and wished him well.

Rachel watched Valerius leave until he disappeared beyond the bend and pondered the question he asked that she didn't have a chance to answer.

✦

In Cyrene ten years ago.

Rachel is almost sixteen. Simon affectionately dismisses her as a child, a little sister whom he wants to protect but who is also a nuisance when she hangs around when he talks with his best friend, Valerius, who visits often. She enjoys watching people in the street from the parapet that encircles their rooftop garden and sees Simon and Valerius coming back from their classes at the academia. She observes the way they walk, the way they move their heads together and gesture with their hands as they talk, and the way they suddenly erupt with laughter. She senses the mysterious bond between two friends who never seem to run out of things to say to each other. Her eyes begin to follow every move Valerius makes. He lifts his shoulders and shrugs. The sunlight hits his hair and turns light brown into burnished copper. A peal of laughter rises from his throat, which makes her eager to know what Valerius finds so delightful. She sees the folds of his white tunic trimmed with blue and wishes she could touch his arm to feel the fine fabric and the hard muscles beneath. She smiles at the thought and is caught because, at that moment, he looks up, straight into her face, and waves and smiles. She smiles back, enchanted. Then she ducks out of sight, embarrassed to have been seen watching him, but catches a broader smile as she pulls away from the parapet, her heart beating wildly in her chest. She is not even wearing her head covering, and he has seen her dark hair tumbling around her shoulders. Her mother would be appalled. She closes her eyes to hold on to the image of his smile. She doesn't quite understand what is happening to her. She has seen Valerius many times before, and he was just her brother's friend. This is different. Unaccustomed warmth floods through her body and rises to her cheeks. She wants to run back over to the parapet and look down at him but doesn't dare in case he is still looking up and catches her watching.

She covers her hair to be proper and descends to the kitchen to prepare their usual tray of fruit, barley wafers, and wine and places it on the table in the courtyard in front of them. Simon doesn't pay attention to her, but Valerius thanks her with another smile. She chooses not to disappear but sits on the rim of the fountain and begins to analyze her feelings. Even without looking at him, she is keenly aware of his presence—the slight hiccup he makes after sipping some wine, the angle of his head as he chats with Simon, the way he balances the cup in his hand. She wonders if he noticed that she stayed in the courtyard, perched on the fountain edge, watching him and ready to fly away like a frightened bird. But she doesn't fly away.

When Simon is called away to accompany Ezra to see a patient, she dares to speak up as Valerius rises to leave. "Oh, don't go! You haven't finished your wine."

He turns and nods to her, lifts his brows, and says, "But you have no wine. Please take a sip of mine." Before she can react, he is at her side, holding the cup to her lips, and she feels the sudden boldness of his gesture as well as her own when she obeys and presses her lips on the rim of the cup where his lips had been. The intimacy of the act thrills her. She holds the precious wine in her mouth and absorbs its flavor, its subtle sweetness, the crisp intensity of the alcohol. His face is close to hers. He reaches out to catch a wayward drop at the corner of her mouth with his thumb. They gaze at each other, and she sees flecks of gold in his eyes before she closes hers, wondering if he is feeling the same thing she is and wishing he would rub his thumb across her lips again.

He puts the cup down, but he doesn't move away so that his face stays close to hers, and they are breathing the same air. She knows that this instant will be engraved in her mind forever. She has no idea how she knows this. Her body tingles with the need to touch. She reaches over and places her hand gently on top of his.

"Rachel," he says. He clears his throat and repeats her name as though he is rolling it around on his tongue, getting the feel of the name and how it sounds, tasting it like he tasted the wine. He smiles and places his other hand on top of hers. She feels sheltered. Cherished.

As the late afternoon sun slants lower and the exotic aromas of drying spices and herbs mingle in the air, she sees that the gold flecks in his eyes darken and merge with the blue. She wonders if her eyes change as much with the light and if he notices. The silence between them communicates better than words. She lifts her eyebrows in a question and gestures toward the empty cup. He shakes his head to tell her he wants no more but does not take his eyes off her face. She hopes the message in her eyes reveals the love for him that she feels.

What happened that day? She was charmed by his smile. He shared a sip of wine. Surely, neither event was momentous in and of itself, but she felt changed forever in a way she cannot describe. Often, she returned to that day to relive it; to understand the feelings that transformed her mind and her body and her heart. From that day forward she could never again look at Valerius in the same way as before. It was a new and exciting experience, and she believed it was the kind of love that transcended what she felt for her parents and her brother; a love that could inspire both kings and slaves. A love that could last forever.

PASSIVE RESISTANCE

TWO DAYS LATER, AN IMPERIAL COURIER ARRIVED at the palace with orders for Publius Petronius Valerius to head south with his legions. The final preparations had to be made so quickly that Valerius had little time to stew about it. Immediately, he called for Quintus to arrange an administrative meeting with his officers at the military barracks outside the city to give them their assignments and marching orders. Weapons were sharpened, helmets polished, cuirasses repaired, boots cleaned, and supplies loaded onto wagons. Army cooks and surgeons scrambled to ready their equipment and load their wares onto carts.

After three full days of hectic preparations at the barracks, Valerius hurried back to the palace toward sunset and was stuffing documents and files into a leather bag when Vitellia entered his office.

"Surely you don't really have to go?" Vitellia swished a cascade of dark curls around her shoulders in her newest revival of an old Roman hairstyle.

Valerius didn't bother to answer.

She brushed up against him. "How long will you be gone?"

Valerius steeled himself as he realized there was no way he could know. He felt like a puppet on a string who had no control over his own actions. "Hard to say. I have orders to gather the troops at the border and keep them in combat readiness to descend into Palestine at a moment's notice."

"You make this sound serious." She drew her finger along his cheek and caressed the outline of his lips. "Why?"

"Caligula's orders."

Vitellia sighed. "My father used to rant and rave about Tiberius's orders to wage war on Parthia, or Aretas—how stupid they were, how unnecessary. Now Caligula is just as bad."

Valerius nodded. "Worse. Far worse."

Vitellia wrapped her arms around him. "If I were you, I would send Herennius Capito. After all, he's already in Jamnia, much closer to Jerusalem. Didn't you say that he complained to Caligula about an incident there? Why shouldn't he be the one to bear the consequences, not you?"

Valerius shook his head. "You better than anyone should know that it's the governor of Syria who is responsible. Herennius Capito is merely an imperial procurator and takes orders from me. Besides, he's hotheaded and impulsive. He's likely to cause a bloodbath. Perhaps I can stop it."

"Bloodbath?" Alarmed, she pressed up against him.

Valerius pulled away from her embrace and realized immediately from Vitellia's expression that she felt rebuffed. He patted her cheek and smiled. "I'll try to avoid a bloodbath."

"What is it that Caligula really wants?"

"He wants to be a god."

"He doesn't need an army for that!"

Valerius laughed bitterly. "How right you are. According to Capito, Jews in Jamnia desecrated his altars, Caligula wants revenge. He knows that the worst offense he could give them is to desecrate their temple in Jerusalem." He refrained from mentioning the more personal reasons Caligula was opposing the Petronius family and didn't want to trouble Vitellia by enumerating Caligula's dangerous vendettas.

"When are you supposed to leave?"

"Tomorrow before sunrise. Which reminds me. I've ordered Quintus to pack my gear and some clothes. Since I'll be leaving so early in the morning, I've arranged to sleep in the officers' quarters tonight, so I won't disturb you early in the morning." Valerius stretched, placed a quick kiss on her cheek, and started for the door.

"Valerius!" Vitellia grabbed him by the arm and spun him around. "How dare you leave me like this? I am your wife, and you are leaving, perhaps never to return, and you give me a peck on the cheek and expect that to be enough?"

Valerius looked at her tortured face and cringed inwardly. "I'm sorry, Vitellia. I didn't mean to anger you. I don't have a choice. I must go."

Vitellia looked up at him with flashing eyes but quickly lowered them and smiled coyly. "Stay here with me tonight." She pulled his hand to her breast. Her voice became soft and seductive. "We've been married almost a year, and there is still no promise of an heir. How is that supposed to happen if you are away?" She stroked the back of his hand and reached up and kissed him full on the mouth.

Valerius was touched by her eager devotion and thought ruefully that he would not get to say goodbye to Sedek and Rachel if he didn't leave soon. He swallowed his disappointment and led her to the bedroom.

The next morning, before light streaked the eastern sky, Valerius mounted Rex and joined his advance guard in double file with two full legions on foot at his back. A Roman army could move swiftly, even on foot, and he knew they would reach the first camping site along the Orontes long before nightfall. He summoned Manius Cornelius, gave orders for the legions to continue under Manius's command, and circled back to the rear. Then, just as his plumed helmet caught the first rays of the sun, he galloped back to Antioch and up to the Epiphania to stop in front of Sedek's gate.

The servants greeted him with sleepy eyes and fetched Sedek. Sedek came running, still in his nightclothes, and knew at once what had happened. "You have orders to take your army to Judea." It was not a question but a statement.

"Indeed." Valerius's horse snorted and pawed the ground. Plumes of steam rose from his nostrils in the cold morning air.

"May the Most High protect you and my people!" Sedek nodded to his servant to bring water for his horse. "You know, Valerius, that I will send couriers to Jerusalem and warn them."

"I know."

Sedek sighed. His lips were blue, and he trembled in the bitter morning wind. "You do know that I must do everything to protect my people?"

"Indeed."

"If you try to place Caligula's statue in the temple in Jerusalem, the entire Jewish population across the empire will oppose Rome. You know that?"

"I know."

"Can you not stop this folly before it begins?"

"If I could stop it, I would. I'll delay the process as long as I can."

Sedek nodded. "Philo plans to leave Alexandria in early spring to bring his delegation to Caligula in person on behalf of our people. Can you at least delay until these last attempts at reason and peace have been tried?"

"I'll do my best to delay as long as I can. But even now the courier who brought orders from Rome is waiting to affirm that I did indeed carry them out. His report will reassure the emperor for the moment. In the meantime, I can assure you that two legions need to make their way slowly and take their time to ensure that appropriate supplies are delivered along the way."

Valerius's horse stepped from side to side and swished his tail with impatience. Valerius tightened the reins, and Rex reared up and seemed dangerously close to coming down on top of Sedek, who backed off under the portico. "Whoa, boy! Steady there!" Valerius led Rex around in a circle and paused again in front of Sedek. "I don't plan to go directly to Jerusalem. In any event, the colossal statue is not ready yet."

Sedek shivered. "May the Most High bless you, my dear friend. You go with my prayers for your safety."

"Thank you, Sedek. One last thing. Please tell Rachel that I leave Antioch with a heavy heart. I'm fully aware that I might never return to Antioch. I beg you therefore to tell her that—" His horse reared again and came clattering down on the cobblestones. "—that I will miss her, that I will do everything in my power to protect her—your people."

Valerius feared he had revealed more than he should, but Sedek merely nodded and extended his arm in a gesture of blessing and farewell.

Valerius saluted and spurred his impatient steed to action. Once out the gate, he allowed Rex to stretch his legs and gallop through the empty streets, out onto the road south toward Apamea. It took only a short while for him to catch up with the supply wagons and the foot soldiers. He pressed forward to rejoin the front and slowed his pace to fall in step with the knights on horseback and signaled to Manius Cornelius. His heart was heavy, but he did not look back.

Rachel received the news of his departure with gravity and courage. After she had seen to Matthaios's breakfast and sent him off to his lessons, she draped a wool cape over her shoulders and went to the peristyle to be alone with her thoughts.

Sedek was already busy preparing messages to send to Jerusalem, Caesarea, Sepphoris, and Tiberias. In passionate tones, he urged his fellow Jews to stand together in opposition to the imperial decrees. "Not with weapons," he wrote, "but with your steadfastness, your courage, your very lives. Throw yourselves in the path of the imperial troops and do not allow the statue of Caligula to pass! In this way, you will be more powerful than the Roman army."

In the peristyle, the wind blew forlornly over empty flowerbeds and fountains. A little brown leaf fluttered and danced over the blue tiles and came to rest at Rachel's feet. She picked it up and twirled the stem in her fingers, then turned it faster and faster until it became a whirling blur. When her fingers stopped, the leaf was still only a blur through her tears.

✦

THE ARMY HEADS SOUTH

VALERIUS HAD NO DOUBT THAT SEDEK WOULD USE all his influence to rally the Jews behind a common cause. He also knew Philo would start a similar epistolary campaign from Alexandria. Both Sedek and Philo had great influence in the Jewish communities throughout the region and were adept at elucidating the political, religious, and military consequences of this latest outrage dreamt up by Caligula. As Valerius headed south with his legions, he knew every Jewish community was receiving letters to resist at all costs the extreme blasphemy of raising a statue of Caligula in the temple in Jerusalem.

He realized his was a thankless role to play. He was a symbol of imperial power, the embodiment of the evil the Jews loved to hate, the mighty sword that had conquered the world. At the same time, he despised Caligula and the arbitrary violence he condoned and promoted. He detested the self-serving quest for glory that motivated both Caligula and many of the Roman commanders. But Valerius knew he could not claim the moral high ground in this fight, for he had sworn allegiance to Rome and to Caesar. Valerius had to study his own conscience and decide which side he was on while knowing he had no choice in the matter. He was a mere pawn in the deadly game Caesar was playing. What angered Valerius most was that it was just a game to Caesar, one Valerius had hoped he would tire of, but one that could cost the lives of thousands.

The slow pace of two legions making their way over mountains, through forests, and across streams allowed him plenty of time to think about potential battle plans, ways of thwarting rebellion among local populations, and tactics for keeping the peace when confronted with an angry and fervent uprising of Jews. The best strategy, he knew, would be to avoid confrontation altogether. He also knew that would be impossible.

Two days south of Apamea, Valerius awoke to screams among a cohort of foot soldiers. A scout came running and reported that a group of bandits killed two soldiers and fled back into the woods with stolen weapons. Manius Cornelius arrived at his tent, already fully dressed and armed and ready to ride out in pursuit. Valerius strapped on his sword and ordered ten equestrians to join him to hunt the bandits down. The chase through the woods led into brambles and heavy undergrowth, but the broken branches also revealed their path of retreat.

Manius yelled, "They haven't gone far. We'll catch up."

In the weak light before dawn, Valerius sensed danger at his back when Rex went tense and swayed to the side without breaking his stride. A dagger flew past Valerius's head to land in front of him. Valerius glanced back in time to see his assailant disappear into the brush. Valerius jumped off his horse and went after him to tackle and wrestle him to the ground. He pulled his knife and held it at his throat while Fabius, the camp prefect, arrived right behind him with his sword, ready to pierce him through.

Valerius stopped Fabius from delivering the death blow. "We need to interrogate this bandit and see how many there are. Tie him up."

By the end of the morning, the centurions had captured

seven bandits and killed five, and at least that many had escaped back into the Lebanese mountains. Valerius knew they would continue to attack their rearguard if they could successfully steal weapons. The chief bandit spoke a strange Latin and claimed to come from the high mountains of Cilicia.

Manius argued for swift justice by the sword. Valerius said that the strongest should be selected to clear passage through rough terrain and forests. Manius protested that it was too risky and obviously disliked being overruled. Grudgingly, he lined up seven brigands in front of Valerius for inspection. Valerius studied all seven and asked their names and was relieved to discover their attack was opportunistic rather than political. Thieves were more easily dealt with than fanatics. He ordered heavy irons attached to their feet, placed them under guard, and singled out the brawniest, named Lacertus, to be handcuffed and escorted to his governor's tent. Valerius liked the way Lacertus stood at attention, the intelligent look in his eyes, and the way he said his name with pride and defiance. When Valerius was the captain in command in Gaul, he had learned that local rebels could often become his best aides because their survival depended on their usefulness, and they knew far more than he did about local dangers and traditions.

After setting up camp just before sunset, Manius appeared at Valerius's tent and shoved a girl onto her knees in front of him. Manius saluted and said, "I went after the rest of the bandits with my men and killed all six of them so we wouldn't lose manpower to guard prisoners. I brought you this tramp who was shivering in their hideout. She's dirty and doesn't speak Latin, but several men want her tonight if you don't want her for yourself." He saluted and started to leave before Valerius ordered him to stop and berated him for carrying out executions without permission.

Manius made a wry face. "Those of us who received the best military training were taught to think on our feet and make judicious decisions. I make no apology for killing the enemy."

Valerius rose and looked him in the eye. "Insubordination is a serious offense. But turning potential allies into enemies creates conditions for unnecessary conflict that should be avoided. You are not to execute anyone without permission. I am justified in taking your *primus pilus* designation away from you. Should there be a second offense, I will do so. Now leave me!"

Manius stalked off, and Valerius looked down at the girl, who was shaking with fear and cold. She reached out her hands in a mute gesture for mercy. Valerius called Lacertus to come into his tent and observed his reaction to the girl at his feet.

Valerius asked, "What is her name?"

Lacertus refused to answer.

Valerius held a knife to his throat.

"Rhaetia."

"Where is she from?"

"The high mountains beyond Cilicia."

"Your tribe goes that far north?"

"In the summer. To hunt."

"You are fond of her?"

Lacertus hesitated and looked at the girl and shrugged.

Valerius called Sestius to enter. "Take this woman to the women camp followers. Tell them to wash and feed her."

"And then?"

"She is not a prisoner. If she wants, she may go."

Sestius grabbed her by the arm and jerked her to her feet.

Valerius stopped him. "Not like that. Treat her with dignity. Her name is Rhaetia."

"Yes, Sir! And this outlaw here?"

"Lacertus will keep the first watch with you in front of my tent, chained to a stake."

"And after the first watch?"

"He can sleep under guard, but he must stay shackled. You can see to it."

Valerius turned toward Lacertus, whose expression was hard to read in the light of the one lantern that hung at the center pole. Valerius sat on his low cot and took off his boots. "Ah! It's always good to let my feet breathe. I've made enemies today. I just don't know how many. What do you think, Lacertus?"

Lacertus did not answer.

Valerius droned on, talking mostly to himself. "For one, Manius is not happy. Then his men who wanted Rhaetia are angry. And you—well, that remains to be seen. I saw your face when they brought Rhaetia in. You are not indifferent to her. She was good at hiding what she felt for you. And, by the way, she understood every word I said. That much we can agree on, don't you think?" Valerius began undressing for bed. "Well, I'm sorry you must do the first watch, but at least you can sleep after that. Quintus will set it up."

As Sestius got ready to take up his post, Valerius told Lacertus, "If Rhaetia comes to you during your watch to plan your escape, be aware that Manius will not hesitate to kill you both, and he would be justified. I will not be able to help you."

Just as Valerius was arranging his sleeping mat, Servius appeared and asked to speak to him.

"Can't it wait until morning?"

Servius shook his head, sat, and cleared his throat.

"Is there something I should know? Are there more bandits out there that you saw? What is troubling you?" Valerius was getting impatient.

Servius studied Valerius's face in the dim light. "I just wanted to say..." He took out his knife and scraped some mud off the soles of his boots. Without looking at him, he said, "We've been through a lot together. How many years has it been?"

"Well, since Gaul. Right?"

"Right. Nine years. Hard to believe, isn't it?"

Valerius nodded sleepily and yawned. He wondered if

Servius was going to tell him why he was there, but Servius finally said good night, rose slowly, and left.

✦

Bright and early the next morning, Valerius held his regular session with his senior centurions and asked about any further incidents during the night. For the time being, all was calm. Valerius decided to make a more detailed announcement of their itinerary and emphasize the purpose of their expedition. The troops were obviously mentally and physically planning for war. Therefore, he hoped to change the expectations by explaining their imperial assignment as a mission of keeping the peace. "Today we will arrive in Heliopolis to buy supplies. Buy, I said. Not loot, not steal. It will not be a strenuous march, and we will stay there for several days. Then we will head west over the mountain toward the coast to Byblos and along the coast to Berytus and on to Sidon. Therefore, for the next several weeks we will be able to have fresh fish along the coast." This announcement was met with a loud cheer, and the regular soldiers crowded close to hear more. "In Sidon, the emperor wants me to supervise the construction of his grand statue that we are escorting to Jerusalem."

"Why are we stopping in Heliopolis when we could get to the coast sooner?" the camp prefect wanted to know.

"A good question, Fabius. I want to ensure we have adequate supplies. You will like Heliopolis. It is a city of beautiful temples." The soldiers moaned. "Oh, I see. Beautiful temples do not interest you. Perhaps you will be more interested when I tell you the most beautiful temple in Heliopolis is dedicated to Bacchus." A loud cheer went up. Valerius laughed. "Right! Heliopolis is in the center of Syrian wine country."

Manius was not cheering. "What I want to know is why we need two legions to deliver a statue."

"An excellent question, Manius Cornelius. A question I

asked as well. I was told the emperor wants two legions to escort it."

"He obviously expects trouble."

"I believe that to be true."

"What kind of trouble?"

"I don't know yet."

"But we can expect it is the kind of trouble for which we would need two legions."

Valerius said, "I doubt there will be trouble in Syria. Therefore, we should respect the people who live here who assure me they want no quarrel with Rome."

Manius would not back down. "But farther south. The Jews will have a quarrel with Rome."

There was no point in avoiding the truth. Valerius realized that Manius Cornelius was going to be a bigger thorn in his side than he had realized. "Indeed, I do believe they will."

✦

In the glorious splendor of Heliopolis where an old Roman garrison built during the time of Julius Caesar housed veteran Roman soldiers, Valerius ordered Quintus to organize the purchase of supplies and encouraged all the soldiers to participate in the local festival that celebrated a statue of a golden god who held a whip in his right hand and a thunderbolt and stalks of grain in his left. A row of priests started the procession. Then, prominent citizens who had fasted for days to be ready for this honor carried the statue along a sacred way through the city. Valerius had warned the troops to observe the proper respect for the local rituals and was gratified to note that the soldiers, who had celebrated Bacchus with such verve the night before, were mostly sober and solemn as they followed the procession to the temple. Valerius thought it was the most beautiful group of temples he had ever seen.

After Heliopolis, the Roman army moved west toward

Byblos and set up tents beyond the tide line along the wide beaches. While Manius was trying to tell the troops that Byblos was the old center for the production of papyrus and the origin of the word *biblion*—the word for "book" in Greek—the troops stripped naked and ran into the water like children, splashing and dunking each other below the waves. A more enterprising group of soldiers had already dipped a net into the water and hauled in fish and seaweed, but, when they saw their comrades frolicking in the sea, they dropped the fish on the beach and ran for the water.

Manius looked toward Valerius and said, "And these are the defenders of the Roman imperium!"

Valerius gave up trying to keep a straight face and laughed as a scavenger of seagulls devoured the whole catch on the sand before the bathers even hit the water.

Manius said, "Serves them right."

Valerius doubled over with laughter, and soon nearly everybody was laughing except for Manius and the fellows who had caught the fish.

Before long, the aroma of frying fish drew flocks of seagulls, sea birds, and wild animals to their campfires, and around noon nearly all the soldiers threw off their tunics to bask in the winter sun. Despite Manius's stern objections, Valerius decided to let the troops enjoy what amounted to a winter holiday.

Valerius looked across the deep blue water and, instead of listening to Manius's raving about how the great general Gnaeus Pompeius had conquered Syria for Rome seventy-five years ago, thought about Homer's description of the wine-dark sea. He closed his eyes so he could visualize what Rachel was likely doing at that moment and smiled.

When Manius finished his speech about the grandeur of past Roman generals, Valerius saluted him and announced that he was appointing him to take over full leadership of the two legions while he would be absent at Sidon to oversee the production of Caligula's statue.

Obviously surprised, Manius said, "You realize that I would want absolute discipline with no lounging about? This—" he swept his arm around to indicate the sunbathing soldiers, "is no way to run a Roman army."

Valerius clasped Manius's shoulder and said, "You are right. You can make them do athletic training and hone their mastery in archery and javelin throwing. They can learn Parthian tricks of archery. Ask Farid about it. Your soldiers can continue to hunt the wild boar in the woods and roast them on their fires. Just remember to follow the rules that even the great Pompeius revered. All soldiers are to be treated with respect. I don't know how long I will be gone." Valerius looked him straight in the eye. "No executions during my absence."

Valerius chose ten men from the first cohort, a standard-bearer, and two engineers to accompany him. At the last minute, he decided to have Lacertus join him, ostensibly to take care of the horses, but mainly because he wanted to test him. He sat down near Lacertus, who was whittling some driftwood he had found on the sand.

Valerius studied his grim profile and said, "I know you grieve for your friends. I'm sorry."

Lacertus remained silent and continued whittling.

Valerius frowned. "There was no need to execute them. Your fate will be determined by how you behave on our trip to Sidon. Tell Rhaetia to start out tonight on the road toward Sidon. She can join us tomorrow."

Lacertus looked like he was about to ask a question, but merely nodded.

At sunrise, Manius strode up just as they were leaving. "You are taking this thief with you?" He pointed toward Lacertus.

Valerius answered, "I am."

"Unshackled? On horseback?"

"That's right."

"You are aware he carries a knife."

"I am. He carves trinkets and uses it to eat. I appreciate your concern."

Manius shrugged. "Well, let no one say I didn't warn you."

Valerius saluted, and his unit set out on horseback along the coast and made their way over lagoons and rocks until they reached the main road to Berytus.

At a watering hole later that morning, Servius walked away from the group with Valerius and wanted to know if he was sure about Lacertus. Valerius and Servius engaged in their usual competition of testing who could hit a designated target with their urine stream. Servius won and laughed but was immediately serious. "Manius is right, you know."

"Manius is a career soldier, who by rights should be the commander of the legions. He resents me. If I could, I would gladly turn all of it over to him."

"I thought you were going to make me legate of the troops. After all we've been through." His eyes pierced him with questions.

Valerius frowned. He wasn't sure he could reveal his misgivings about the nature of their mission and feared for Servius should he have to take over for him. Finally, he told Servius he wanted to give Manius the opportunity because he realized he was more fiercely ambitious than Servius. As Valerius rode ahead, he glanced back at Servius and caught him glaring daggers at his back. Immediately, Servius looked away, but Valerius noticed that he sat stiff and rigid in his saddle, his face taut with strain, his lips curved downward in frustration. Valerius wondered if his promotion of two equestrians after the attack had triggered Servius's discontent.

Near Berytus, Rhaetia emerged out of a tangle of saltwort spikes from behind a terebinth tree. Lacertus jumped from his horse, lifted her on, climbed up behind her, and, without breaking their stride, they continued south toward Sidon.

✦

THE FOUNDRY AT SIDON

COMPARED TO THE TRUDGING PACE OF ROMAN legions, it was liberating to travel with a small team on horseback. Valerius decided they would camp on the hillside, where they could look down on the city. He pushed on alone and was soon encircled by the walls of Sidon and the strong smell of the foundry that made even the city well water taste metallic. The announced purpose of the visit was to meet with the director and engineers of the foundry to expedite the creation of a colossal statue of the emperor. Valerius had a different objective in mind and was hoping to find ways to delay or even impede production.

The foundry itself was huge and stifling and noisy. Most of the workers wore leather body-covering aprons with huge gloves and little caps to cover their shaved heads. No body hair was allowed in case of sparks, but even so, nearly everyone Valerius met had burn scars on every piece of exposed skin. Some wore protective glass over their eyes, but many workers went blind after a few years in the foundry. The fires in the furnaces burned so hot they glowed yellow. The heat was overwhelming. But worse was the din of huffing bellows and clanking tools that meant Valerius could hardly hear what he was being told about the different stages of forming a statue.

There was a gallery separated by glass from the ovens, but even there the heat caused onlookers to leave quickly for the outside air and the sandpits where bronze, iron, and steel objects simmered at various stages of cooling. The fumes of charred metals hitting sand were particularly offensive.

When the director heard that the governor of Syria had appeared on the premises, he came running to pay his respects and immediately demanded his payment for barges of raw materials that had already been delivered for the project. Valerius was taken by surprise because not one of the imperial messages had mentioned cost. Valerius had assumed that the emperor's envoys who had provided dimensions and some wax and clay impressions of Caligula's head had already sent funds. Valerius realized that he had been given a welcome opportunity for delay and promised to send an urgent message for the money to Rome.

Rubellius, the director, was a veteran of several Roman wars and had been appointed overseer of the foundry during the last years of Tiberius's reign. To greet the governor, he had removed his leather protections and stood with a naked torso in front of Valerius, his chest and arm muscles huge and rippling and glistening with sweat. Valerius guessed that some of the scars on his chest and face were not from pouring iron and copper into vessels, but from battles he had fought for the Roman imperium.

They had hardly begun the tour before Rubellius pointed to glistening steel hooks that moved along railings hung from the ceiling and tipped the contents of buckets into forms below in a procession that reminded Valerius of bowing priests in the ritual at Heliopolis. "Brand new," Rubellius bragged. "And down there—you can hardly see it from here—is a large sprocket wheel two men turn slowly, and we just discovered how to regulate the speed with precision. No other foundry has anything like it to make vessels of iron."

Nodding and trying to show interest, Valerius wandered through a maze of halls and rooms behind Rubellius as he explained how they were going to create the bronze statue of Caligula. From the dock where the raw ores were unloaded to the rooms where the ores were stored, to rooms for modeling, casting, cooling, refining, chasing, detailing, and polishing Valerius learned that every step in the process took precision, attention to detail, and a lot of time. When he realized that the statue was still in the earliest stage of creation, that it existed only potentially in the raw material still floating in the barges, he heaved a sigh of relief. It would be months before any statue could be ready.

Rubellius was eager to please and pointed out that the process could be sped up by using a large statue of Hercules or even of Zeus and just switching the heads, but Valerius protested. "The emperor must be larger than life, more imposing than Zeus, for he sees himself as the greatest of all gods. But it must be his body." Valerius managed to say this with some conviction, hoping this tactic could delay completion even more. Rubellius grunted that it was not the original agreement.

Over ale at the local tavern, Rubellius asked, "So this bronze Caligula we're making is headed for the temple in Jerusalem. Isn't that rather provocative?"

Valerius almost choked on his ale. "Rather," he managed to say.

"So, Rome now starts wars in temples?"

"It wasn't my idea."

"I guess not. You got the short straw?"

Valerius shrugged. "You could say that."

Rubellius scratched his broken nose and seemed thoughtful. "It's odd that our two biggest projects at the foundry right now are for the temple in Jerusalem."

"Caligula ordered two statues?"

"No. Two guys are here with designs for a new temple

door. A huge one. It will weigh more than Caligula and take twice as much bronze. Probably a lot more."

"I didn't know the temple would have that much money."

"Somebody in Alexandria is paying for it and sent his engineers here to make sure we cast it right. Two brilliant guys. Young. One of them just designed that delivery system I was showing you."

Valerius wondered if Simon knew about this project for the temple. "When were they here?"

"They're still here. They want to make the molds themselves. But they are way too ambitious."

"Explain."

Rubellius shook his head. "I've warned them about the weight and the cost. What they propose to build is forty cubits tall and so heavy it would take at least twenty men to open and close each side."

"By Neptune! That's enormous. It will cost a fortune. Is it even feasible?"

Rubellius drank and wiped his mouth. "The amount of bronze they want will mean this is the biggest project my foundry has undertaken. And that's not all. They tell me they are going to add an overlay of silver and gold. I questioned them, but they declared they have money we can draw down from various accounts at each stage of the production. How they hope to transport the door to Jerusalem they didn't say." He finished his ale and plunked the cup down on the table.

Valerius thought the issue of transport might provide another hope for delay.

After a moment, Rubellius belched and said, "You understand that I cannot proceed on your project until I get payment. Half now. Half at completion. Even the emperor must pay."

Valerius nodded and thought it strange that Sidon was in the middle of a contest between the God of the Jews and Caligula.

✦

When Valerius learned that Sosias was one of the young men who was planning the bronze door for the temple, he met up with him at the local inn and was introduced to Nicanor, a young sculptor from Alexandria. Both Sosias and Nicanor were so excited about their project that they stumbled over themselves trying to explain how it all came about. Valerius made them start from the beginning and finally understood that they had won a contest to design and build the door, and that the project was being financed by Alexander Lysimachos, the alabarch of Alexandria, and that Agrippa, the king of the Jews, had promised to provide laborers and oxen to transport the door from Sidon to Jerusalem and to mount it in the temple.

Nicanor spread out elaborate drawings and explained the details of the ornamental designs that would embellish the door. When asked what he thought of the decorative designs, Valerius said, "It is not as grand as the friezes on the temple to Jupiter in Rome."

Nicanor frowned and said, "It is not the Jewish way to make images of God."

Properly chastened, Valerius said, "That is most wise."

Sosias unrolled technical drawings with measurements, angles, details about fastening rods, and the weight of each side of the door with the counterweight needed to lift them. Nicanor was more concerned about the aesthetic impact of the door and showed no interest in the engineering process. Sosias, by contrast, expressed the need for precise measurements to make their enterprise successful and predicted it would become a marvel of technical achievement.

Valerius sensed an undercurrent of tension between the two men and assumed they did not agree on construction details. Nicanor was not even listening to Sosias's account and had turned back to his drawings.

When Sosias finally stopped to take a deep breath, Valerius asked if he had any news from Aurelia.

"Aurelia is fine. At least she was when we left Alexandria. She had a baby. A little girl."

"And the boys?"

"They keep getting into trouble. They've outgrown playing with wooden swords and are taking lessons in sword fighting, javelin throwing, and wrestling. They still pretend they are part of your legions. They think that is a glorious life."

Valerius winced. "If they only knew." Then he told them why he was in Sidon and why a few miles from there two Roman legions were on a mission to Jerusalem. Nicanor went pale because he understood the implications immediately, but it took Sosias a little longer to grasp the full scope of the calamity Valerius faced.

Sosias suddenly gazed in horror at Valerius. "This is insane. I remember when you told us that the emperor had summoned you to Rome, but I couldn't imagine it would lead to this. I didn't understand then why Aurelia was so upset. I understand now."

Valerius invited Sosias and Nicanor to come out to their camp on the hillside to share soldiers' rations with his team. "I need to make a progress report on the foundry, and you can certainly explain how a statue is made and why there will be delays far better than I."

While Valerius ate his supper on the hillside, Nicanor stayed aloof and gazed off into the distance. In contrast, Sosias mingled with the Romans, shared jokes, and even repaired a leather harness, sharpened a broadsword, and fixed a broken knife. Valerius wondered if there was anything Sosias didn't know how to fix.

The next day, Valerius met with Sosias alone outside of Sidon at the sea. Sosias took off his sandals and waded into the water up to his thighs and joyfully gulped in clean sea air after breathing acrid fumes in the foundry for months.

When they sat down on an outcropping of rocks and dangled their feet in the water, Sosias was curious about the group of men he had met on the hillside. His first question surprised Valerius. "Where do their loyalties lie?"

"What do you mean?"

"Quintus, for example. Does he profess allegiance to you, to the emperor, or to Rome?"

"They should all be the same."

"Should be. But are not. He impressed me as the one most loyal to you. If I'm right, that would be a good thing."

"What about Servius?"

"I sense some friction. Is he uneasy with your mission, or is he just tired of the army?"

"Perhaps both."

"And Sestius?"

"He was quick to tell me he has served under the best commanders Rome has to offer and is proud of it. I don't think he was speaking of you."

Valerius nodded. "He idolizes Manius Cornelius and wants him to adopt him since Manius has no heir."

"Who is Manius Cornelius?"

"The legate and highest-ranking officer. He would be leading this expedition if the emperor had not placed me in charge."

"He is your rival, then, and the men will take sides."

"I see that already. What did you think of the two engineers?"

Sosias gave a derogatory snort. "Engineers? I have no doubt they know how to operate battering rams, catapults, *ballistae*, and maybe how to build them, but they don't understand the principles that make them work."

"I guessed as much when I observed your face when you were talking with them. What about Lacertus?"

Sosias shook his head. "He's a mystery. I cannot tell whether he is enemy or ally, or possibly indifferent. At least we know that Rhaetia is smitten with him, which could be a good thing."

"Where did you learn to assess character like this?"

"A question of survival for an orphan like me. Philo taught me how to be a spy."

"A spy!"

"I was just thirteen when he hired me. I learned to hang around guys who looked like they were plotting against Jews. I also had to watch out for Simon and try to keep him out of trouble. That was the hardest part because Philo didn't want Simon to know he was trying to protect him."

Valerius smiled. "I can agree that would be the hardest part."

"I don't do that anymore. Spying was easier when I was a kid, and I could slither in and out of places unnoticed. One trick Philo taught me that I often find the most helpful is to listen carefully to what people do not say."

"How do you do that?"

"You watch gestures. You notice their expressions, what they look at. You try to find out what they like and what they fear by how they react to others. Rhaetia, for example, is very expressive without saying a word. And even when people speak, it's often clear they are hiding something."

"Indeed. Even I figured that out. I am grateful for your skills, but something troubles me. You and Nicanor. You are a master at assessing character, but I sense friction between you. I don't think it is just about how you want to build the door. I think it is deeper than that."

Sosias looked away and did not answer.

Valerius was quick to apologize, but Sosias shook his head and said, "It's not easy to talk about it. What would you say about your friendship with Simon? Are you always in agreement?"

"Of course not. In fact, right now he sees this mission imposed by Caligula in a totally different light than I do. I am not sure our friendship will survive."

"So, you will understand. How would you feel if you and

Simon were in love with the same woman?"

Valerius reared back and groaned.

"I asked for Rhoda's hand a long time ago, but her family won't allow it because I am not a Jew. I am an orphan. I have no idea who my parents were. Are."

"And Rhoda?"

"She loves me but won't go against her family."

"I see."

"No, you see only a small part of it. Nicanor and I have been friends for a long time. So naturally, I took him with me to meet her—" Sosias picked up a pebble at his feet and hurled it into the sea. "I feel betrayed."

"Then Rhoda should choose."

"That's not how it works. The family has chosen."

"And he is a Jew." Valerius wiped his hand across his eyes and shook his head. "I'm sorry."

There was a long silence between them. After a moment, Valerius said, "I understand how you feel."

Sosias nodded. "Rachel."

"Be patient. Things may turn in your favor."

As they walked back to Sidon, Valerius asked, "What advice do you have for me in dealing with my legions?"

"Give Manius as much power as you dare so the soldiers will blame him more if things go sour."

"And Rubellius?"

"He won't go forward with the statue until he has the money in hand. He also won't allow his crew to make an inferior product. You have time on your side."

"And not much else," Valerius responded.

TWO BULLS AND A BOAR

BACK WITH THE LEGIONS, VALERIUS NOTED THAT Manius Cornelius had instituted athletic competitions among the soldiers and praised him for his innovative leadership. Manius ordered the soldiers to separate into teams by legion and escalated the tension by setting the winners of each legion against each other. Manius was quick to note that Valerius had announced no new marching orders south and objected. Valerius blamed the delay on the absence of a statue and quite logically argued that descent into Jewish territory would start premature conflict. He sent a letter to Rome about the needed finances for the statue and finally received an answer three months later. The emperor wanted him to raise taxes in Jerusalem for the project. Raising taxes to pay for a statue that would desecrate the temple would cause outright rebellion, a tactic Caligula might even be embracing. Valerius decided a promise of tax money would not set Rubellius into motion and placed the order in the files for later action. To leave for Jerusalem, he had to have the statue. To obtain the statue, he was supposed to raise taxes in Jerusalem. The impasse the emperor himself had created provided delays.

Summer was coming, and the troops enjoyed being near the sea. Valerius decided it was wise to stay near the coast and keep an eye on developments at Sidon and wait.

Manius became increasingly impatient with arguments for delays and warned that the army would lose all discipline without specific goals and leadership. Valerius agreed and asked Manius to continue with the competitive games he had set up. Quintus suggested they could emulate the old Olympic games and crown winners with laurel wreathes and grant a full day off from their duties.

Meanwhile, Manius challenged Valerius to games of chance. During these sessions, Valerius usually lost, which prompted Manius to start placing bets. Other officers began to place bets on their games as well, and Valerius feared they were turning the camp into casinos because the soldiers were soon following in their footsteps. Even Farid got into the act by challenging tribunes and centurions to games of chess. After Valerius discovered that Farid was acquiring a sizable sum, he tried to put a stop to the betting before it got out of hand. Valerius suggested that valor and strength should replace money. Servius looked at him with a warning in his eyes, but Valerius failed to foresee what would happen next. The two legions set up a pyramid of successive contests and declared the final winner would face the governor of Syria, who could choose his style and weapon of combat. Aghast, Valerius quickly argued that Manius Cornelius, the chief centurion and experienced legate of the army, should have that honor. Thundering applause greeted this suggestion, and much to Valerius's consternation, it was decided that the final contest would be between Manius and Valerius. Valerius would represent the Tenth Legion, whose emblem was a boar and whose protective god was Neptune. Manius would represent the Third Legion, whose emblem was two bulls and whose protective god was Mars.

Trapped by his own suggestion, Valerius hoped to drag out the process by giving every soldier who wanted it a chance in the arena. Arenas were set up on the plain, and the combats began. For the moment, Valerius decided that this diversion was a gift of the gods, given that it was an entertaining occupation for two legions waiting in the countryside for a statue. He told Servius he should have asked the legions to build an aqueduct over the Beqaa Valley into Berytus instead. "If we have further delays, I will suggest such a project."

Servius thought it was a better idea than having the two highest-ranking officers fight each other. "No matter what happens, you will have half of the troops mad at you!"

"I don't know, Servius. I think it should all be done in fun. The soldiers will be amused to see their commanders struggle and fail. It might do more good for their morale than you think."

"I think it is undignified. You should let me fight in your place."

"You! Why would you want to do that?"

"I could bring him down where he belongs." Servius mimed a fistfight and growled deep in his throat.

Valerius assumed he was joking and laughed.

"You are not taking this seriously enough. Manius is practicing, although he will deny it. What about you?"

Valerius was about to say that this was child's play compared to what they were about to confront in Palestine, but finally agreed to secret practice sessions in the sand near the beach. The ten warm-up exercises taught by Dhaki, the Parthian wrestling master in Cyrene, were ingrained in his memory. In fact, his muscles remembered them in their proper sequence without conscious effort on his part. Servius stood watch with his lantern and realized he needed someone to help Valerius practice. He thought of Lacertus, who had been training some of the soldiers, and the night sessions began in earnest. Lacertus fought like a mountain lion with fierce instincts and slithering moves that caught Valerius by surprise. He was the master of a running jump that launched him higher than an opponent's head, and Valerius was an agile student. The change was good for Valerius and made him quicker to react and more alert. At the end of the sessions, they sat for a while to catch their breath and gazed at the stars. Lacertus slowly warmed to Valerius's offer of friendship and learned the fluid, dance-like backward roll that allowed Valerius to land on his feet. One night, after a grueling practice session, Lacertus said that he had had many opportunities to kill him.

Valerius nodded and said, "I know. Why didn't you?"

Lacertus thought for a moment and answered, "It wouldn't be right. There's no valor in murder."

Valerius sighed. "Sometimes I wish you had."

After a long silence, Valerius explained what awaited them in Palestine. "If we fight, thousands die. If we don't fight, I die. Therefore, you see, you would have done me a favor."

When the time finally came for the big match, the soldiers had worked up such anticipation and excitement that the whole idea of encouraging competition without bets fell to pieces. Outsiders from Sidon and Berytus and surrounding villages lined up along the sidelines and were placing money on their man. Half of them were waving signs for the two bulls and the other half flags for the boar. It was the biggest event in the region since gladiators had fought in the amphitheater in Sidon. Even Rubellius appeared with Sosias and Nicanor to see what all the commotion was about.

Valerius decided he would introduce the event with a lighthearted speech. He emphasized that the rivalry between the two legions was done in the spirit of encouraging valor and honor along with some fun in a friendly competition. Then he said, "My friends, after careful reflection, Manius and I have decided not to use weapons because we are afraid, we might hurt each other." The crowd roared with laughter. Valerius grinned, and both Bulls and Boars cheered back. With that, he took off his military belt, tunic, and sandals until he stood in his loincloth and walked slowly through the sand to the center of the arena that had just been roped off for their match.

Manius entered the arena in his loincloth and saluted. The simplicity of white loincloths against tan skin announced that neither carried a weapon. He bowed toward Valerius, who bowed back. His face was deadly serious. Then Manius said, "My dear fellow soldiers, any one of you in front of me today could fight more valiantly than I ever could. I salute you all! May the Bulls protect me!"

They stood across from each other in the arena. Almost equal in height and weight, Manius was older, his muscles tighter, his straight back accustomed to long military marches and standing guard without moving a muscle. Valerius stood more at ease, exhibiting the poise of an athlete more than a soldier. He looked less fierce and determined than Manius, and some of the Boars started yelling encouragements that set off the Bulls, who yelled louder. They advanced toward each other and leaned in to touch foreheads in honor of the old and venerated Greek Olympic starting position, their arms loose at their sides. They took two steps back to flex their muscles before the fight began.

Despite the levity and the dismissal on both sides that it was just a game, it was immediately apparent that the two principal actors in the arena were not out to provide a mock fight or light entertainment. Their determined expressions announced a contest of wills, a battle of endurance, a raw display of strength.

Manius sprang into action, plowing into Valerius with such vehemence that Valerius was pushed back against the rope. Staggered by the force of the blow, Valerius walked off to the side to catch his breath. Suddenly, he sprinted forward for a high jump off the ground that sent him higher than Manius's head. As he came down on top of him, he grabbed his opponent's shoulders and forced his knee against his chest, causing Manius to fall backward with Valerius on top. Impressed by his unexpected high-flying move, the

Boars yelled and whistled and stomped their boots against the ground. Then the Bulls screamed victory as Manius threw him off. On his feet again, Manius charged like a battering ram, using his head as a weapon, then forced Valerius into a backward dance as they struggled chest to chest, arms and shoulders locked, straining and panting, two steps forward then two steps back, until Valerius grabbed Manius's shoulders and knocked him to the sand. Manius slithered out from under Valerius's hold, surging to his feet, swinging his arms low to tackle Valerius around the hips. After a scrambling struggle where the sand flew up in puffs at their feet, Manius shoved backward. Valerius pushed forward. They stayed joined together in a brutal embrace that led nowhere.

Fabius sounded the gong for the end of the first round.

During intermission, Manius called for his sand burns to be treated and his body rubbed down with fresh oil. Valerius called for water. His muscles screamed for rest, and he would gladly stop. He sat back and felt foolish. Why did he agree to this? He felt far away from Dhaki's teaching about wrestling which inspired his youth. He remembered how Dhaki kept reminding him that muscle had little to do with winning. "Wrestling is a discipline of the mind. Anyone can develop muscles. Developing the mind is far more difficult and important. Inner strength is everything." Valerius realized that inner strength was an attribute he had not possessed in a very long time. He started breathing deeply to seek calm and focus and tried his old trick of placing himself outside the arena to gaze at the fight from afar as though he were not involved.

Sosias came by and grinned at him. "You are more athletic and dramatic, and the crowds love that, but—"

"But what?"

"You lose if you win. And you win if you lose."

"What should I do?"

"They want to see you clobbered. Secretly, even the Boars are rooting for Manius. He's like them. He's a soldier. A lot of them see themselves rising in the ranks to become centurions or legates. No one thinks they could become senator or governor."

"Ergo: I let him win?"

"Never! You make his victory real."

"How?"

"Remember, it's like a chess game. Sometimes the weaker becomes the stronger."

"You've been talking with Farid."

The fans yelled for the fight to resume. The second round started with a slow dance as they circled each other, Valerius walking backward around the arena with the rope at his back and Manius in relentless pursuit. Twice Manius feigned a sudden attack, but Valerius remained still. When Manius finally pounced, Valerius stepped to the side and spun out of reach. Quick to pick up on Valerius's tactics, Manius deflected an assault at the very last moment so that Valerius stumbled forward into the sand, a victim of his own momentum. Immediately Manius was on top of him and slammed a fist into his jaw. The Bulls cheered. Valerius ducked another punch and spun back to clasp Manius's neck and shoulder in a stranglehold that bent him backward onto the ground. The Boars cheered. Manius scrambled up, charged Valerius like a bull, and pushed him face-down into the sand. As Valerius came up sputtering, Manius seized Valerius's legs and tilted him off his feet. As he fell, Valerius pulled his head in, curled his body into a backward roll, and landed on his feet. More cheers. Louder this time.

They stood facing each other, breathing heavily.

Manius crouched and started up at a run, slamming his full weight into Valerius, who stepped to one side—the side he usually favored—so that Manius anticipated his move, changed the angle of attack, and rammed his full body weight into him and pinned him down. Hard. Everyone waited. They expected a countermove. None came. Manius kept him pinned to the ground.

The gong sounded. It was over.

Valerius lay in the sand and looked up at the sky. No part of his body did not ache. He tasted blood in his mouth and felt it running down his face. And yet he was happy. It had been a decent fight. No one could fault him for not doing his best, and the cheers that echoed through the camp were for Manius, who was being carried in triumph on the shoulders of chanting legionaries. Above him, someone poured water on his head and urged him to sit up. Servius washed the sand from his skin and tended to his wounds.

Manius Cornelius, chief centurion and legate, was crowned with laurel leaves on top of the victory platform. Publius Petronius Valerius, governor of Syria, limped up to the foot of the platform, saluted, and hailed him as the victor.

✦

The whole camp turned into a carnival. Musicians brought out their instruments; bakers had been busy all day preparing rolls and buns dipped in honey; Valerius had authorized the slaughter of several cows that had been roasting since dawn; the enticing aroma of fresh meat wafted over the camp all day. Fabius brought a splendid hunk of beef to Manius and served it with flair. The soldiers cheered and rushed to get in line for their portions. Valerius was not hungry and retreated to his tent to rest. Sosias and Nicanor came to congratulate him on his performance.

"It was not a performance. I really didn't see that last move coming."

Sosias got right to the point. "We have a big problem. There's not enough ore available to make the door as well as the statue."

"What has changed since I talked to Rubellius?"

"The amount of raw ore available even as far away as Britannia and Germania will not be enough for both the door and the statue. It will have to be mined first. It may take until next spring or longer. It's not just the money, although he wants that too."

"That's insane! If the emperor wants his statue, he will have to send the funds."

"Rubellius won't let us proceed until he has the materials and money for both. We can finish the molds, and then we must stop."

Valerius raised his hands in a gesture of helplessness. "I know how frustrating this is for you both. I'm afraid I have no solution. Caligula is running this show, and if we don't get the money we have to delay. If we don't get the ore, we have to delay. You cannot create the door until we have both. If this means Rubellius won't let you proceed, I can do nothing about it."

Sosias and Nicanor begged him to intervene, but Valerius shook his head. "What do you think will happen, if we ever manage to get the statue to the temple in Jerusalem?"

"War."

"Right. The people will rebel and could destroy the temple in the process. Then there would be no reason for a new door. In the meantime, make the most beautiful molds ever for the temple and hope that someday this madness will cease. One way or another, it will have to."

As Nicanor made to leave, Sosias stayed back and reminded Valerius of a moment years ago in Cyrene when he watched him kiss Rachel.

Valerius smiled. "How could I ever forget? We thought the future was bright and we could simply love each other. Things are never as simple as we think."

"But sometimes we get the chance to make a few things right?"

"You are being mysterious. What do you have in mind?"

"Remember Hallas?"

"Of course—the thug who helped Meidias and got away with it?"

"Right. He was in Sidon with his boat last week on his way to Tyre. After Rachel was abducted by Meidias, Hallas started a business of abducting children and young women in Cyrene and Alexandria and along the coast to sell them to slave merchants. He brags that it's a lucrative business. Simon told me there is still a Roman warrant out for his arrest. Ten years ago, he was declared an enemy of Rome by the prefect of Egypt, Vitrasius Pollio."

Valerius promised he would try to find out more about Hallas and expressed his regret about the door. After they left, he inspected his tortured body, and Farid entered his tent to rub olive and peppermint oils into his limbs and back.

Valerius sighed with contentment. "Ah. Where did you learn these skills?"

"In Parthia."

"That makes sense. I learned to wrestle from Dhaki. A Parthian genius."

"His methods are famous in Edessa. His students always say that your strength is in your mind, not in your muscles."

"That's easy for him to say when his muscles don't hurt."

"They will heal. You are upset for Sosias and Nicanor."

"Rubellius is being stubborn. And the emperor is not about to pay."

"Do you want me to try to find out more about Hallas?"

"How would you do that?"

"I know a lot about crooked slave dealers. Have you forgotten that I used to be a slave before you rescued me?"

WHO IS THE ENEMY?

AFTER THE FIGHT, VALERIUS THOUGHT HE WOULD not be able to sleep. He was in considerable pain, and the fact that Sosias and Nicanor had become additional victims of Caligula's whims didn't make things easier. When he finally dozed off, he dreamt of Rachel. When he awoke, he knew he owed it to Rachel and to Simon to find out what Hallas was up to. Before he rode off to Tyre to investigate, he decided to meet with Manius to plan the next steps toward fulfilling the emperor's demands. Valerius had no idea how Manius would respond to him after the fight.

Valerius started with a thoughtful analysis of the history of the Jews and how Emperor Augustus and former governors of Syria like Vitellius had shown deep respect for their religion, traditions, and heritage. When Manius sat silent for a long time, Valerius worried that their approaches to military leadership and their mission would be more at odds than ever.

Finally, Manius jumped up from his stool and suggested they take a ride along the coast. As they rode south side by side, Manius abruptly urged his mount to a fast gallop and challenged Valerius to a race. The tide was out and revealed a fine racing track of packed sand. Manius was way ahead before Valerius could even react, but they finished in a dead heat.

Manius erupted in laughter, jumped off his horse, and sat down on a rock. Valerius suspected that Manius was demonstrating he had no residual pain from the fight, but Valerius could not claim the same and gingerly moved his limbs to avoid sharp stabs of pain.

"Come sit down. We need to talk. I predict we will either be the worst of enemies or the best of friends." Manius lifted his waterskin to his lips.

Valerius raised his eyebrows in surprise and obeyed.

Manius said, "I am a soldier. You are a statesman. I know we do not see eye to eye on how to treat prisoners. We are not likely to see eye to eye on tactics. I like clear strategies. I like to fight battles we win with superior manpower and with clever planning. But you are doing everything to avoid confrontation. You want to avoid war with the Jews."

"True."

"You claim the Jews are planning a strategy of resistance by obstruction but without weapons."

"True."

"How do you know this?"

"Every day I receive petitions from prominent Jews all over Syria and Palestine warning that they will resist the progress of the Roman army by lying down in the road and refusing to let the statue pass. They are willing to die to protect the sanctity of the temple and will refuse to fight."

"And your strategy is to delay as long as possible. How will this end?"

"I cannot send an army against people who will not fight."

"I ask again. What happens when you do not fight?"

"The fury of Caligula. He will demand my death."

Manius stared at him, his eyes puzzled, trying to grasp the ominous implications of what he had just said. "You say this with conviction. Without hesitation. You are willing to die to save Jews?"

Valerius turned away from his gaze and stood. He felt smothered by a new sense of dread and was even afraid to admit he was afraid. Finally, he turned toward Manius and spoke. "It is not a decision to make lightly. Do I even have a choice? At least not one I can live with. My father once stood before the senate and proclaimed that you can only die once and then fell on his sword because he had defended a comrade in arms and was falsely accused of treason. What I am about to say could be construed as treason. What Caligula wants is wrong. But he is the emperor. He will demand that I fall on my sword."

"And you are willing to give up your life?"

"I will confess to you that I am afraid. But I will not fight unarmed Jews with our legions. You can report me to the emperor." Valerius sighed but felt relieved that he could express both his fear and his resolve.

"Hold on. Let's think this thing through. What happens then?"

"Manius, as second in command, you know that as well as I."

"So, Caligula commands you to fall on your sword. Then you expect me to carry out a massacre of unarmed Jews and place the statue in the temple that the Jews will promptly tear down?"

"Caligula will expect you to do that. Not I. Otherwise, you have understood completely."

Manius sifted sand through his fingers and looked out to sea. He rose and walked over to the edge of the water and kicked a few pebbles with his boot. Valerius studied his grim expression and wondered what he was thinking. Then Manius turned to Valerius, handed him his waterskin, and gave a hollow laugh. "Here. Drink. It's suddenly in my interest to keep you alive."

Valerius took the proffered waterskin and drank. "I'm not sure what you mean."

"Your real enemy is Caligula."

"Agreed. But I cannot fight Caligula."

"So, you oppose him at every turn."

"Correct."

"I see now what you are trying to accomplish. We must continue to stall, hoping Caligula will change his mind."

"I wouldn't count on that."

"In the meantime, I promise to do my best to support you and to keep the legions occupied with military training. As long as they get their pay and daily rations, they will be happy not to fight."

"What happens after I am ordered to fall on my sword? Would you defy Caligula's orders?"

"That's the big question. Isn't it? I've been standing here thinking about why I should risk my life to save Jews. But I also have no desire to follow through with unheroic and senseless massacres after your death."

"Surely, you want your military career to be noble rather than absurd, and you will refuse to slaughter unarmed civilians?" Valerius tried to read his face for a reaction.

They studied each other for a moment, and Manius was the first to grin as he clasped Valerius by the shoulder. "We can always hope that the winds of war will change."

"You cannot count on that."

"No," Manius agreed. "I don't count on Rome becoming sane again. But I will support you. If, indeed, I must take over, I will make my decision at that time."

Valerius said, "This must remain between us. Our announced purpose is the same—to deliver the statue to the temple in Jerusalem."

"Understood."

As they mounted their horses to return to camp, Valerius suggested they ride a few more miles south to Tyre, where they might stop a criminal from selling stolen goods.

They rode into Tyre over the causeway that led to the old

part of the city, where they found the slave markets in full swing. Merchants in fine silks with bright gems festooned around their necks bowed to them and offered their wares from eastern lands. Veiled women who were elegantly dressed and naked men of different races stared at their military dress with defiance. Valerius pressed on to examine a group of slaves who looked bedraggled and cowed and asked about their provenance and where he might find the merchant who was selling them. Immediately, a suave businessman pushed forward through the crowd, bowed, and offered to sell them for a high sum. It had been ten years since Valerius had interrogated Hallas in Cyrene after Rachel was abducted. He doubted he would recognize him. Manius stood by and watched Valerius haggle over prices and seemed vaguely amused before suggesting they visit the city magistrate to inquire about the slave trade along the coast.

The city magistrate, a jolly fellow who also served as tax collector for Rome, knew the merchants who plied their trade up and down the coast, but had not heard of Hallas. Valerius sensed that, as long as a business was lucrative for Tyre and paid the requisite taxes and kickbacks, there would be little incentive for the local administration to shut it down. As they rode back to camp, Valerius decided to tell Manius about Rachel and why he had a personal interest in bringing Hallas to justice.

Manius offered to ask Fabius to track down Hallas. "He is good at this sort of thing."

Once back at camp, Fabius and Valerius met up with Sosias and Servius to gather information and check shipping records at several ports. Two weeks later, Valerius was appalled to learn that the number of slave traders who sailed up and down the coast exceeded the number of ships loaded with wheat, barley, and olive oil. Most of the slave traders owned villas along the coast and were considered respectable businessmen in the communities where they lived. The local police, known as *vigiles*, did not have the manpower to check where and how the slaves were acquired, and most of the magistrates openly agreed that a good proportion of slave trafficking was illegal, but they had no way to prove it.

Frustrated, Valerius declared that it was high time new laws were passed by the senate to counteract what he called slave piracy.

Manius said, "I couldn't agree more, but how many senators in Rome live in villas financed by the illegal slave trade? Unfortunately, you must be rich to be a senator in Rome."

Servius asked, "How rich?"

Valerius said, "Under Augustus, you had to prove you owned property worth at least a million sesterces. Unless you are appointed to the senate by the emperor, or you have achieved military glory on the battlefield."

Servius turned to look directly at Valerius. "Or if you are the son of a senator, and you assume you inherit the title." He said this with some rancor.

Valerius smiled. "Not always. But even when that's true, senators must own enough property to sustain themselves because senators receive no pay for their service. And it might be good to remember that many senators died under Tiberius when they were falsely accused of treason. You might be safer on the battlefield."

Manius laughed, but Servius mumbled an embittered oath to Jupiter.

Toward evening, Valerius summoned Servius to his tent and suggested they walk along the beach. For Valerius, the peacefulness of their limitless view out to sea made the prospect of war and bloodshed in Palestine incongruous and senseless. After his surprisingly uplifting encounter with Manius, he felt justified in his choice of legate, but realized that Servius perceived it as an offense to their long friendship. Until their discussion today, Valerius had not realized that he had senatorial ambitions.

Valerius stopped to admire nature's light show as the sun melted into the sea and turned to study Servius's face in profile. He looked subdued and sulky and made Valerius think he expected to be reprimanded. He realized that his desire to protect him from the consequences of Caligula's anger had damaged their friendship. "I have news from Parthia."

"They are at each other's throats again?"

"Worse. Regicide. It's hard to keep up with the different feuds between royal families, and the governor of Asia needs our assistance. I am not in a position to help. But you are. I want you to command Roman troops to go to Parthia and reestablish order, if not peace. I know it is much to ask in the middle of this campaign, but I can think of no one more qualified to engage in this mission."

Valerius saw excitement flare into Servius's eyes, but his voice was calm. "How many troops?"

"You can pick up one legion in Antioch and take a good portion of our cavalry. They are less useful in our march toward Jerusalem."

"What is going on in Parthia?"

"You will have to find out. Artabanus died. It is likely he was killed by one of his sons. Vardanes and Gotarzes are fighting for the throne. Brother against brother. It will be a challenge. But you will have full command. You will be the legate. You can appoint your own commanders among the centurions and decurions. At least, the worst of the winter is behind us, and you will be heading into spring. You will have to confer with Marcus Vinicius, the current proconsular governor of Asia who will bring his legions."

"What's he like?"

"I've never met him. He is somehow related to Tiberius. He is known as an orator. I have no idea about his military skills. I don't know if he will be as much help to you as Lucius Vitellius was to me, but you know a lot more about Parthia than I did when I tried to secure the border."

"Any advice?"

"Just one. Don't marry a princess."

They both laughed.

"And remember that glory on the battlefield often means avoiding a battle altogether."

Valerius clasped his shoulder and gave him a friendly shove. He was not convinced that Servius was ready for the chaos that Parthia represented and sent a silent prayer to Mars, hoping he had made a wise decision. He felt better when he decided he would send Farid with him. Farid had proven to be a valuable advisor.

Later that evening, Valerius walked through the camp and stopped to talk with several soldiers. Some were playing with dice; others tried to toss bean bags into a bucket; two were lining up pebbles, trying to arrange three in a straight line and block his opponent from doing so. Another soldier was drawing crude images of gladiators on blanched papyrus he had cut up in squares. Valerius stopped to look at a few and saw a caricature of Fabius with his head sticking through a hole in his shield. He recognized Servius arcing urine high into the air to target Mount Olympus and Manius with a laurel wreath askew on his head. Valerius asked, "Where is one of me?"

The soldier's face went red as he claimed he didn't have one, but Valerius knew better and demanded to see it. With trembling fingers, the boy held out an image of Valerius that showed him on a crutch with two bulls attacking him. Valerius pointed to big blobs dripping down his face. "Blood or sweat?"

"Both."

Valerius erupted in laughter. "Very good. You captured the dip at my nose and my grimace of pain. You could illustrate my reports to the senate and make them far more readable."

A soldier jabbed the flustered cartoonist playfully in the ribs. "He also does juicier ones." He fished one out to show him and laughed. "They cost more."

Valerius nodded. "I think I've seen some like that in the latrines." They all laughed.

Before he walked away, he said, "I suggest you refrain from making caricatures of the emperor. He might not laugh."

✦

PTOLEMAIS

AFTER SERVIUS HAD LEFT WITH HALF OF THE CAVALRY to join up with the Twelfth Legion in Antioch, Manius suggested it would be wise to keep the troops moving south toward Jerusalem. Valerius disagreed, for he knew that as they made their way south, the number of Jewish petitioners would increase, and the pressure and tension would escalate. Manius's point of view prevailed when a group of Roman soldiers looted a nearby village because they were restless and bored.

The legions set out to follow the coast as far as Ptolemais, and what Valerius had feared became true. Jewish women and children and old men on crutches and young men with provisions strapped on their backs swarmed in from the surrounding countryside and would not go home. Valerius steeled himself to listen calmly and patiently to their insistent pleas but could offer little beyond concern for their wellbeing. He urged them to return home and start planting their crops. He had to be cautious in what he said, for every pronouncement to the troops or to the petitioners could reach back to the ears of the emperor.

What he found most disconcerting was the number of women petitioners with their children who pushed onto the roads, blocking the progress of their supply wagons. The troops made wide detours around them except south of Tyre, where high cliffs stretched out to sea and interrupted coastal roads so that they had to travel further inland before making their way back toward the sea. It was a relief to reach Ptolemais where the troops made camp outside the city, and the officers moved into a fortress built by the ancient Phoenicians. It was a dark and drafty place where birds roosted in the rafters, and bats swarmed out at night.

After several weeks, the population of Ptolemais doubled with the crush of Jews coming to petition, and Manius began to worry that their strategy would not work. "We have underestimated their fervor, and I bring bad news. Herennius Capito, the procurator of Jamnia, has just arrived with eighty men and demands to see you. He is riling up our troops and declaring that he will lead the way to Jerusalem if you don't. He has no patience with our strategy. Capito wrote to Caligula to denounce the Jews for destroying a brick altar in the emperor's honor. Capito claims to have a personal command from Caligula to expedite the placement of his statue in the temple. He is on his way to see you as I speak."

"Surely, he is bluffing."

Manius shrugged. "Bluffing or not, he has already created a following among our troops."

Valerius acknowledged Manius's words with a solemn nod. He could tell by the warning in Manius's eyes that a serious conflict was brewing, and he was in no mood to argue with a man who considered his role superior to the chain of command and went directly to the emperor.

When Herennius Capito came storming into Valerius's presence, he slammed his high-plumed helmet on the table, omitted the normal courtesy of a military salute, and pounded on his desk. "Why are you lingering here when you should be in Jerusalem?"

Valerius studied the man who stood before him. He was stocky and short with a bull neck, deep-set eyes under bushy brows, and a belligerent stance. His lips twisted in a sneer.

Valerius said, "Please state your name, position, and reason for bursting into my office unannounced."

"Why are you sitting here when you have clear orders to get to Jerusalem to place the emperor's statue in the temple?"

Valerius ignored the question and picked up a document on his desk.

Capito sputtered in fury. "Answer me!"

Valerius looked up slowly. "You obviously refuse to follow proper procedures, and I'm sure you are aware that the temple in Jerusalem is a sacred place to all Jews."

Capito threw his head back and stared at Valerius in disbelief. "I obey orders without question. Gods, goddesses, temples—mean nothing to me. I have a clear command from the emperor, and that means something."

Valerius went back to the document in front of him.

"I have full authority from the emperor. You sit here and do nothing, and the Jews are gathering forces in the thousands."

"Forces in the thousands?" Valerius laughed. "Do you really call the people out there—old men, children, women—yes, there are some young men too—do you really call them forces?"

"I do."

Valerius shook his head. "These people are unarmed. In fact, they approach headquarters here in Ptolemais with their hands behind their backs, lest we think they want to fight. The very fact that they are not armed, that they are not forces, creates the problem. If only it were an army! We could fight on an even footing. If we plow into them now, it would be butchery. Slaughter."

"Give fair warning and start killing. They'll get the message."

"And after you kill ten, what then? Fifty? One hundred?

Four hundred? How far do we go? There are thousands out there, and they keep coming. Entire villages and entire cities have joined their holy mission. They are not tending their crops. The entire countryside will be a wilderness for generations if we cannot get these people to go home. The only way to do that is through persuasion, not war."

Capito slammed his fist on the table. "You can't be serious!"

"I will not slaughter thousands."

"The Roman army will not put up with a commander who is a weakling. You are a coward."

Valerius rose and looked down at him. "Those are big words for such a little guy."

Capito's hand went to his sword.

Valerius caught his wrist and twisted it sharply in a crocodile clamp.

Capito flinched but stared unblinking into Valerius's eyes.

"What were you saying?"

Capito spoke defiantly and rubbed his wrist. "Since you are too afraid to try, I'll have my soldiers do it. I will order them to start killing Jews tonight. On orders from Caligula."

Valerius said, "Your soldiers, including you, are under my command. Take all your men immediately back to Jamnia. Understood? You are dismissed." Valerius turned back to his work on the desk, dipped his pen in the inkpot, and started to write.

Capito spit out vile invectives, his face turning red with rage.

Valerius ignored him.

When he finally ran out of words and started sputtering and coughing to catch his breath, Valerius spoke calmly. "I have just written a letter to the emperor relieving you of command in Jamnia. This will get the emperor's attention, and we'll see who really has the ear of the emperor. I will send it by special courier if you do not leave now."

"You can't do that!"

Valerius called for Quintus to escort him out of his office. "I have ordered him and his men back to Jamnia! Tonight. Arrest him if he causes any more trouble."

Furious, Capito picked up his helmet and plunked it on his head. As he was led to the door, he turned. "I will inform the emperor of your treason. I will win this battle. I have direct orders from the emperor." His eyes flashed. His mouth contorted into an arrogant grimace as he was pushed out the door.

Valerius cringed at the word "treason" and knew that Herennius Capito had become a dangerous enemy. It was hard enough dealing with the Jewish population that kept beleaguering him with petitions without having to deal with insolence and dissent in his own ranks. What he feared most was some thoughtless incident that could, like a small spark thrown in a pile of brushwood, set the whole camp on fire. He rubbed his eyes.

For a long time, he had not slept well, and the last few days had been particularly trying. Six delegations from various Jewish groups had confronted him with petitions. He listened patiently to each one. Long tirades and longer petitions, to the accompaniment of women keening in the background, set his nerves on edge.

Manius came to warn him that Capito was walking among the soldiers and calling for them to revolt against the governor of Syria. "He is calling on them to follow him since he has direct orders from the emperor while you, he claims, do not."

"How are the soldiers responding?"

"Capito already has a following. Some are openly defiant. Some are threatening mutiny. I think we should arrest him before he causes more damage."

Valerius agreed and asked an orderly to fetch a light supper and turned to the stack of mail with a sigh. There were letters dealing with affairs of state, mostly routine business forwarded from Antioch. There were also three personal letters, one from Sedek, one from Vitellia, and one from Philo. He read the official letters first and affixed his directives on the margins, then turned to the letters from Antioch.

Sedek was hopeful that the crisis would be over soon and told him that Simon was on his way from Antioch to speak to him. "I hope you will give what he has to say your full attention," he wrote. He made no mention of Rachel.

Valerius grimaced. How many special delegations would come to plead the Jewish cause? He groaned and felt a surge of violent resentment. How dare Simon be glib about the danger when he himself was not affected? How dare he presume to talk of sacrifice? How dare Simon come and beg him to lay down his life for the Jews? Simon must think a Roman life is expendable.

Valerius crushed the letter in his fist and bolted to his feet. The constant roar of the sea slapping against the fortress walls irked him now and seemed to phrase relentless, taunting questions. He paced back and forth.

How long would Caligula persist in this madness? Valerius knew the answer before he asked the question, and he became more and more aware that he had no more control over his own destiny than his father before him. What would his father do in his situation? No doubt his reasoning would have been closer to Herennius Capito's than his own. He sighed and picked up the letter from Vitellia.

He cut through the proud seal of the Vitellius family stamped in the wax and read the bold, slanting script that announced the arrival of a son, an heir to the Petronius name: "Since you never sent me your preference for names, he will be called Lucius Petronius after my father. His loud and lusty cries indicate he will be a general, if not an emperor, when he grows up."

Valerius stared at the letter and reread the news again. He had a son! With the ever-mounting tensions in his army and the persistent wailings of the Jews, he had pushed the news of his wife's pregnancy from his mind. He tried to picture his son cradled in Vitellia's arms. Despite his gloomy mood, a smile lit up his face. "Little Lucius, become an emperor and bring some sanity into the world!"

The thought of his son assuaged an old longing in his heart. An heir! Someone to bear his name after he was gone. There was some comfort in knowing that the torch would pass on to the next generation. He began to visualize what he would do for his son. Then he frowned with the sudden awareness that the boy might never be more to him than the dreams he cherished for him and that he, in turn, would be but a meaningless name to him as he grew up without a father. The way things stood now, it was highly unlikely he would ever get to see his son.

Night had fallen, and he had not touched his supper. He felt an urgent need for fresh air and left the fortress by the side door to walk along the stone cliffs that fell sharply off into the sea. He could hear the soldiers' jeers and cheers as they prepared for another evening of wine, women, and games. There was no doubt in his mind that he would have to move at least part of his army soon. They could not go on like this, or he would lose their respect and all discipline.

He gazed up at the stars and, suddenly, he knew what he wanted to do.

Without the statue, it was folly to proceed south toward Jerusalem, nor did he want to move the army back north and give the impression of retreat. He decided instead to move half of the troops he had left due east over the hills to Tiberias in Galilee and leave the rest in Ptolemais for the moment. A smaller group of soldiers would appear less threatening to the population, and Tiberias, the splendid new capital named in honor of Tiberius, offered a strategic location for his camp. In addition, smaller groups of soldiers would impose less burden on local resources. From Galilee they could send a cohort to fetch the statue in Sidon and then bring the army down the Jordan Valley to Jerusalem.

He went to discuss his new plan with Manius, who told

him that Herennius Capito was nowhere to be found. "Alert the guards to arrest him and have the centurions meet in my office to discuss departure for Galilee."

After seeing to the last details of departure, Valerius closed himself up in his room, overcome with fatigue. As he was packing up his personal affairs, he found Philo's letter and learned that Philo's delegation of Alexandrian Jews to Rome had been an utter failure.

Valerius sighed as he reread the last sentences of Philo's letter: "I am convinced that the emperor will not be appeased and that reasonable men cannot prevail upon him. We were fortunate to escape with our limbs and lives intact. In fact, there was a moment when he flashed such an annoyed and angry look at us that I thought his next words would be a command to put us all to death."

Philo's final admonition to Valerius was to employ every delaying tactic he could possibly think of.

Valerius hurled unspoken curses against Caligula, pounded his fist against the rough wall of the fortress, and finally slumped down on his cot, doubting he would be able to sleep.

In the middle of the night, he sensed something was amiss and awoke. He lay perfectly still and listened. Somewhere close by he could hear breathing.

In a heartbeat, someone was on top of him, grasping his neck in a chokehold. Valerius struggled against rough hands and tried to claw them away, but the weight of his assailant pushed him into the folds of the cot, and he could no longer breathe much less call out. The realization hit him that he was about to die. He thought of his son in Antioch and passed out.

When he came to, gasping and sputtering, he saw a flame flicker in a lantern. His throat was too raw to speak. Slowly, he moved his head so he could focus on the room and saw Lacertus with a knife above him. Their eyes met. He closed his eyes again and thought Lacertus should go ahead and finish the job and spare him the torture of slow death, but Lacertus moved away and positioned the lantern so that Valerius could see a man slumped against the wall, his hands roped at the wrist. A gag covered part of his face, but Valerius recognized Herennius Capito.

Lacertus offered to wake Manius, but Valerius shook his head. "Get Quintus." His voice was raw.

Quintus was alarmed when he saw Valerius's throat and heard the weakness in his voice and wanted to call the medic and take over the prisoner, but Valerius stopped him with a gesture.

After a drink of water when he could barely speak again, Valerius stripped Capito of his command and ordered Quintus to fetch Capito's officer, who was next in line.

Valerius studied Capito's face. All he could see above the gag was the burning hatred in his eyes.

Valerius drank again to clear his weakened voice. "Herennius Capito, either you leave under your centurion's command for Jamnia, or I will send the letter to the emperor I have already written, relieving you of all your duties, and ship you as a prisoner in chains to Rome for the emperor to judge. Caligula must decide what he would like to do with a Roman officer who tried to murder a governor appointed by Caesar." He coughed until another cup of water helped him finish.

When Quintus appeared with a centurion, Valerius appointed him to command the garrison at Jamnia and had him swear loyalty to Rome.

Then he turned to the seething Capito and said, "You will be locked up and under guard until your troops leave at sunrise." He gestured to the guards to haul him off.

When Manius learned what had happened, he stormed into Valerius's quarters and argued with him. "You are allowing him to leave?

"He's no longer in command. He has to follow his centurion's orders."

"You think that will stop him? You cannot turn him loose

to cause more havoc. Send him in chains to Caligula!"

"And whose side will Caligula take? The emperor will agree with the commander who is the most eager to carry out his orders."

"Then you are a fool to give him a choice. If he is smart, he will choose to go to Caligula. Execute him now while you have every right to do so. He tried to murder you! You have justice and the law on your side."

When Valerius refused to change his mind, he agreed that the sooner Capito left the better. "Order the cavalry and one hundred men to escort him and his troops back to Jamnia."

Manius warned, "Someday this decision will come back to haunt you."

Later that day, Valerius told Manius, "You were right. I should have had him executed. At least, he and his soldiers are out of here before they could do more harm. If the threat of my letter to Caligula doesn't hold him in check, Fabius tells me he has proof of the tax monies Capito has been skimming off for his own use."

Manius shook his head and advised, "That won't keep him from causing trouble. Letting him go free with mild threats is reckless. From your point of view, your threat of imperial retribution seems adequate. But you have humiliated him in front of his troops. A man like Capito will seek revenge."

Valerius sighed. "Even Quintus agrees with you." He felt exhausted.

Manius added, "But you were right about Lacertus."

Valerius lifted his shoulders. "Maybe. Maybe not."

✦

AN URGENT REQUEST

FROM THE MOMENT RACHEL GAZED UP AT SIMON'S face, she knew that something was badly amiss. She had been about to exclaim her joy at his unexpected visit. Instead, her hand went to her throat, and her first thought was that something had happened to Aurelia or their children. She whispered, "What's wrong?"

Simon clasped her in his arms and ruffled her hair in the way he used to when she was a child, and he was the protective older brother. His voice was hoarse, scarcely audible. "I'm so sorry, Rachel. Father—is dead."

"Father!"

Simon relived the last month of anguish in the telling: the urgent summons from their mother, the hasty trip to Cyrene, his vain attempts to ease pain, his father's last words.

Rachel lingered in her brother's embrace. "It was not so long ago that he was here. He seemed so vigorous and alive, always full of stories of his journeys. I'm so glad you were able to be at his side. You must have been a great comfort to him."

Simon pulled back and studied her face. "Hardly. You were far closer to him than I ever could be, and yet you seem more reconciled to his death than I."

"Perhaps that's the reason. I was never the target of his anger. He was gentle with me. I loved him and feel very sad. During his last visit, he promised to visit you in Alexandria."

"He did."

"And?"

"Aurelia invited him. He loved the children. We argued as usual."

"Oh, Simon! When he visited us, he talked about you all the time. He was so proud of you but too proud to tell you. He didn't even know that you were once physician to Tiberius. He was quite impressed with that."

"I take no glory in that. Especially now that Caligula is so much worse. We face grave dangers. We must be brave."

"You are worried about Valerius?"

"I am. But there is far more to be concerned about."

"It was good of you to come and bring this sad news in person."

"That's not the only reason why I've come."

After their evening meal, Simon asked to speak to them in the peristyle. Rachel was caught up in mourning the loss of their father and was hardly listening to what Simon was telling Sedek about the situation in Judea. When Simon stopped pacing and turned to Rachel, she realized that both Sedek and Simon were waiting for her reaction. She made him repeat what he had just said.

"You must go to Valerius and beg him to retreat with his legions before it is too late."

Rachel rose abruptly and faced Simon. "I will not do what you ask!" Her voice was shrill, her shoulders tense, her face flushed with anger.

Simon looked at Sedek for help, but he sat in his chair and did not look at her.

Simon placed his hands on her shoulders and pressed her down on her stool. Then, like a schoolmaster, he stood in front of her. "Rachel, we have run out of options. There are no choices left. You know that I've already begged Valerius to bring his legions back to Antioch. In vain." He pointed to the letter. "Vitellius sent a new message to Valerius, warning him to follow the emperor's orders immediately. You know the consequences of that order. Thousands, many thousands will die. He's also worried about the consequences for Vitellia, his daughter."

"I believe you."

"Well then. It's up to you now."

Rachel shook her head. She felt like screaming at him, screaming at both of them. Simon's passionate pleas made her feel she was about to suffocate, and she gulped for air. But worse was Sedek's stony silence. How dare they come to her with such a request?

Simon turned to Sedek. "You must help me persuade her." There was exasperation and panic in his voice.

Sedek did not answer.

Simon took her hand. "You must consider what is at stake. There are thousands of lives at stake. People like you and me. Children who will be killed, maimed, or orphaned, women who will be slaughtered or widowed, men—good men—who will die if you don't do this. As we speak, he is getting closer to Jerusalem. I got a message that he's already in Tiberias. Soon it will be too late."

"You are asking the impossible—"

Simon sighed and began pacing in the peristyle. Purple heliotropes glistened in the spray from the fountain, and shimmering waves of late summer heat rolled off the marble floors and engulfed them, stifling them. Rachel remained motionless, staring forlornly at the tiles at her feet.

Finally, Rachel raised her head and glared at Simon. "Why me?"

Simon stole a glance at Sedek and answered. "Because Valerius loves you, and he will do what you ask."

Rachel shook her head and turned to Sedek, aghast. He held her gaze. Then—almost imperceptibly—he nodded. She felt her face flush with mortification. Sedek's eyes seemed to penetrate her soul, and suddenly she realized what her anguish had already told them.

Sedek spoke, his voice solemn and low. "Rachel, I have known for a long time that you love him. It is a reality I learned to live with long ago."

Rachel bounded from her stool and fell at Sedek's feet and clasped his knees in the age-old gesture of the suppliant.

Simon's voice was cold. "My one goal is to save as many lives as possible. Personal feelings cannot get in the way."

Rachel crumpled against Sedek's knees.

Sedek said, "Rachel, this is not nearly as difficult as you make it out to be. You have been through far worse. You remind me of the first night I met you. You cried like this until all your tears ran dry. You recovered then, as you will recover now."

Rachel shook her head. "You cannot make me do this!"

Simon grabbed her by the shoulders and pulled her to her feet. "You must do a noble thing for a noble cause."

Rachel shook her head. His grip on her shoulders was painful, the fierce look in his eyes frightening.

Simon began to shake her in anger. Abruptly, he let go and addressed Sedek. "Tomorrow, I leave for Tiberias to see Valerius. She will accompany me!" He turned on his heel and stalked out of the peristyle.

Rachel regarded Sedek with pleading eyes and waited for him to speak. When he remained silent, she whispered, "When I was a slave in this household, I was treated with more dignity than this."

Sedek winced. "Rachel! You cannot mean that! You must forgive Simon. You know his temper, his determination. He does not understand how you can put your feelings for Valerius above the lives of thousands. He does not feel he is asking that much of you."

"And you? How do you feel?"

"I would gladly go in your stead if it would do any good."

"Then you think me wrong?"

Sedek sighed. "I am not your judge."

"That means you think I should go."

"I think you should go."

Rachel put her face in her hands and sobbed anew.

Sedek remained silent and did not try to comfort her.

"I cannot believe my husband and my brother would use me in this fashion. It is unworthy of you."

"Is it unworthy to attempt to save thousands?"

"You are asking me to throw myself at him, to abuse his feelings for me. You are asking Valerius to die."

"Remember the purpose of our request."

"As my husband, you should want to protect me, shelter me from this turmoil."

"My dear Rachel, these are terrifying times we live in. All of us need to make sacrifices for the greater good. If I thought you were walking into a dangerous situation, I would not let you go. But you know as well as I that Valerius would never harm you."

"Sacrifices! I don't see sacrifices being made here. You are asking me to persuade Valerius to make the supreme sacrifice of his life! Surely, any sacrifices we are supposedly making are nothing compared to that."

"I'm not so certain."

Rachel studied Sedek's face. "What do you mean?"

The sun was already sinking in the west, casting long fingers of shadow into the peristyle.

Sedek reached down to her tear-stained face and caressed a wayward curl, smoothing it behind her ear. "The fact that I must explain seems to make it worse. For too long we have avoided speaking the truth. Simon dared to say it this afternoon. You love Valerius. He loves you. How do you suppose I feel sending you off to him? Who is making sacrifices now?"

Rachel regarded him in troubled silence.

Sedek continued. "Do you think I did not see your blush of pleasure every time he came? Do you think I did not notice how your eyes lit up when he spoke, how he looked at you and seemed to forget what he was saying, how you watched for him when you knew he was coming? Do you think I did not notice how distraught you were when he left for Judea?"

Rachel lowered her eyes.

"Rachel, you have brought joy to me in my old age, and I am blessed. But do not make light of my sacrifice."

"Sedek, you are asking too much. You are my husband, and I love you."

"Do you?" He clasped her hand in his and held her gaze. "To send you away breaks my heart. But the Most High has given us courage according to our needs. He asks a great deal of me. He asks a great deal of you. You are in the position of Esther of old to be the instrument of salvation for our people. Remember what she said: '*For how can I look on while my people suffer what is in store for them? How can I bear to witness the extermination of my race?*' We cannot let personal feelings get in the way."

Rachel felt way too insignificant to be compared to Esther. She struggled for words. "It is not fair for me to be the one to ask Valerius."

"Why not?"

"Because he might grant my wish if I ask."

"That is precisely why you must go."

Sedek stood abruptly and looked sternly at her. "You must choose. I ask you to go. For my sake."

"But—"

"Your refusal to seek to save thousands will mean only one thing. It will mean that you love him so much that you cannot bear for him to come to harm. Your willingness to save our people is a sacred duty and will express your desire to please me. You must choose. It is either Valerius or me. If you choose me, you must go to him and ask him for the supreme sacrifice. He has known for a long time that it would come to this. The morning he left Antioch, he was the one who assured me he would avoid bloodshed at all costs. Now you must remind him of his promise."

He turned quickly to avoid looking into her tortured eyes and left the peristyle. She heard his footsteps hesitate at Simon's door, then continue along the corridor to his study.

✦

IN GALILEE

WHEN THEY CRESTED THE HILL OVERLOOKING THE Sea of Galilee, Rachel stared out at the rolling green meadows that cradled the city of Tiberias. On the south edge of town, the tents of Roman troops stretched as far as the eye could see. Her heart lurched, thinking of Valerius walking among them. Then her gaze swept eastward over the sea. From the heights, it looked like glass, peaceful, as though no turmoil could ever touch its face. The sky above was leaden blue. Late fall vegetation beneath the horses' feet gave off the strong scent of bruised grass, and she could smell the special pungency of olives ripening in the sunlight. Their aroma lingered even after she was in her room in a tiny inn on the edge of Tiberias. Simon admonished her to get some rest while he galloped off to find Valerius.

When Simon reached the outskirts of Tiberias, he could hear the keening dissonance of the crowd that squatted on the hillside. In front stood Valerius in full military dress, his back to the sea. The scarlet crest of his helmet rippled in the breeze like undulating wheat in a summer field. The wind snatched Valerius's words from his mouth and made Simon's loud cry of greeting disappear unheard into the hills.

For a moment Simon watched the drama in front of him. The Jews had lined up a row of petitioners who spoke earnestly one after the other. Halfway up the trampled vineyard, men, women, and children sat on their heels, shifting their weight from foot to foot above the cool ground. A small ring of Roman soldiers stood to Valerius's left, while a scriptor wrote down petitions on wax tablets. Simon edged through the crowd. He was just about to call out again when Valerius turned and saw him.

Valerius froze midsentence. His greeting to Simon was cordial, but his eyes seemed veiled and cold. He summoned Manius Cornelius to take over, had his horse brought to him, and threaded his way through the pressing crush of people who tried to block his path.

Valerius pulled away from an eager petitioner who had grabbed his cape and turned to Simon. "When did you arrive in Tiberias?"

"This afternoon."

"Where are you staying?"

"At what is called Cochas Inn." Simon thought of Rachel at the inn and studied Valerius's face. He looked worn and drawn.

"I have quarters with Aristobolus at his palace. Do you know him?"

"No."

"Agrippa's brother. As you may or may not know, Agrippa is back in Rome petitioning for your people. I must say that I have never seen so many petitions fly back and forth as I have in the last several months."

Simon nodded.

"And I assume you bring even more." Valerius sighed. "Have you just come from Antioch or from Alexandria?"

"Antioch."

"I see. My true petitioner is Sedek, I presume, and not Philo this time."

Simon frowned. "Not just Sedek."

They made their way along the narrow streets and then turned left up the hill to the palace. His headquarters of two rooms were in convenient proximity to the central palace but offered complete privacy and freedom to come and go as he wished without disturbing the household. Usually, he dined alone in his office, preferring solitude to company.

He called for wine. Then he unfastened his helmet, loosened his sword belt, and removed his greaves, military cuirass, and boots. A servant brought a basin and an ewer of warm, fragrant water that he poured over their hands and feet.

While the servant toweled them dry, Valerius said, "I am weary of petitions. For almost two years I have been on this grim mission for Caligula and have heard petition after petition. Will there be no end to it all?"

"As long as the very heart of the Jewish people is threatened, there will be petitions." Simon showed little sympathy for Valerius's predicament.

Valerius sighed and dismissed the servant. "Well, we don't need to discuss business right away. How is my sister? Your family?"

Simon's eyes lit up. "Aurelia is fine. Our children are a handful. Rufus and Alexander have grown so much you would hardly recognize them. And Antonia can walk already and is talking."

"You are not afraid to leave them in Alexandria during the turmoil there?"

"I am always concerned for their safety. But we are fortunate to live on Philo's estate, and though Caligula has not restored citizenship nor rights to the Jews of Alexandria since the massacre, the city has been reasonably calm since Flaccus's departure. I dare say it is safer to be in Alexandria than in Tiberias right now."

"Did you stay with Sedek and Rachel?"

"I did."

"How are they?"

"Doing well but as disturbed as everybody about what is going on here."

"Disturbed? Of course. It's easy to be disturbed when you are far away and are not in danger. Let me be completely frank with you. So far, I have succeeded in averting bloodshed and war. I've tried to think of every possible way to satisfy your people while I obey Caligula's orders, but there is simply no way out of this."

"I assume you know what Sedek says about that?"

Valerius shook his head with some indifference.

"He says there will always be a way. The Lord will provide one."

Valerius snorted. "Ha! If that were the case, the Lord should have appointed a different emperor. That would have spared everybody this agony. Even if we could arrange for some harm to come to the colossal statue being crafted in Sidon, I have heard that Caligula has become impatient and ordered a new and gilded statue to be readied in Rome. He plans to bring it to Jerusalem. In person. There is no stopping this obsession of his."

"Yet you have the power to stop it."

"How?"

"Caligula can accomplish nothing without the strength of his army to back him up. You simply refuse. You are, after all, the most powerful man in this region. You control the army. You take your legions back to Antioch. He will be left to fend for himself, and the crowds will lie down on the roads in front of him and his statue and will not let them pass."

Valerius plunked his wine goblet on the table. "Mutiny! Treason! Is that what you so glibly recommend? It all seems so simple to you, doesn't it? At every turn, I get yet another petition to save your precious temple." Valerius got up and kicked his helmet to one side. "I told you before, the only thing I can do is stall and delay. I've been doing that for two years now, and I've run out of options. Getting me out of the way will do no good. Caligula will appoint another military commander who could quite happily obey him promptly."

Simon remained silent.

Valerius fumed. "You sit there calmly asking me to save the temple. Is the temple, then, so much more important than my life?"

Simon said calmly, "Thousands of lives."

"All right, so it is a question of numbers, not of religion and principle?"

"Lives must be saved."

"And the temple?"

"The temple is the very symbol and heart of our people."

Valerius looked into Simon's eyes and said coldly, "The temple is a structure of stone, one stone put on top of another. A statue is a big chunk of metal or stone shaped to look like a man. Are they so sacred, worth dying for? I grant you that it is a beautiful temple, and I don't want to see it destroyed. As a Roman, I have never entered the courtyard, but I can admire it and wish to preserve it."

"You are a typical Roman."

"What does that mean?"

"You believe that beauty itself is holy. We believe that holiness is beautiful. The importance of the temple has nothing to do with a work of art. It could be ugly, grotesque even, and it would still be a holy site. It represents the soul of our people."

"I have no wish to see your temple, or your people, destroyed."

"Then retreat with your legions back to Antioch."

"Damn you, Simon! You might as well pick up this sword of mine and run it through me right now." Valerius slapped both palms against his forehead. His voice quavered. "I've done all that can be done. I held my officers at bay and kept my soldiers from harming your countrymen. I even wrote to Caligula in protest, risking my life. You have no right to ask me for more."

"For this we are grateful."

"Your gratitude is like a snake coiled around my neck that chokes me to death."

"The fate of thousands lies in your hands."

Valerius's voice rose in fury. "The fate of thousands lies in Caligula's hands. In the gods' hands. Not mine! Your preposterous notion that I am somehow responsible is outrageous. Your lack of sensitivity is exceeded only by your arrogance."

"I don't care how angry you get at me, provided you retreat."

"I have been attacked by assassins. My death would make matters worse. Manius would take over. If he fails to do the emperor's bidding, he will be replaced. Don't you see? The only tactic I have is to stall and delay. At some point, the strategy will crumble, and Caligula wins."

"Not if you retreat. Caligula needs the army."

"Simon, does Aurelia know what you are asking of me?"

"No."

"I cannot believe Aurelia would support you in this. You abuse our friendship, our family ties. You are callous, unfeeling, cruel. You will use any means to justify your cause. You would stoop to bribery and deceit to save a Jewish life. Does a Roman life not interest you? Your own brother-in-law?"

When Simon did not answer, Valerius said, "You have more concern for a thousand nameless Jews whom you don't even know!"

"I have saved countless Roman lives through my practice of medicine."

"What about Rachel? She is your sister! Does she support your mission? Does she?" Valerius's voice rose higher with each question.

"Yes."

"That cannot be true."

"But it is."

"I don't believe it. Rachel would never be so cruel."

Simon shook his head. "After all these years, you still love her."

Valerius looked away and did not answer.

Simon rose. "You do not need to answer. I can read the answer in your face. You should know, though, that she is in Tiberias and that I will bring her here tonight to talk to you. I hope she will succeed where I have failed."

Valerius went white. "You couldn't! She wouldn't. How dare you?" He looked at Simon in disbelief and horror.

"Tonight then." Simon was already at the door.

Valerius didn't answer. Rage and despair constricted his throat.

He was stunned. They were going to use their most powerful weapon to get him to bend to their will. How could they use Rachel in this way? How could she? He ran his hand across his face and tried to sweep the jumbled cobwebs from his brain. The wine had left a bitter taste in his mouth, and he felt like retching. He threw himself on his cot, feeling like a prisoner who was to be executed the next morning and was allowed to spend his last evening relishing his favorite meal. He could suddenly appreciate the full irony of that custom. At any other time, he would have been thrilled for Rachel to enter his chambers and throw herself in supplication at his feet. Now he recoiled in bitter denial and was tempted to flee for a long night in the Galilean hills and let her find his quarters abandoned, his room deserted, his heart empty.

He pressed his palms against his burning eyelids and groaned. Too many questions flew through his head that he could not answer. Had she asked to come? Did Sedek encourage her to come or try to restrain her? Was this Simon's doing? Was she forced to be here against her will? Was she as miserable as he? What would she say? How would she seek to persuade him?

Often, he had dreamt of some fortunate circumstance that would have thrown them together so they could discover each other's intimate thoughts. All he had from her were the messages her eyes could not hide. They had conveyed a great deal but had always left him feeling bereft and alone. Now she was coming to ask him to die for people she did not even know.

He went to the door and looked down the slopes at the rooftops of Tiberias. The lake beyond seemed to writhe with passion, touched by the sparks of the setting sun. He drank in the evening air and realized suddenly that the anticipation of seeing her again had sharpened his senses and made him feel alive again as nothing else could.

A WONDROUS GIFT

"ANTICIPATION OF DISASTER IS OFTEN WORSE THAN the disaster itself," Rachel said earnestly, holding fresh grapes in one hand and absently pulling them off the stems with the other. Her gaze rested on Valerius, whose smile of genuine pleasure calmed her somewhat. When Simon warned her that Valerius was in a sinister mood, she had made one last desperate attempt to get out of seeing him at all, but now she was vaguely relieved to see him face to face and see him smile.

He reached out and placed his hand over her fluttering fingers to still them in their obsession with grapes. She was both comforted and excited by his touch and wished she could hold on to this moment forever. It would be proper for her to retrieve her hand, but instead, her whole being seemed focused on their tenuous embrace of fingers. She hardly expected an answer to her statement and was startled when it came.

"You are right, Rachel. I often lie awake at night wondering about the future, and each possible scenario ends in disaster." His voice was barely above a whisper. "But you know I may be wrong to anticipate such doom. After all, not in my wildest dreams did I think that I would get to see you here—

alone." He laughed bitterly. "My dear, dear Rachel, how often I longed to tell you what is in my heart. An odd twist of fate has given me the opportunity—a cruel fate, but in some ways, it is more than I had hoped for. To get to see you! To have you here with me now. To touch your hand and feel that you are real." He lifted her trembling fingers to his lips and closed his eyes. He could feel, almost hear, his heart pounding and he opened his eyes to see that hers were closed, her dark lashes brushing her cheeks, her whole body leaning forward, concentrating on their mutual point of contact.

Valerius did not believe in the gods and the countless rites each cult seemed to invent for avid worshipers. But now he felt a sense of mystery and awe, as though he were participating in a new and magical ritual. He said hoarsely, "Rachel, what I feel for you transcends any emotion I have ever had."

She smiled and put her finger across his lips as though to keep them from expressing the mystery, but he caught her finger with his lips and caressed her hand. "Rachel, what I feel for you cannot even be summed up in the words 'I love you.' Whatever happens, I will hold onto this very moment with you. Now. Forever. Your brother spoke this afternoon of the beauty of holiness and the holiness of beauty. He was speaking of the temple. But I see that in you. You touch my heart with such beauty that I can only think of my feelings for you as holy, and I am not even a religious man. I love you, Rachel."

He took her wrist and encircled it with his fingers. Rachel smiled, and he knew that she understood. He wanted to go over the *what ifs* that he had dreamt about so often—*what if* she had not been abducted; *what if* he had been able to rescue her; *what if* Sedek had not married her—and he knew it was useless and stupid to dwell on the past and that it was useless and stupid to speculate about the future as well.

"I wish this moment could last forever." Valerius sighed and thought he heard her sigh as well.

She shook her head slowly, rose from her seat, and walked

away from the table. Turning her back to him, she said, "Valerius, you know why I am here. If—"

"No, I don't!" Valerius rose as well, and his interruption was more vehement than he intended.

"Of course, you know that I'm here to beg for the lives of my people. And—"

"Was this your idea?"

"—and I hope to be able to persuade you to return—"

"Who sent you?"

"—to return to Antioch with your legions. I—"

"Rachel!" Valerius caught her arms and forced her to look at him. "Rachel, I have a right to know the answers to my questions!" He held her close, and he could see the pulse throbbing at her neck. She twisted to break free, but he held her tighter and pulled her closer. He cupped her chin in one hand and forced her to look up into his face. "Was this your idea?"

Rachel shook her head.

"Did you want to come?"

Rachel shook her head.

"Was this Simon's idea?"

Rachel looked down and didn't move.

"Why? Why did you agree to come? You knew what you were asking of me. If you had any feelings for me at all, you would not have come. What were you supposed to do? How were you to persuade me?"

Rachel refused to look into his eyes.

"All right. If that's the game we are playing, let me paint the whole picture for you. Simon made you come. Somehow or other he was able to persuade Sedek to let you go. How, I don't know, because Sedek is no fool, and I've often caught his gaze on me, and I felt that he knew that I loved you and knows that I've loved you for a long time. On purpose, I would talk about childhood memories in Cyrene, knowing those would exclude him from our conversation, and I often saw his eyes observing us both with sadness. Why would he agree to your coming here? Well, the obvious idea behind leaving you alone in my quarters is to bribe me into giving up my life for your people." Valerius laughed a hollow, bitter laugh.

Rachel remained motionless, her eyes averted.

He clutched her shoulders tightly. "Why would you agree to this? Why?" Abruptly he let his hands fall to his side and he clenched and unclenched his fists in frustration. "Tell me, what were your orders from Simon tonight? *'Look your best! Make yourself beautiful for Valerius! He is very fond of you, so it won't be difficult to seduce him. You will need to make him want you so badly that he will do anything, anything at all, to possess you.'* Is that what he said?"

Rachel stared at the floor.

"Was that the arrangement? You were to come here and get me to give up my life for your people." He grabbed her shoulders again and shook her. "Rachel! You owe me an answer. In your plans, I am about to die. What was my consolation prize to be?"

Rachel looked up then so he could see the tortured expression in her eyes.

Valerius steeled himself against the rush of compassion he felt and stepped away from her. "Rachel, I deserve to know. You and Simon and perhaps Sedek set up a play in which I'm the principal actor. I have a right to know my role. You have decided that I am the tragic figure; that I am to die?"

Rachel did not move.

"Did Sedek want you to come?"

"Yes."

"Did you want to come?"

"No."

"Were you then forced to come?"

"Yes."

"Did you dread coming tonight?"

"Yes."

"And your mission is to get me to defy the emperor's orders

and retreat with my troops to Antioch?"

"Yes."

"And what do you offer in return?"

There was no answer. She stood trembling and pale, her eyes averted, tears running down her cheeks.

"Yourself?"

She nodded almost imperceptibly.

"For one night?"

She turned her face away.

"One night of pleasure for my life? No, you don't have to answer that. Do you know what that makes you? Do you realize what your brother and husband are doing to you?" Valerius's voice rose in anger, and Rachel began to shake. "No, you need not answer that question either. I will say it for both of us to hear. A harlot!" Valerius repeated the word louder, spitting it out in disgust.

The word hung in the air and echoed through the room. She squeezed her eyes shut, took two steps forward, swayed, and collapsed.

Valerius caught her in his arms and carried her to his bed and placed a warm sheepskin over her. He stroked her hair and caressed her cheeks, which were moist with tears. He was angry at the Jews, at Rome, at Caligula, at Simon, at Sedek, and above all at himself. What had happened? He had had no intention of degrading her in this fashion. For years he had dreamt of caressing her and making love to her, and now, when he had that very opportunity presented to him, he had lashed out at her and humiliated her.

She moaned, and he bent down and kissed her on the lips. They were cold and unresponsive, but he could not stop, and he tried to revive her with the warmth of his passion.

Her eyes opened and she sat up abruptly and pulled the sheepskin high to her neck in an instinctive gesture of self-defense.

"Forgive me, Rachel!" He reached for her limp hand and stroked her fingers.

"Please let me go home."

"I think you had better stay here. I want you to listen to me first. Please forgive me for being so brutal with you. Do you know what I feel for you? When I first became ambitious to be a military leader, it was because of you. I thought I could conquer the world to lay it at your feet. At the very least, I was going to be the person to rescue you from the clutches of Meidias. Even the most casual acquaintances noticed the difference in me after I learned about your horrible fate. Rachel, it is not an exaggeration to say that most of what I have done in my life I have done out of my love for you. In Gaul, I conquered fear and learned to lead my troops, trying to become worthy of you. I even gained my father's approval before he died. And do you know how that miraculous change came about? I owe it to you. When I heard that you had been found and were married to Sedek, I rejoiced that you were still alive, but I was stunned. My beautiful dream, my fantasy of courting you, lay shattered at my feet. For years I tried to forget you. I even married Vitellia, thinking that family life would soften my painful longing. But no matter how hard Vitellia tried, she could not satisfy my deep longing for you.

"When Caligula appointed me to be governor of Syria, I could not believe it. To be in the same city with you and know that you could see the same clouds and feel the same breezes was at first a thrilling thought. But it was also frightening. I knew I could not come to see you casually and not betray what I felt. Every day I didn't go to your villa cost me a supreme effort in discipline and willpower. Yet every time I did see you, you inspired me to—to become worthy of you, even if I could never call you mine. In all my dealings with your people, I try to be just and kind and understanding. Do you know how I accomplish this? I imagine you are somewhere in the crowd—a veiled face watching me—and I become wise and caring and just, and you become the touchstone by which all I do is measured. If I thought you wouldn't approve, I didn't do it."

He kneaded her cold fingers and grazed them with his lips. "What a joy it was to slip away from the headaches of the day and spend an evening in your peristyle, surrounded by your flowers. I knew that my feelings for you were written all over my face and that even Matthaios noticed his uncle's unusual affection for you. But you must realize that I could read your feelings in your eyes as well, and the fact that you were obviously pleased to be with me made the situation even worse. If I had been rebuffed or reprimanded, I would have stayed away. But Rachel, every day I saw you, your eyes gave me messages your mouth contradicted."

Rachel began to protest, but Valerius put his finger on her lips. "Even now! You try to object, but your eyes tell me a different story." He smiled when she clamped her eyelids shut. "Rachel! I don't tell you all this as an excuse for my harshness, but so you will understand. I am grateful to you because you made me the person I am today. I owe the best that is in me to you. And tonight, you saw a different side of me. Not the noble Valerius, but the Valerius who suddenly found himself in front of the person he most cherishes, and that person was demeaning herself because of me. Because of me!" A sob rose in his throat. He stopped to catch his breath.

"There is nothing I would rather do than take you in my arms right now and make love to you. Ironically, tonight even your husband permits it! Wants it! Don't you see, Rachel? It can't be this way. I cannot make you into something tarnished and used. If I make love to you, it must be because you want it as much as I do. It must be because you come to me of your own free will, not as booty in some tug-of-war or as a prize in a diplomatic deal to save your people."

He had never bared his soul to anyone with such candor. "Rachel?" He waited.

She did not move.

"I realize I made you suffer because I was suffering, and I had no right to do so. Rachel, please forgive me."

Her eyes remained closed. He could not gauge the effect of his words, for she lay perfectly still, while he waited patiently for a sign from her about the role he was to play. He would take his cue from her, and he knew he could wait as long as that would take. In the meantime, it was a pleasure, simple and innocent, to run his hands through her dark hair that curled so willingly around his fingers.

His face was so close to hers that he could feel her breath. Softly, tenderly, he brushed his fingers along the contours of her cheek.

Suddenly, with a jagged sob, she reached for him and buried her face against his chest. Then she clasped his head to her breast and ran her fingers through his close-cropped hair. "I've always wanted to do that!" she confessed.

Valerius laughed suddenly against her breast, and, feeling the thrilling boldness of her gesture, he pulled back slowly to read her expression. She opened her eyes. He was so close that he could see tiny flecks of bronze in their dark depths. He understood their wordless plea and their unstinting bestowal of love. Awed by the wondrous torment of her gift, he longed to bring her joy and caressed her gently.

They made love with great tenderness and devotion, joined together as lovers who had earned the solemn right of fulfillment.

NOT AN ORDINARY BREAKFAST

A RED GLOW IN THE EAST ANNOUNCED A NEW DAY, and Valerius rose quietly to dress. He looked down on the still-sleeping Rachel with awe. Dark curls framed her face, and her arm still lay slightly crooked where she had held him in her embrace. A hint of a smile quivered on her lips. He rebelled against waking her, but he knew their moments together were numbered. Gently, he touched her forehead and bent to brush her cheek with his lips.

Her eyes fluttered open. "Valerius!"

"Good morning!"

Rachel squinted at the square of dim light where Valerius had opened heavy drapes and shook her head to clear her thoughts. "I was just dreaming that you were my husband."

Valerius smiled. "And how did that feel?"

"Wonderful!" She laughed and then suddenly remembered. A dark cloud fell over her face. "What are we going to do?"

"I don't know. Simon will be here soon to return you to Antioch and to Sedek!"

Rachel frowned. "I cannot."

Valerius called a servant at the door to bring hot water and began to lather his face with soap in front of a small mirror. As he raised his knife to shave, he turned to Rachel and asked, "You cannot what?"

"Return to Antioch and to Sedek."

Valerius scraped one side of his face with even strokes, stopped, and turned to Rachel, his eyebrows raised in a question. "What do you mean?"

Rachel pulled the sheet around her tightly and murmured, "How could I return to Sedek and behave as though—this hadn't happened?"

Valerius stopped his blade in midair and frowned. "Sedek wanted you to come. Surely, he wants you back."

"How could I return to Sedek and be his wife as before?"

"He knew you would be upset. Still, he wanted you to come."

"He made me choose. He said that I would demonstrate how much I truly loved him by coming, that my reluctance to go proved how much I loved you, because I would want to save your life."

"And do you? Want to save my life, that is?"

"Of course, I do. Is there a way?"

"Not without bloodshed."

"You could retreat and see what happens."

"You underestimate the power of the emperor and the power of his anger."

"What could he do against you and your army?"

"The army is not mine. True, they must follow my orders, but I must follow his. Have you forgotten what happened to my father and what happened to Flaccus? There is no place in the world safe from the arm of Caesar."

"We could die together."

"What would that accomplish, and how would that save your people?"

"It would spare me the anguish of being separated from you again."

Alarmed, Valerius realized the experience that had given him a new will to live had taken hers away. He forced himself to smile. "The only way I can help your people is by staying alive and attempting to remain a voice of reason. Our emperor is mad. Consistent he is not."

Valerius noted with mounting dread that she was no longer listening. The faraway gaze of her eyes caused his heart to leap in sudden fear. "Rachel!"

She turned her eyes to his half-shaven face, but her thoughts were obviously elsewhere and obviously grim. Her gaze was now on the steel blade of his shaving knife.

Valerius ran smooth strokes along his other cheek, wiped his face, and stood. Then he put the knife, honing stone, and soap away, placed the water basin at the door, and retrieved a fresh basin of hot water. Finally, he picked up the small mirror framed in silver and held it so that Rachel could see herself.

"Rachel, you must banish such thoughts from your mind. Even if something happens to me, you must live for the sake of Matthaios. Promise me that!"

Rachel didn't answer but clung to him in despair. After a moment, he straightened and pulled her to her feet. "Rachel, you must get dressed. Here is a basin of water for you. Simon will be here soon. Listen carefully to what I have to say."

Numbly, she obeyed.

"We must compose ourselves and play the roles we have been assigned. You can tell Simon what you will, the truth if you like. But expect his anger both at you and at me. And I'm sure you are aware that your brother's anger can be formidable. Remember, it's in your best interest to note that nothing has happened here that concerns either Simon or Sedek. Or the fate of the Jews, for that matter. Far better for you to tell him nothing and for us to sit here at this table in calm conversation when he comes. We must continue to play our roles in his presumptuous little drama. Except we will rewrite the script. He must be made to realize that his scheme didn't work. You gave yourself freely. You did not exact a price. And I gave myself freely with the same devotion for your welfare as I have for mine. You agree?"

Rachel nodded.

"I made no promises to you except the one that I will always love you. You must hold on to that fact. You do believe me?" He encircled her wrists and pulled her to him.

"I believe you."

He smiled. "Good. Then you must be ready to back me up in the role I'm about to play." Valerius swallowed hard, squelching the urge to take her in his arms again. "I hear some commotion outside. That could be Simon." He went to the door, looked out, and returned. "Simon is already returning to exact his price." Valerius pressed his lips against hers and pulled back. "I may not get to do that soon again, perhaps never again. Remember, you take your cue from me, but you must promise to remember how much I love you, and you must take care of yourself. For my sake, if for no other. No one knows what the future holds. We both deserve to fight to have one."

Rachel nodded.

Valerius insisted. "Promise!"

"I promise."

He steered her to the other side of the table and called his servant to bring breakfast.

When Simon pounded on the door, he was greeted by a tranquil domestic scene. Rachel sat opposite Valerius, eating bread, while Valerius cut an apple and dipped it in Galilean honey. A servant hovered with a pitcher of fresh goat's milk. Simon was prepared for most anything except this.

"Welcome, Simon! You are just in time for breakfast."

Simon grunted, glared at his sister, and took the proffered stool. Then he reached for the fresh bread, broke off a huge chunk, and began to chew.

Valerius seized the opportunity to speak first. "I will refrain from calling you by the name you truly deserve and hope that peace can return to the Toubias family. No sister should tolerate a brother who has betrayed her most fundamental dignity. I could never under any circumstances see myself stooping so low as to treat Aurelia the way you have treated Rachel. I do not know whether she will find it in her heart to forgive you. I do know that I cannot and will not."

Simon held up his hand to interrupt, but Valerius forged on. "Despicable, utterly despicable! Rachel and I have had a long talk—after all, you insisted on her staying here—and it is quite clear that she was trapped by you and Sedek into coming into a most intolerable situation. You, who were responsible for her being sold into slavery once before, have tried to sell her once again. You have used her, abused her, and treated her no better than a slave!"

Simon rose in anger. "How dare you—"

Valerius rose as well. "No, how dare you treat another human being this way? Your sister! Does she mean so little to you?"

"But—"

"But no! You are in my quarters here, and I will have my say. No matter what noble motivations you profess to have, you have stooped to the very lowest level in betraying your sister in this way. 'To save Jewish lives,' you will say. How noble! So, this treatment of your sister should be an example for the blustering, dissolute Roman to follow? Ha! Spare me your lecture on the higher good, your so-called superior ethic you claim as your sole possession! What have *you* sacrificed to save your people? How many personal friends and family members have you betrayed to your noble cause?" Valerius's voice broke, and he paused. One glance at Rachel's alarmed expression made him lower his voice and continue with cold, deliberate scorn.

"For years I have kept my army and my officers in line to protect the people, whether in Gaul, Asia, Parthia, Syria, or here in Palestine. I will continue to do so as long as I can. But I do not accept bribes. You can have your sister back. Take her back to Sedek! You have accomplished nothing but her humiliation."

Simon looked from the accusing set of Valerius's face to Rachel, whose features had crumpled in silent sobs of dismay. He gulped for air. "You are the one humiliating her now. Look at her! She was calmly eating breakfast before you spoke."

"She was calmly eating breakfast before you came. Stick to the point. I am not the source of her humiliation."

"Sedek and I—we thought—you—" Simon groped for the right words. He cleared his throat and began again. "The point is, there are thousands out there who will lose their lives. Do you want that much blood on your conscience?"

Valerius shook his head. "You seem to forget that I am not the one responsible for all those lives you would like to bring down upon my head. I did not issue orders to desecrate your temple. For two years I have been the instrument of peace and have held off bloodshed and death at great personal cost. I am the instrument of reason. I cannot alter the fact that when reason confronts insanity, insanity usually wins."

"The reasonable thing to do would be to retreat with your troops to Antioch and let my people go home."

Valerius snorted. "What would be Caligula's reaction within the hour of his hearing of a retreat to Antioch?"

"I don't know."

Valerius's eyes narrowed, and he shook his head. "Don't add deceit to your list of character traits. You know full well what would happen. By return courier, I would meet the fate of Gemellus, Flaccus, Macro, Gaeticulus, Ptolemaios, Lepidus, Titius, and—"

Simon did not answer.

Valerius detected the quick flutter of eyelashes as Rachel blinked to hold back tears. He sighed jerkily, suppressing his own desire to sob, and turned to Simon. "Believe me, I would like nothing more than to return to Antioch to be with my wife and my son whom I have not yet seen, but I cannot."

As he said those last words, he stole a quick glance at Rachel, knowing the effect this news could have on her. She had regained her composure somewhat and showed no signs of alarm.

It was Simon who seemed suddenly stricken by the news. "You did not tell me you had a son!"

"You did not ask. You were presumptuous to throw your sister at me as though you were baiting a lion with raw meat." Valerius chose the crudeness of his image on purpose and quickly shot a meaningful glance at Rachel. He was relieved to note that she seemed calm. He sensed that this was perhaps the only means he had to save her from herself and her own conscience.

Simon looked from Rachel to Valerius then back to Rachel. "But I thought—"

It was Rachel who now rose and confronted Simon. "You thought wrong. I suggest you take me back to Cochas Inn and we set off for Antioch. I tried to stop this useless mission and spare all of us the trouble and the humiliation, but you wouldn't listen. Please, take me home now."

With great poise and dignity, she turned and offered her hand to Valerius. "Thank you, Valerius, for your hospitality. We do hope the emperor will come to his senses and back down so that you can return to Antioch soon." She turned to Simon and smiled ingenuously. "Simon owes you an apology for this imposition. I apologize on his behalf."

Slowly, she pulled her hand away from Valerius's warm clasp. She had played her role deftly and convincingly, and he knew that she understood that his denial of passion was in truth his most ardent expression of love.

✦

THE CHALLENGE OF DIPLOMACY

"ARISTOBULUS REQUESTS THE HONOR OF YOUR presence at his table tonight." The servant bowed and awaited orders. Valerius nodded distractedly, washed the blood from his hands and arms, and shook the dust from his cuirass and boots. He wished he could shake the image of distraught petitioners as easily from his mind.

As he put his large boots aside, he kicked them in disgust, thinking of Caligula's nickname the Roman soldiers in Germany had given him when he was but a child. Caligula was no longer a child, and the games he used to play with toy soldiers were now in deadly earnest. Deadly was the apt word.

The crowds on the hillside had become more desperate and strident. Rumors were rampant. One young agitator proclaimed that the emperor had set sail from Puteoli with a new statue to erect in the temple at Jerusalem. Brigands robbed the local merchants of their wares and ambushed fishermen as they landed on shore with their catch. To maintain order, Valerius brought more than twenty young men to trial and imprisoned them in the old garrison in Sepphoris. Feeding the crowds and his legions placed an inordinate burden on the population of Galilee, and he had no doubt that Aristobulus was going to add his name to the persistent petitioners.

Once again Valerius struggled with the realities of his plight: his troops were restless and cold; his officers flaccid and short-tempered. The discontent Herennius Capito had sown among the officers had affected morale, and Valerius realized Manius had been right, and he should have sent Capito off in chains to be dealt with by Caligula. Despite illness, dwindling food supplies, and the lack of firewood, the crowds would not go home and abandon their single-minded obsession. That morning, a woman from Bethsaida had given birth in a dank and trampled vineyard.

Valerius ran toward her screams and stood in paralyzed horror when he saw she was giving birth in the mud. "Enough!" he yelled. "How can you bring an innocent child into the world like this?"

The woman heaved again and groaned, and the baby emerged into the hands of a young woman who was splattered with blood and mud. Immediately, the mother turned her dirty face to Valerius and raised an accusing finger. "I will not move from here until you promise to protect our temple. Without the temple, my baby has no birthright."

Valerius stared at her and then at the baby boy, whose bluish tint caused him to yell anxiously at the inexperienced midwife. "Clear out the throat. You must get him to breathe on his own!"

The young woman gaped down at the inert, slippery ball of flesh she held at arm's length. Valerius jumped forward and grabbed the baby, turned him over in his palm, and thumped him on the back. To his great relief, the baby whimpered as a clog of mucus emerged from his mouth, then squinched up his eyes and yelled lustily.

Valerius laid the baby back on the mother's belly and warned gruffly, "Cut the cord!" He looked from one petrified face to the other. "There isn't a midwife among you, is there?"

They shook their heads.

Valerius looked at his aides in disbelief. "I can't believe this! Surely, there is a midwife in Tiberias." He looked from one of his men to the other in consternation. "Marcus, Drusus, Sestius?"

None moved in compliance with his unspoken request.

"Well? Isn't anyone going to get a midwife for this poor woman before she dies?"

Marcus turned on his heel and stomped away, fuming at the indignity of a Roman soldier charged with fetching a midwife for a Jewish tramp. It was Drusus who stepped forward, pulled a thread from his tunic, tied it around the navel stub, and grasped his broadsword to cut the cord with a deft stroke. He wiped his blade on a grape leaf, sheathed it, and mumbled about the litter he had at home for whom he had done the same.

Valerius turned to Drusus and placed some coins in his hand. "See that this poor woman gets proper care in town. Warm food. A midwife and a doctor."

Abruptly, he turned away, feeling a burning nausea in his throat.

Caught up in his dreary thoughts, he had forgotten Aristobulus's servant, who was waiting patiently, watching him kick his boots. "Tell your master I'll be honored to be his guest tonight."

The servant bowed and left. Valerius sat on his stool and stared blankly at the wall. For days after Rachel had been there, he could smell the faint scent of jasmine on his pillow. When it disappeared in the first change of linens, he felt bereft. He'd found a hairpin made of bone that had held her hair, and he clasped it now in his hand like a sacred relic.

"By Jupiter and all the gods, I cannot stay here for the winter!" he said aloud and shook his head. The feel of the baby in his palm haunted him. He kept seeing the black shock of matted hair, the flailing arms, the small uvula in the cavern of his throat, his warm and trembling wetness. A gagging moan rose in his throat. He thought of the birth of his own son, the son who was now more than a year old whom he had never seen, and an unbearable longing seized his heart. He balled his fists and held them to his burning eyes, swollen with unshed tears.

Could one man have the power to cause so much misery? Was there no way to defy Caligula and escape unscathed? Damn his arrogance! Vitellius was right. There were two paths to follow. One was the path of obsequious flattery that Vitellius had chosen. The other was open defiance. The former was disgusting but safer; the latter was bold but dangerous. Caligula had absolute power on his side. Valerius had the winter on his side and the slow pace of ship traffic bearing messages. Could he even stay in Galilee and maintain law and order under current conditions?

A bath and massage restored his weary bones enough for him to make a tolerable guest at Aristobulus's table. At the end of the dinner, his host warned, "A group of young rebels meet secretly in Galilee and plot against Rome. They carry small knives and hide in the caves high up on the precipices near Arbel. They have sworn to strike down Roman soldiers, commanders, and Jewish leaders friendly to Rome. Their prime target is you."

"I am not afraid of them."

"We are."

Valerius smiled. "You want me to flush them out and subdue them?"

"No, we want you to take your troops back to Antioch. Winter is coming. Our people are dying out there."

"They need to go home."

"If you stay, they stay. True concern for their plight would require you to retreat so they can go home. You fear the distant danger of Caligula. The current danger to our people is sickness, starvation, and a slow death. Entire villages and entire cities have joined the holy mission of saving the temple. They have forsaken their harvests. Fruit is spoiling on the trees; grain is bursting on the stalks; grapes are rotting on the vines; animals have been left untended in the fields. They will not back down, and their deaths will be on your conscience."

Valerius rose and walked up and down in the grand dining hall of Aristobulus's palace. Aristobulus and his friend Helcias remained silent, watching him. There was some truth to what Aristobolus said. Every day people were dying of cold and hunger and illness.

Finally, Valerius stopped pacing. "I will write to the emperor once more informing him of my decision to return to Antioch for the winter months for strategic reasons. I'll make it very clear that he must give up on his grand scheme of being worshiped as a god in Jerusalem."

Aristobulus shot a relieved smile at Helcias, who was frowning. Helcias spoke cautiously. "Caligula will see your retreat as treason."

"I know. Perhaps I am simply tired of playing the waiting game. The emperor can ask me to lay down my life only once. I—" Raw, shattering fear strangled his voice, for he suddenly heard the echo of his father's words in his ears.

Aristobulus rose from his couch like a camel by first rocking forward and then backward and then forward again to heave his heavy bulk from the cushions. "Farewell, Publius Petronius. You are a true friend of the Jewish people, and we call the Lord's blessings upon you. May peace be with you."

Valerius looked down upon Agrippa's younger brother and said, "May the Lord cause his countenance to shine upon you and give you peace." The Jewish blessing came as a surprise, and Helcias and Aristobulus watched him leave in stunned admiration.

✦

Early the next morning, Valerius asked Manius if he was willing to supervise the supply wagons and foot soldiers while

Quintus led the cavalry. He showed him the map. "Lead the troops via the Roman camp at Arbel. Watch out for Jewish insurgents in that area. Romans are their target. The cavalry will join us here near the crossing of the Jordan. Proceed along the Jordan on the road toward Damascus until Hazor, where we will fork to the west."

"But—that is not the way to—" Manius looked alarmed.

"Jerusalem? No, it's not. We are returning to Antioch. I made the decision on my own without you, so you can truthfully tell Caligula—if he asks—that you had nothing to do with it."

Manius shook his head and cleared his throat. "This takes me by surprise. Are you sure? We have managed to come this far together, and now?"

"No blame can fall on you for following my orders. You can refuse to retreat if you wish. Either way, you are not responsible for my decision."

There was a long silence between them. Valerius averted his eyes from the gut-wrenching anguish that was written all over Manius's face.

Finally, Manius said simply, "I honor your decision." Before leaving to meet with his officers to convey the new orders for the troops, Manius gave Valerius a solemn salute. "*Ave et vale!*"

Valerius returned the salute and guessed that Manius was probably wondering the same thing he was. Would they see each other again before Caligula ordered him to fall on his sword?

Valerius summoned Sestius to his office and told him they were returning to Antioch.

"You have received a command from the emperor to—?" Sestius looked baffled.

"To retreat? I have not."

"But Sir, with all due respect, Sir, Caligula could—"

"I take full responsibility for the decision."

"But—"

Valerius became impatient. "Enough! Pack my things! Get my horse ready! Call Septimus Scuros right away. I have this message for him to carry to Rome."

Sestius swallowed hard, saluted, managed a weak "Yes, Sir," and left.

Valerius stared after him, tapping the letter he had written to Caligula against his open palm. He still had time to countermand his orders and stop the retreat. He could still tear up the letter in his hand and cancel his session with the stubborn Jews on the hillside. Sestius's reaction caused him to shudder. If Sestius could immediately see the consequences of his act, then rationalizations about political and military logistics would not convince anyone, least of all the emperor.

Valerius unrolled the letter to reread the last sentences: "*Surely, you deserve a likeness of purest gold. It should be erected in Alexandria, Ephesus, or in Athens where the populations of the world can fall to their knees in admiration of your glory. But not in Jerusalem. Your statue in Jerusalem would not be seen. It would be hidden away in a secret, inaccessible room in the temple, and the blood of an entire people would be on your hands.*" He could not be more direct than that.

Septimus Scuros stood patiently before him. Valerius rolled the letter up, dribbled hot wax over it, and pressed down his seal. He stared at the image of Neptune his ring had left behind. The prow of the ship was indistinct, and it looked like Neptune was shoving it away. Even the gods would not be able to grant him protection now.

He handed the letter to Scuros.

After placing the roll in a protective tube, Septimus Scuros fastened it with a chain to his belt, saluted, and ran for his horse. He would be in Tyre before nightfall and catch the next ship along the coast.

Valerius closed his eyes. The die was cast.

He called for his basin and washed and shaved. Even if he had not slept at all, he knew he must look fresh and strong for his speeches to the soldiers and to the crowd. There would be no time in the days ahead to heat water for such luxuries.

✦

Out on the hillside, a light rain was falling, and muddy rivulets tumbled into the lake. Valerius surveyed the crowd, feeling the tension in the air. The petitioners knew the wagons were being loaded and that the tents were flat on the ground, being folded for transport. He asked Aristobulus and Helcias to join him on the platform. The figure of the rotund Aristobulus beside the lanky Helcias provided an amusing contrast. Both were sheltered from the rain by a fringed canopy held by four slaves.

Valerius stepped forward. "The time for waiting is over." A hostile uproar greeted his words, and Valerius wiped the rain from his face and waited. Then he held up both hands to calm the crowd. "I beg for silence. The longer it takes for me to be heard, the longer you will be away from your homes. I have given orders for the Roman troops in Tiberias, Arbel, and Ptolemais to return to Antioch."

Before he could speak again, a wild roar of triumph erupted, and several men intoned a chanting prayer, holding their arms up in gratitude to Yahweh.

Valerius joined Aristobulus and Helcias under the canopy and waited. It was a moving moment to hear more than ten thousand voices raised in thanksgiving. Aristobulus leaned toward Valerius and shouted in his ear. "Today you have become a hero!"

Valerius felt drained, distraught, and despondent. He shook his head.

Aristobulus was singing the psalm with tears in his eyes, and his deep and pleasant voice rose above the crowd. At the end, he turned to Valerius and embraced him. Another roar of triumph arose, and Aristobulus stepped forward to speak. "You have been part of a great host to protect our temple. You have done your duty, and the Most High has protected us."

The crowd roared again. The rain had stopped, and shafts of sunlight fell across the land and warmed their wet faces. Waving his draped arms like banners in the wind, Aristobulus tried to silence them. "My fellow countrymen, my brother Agrippa has interceded on your behalf with the emperor. But you must know that Publius Petronius had orders to kill all who would thwart the emperor's wishes to be worshiped in our temple. For two years he has held back his army and preserved your lives. Hail to Publius Petronius, governor of Syria!"

Aristobulus bowed to Valerius, and a great swell of cheers greeted him. Valerius ignored the anxiety in his aides' eyes. The roars of the crowd reminded him of the ebb and flow of the waves of the Great Sea beating against the rocks at Ptolemais. Finally, they lifted their eager faces, ready now for the speech they had interrupted an hour earlier.

"My friends, I have this day sent a message to our august emperor, telling him of your resolve. I cannot have regard for my own safety when you are willing to die for your laws that have come down to you from your forefathers. I cannot suffer your temple to fall into contempt. I beg you. Go home! Finish the harvest! This very day we are returning to Antioch. As long as I am your governor, you can live in peace. I will protect your temple." He paused and let his words sink in and resumed after the crowd began to murmur among themselves. Valerius knew his message might be only a reprieve. "Today you are free to go back to your homes, but I must warn you that the emperor can easily find a general to replace me. And then—" He could not finish his sentence.

There was a moment of stunned silence as the magnitude of the risk he was taking sank in. Several women dropped to their knees and started to pray, but they were soon drowned out by cries of gratitude and renewed shouts of joy.

Valerius turned to Aristobulus and Helcias and embraced them in farewell and was about to descend the steps of the platform when Drusus came running, anxiety written all over his face.

Drusus saluted and gasped for breath.

"Out with it, Drusus! What's the matter?"

"The baby!" Drusus looked like he was on the verge of tears, and Valerius laughed, finding the spectacle of his robust country soldier undone over a baby incongruously funny. "What about the baby?"

"Well, remember you asked me to find a place in town for the mother and baby and see that they were cared for. I went to check on them this morning, and I found the baby sucking at his mother's breast and—" Drusus could hardly continue.

Valerius was getting impatient. "And what, Drusus? Out with it!"

"Well, Sir, the mother was dead! She died during the night."

Valerius shivered slightly and realized Drusus's superstitious soul would be greatly affected by this incident. "And what did you do with the baby?"

"Nothing, Sir. But then I thought I must come and tell you since you saved his life yesterday and—"

"And the baby is still breathing?"

"Still trying to nurse."

"Drusus, you were right to tell me." Valerius glanced at the astonished faces of Aristobulus and Helcias and explained what had happened. "I ask a favor, Aristobulus. You could certainly take in a poor orphan?"

Aristobulus frowned. "Who is the mother, and more importantly, who is the father?"

Drusus shrugged. "No one knows. Even the women around her didn't know."

Aristobulus snorted and turned to Valerius. "You are asking me to take in a brat whelped on the hillside by some harlot you don't even know? Never! I check and double-check the pedigrees on all the slaves in my household and would never allow such a bastard among them."

Valerius was struck dumb and looked at Drusus, who was fidgeting in his cuirass as though he'd been bitten by fleas. Suddenly, he saw the little creature, hardly bigger than his hand, trying desperately to suck life from a dead breast. On impulse, he ordered Drusus to fetch the baby.

Drusus started to run back to Tiberias. Valerius called him back. "Hire a wet nurse and find space for them in the wagons. Then join me at Arbel where we will spend the night." Valerius handed him some coins, and Drusus scrambled down the hill. Valerius made a mental note to recommend Drusus for a raise in wages. He was obviously a good sort.

He turned then and looked Aristobulus straight in the eye. "I regret the innocent baby is not worthy to be among your household slaves. If the baby survives the journey back to Antioch, I will adopt him as a member of the Petronian *gens*."

For a moment he relished the deep shock that registered on Aristobulus's face and turned to have his horse brought to him. It had been a reckless thing to say, he thought. But then, this was not the only reckless thing he had done that day.

He mounted his steed and galloped off to inspect the progress of his troops as they readied for departure.

When Drusus had not arrived in Arbel by nightfall, Valerius deferred the departure of his troops. A nameless Jewish baby held up the Roman army for an entire day.

When the wagon arrived, Drusus was seated on a keg, the baby's face crushed against his cuirass, while the baby hungrily swallowed sustenance from a makeshift breast Drusus had formed with a sow's bladder. Guffaws from the surrounding soldiers were hardly a welcome expression of gratitude for what Drusus had endured, and he reddened defiantly, then held the baby out toward Valerius and said, "Here's your baby, Sir!"

Valerius couldn't help himself. He bent over his horse's mane, his face contorted with laughter, his entire frame shaking in spasms that were worse because he was trying so hard to suppress them.

Drusus's puzzled look turned to anger as he stood there with the baby squealing and goat's milk running down his front into his boots. The soldiers laughed until they started choking.

Valerius pulled himself together long enough to praise Drusus for his inventiveness and charged him to take care of the baby until their arrival in Antioch.

Drusus shook his head in disbelief as Valerius let his laughter burst forth in full force until tears streamed down his cheeks. Gasping, he had to dismount to regain his composure.

"I'm no wet nurse, Sir!" Drusus was still holding the baby at arm's length.

"There's no doubt about that, Drusus! But you have done wonders with him. Where did you learn to manage a baby?"

"I have seven of my own, Sir. When the wife is sick after birthing, there is more than one way to pluck a goose."

From the back came a soldier's voice, loud and taunting. "But you can't press milk from a toad!"

Valerius sensed immediately that things had gone too far, and he looked at the furious Drusus. "For your service beyond the call of duty, I award you special remuneration and appoint you as personal aide. On our return to Antioch, I'll grant you a special six-month dispensation from the army so you can visit your family."

"Thank you, Sir!" Drusus grinned and stepped from the wagon, holding the baby aloft like a banner of victory.

During the slow march back to Antioch, Drusus managed to keep the baby alive. The soldiers took turns holding him in the wagon and gathering fresh milk from the local farms. As they crossed the range of Mount Lebanon, Drusus found a goat and managed to place its teat in the baby's mouth. For the first time, the baby sucked properly and got his fill. Valerius thought of Romulus and Remus, founders of Rome, who were nursed by the legendary wolf, and decided the baby's survival was an augury of good things to come.

Just as the walls of the city of Antioch came into view, Valerius stopped to say goodbye to the troops who headed east to the barracks. As they filed past, many shouted their wishes to him for good fortune and health. Valerius could read their concern for him in their eyes. When the rear guard had finally gone on by, Lacertus came even with his horse, with Rhaetia seated in front of him.

Lacertus gave him a Roman salute.

Valerius responded in kind and asked, "What are your plans?"

"Home to Cilicia."

"I wish you a fair journey and much happiness."

Lacertus nodded and thanked him for buying him a horse.

Valerius said, "It was the least I could do after you saved my life."

Valerius watched them head due north until they were out of sight and turned to look down on the city of Antioch glistening in the sunlight. His pulse quickened. He steadied his horse before his descent into the valley of the Orontes, for Rex, too, felt the pull of the familiar and wanted to gallop ahead to the home stables. To be home after more than two years and to breathe the crisp mountain air that blew down the valley were experiences he had feared never to have again.

The thought of his son caused his heart to swell with tenderness, and he knew that Vitellia would be eager to show off their new offspring. He had ordered Drusus to deliver his new fledgling to the palace at sundown. He chuckled, remembering his awkward role as a wet nurse. Then his smile faded as he worried about Rachel.

✦

Word of the returning legions reached Antioch days before their arrival, and Vitellia found herself pacing back and forth, waiting for the gates to open to her husband and his aides. She refused to be troubled by the persistent rumors in the city that he was retreating in defeat and that he was a doomed man.

She planned the reunion so carefully that she even memorized what she would say. Nothing could go wrong. She wouldn't let it. It would be a blissful resumption of their married life, and she could proudly thrust little Lucius into his arms. Valerius would be moved by that, and she thanked all the gods and goddesses of the household that she had borne him a son and that he was healthy.

She chose a white linen robe with a wide green sash that fell diagonally across her body and long dangling earrings in her ears with a gold necklace. She decided to forego her favorite attar of roses and dabbed oil of jasmine on her neck, ears, and breasts and outlined her eyes in black kohl until they resembled the elongated features of old Egyptian wall paintings.

At the sound of the gate, she ran to the top of the stairs to greet him, her heart pounding in her throat. One look at his haggard face and two-week-old beard caused her to gasp, but she ran to him and clasped her hands around his neck.

"Oh, Valerius! I thought you would never come back to me."

Valerius smiled wearily. "Well, I did. But I'm dirty, unshaven, tired, and feel old." He unclasped her arms from around his neck. "Your beautiful dress will smell like horses, sweat, and garlic. I can think of nothing I would rather have than a good hot bath, a massage, and a cooked dinner with real plates."

Hurt to the quick, Vitellia thought wryly of Clytemnestra, who welcomed her husband home after ten years on the battlefield and didn't even get a kiss before her husband demanded his bath. Vitellia understood fully why Clytemnestra had murdered Agamemnon in his bath.

"Don't you want to see your son?" She could not keep the whine out of her voice, but she managed to smile.

"Of course, I do. I thought maybe he was sleeping. Where is he?" His face was suddenly alive, and he looked at her eagerly.

She stiffened and led the way to the nursery. Little Lucius lay asleep on his back. Already more than a year old, he was big and strong compared to the poor newborn on the hillside.

"Beautiful," Valerius whispered.

Vitellia nodded. That line had been part of her imagined scenario, but it had not been addressed to her son.

"Do you want me to wake him?"

Valerius shook his head and tiptoed away from the crib. "Let me get cleaned up first, and then I have a surprise for you, too."

"Then hurry, Valerius. I can't wait to hear about it."

After his bath, Valerius sat at the table with her and jostled little Lucius on his knee. When he had finished eating and was allowing Lucius to demolish fistfuls of barley cakes, she reminded him of his surprise.

Valerius called a servant to fetch Drusus.

Drusus appeared with the baby in his arms.

"Vitellia, this is Drusus, my personal aide. He's carrying the newest member of our family. I have adopted the boy in his arms. On purpose, he has not yet been named, because I thought you"—he turned to Vitellia—"you would like to name him."

Vitellia glared at the baby, who had begun to scream, and all color drained from her cheeks. The heavy kohl around her eyes made her look fierce and forbidding. "This is the surprise?"

Valerius nodded. Lucius started screaming as well, either because the barley cakes were all gone or because he was not to be outdone by the intruder.

Vitellia snatched Lucius from her husband's knee and scowled. "How dare you bring your illegitimate offspring into my house!"

Valerius was stunned. He looked from the frowning

Drusus to his screaming wife, who had drawn herself up to her full height and was screeching above the two babies. "How dare you do such a despicable thing! Get this baby out of my house. Immediately! After all I've been through, you do this to me! Don't you understand what I've endured?"

"Let me explain!" Valerius tried to be heard above the screaming. With consternation, he watched his wife run from the room with Lucius clutched to her breast. Then he turned to Drusus, who looked at him with compassion in his eyes.

"I can take care of it one more day until you decide what to do."

"Do that for me. I'm sorry for the misunderstanding."

Drusus nodded. "I know you don't need no advice from the likes of me, Sir, but a hen is not going to take care of another's chick and watch the rooster crow about it."

Valerius smiled in spite of himself. "Drusus, your wisdom far exceeds mine. I've made a big mistake. I'll let you know my—our decision tomorrow."

Drusus hurried from the room, and Valerius went to find Vitellia. So far, he had managed to keep peace between a hundred thousand Jews and two Roman legions and a mad emperor, yet the most crucial challenge to his diplomatic skills lay ahead in his own bedroom.

He found her in the nursery, cooing endearments to Lucius. She didn't look up as he entered the room, but her back stiffened visibly, and he detected a slight tremor in her halting lullaby.

He touched her shoulder gently. "I'm sorry, Vitellia. I didn't mean to upset you. I never realized what you would think, and I was—"

She placed her finger over her lips.

"Then let's go to our room where I can try to explain. Please."

She rose and preceded him through the corridor to their room.

"Vitellia, it's so good to be home. I don't want to fight with you. I would like to explain. The child—"

"The child must go."

"May I explain first?"

When he had finished his account, Vitellia spoke through clenched teeth. "The baby must go!"

"Don't you see, Vitellia? The baby seemed like an omen that gave me new life. It made me have new resolve. The next day the mother died. I naturally felt I should—"

Vitellia looked Valerius full in the face. "How dare you drag that thing in here like some stray puppy? Do you even understand what I've been through in the last two years? And why would you get so attached to it if it isn't yours? You have a son!"

"I'm very happy to have such a beautiful son. Lucius is another reason why I am here. I wanted to see my son before I—" His voice caught, and he didn't continue. Suddenly, the argument seemed stupid and inane. "Vitellia, I want no quarrel with you. I'll do whatever you say."

"Get rid of that baby. I don't want to see it ever again."

"All right." Valerius began to undress.

Vitellia pulled the pins from her braids with sudden fury. Two hairpins popped onto the floor, and Valerius watched her dark tresses tumble down her back and felt an unmanly sob mount in his throat. He picked up the pins and realized they were exactly like Rachel's and yet felt so different in the palm of his hand.

"Would you like for me to brush your hair?"

Vitellia glanced up in surprise. She shrugged. "If you want."

He closed his eyes and brushed with long, even strokes. Suddenly she sniffed like a schoolgirl. Valerius hesitated, then pulled her head around to see dark streaks of kohl staining her cheeks like the faces of clowns at festivals. He hugged her gently to his chest. "Oh, Vitellia, I looked forward to my homecoming so much, to seeing you again, to seeing my son—our son—for the first time. He is magnificent. I wanted nothing more than to be at home and find peace. Please, let there be peace between us."

Vitellia nodded but said nothing.

"Vitellia, forgive me. It never even occurred to me that you might think he was mine. He's an orphan."

"A thousand orphans die every day."

"But I don't see them. I don't feel responsible. They are nameless."

"As this one is."

"You're right. We'll never mention it again. In the meantime, should not a husband who has been gone for more than two years be welcomed into his wife's arms and bed?" He pulled her to her feet and kissed her hard on the mouth. The scent of jasmine filled his nostrils and caused a raw ache to sear his throat as he lifted her and gently placed her on their marriage bed.

The fates had allowed his most fervent wish to be fulfilled. He had gotten to see his son. He had come home. So far, he had avoided war. He had maintained peace without a massacre. Though his life hung by a thread, this would have to be enough. It was more than the last years of hardship had led him to expect.

✦

A HERO'S WELCOME

SEDEK THREW HIS ARMS WIDE. "WELCOME, VALERIUS! Our hero! May the Most High be glorified!" He clasped Valerius in his embrace and led him into the house.

Rachel rose stiffly as they entered the atrium, where burning braziers threw dancing lights on the walls. Valerius guessed that the flush on her cheeks was not just the effect of the glowing embers.

"Rachel!"

"Welcome, Valerius! We are delighted to see you back in Antioch."

Sedek beamed and chided, "Well, aren't you going to embrace your brother-in-law? He deserves a hero's welcome."

Rachel stood transfixed, her hand clutching her throat, but Valerius stepped forward and pulled her hard against his chest, then daringly planted a smacking kiss on her cheek, close to her mouth, and squeezed her hand.

Sedek called for wine and ceremoniously proposed a toast. "To Valerius! Your deeds will be recorded in the history books for posterity." His eyes glistened. "In fact, before you leave, I have a surprise for you."

Valerius turned a questioning gaze on Rachel, but she said, "It will be a surprise for me as well."

Valerius nodded. "Well, it won't be the first surprise you prepared for me. It was quite a surprise to receive Rachel's visit in Tiberias." Valerius looked Sedek full in the face, and Sedek cleared his throat, not knowing what to say.

It was Rachel who had the presence of mind to change the subject. "How are Vitellia and your son?"

Valerius hadn't heard. He was still staring at Sedek. Valerius had the sudden urge to declare his love for Rachel right then and there, so there would be no more half-truths between them. He took a deep breath and glanced at Rachel, but she was speaking again.

She repeated her question.

"My son is amazing." Valerius smiled proudly. "Lucius is vigorous, alert, demanding. He's already ordering everybody around in our household."

Rachel laughed, a light, airy sound that bubbled forth and thrilled him. He glimpsed the tip of her tongue between white teeth and followed the ripples of her laughter along her throat to her trembling breasts and realized that making small talk could become as torturous as dealing with obstinate Jews.

Sedek proposed to arrange a huge banquet to celebrate.

Valerius shook his head. "This is not the time for celebration. We are still very much in danger."

"You mean the other cities outside Jerusalem?"

"My last letter back to Caligula will stir up a hornet's nest. I defied him openly. I recklessly refused to follow direct orders from the emperor. For only thinking that men were condemned and died under Tiberius. My father was merely a friend to someone they suspected of supporting the opposition, and you know what happened to him. And all who know both emperors will quickly affirm that of the two, Caligula is the cruelest. When he gets my letter, heads will roll, most notably mine."

Rachel said, "Surely, you have not come through the last years of agony only to lose—" Her voice broke.

"For the present, we have winter winds to thank for the slow pace of messages back and forth. My latest letter will elicit a response. I have no doubt I will be accused of treason."

Sedek asked, "You think he will ask you to fall on your sword?"

Rachel gasped.

Valerius merely nodded.

Rachel protested, "You defied the emperor once. Surely you can again?"

Valerius shook his head. "If I defied such an order, my whole family would be endangered, and all my possessions would be confiscated by the empire. Not only would I lose my life in the end, but I would also endanger my mother and Vitellia and her family. I would deny my son the possibility of a future. Who knows, his wrath might even extend to Aurelia, to you as my brother-in-law, and your family. I could not have that on my conscience. I—" He stopped when he saw tears well in Rachel's eyes.

Sedek said, "Surely—"

Valerius interrupted. "I'm sorry to dampen your zest for celebration. We have reversed our roles. I used to be the optimist, believing there would always be a way for me to outsmart a madman, and you were the warning voice."

Valerius noted with alarm that Rachel's cheeks were now wet with tears. He bent toward her. "I'm sorry, Rachel. I did not mean to be so blunt."

Sedek refused to be daunted. "The Most High has brought you through unscathed this far. You must have faith. Surely you cannot object to celebrating the current peace, such as it is."

"Such as it is."

Sedek nodded eagerly. "We will make it a celebration for both families. In the meantime, if there's anything I can do, let me know."

Valerius looked at Sedek's earnest face. "There is one favor I would ask. You will want to think about this before you give me an answer. On the day I decided to defy the emperor, a baby was born on the hillside outside Tiberias. In some mysterious way I have yet to understand, the baby had a lot to do with my decision to retreat."

Having learned the hard way that he must tell the full story, Valerius chose his words carefully and described his adventures with the Jewish baby even down to the detail of Drusus's role as wet nurse. They erupted in laughter at his description but sobered quickly when he recounted the scene in his household, accepting the blame for being insensitive to Vitellia's feelings.

Before he could phrase his request, Rachel interrupted. "Yes, Valerius, I—" she stole a hurried glance at Sedek— "we will take in this poor baby and rear him as our own!" She slid to the floor in front of Sedek and clasped his knees in eager supplication. "This baby helped bring about peace. This baby is a gift from the Most High. Please, Sedek! He deserves a mother and a father. Matthaios needs a little brother, and—"

Sedek interrupted. "Of course, Rachel, we can do this. But calm yourself."

Rachel turned to Valerius and clasped both his hands in hers. "Valerius, when can you bring him? I'll find a wet nurse right away. What do you want his name to be?"

Valerius squeezed her hands. "You must name him."

Sedek rose. "I need to fetch my surprise." He smiled eagerly and hurried from the room, leaving Valerius and Rachel lost in each other's gaze.

Valerius stole a quick kiss on her lips, and she backed away. "Please, Valerius, I cannot bear it."

Valerius whispered, "You have invaded my very soul and leave me no peace. Even your perfume invades my senses, and all I want is to take you in my arms, to hold you, to make love to you like in Galilee, to—"

"Hush! You must control yourself." Rachel turned her back to him, picked up a poker, and busily stirred the embers in the brazier. The sudden glow across her face showed her firm determination. "It's enough for me that you are alive. That's all I ask." She looked back at him. "I will love the baby as though it were our child."

At that moment, her face glowed in anticipation of the baby, and he clasped her shoulders and pulled her back into his embrace.

She took a step forward and away. "You are playing with fire."

Valerius laughed hollowly. "You're the one with the poker in your hand."

She looked at the hot poker as though she had been unaware of its presence and quickly walked to the other brazier and stoked the fire. At that moment, Sedek returned with a scroll under his arm.

"Here it is, Valerius! I have written it all down. Except for a few details that you must help me with, I think it is all here." He looked at Valerius's face and realized that Valerius had no idea what he was talking about. "Forgive me! I have not made myself clear. This is the account of the conflict between Caligula and the Jews. I told of your role in this whole affair. There is no question that you are the hero in this drama."

Valerius was moved. "All this?" He looked at the thick scroll.

Sedek nodded. "There are some gaps only you can fill. Please read it and note corrections. It's not urgent unless something happens to—"

Valerius understood. "I'm overwhelmed. You think the story is worth telling?"

"Absolutely! Philo agrees as well. He, too, is writing about it as part of his essay on God's providence, and I have promised him my account."

Valerius was stunned. "I'll be delighted to read it." He

bowed toward Sedek and then toward Rachel. "When do you want me to bring the baby?"

"As soon as possible." Rachel smiled eagerly. "I'll be impatient until he comes." She looked straight into Valerius's light blue eyes and added, "I already love him."

✦

THE WAITING GAME

THE FEAST OF THE SATURNALIA CAME AND WENT, and there was no news from Rome. Valerius supervised the completion of the harbor in Seleucia Pieria, adjudicated the backlog of legal cases, wrote letters to city magistrates along the coast to be on the lookout for the outlaw Hallas, worried about Servius in Parthia, and waited. Valerius thought that nothing could be more intolerable than the endless petitions and uncertainty in Ptolemais and Tiberias. Yet waiting in Antioch proved far more nerve-racking because the very aura of normality mocked him. He knew that he had flung the ultimate dare into Caligula's face, and it was just a matter of time before all would come crashing down upon him. It was like that eerie moment of suspense Vitellius told him about during the earthquake when the earth shook and trembled underfoot, and the columns on the temple of Apollo swayed back and forth, and, for a suspense-filled moment, everything hung motionless in the air. Then amidst a rumble befitting the death cry of Pluto, the temple had toppled in a cloud of dust. The superstitious had interpreted the event against Rome and shook their heads and clucked their tongues. The finger-point-ing and repercussions in the aftermath of that earthquake were nothing compared to what could happen in the wake of Caligula's wrath.

Since the news from Parthia was troubling, he won-dered what Caligula's response would be to so much unrest on the eastern border. Would he pull back from his obsession with being deified by the Jews to deal with Parthia? Valerius doubted he would be released from his torment by a new mil-itary assignment.

In the meantime, Sedek held his promised banquet in Valerius's honor at which Sedek spoke of God's deliverance. At that same banquet, Sedek and Rachel celebrated the arrival of their new son, and, because they saw him as a symbol of God's grace, they named him Yohanan.

Vitellia and Rachel hardly exchanged three words with each other, and had Valerius been an impartial observer, he would have been amused by Vitellia's haughty disdain of both Rachel and the little waif born in the mud on a hill in Galilee.

In a cold and condescending voice, Vitellia said, "So good of you to take in the poor urchin. But dear, don't you think it risky? No telling what he'll be when he grows up. No one knows his background. From what Drusus tells me, the mother didn't have a clue who the father was." She sniffed and sipped her wine.

Valerius saw the pain in Rachel's dark eyes and silently congratulated her when she did not answer.

Instead, Rachel clutched the baby to her breast and rose from the table. "I must put Yohanan to bed," she murmured. "Please excuse us." She bowed to Vitellia, and her eyes just barely skimmed over Valerius.

Rachel seemed so totally wrapped up in her new son that Valerius felt vaguely resentful. He knew it was irrational to feel jealous of a baby, but her maternal preoccupation with her new fledgling obsessed her to the exclusion of all else.

Days flowed into weeks, and weeks became months. In March, early signs of spring touched the surrounding mountains with fresh green, and hope was harder to hold at bay. Valerius knew full well that the coming of spring meant the arrival of messages that would determine his destiny.

Early one morning near the Ides of March, Valerius awoke to a commotion outside the palace. Hurriedly, he descended the steps where servants were already trying to keep an unruly crowd from entering the courtyard. Valerius's first thought was that there was a local rebellion against Rome, so he paused to arm himself and donned his military cuirass. When he emerged at the top of the stairs, he noticed a messenger below whom the gate sentry had let in and recognized Septimus Scuros.

"Ah, my friend! You're back from Rome, having traveled much. Welcome! I hope you bring good news."

Scuros saluted. "Caligula is dead."

Valerius lifted his eyebrows in surprise. "What?"

"Caligula is dead. I came as fast as I could."

"How?"

"Murdered. The praetorian guard. Tribunes mainly. A conspiracy that was widespread. Caligula was at the festival—the *Ludi Palatini*—when the tribunes Chaerea and Sabinus lured him out into a passageway and stabbed him to death. The praetorians joined in."

"When did all this happen? Tell me all you know!" Valerius grabbed him by the shoulders.

"Some weeks ago. When I heard, I rushed to the arena to see for myself. I got there just in time to see his German bodyguard carry him out. At least ten stab wounds, perhaps more. Completely covered with blood. A ghastly sight. His eyes were open and glazed like his statues. Real eerie to look at. I'll never forget it. I heard his wife and daughter were murdered too, but I didn't see them. I ran back to the barracks to wait for orders. Confusion everywhere. That's when I decided I should get a message to you. I galloped all the way to Ostia and caught a Cypriot freighter about to sail. Told the ship's captain. He was eager to be the first to bear the news. A storm blew us off course near Crete. We limped into Myra. From there I came straight to Antioch."

Septimus was quite out of breath from his long speech and pointed to the crowds at the gate.

Valerius called for a water flask and watched Septimus drink.

Septimus wiped his mouth and grinned. "Good news, eh?"

Valerius smiled and let go of a long sigh. He had not realized that he had been holding his breath. "Excellent news. I'm surprised the praetorians had the courage. Any word on his successor?"

Septimus frowned. "Rumors. One that the senate wanted to re-establish the republic. Another that the praetorian guard found Claudius hiding in a closet and asked him to be emperor. I left to bring you the news before I could hear more."

Valerius clasped his arm in gratitude. "Septimus, you've served me well. Let us hope that Rome does not fall into anarchy." He placed his helmet on his head and went to address the crowds at the gate.

By nightfall, every man, woman, and child in Antioch knew the emperor was dead. Dancing and rejoicing took over the streets. Taverns opened early and tapped their new ale for the first time.

That evening, Valerius dictated letters to all the garrison commanders in Judea, cautioning them to maintain law and order and to respect the religious freedom of the Jews. One of his warnings went to the new commander at Jamnia where Herennius Capito used to be procurator. Then he wrote to the high priest in Jerusalem and to Aristobulus, assuring them of Rome's desire for peace during the transition period. When those letters were copied, he wrote to Marullus, the Roman procurator in Caesarea, to alert him to the guarantees of Roman justice and peace that he had promised the

Jews. Finally, he dictated a letter to Servius to warn him that a new emperor would be giving instructions about the war with Parthia and that he should keep order at the border and refrain from engaging in battle.

Then he picked up his pen and wrote the next letters himself. He knew that his mother would have heard of Caligula's death long before he had.

He hesitated over the last letter. He was still furious with Simon and chafed at being conciliatory. But then he thought of his sister and invited the whole family to Antioch to celebrate.

When the letters had been sent, he picked up copies of the official documents and threaded his way through the crowds to see Sedek and Rachel.

Rachel greeted him with open arms, her heart in her throat. He cradled her head against his chest and reluctantly let go as Sedek entered the room and embraced him as well.

"My dear Valerius, so shall the wicked perish from the earth! Let us rejoice!"

Valerius laughed. "You are right, this is a day for celebration! It's not just freedom for the Jews, but freedom for all men everywhere. Perhaps now we can fulfill the dream of Augustus for the *pax romana* and we can all live in peace."

Sedek still held him in a close embrace. Rachel stood behind Sedek, her face flushed with joy, relief, and love. Valerius winked at her and laughed again. The agony of the last years was swept away in one stroke, and he felt lighthearted, boyish, even reckless. He escaped Sedek's arms to gather Rachel once more to his chest and kissed her full on the lips. "My God, Rachel, I never knew the immensity of my burden until now, and it is suddenly lifted from my shoulders, and I can breathe again."

He turned to Sedek. "I brought you copies of letters I sent today. I also brought back the fascinating account you wrote. Now you can write the conclusion."

Sedek took the documents with the eagerness of a child

receiving a present. "Do you have suggestions? Corrections?"

"Admirable. It's very well done, but you must add one thing."

"What is that?"

"You are generous with your praise of me, and I am most touched by it. But the true hero of this story, you don't even mention."

Sedek looked puzzled.

Valerius turned toward Rachel and bowed to her. "She is the true heroine. It was always because of her that I tried to save your people. Yet, she is never mentioned in your account." He enveloped her in his arms once more.

Sedek groped for words. His eyes darted between Rachel and Valerius. "I—I don't understand—"

Rachel shot Valerius a warning glance and retreated from his embrace, but Valerius persisted. "Ah, but you must, my dear Sedek. From the beginning, Rachel symbolized all that is beautiful and good and noble among your people, and she became my ideal. Whenever my patience ran thin, I would summon up her image in front of me to give me strength to continue. Even when all seemed utterly hopeless, it was my solemn promise to her that gave me courage. You must know, Sedek of Antioch, since you are a dealer in fine jewels, that the most precious jewel in your household is Rachel!"

Sedek saw that Rachel's face showed both alarm and pleasure and said, his voice barely audible, "You love her." It was a statement of fact, not a question.

"More than my own life and I always will."

Rachel gasped and fled to Sedek's side.

Valerius continued. "Let no clouds mar the beauty of this day. Let no false rivalry sully what we both feel for her. She is your wife, and I honor her! We are both honorable men and respect one another. But I loved her long before you ever knew her and cannot remain silent today on this day of deliverance and accept all the accolades of your people while hiding the truth. The truth must be known, at least between us. Sedek, I owe you respect and sincerity. You deserve to know that Rachel has been the guiding principle in my life and continues to be. I have no apologies to make for that. Your account is fine as far as it goes, but it omits the most important person in this drama: Rachel!"

Rachel's eyes were moist with emotion.

Sedek chided, "I thought you were motivated by your sense of justice and that God gave you wisdom."

Valerius smiled, feeling suddenly that he could conquer the world. "Justice and wisdom are cold words without passion. It is the passion for justice and the passion for wisdom that make the difference. For you, it is your faith. For me, it is Rachel."

Sedek shook a finger in Valerius's face. "Rachel is more priceless than any jewel on earth, but not more so than the love of God."

Valerius said, "I know little of such things. I studied your religion and found your teachings to be wise but harsh. A god who demands too many sacrifices is hard to accept and follow."

"Rachel's brother carried the cross of one who showed us that God is a God of love."

"You are, then, part of this new religion?"

"We are followers of the Christos, the anointed one, the one who showed us the way to God. Some time ago, people here in Antioch called us Christians in contempt, but we adopted the term as both accurate and glorious, and we've used it ever since."

"And what will you have Matthaios be?"

"When he is old enough, he will choose for himself."

"You truly believe your common religion can bring people together who have hated and fought each other for generations?"

Rachel seemed unshakable in her conviction. "It already has."

Valerius turned to Sedek. "You are both dreamers. It's preposterous to think that your new religion can bring unity. It is already tearing families apart."

"All things are possible if we stay focused on the one who showed us the way. His message is a simple one of love and peace. In fact, not far from the very hillside on which you struggled to maintain peace in Tiberias, he said, 'Blessed are the peacemakers, for they shall be called children of God.' Today we know that God has answered our prayers and you were an instrument of that peace, whether you believe it or not."

Valerius regarded Sedek with surprise. "You prayed for Caligula's death?"

"We prayed for the deliverance of our people, and you have been an agent of God in bringing about peace." Sedek's eyes glistened with a faraway look. "God moves in mysterious ways."

There was a long silence. Valerius was startled by the ping of the water clock and roused himself from his chair. "It's late. It has been a long, eventful day. The self-proclaimed god of Rome is dead, and you believe the god of Jerusalem has won."

Sedek corrected. "The God of the whole world."

Valerius bowed. Rachel returned his gaze with solemn intensity.

On his way home, Valerius allowed Rex to saunter as he looked up at the wide expanse of the heavens and the blinking stars. A sudden terror of the unknown seized him, and he longed for Sedek's faith. Then his thoughts turned to Caligula and the celebrations taking place all over the empire. When Tiberius died, the same cries of jubilation rose from a million throats, and Caligula became emperor. Could Caligula's successor be even worse? Valerius shivered and spurred his horse to a trot. He was too tired even to conceive of a greater evil than Caligula.

✦

A LETTER FROM ROME

WHEN AURELIA AND SIMON ARRIVED IN ANTIOCH for the family reunion and celebration, Vitellia welcomed them warmly and showed them to a lavishly renovated guest room with a suite of rooms for their children. Aurelia had steeled herself for a cool reception from her brother's wife and was surprised at how graciously she showed her concern for the welfare of the children. She even offered to show Aurelia the new gown she was going to wear for the celebration. Made of emerald-green silk with gold and jeweled trim, it must have cost a fortune.

Aurelia said, "I have never seen anything so fine. You will look like an empress."

"Hush, Aurelia. They might accuse you of treason just for saying that."

Aurelia wondered if Vitellia was making light of the ordeal that Valerius had just lived through, but Vitellia was already setting a tray of cosmetic jars and bottles in front of a huge mirror. "Vitellia, you have more pots than Simon has for his medicines."

Vitellia smiled mischievously. "You should learn the art

of cosmetics. Here, I'll show you how to look like a bride for Simon tonight."

Aurelia laughed. "After three children, I hardly feel like a bride!" Still, she let Vitellia perform her magic. After a perfumed bath, three maids slathered oils on her body and scraped her skin with silver strigils. When Vitellia dressed her, she bound her stola's girdle high under her breasts, giving her profile the shape of the Egyptian maidens in hieroglyphs.

"Look in the mirror! See how young that makes you look?" When Aurelia frowned at her reflection, Vitellia said, "These things are important. Valerius always needs a little encouragement." She clucked her tongue as she studied Aurelia's pensive expression and said, "What about Simon? Does he come late to your bed and sleep before his head hits the pillow?"

Aurelia lowered her eyes and realized with a catch in her throat that she was afraid to give honest answers because she was uncertain about what they would be. The horrible years of Caligula's reign had taken their toll, and Simon seemed distant and obsessed; obsessed in the same way he had been when Meidias was the object of his single-minded pursuit, except now it was an enemy with no name and no face. Once she had accused him of being a *goel* for all Jews everywhere, and he had agreed, saying, "As a Roman, you cannot begin to understand."

Vitellia regarded her knowingly. "Do you want to talk about it?"

"There's not much to say. Since the horrifying massacre in Alexandria, Simon has been away more often than at home." Aurelia caught herself. "I'm sorry, Vitellia. I forgot that Valerius was gone for over two years. That must have been dreadful."

Vitellia sighed. "That's why tonight is so important. We celebrate the new emperor—Claudius! But I'm celebrating years of worry dropping off Valerius's shoulders. Now he will be free to be an enthusiastic husband and father, and he must forget about politics. Simon must do the same." She gave Aurelia a quick kiss and began to pile her hair in curls on top of her head and fasten them with jeweled combs.

"There, look at yourself and marvel. You could rival Cleopatra herself!"

Aurelia regarded her image in stunned silence. The maids danced around her in gleeful admiration, and Vitellia bent forward and whispered in her ear. "I swear by Venus and Cupid, tonight you will need no aphrodisiacs. Simon will melt in your arms, and he will promise you anything in the whole world."

In her heart, Aurelia knew Simon would be indifferent to such things. She felt a sob rise in her throat and turned away.

Vitellia was quite pleased with her handiwork and confided in Aurelia that Valerius had spared no expense for the banquet. "It is going to be so very fine, as grand as any banquet hosted by the emperor."

The elite of Antioch was invited: merchants, magistrates, priests, centurions, tribunes, and knights all assembled in the grand hall of the old palace built by the Seleucids.

In each corner stood a bronze tripod with a huge crater of wine ready to be tipped to pour libations for the diners. Slaves dressed in saffron tunics brought in platter after platter of delectable dishes: stewed fish in pepper sauce, mallows in garum, boiled squash mixed with cumin and dried mint, and peas in barley broth. Sausages from Epirus, Apician cheesecakes, black beets, pungent leeks, and endives dipped in cream, truffles spiced with juice of colewort, and cuttlefish croquettes.

Valerius had never presided over such a sumptuous banquet and nervously walked from guest to guest to ascertain they were well and properly cared for. Lithe Syrian dancers moved to the music of pipers, and in between courses young flower girls strewed rose petals over the diners. At the head of the table stood a large, empty chair for the absent guest of honor: Emperor Claudius. Long proclamations of praise and thanksgiving were being signed by his guests to be shipped off to Rome.

While finger bowls and fresh towels were being distributed in preparation for the next course, Valerius rose to speak. "It is an honor to be one of the first provinces to acclaim our new Caesar!" Valerius acknowledged the cheers and held his goblet aloft.

At that moment, the ostiarius slid into the room and whispered something to Valerius. Rachel sensed something amiss and watched them confer for a moment and leave the hall. Simon sat between Rachel and Aurelia and seemed disengaged from the cheering hubbub around him.

Vitellia nodded for the next unit of slaves to bring in the Parthian kid with onion pies, the capons and hens stuffed with chestnuts, the wild boar in wine sauce, and the roast veal smothered in lovage and basil. When Valerius returned with an unkempt stranger in tow, the fruit and desserts were already making their rounds, and Valerius had missed the main course.

As the dancers served iced sherbets prepared with fresh snow from Mount Silpius, Valerius sounded the gong for silence. "My distinguished guests." His voice quavered slightly, and most of the diners looked up from their plates in surprise. "It is not often that we get to hear a voice from the grave, but I heard one tonight. This poor fellow here at my side, who is trembling with fatigue, has just arrived with a message from Rome. Statilius Domitius, please tell these people of your journey."

Statilius was pushed to the middle of the room where everyone could see his torn mantle and his threadbare tunic. A thick growth of beard almost hid his emaciated features.

Vitellia frowned at the intrusion, but Rachel held her hand to her throat as she examined Valerius's face. He met her gaze and did not smile.

Statilius cleared his throat. "Well, it's like this. The emperor's high officer, he give me this letter. See. 'Urgent,' he say. For the governor of Syria. Two days out to sea, we get kicked by Neptune. The ship crack to pieces. I couldn't see nothing. Water all over. I holds onto this beam and makes it to Melita. In Melita we was stuck. Four weeks. Waves high like the columns here. Finally, this freighter goes for Crete. And Neptune done us in again. We was blown clear across the sea. When I sees land again, I says to myself, 'Statilius, you ain't getting on no more ships. Twice I cheat Neptune. Not three times!' So, I walks to Ephesus, and I rents this donkey. For weeks I rides here and gets this letter to the governor. No one going to say Statilius Domitius don't do his duty."

The guests burst into applause. Then there were shouts to bring him food and drink. Statilius seemed revived by his sudden fame and turned to Valerius for permission to eat.

"Before you eat your well-earned dinner, Statilius Domitius, please tell me when you left Rome."

"The Ides of Janus, Sir."

"And your message?"

He threw his shoulders back proudly. "You have that, Sir. I delivers it like I says, straight into your hands."

While the guests cheered Statilius anew, Valerius unrolled a tattered papyrus that had been saved from seawater by a tin casing. He looked up solemnly while an expectant hush fell over the room. "You realize that this was sent in the middle of January and has just arrived now. It is addressed to P. Petronius, governor of Syria from Gaius Caesar, emperor."

Valerius paused, and a murmur arose in the hall. Valerius held up his hand. "Indeed, this is a letter from Caligula. No doubt one of his last. He accuses me of treason. To save the honor of Rome and to prove by example that an emperor's orders cannot be disobeyed, I am commanded to fall upon my sword."

Rachel gasped. Then a loud rumble swept across the room, and some raised fists in rebellion.

Statilius stood, legs apart, his mouth agape. Then he caught himself and protested, "Now, Sir, I didn't know, Sir. Sorry, Sir."

Valerius calmed him. "The messenger need not take responsibility for the message. Statilius, we are gathered here to celebrate the new emperor, Claudius."

"Claudius, Sir?"

"Caligula was assassinated less than ten days after you left, and Claudius, his uncle, was proclaimed emperor by the Roman senate."

Statilius blinked, trying to take it all in, and shook his head.

Valerius continued. "My friends, we are here tonight to celebrate a new emperor! What I hold in my hand is the last message I will ever receive from Caligula. By chance or by the will of the gods, this message was delayed by two violent storms. My pledge to Syria and to Rome and to all of you gathered here tonight is to maintain peace. Let us live together in peace and prosper! Long live Claudius!"

The men scrambled to their feet and lifted their goblets to Valerius and echoed his toast to the emperor. Several took the floor to speak. Manius made a bold speech that started with praise for Claudius and ended with the words: "If the position of emperor were to be chosen on the basis of merit, you, Valerius Publius Petronius, would be our new emperor by now!"

Valerius laughed. "Careful, Manius, I have just been accused of treason by the former emperor; let me not give cause to be accused of the same crime by Claudius. Long live Claudius! May he rule in peace!"

Sedek rose and bowed to the assembled dignitaries. "I welcome the new emperor and hope he intends peace. But the ones who deserve our accolades most this night are our most gracious hosts, Publius Petronius and the Lady Vitellia. It is the governor of Syria who maintained peace at great personal cost, and we owe him a lasting debt of gratitude."

Thunderous applause filled the hall.

Sedek continued. "Publius Petronius, governor of Syria, you have risked your life to save our people, and the Most High has saved you from the fate Caligula designed for you. The wicked perish, and the righteous prevail. No one needs further proof of God's providence than this. May the Lord bless you! May his name be praised!"

Manius held up his goblet and poured a drop out on the floor. "We must thank the Roman gods as well! Above all, Neptune, who delayed the message with his powerful storms. It's good that you wear his emblem on your finger. I stand in awe of your good fortune, Sir." He grinned from ear to ear. "My friend and commander, this reminds me of all those plays where the god comes down in a machine at the last moment and snatches the hero from the jaws of death!"

Valerius studied Manius's smiling face and remembered the many times he himself had compared his predicament to an actor's role with an unfamiliar script. "My dear Manius, the play is finished. And I owe it all to you and to our loyal Roman troops who stood by me. It is a truth most pleasing that you, among all my soldiers, set such a splendid example."

Vitellia rose to be at her husband's side and gave him a juicy kiss on the cheek that was greeted with blustering guffaws. She laced her arm through his and swayed in tipsy rhythm to the pipers' song. The cheers continued until their throats were hoarse. The craters were tipped until they were empty. The dancers twirled until they collapsed.

But Simon sat through the entire banquet without cheering, his eyes fixed on some distant horizon. When Valerius glanced his way, Simon lifted his goblet halfway in salute, but did not add speeches and toasts to the evening's celebrations. He had not even remarked on Aurelia's dazzling appearance.

✦

Long after the guests had left and the large palace had settled down to sleep, Aurelia basked in the afterglow of the evening. Simon extinguished the lamp and crawled into bed with a deep sigh.

Aurelia rubbed his back. "Wasn't Valerius wonderful tonight?"

"Hmm?"

"Can you imagine what it must feel like—getting a letter like that from a man already dead? Valerius is a real hero, isn't he?"

"Hmm."

"What's the matter, Simon? Are you jealous of my brother? You hardly said anything the whole evening."

Simon snorted. "Of course not."

"What, then? You don't rejoice with us."

Simon rolled over to face Aurelia. "Of course, I'm glad that Valerius's long ordeal is over, but the real heroes are the Jewish people. I fear—" He stopped.

"You fear?"

"I fear for Alexandria again."

"Alexandria?"

"Somehow the fact that Caligula was a madman helped keep things calm after Flaccus's death. Already different groups in the city are at each other's throats to appeal to the new emperor. The Jews will want firm proof of their rights, property, and citizenship. The Alexandrians won't want to give up the property they confiscated under Caligula. Blood will flow again."

"Simon, you said there was no way out for Valerius without a massacre, and you were wrong."

"Another thing I must warn you about. I had a long talk today with Sedek, and he and my sister have joined the group that calls itself Christian. Even Matthaios talks like his father. I don't want our children to be influenced by that."

Aurelia fumbled for the lamp and went to light it at the hall torch. When she came back, she sat on the edge of the bed at his side and held the lamp to shine on his face. "We need to talk. You've been away so much you hardly know what's going on in your own household. There's a large group of Christians in Alexandria as well, and I have joined them. We—"

"You what?" Simon sat straight up in bed and looked at her in alarm. "You are talking about a group of fanatics who hold childish beliefs in miracles and profess their leader rose from the dead. I never asked you to adopt the Jewish religion. But this now? This is insanity."

Aurelia frowned. "Simon, you've closed your mind to everything but your own dark view of the world. What happened to our vows that we would share everything with one another?"

"Share! You're the one who keeps dark secrets from me. You've probably already poisoned our children's minds with such nonsense as well."

"Rufus and Alexander are old enough to decide for themselves. I take them to meetings. We sing psalms together. We listen to a simple homily. Then we eat together. There's nothing harmful in that."

Simon's face flushed in fury. He grabbed her wrist, pulled her toward him, and looked into her eyes. "You took our sons to these rituals?"

"They—they enjoy going with me."

In a cold voice, he said, "I forbid you to take my sons anywhere. Do you understand?"

Aurelia turned away in shock. "You judge before you understand. You are being unfair."

Simon's jaw worked back and forth.

She read impending doom in the set of his face, the glare in his eyes. "Simon, please don't look at me like that. I had no intention of upsetting you."

"If that's true, you'll put aside this nonsense and go to sleep." He turned away from her and pulled the covers to his neck.

She knew the conversation was over and went to her side of the bed and blew the light out. Gingerly, she eased under the covers and curled into a miserable knot. For a long time, she listened to Simon's deep, even breathing while she clenched her teeth and stared wide-eyed into the night. Then she slipped out of bed and went to check on the children.

Rufus and Alexander were sound asleep. The way Rufus balled his fists near his chin reminded her of Simon, who did the same thing in his sleep. He had already kicked the bed-clothes to the floor. She covered him up again and smoothed the hair from his forehead.

Alexander slept more peacefully. In the dim light from the hallway, he looked so much like Valerius when he was a child that she caught her breath, remembering their childhood in Cyrene.

She tiptoed to Antonia's crib. "My baby," she whispered. Antonia slept sprawled on her back, her doll clutched in one arm, her other hand open on top of the sheet. Aurelia studied her sweet little face and felt nostalgia for her own lost innocence. She bent to kiss the moist, open palm. When she raised her head, she saw her daughter's eyes flutter open. Antonia gazed sleepily at her mother and held pudgy arms up to greet her.

Aurelia clasped her to her breast and smothered her with kisses. Aurelia realized whatever else she had to deal with, the happiness and welfare of her children must be uppermost. Long after Antonia had nodded off to sleep again, Aurelia walked up and down, drawing strength from the warm weight of her daughter clutched in her arms.

The next evening, after a strenuous morning of packing and a farewell visit to Rachel, Aurelia wandered through the old Seleucid palace in search of Simon. When she couldn't find him, she explored another wing of the palace and found a steep stairway that led to a tiled room decorated with painted flowers. She was about to retrace her steps when she noticed Valerius at the window.

"Valerius!"

He jumped and turned toward her in surprise.

"I'm looking for Simon."

"I haven't seen him this evening." He smiled at his sister and held out his hand. "Come, sit by me. I'm glad I decided to accompany you as far as Jerusalem. I owe Agrippa a visit, and we have many issues to discuss. It's ironic that I would normally visit Jerusalem to deal with matters of state twice a year, but, during this stand-off with Caligula, Jerusalem was the last place I could enter."

Aurelia said, "I hope you and Agrippa are still friends after all that has happened. Simon is anxious about Alexandria."

Valerius sighed. "We had a long talk about it this afternoon. He is convinced there will be trouble."

"There's always something to worry about. What do you know about Claudius?"

"I know only that no one expected him to become emperor."

"Antonia once told me that he had a miserable childhood because everyone thought he was a fool, but she claimed he was the wisest of her children."

"Antonia was a clever and powerful woman. Let's hope she was right."

Aurelia studied her brother's face. She saw deep lines of worry around his eyes and thought he should be relieved and triumphant after what he had just been through. Instead, he seemed troubled. Impulsively, she flung her arms around him and exclaimed, "Oh, Valerius, I'm so proud of you. Father would have been so pleased. You are a true hero!"

Valerius smiled at her enthusiasm. "You know, through all this, it did seem to me that the God of the Jews was protecting not only the Jews but me as well. I can see why you found their religion so appealing."

Aurelia studied his profile. "Did Simon seem upset this afternoon?"

"Quite upset. But then, there haven't been that many times I've seen Simon when he wasn't."

"What was he upset about?"

"Mainly the situation in Alexandria."

"Did he talk to you about me?"

"Some."

"What did he say?"

Valerius sighed. "Why don't you ask him?"

"Is he still angry at me?"

Valerius nodded.

Aurelia looked away from his probing gaze. "Please, tell me what he said."

"He said that you had defied him, that you had joined this new movement without his knowledge, that you had taken advantage of his absence to influence Rufus and Alexander."

"Tell me, Valerius, what should I do?"

"I don't know. I was surprised at his anger."

"It hurts that he believes I am trying to oppose him deliberately. Our new group is mostly Jewish but welcomes everybody. I thought if Jews were there, Simon would have no objection."

"But you didn't feel free to tell him."

Aurelia lowered her eyes and nodded.

"Then you must have thought he would not approve."

"You are right. I should have told him. But he was so worried about more important things that I..."

"What attracts you to this community?"

"We are a community that loves one another and ministers to the sick and old. Is that so different from a physician's calling? Rachel, his own sister, has been a follower for a long time, and she told me not to give up; to be firm."

"You spoke to Rachel about this?"

"This afternoon. She said that our love for each other would overcome all obstacles in the end."

Valerius said nothing and seemed lost in thought. After a while, he said, "A few days ago I would have been a cynic who said that love is powerless, but I have witnessed a miracle.

I've been spared and I'm grateful. I hope that Rachel is right. There's too much misery in this world as it is, and I vow not to add to it."

"You sound like a Christian."

Valerius laughed. "Hardly. It's preposterous to think that one religion would have a monopoly on truth, much less on love." After a long silence, Valerius added, "Some days, Aurelia, I feel very old. The last few years have made me long for a simpler life, a life secluded on some plot of land where I could live in peace."

"Peace. That's what Simon keeps talking about. Yet we hardly have peace between us. I must go find him." She rose.

"Find him or fight him?"

"Maybe both."

"I hope he's calmer now than when he left me this afternoon."

"So, you had a fight with him too?"

"Of sorts."

"About what?"

"About our sisters."

"Did you win?"

Valerius didn't answer.

Aurelia smiled mysteriously, gave him a sisterly hug, and dashed down the steps in search of Simon.

✦

Simon was sitting outside in the garden with Rufus and Alexander, and Aurelia could tell from the expression on his face that he was scolding. The boys stared down at their feet and listened politely, glancing occasionally at each other, knowing the flow of their father's words would eventually stop and they could go back to their wrestling practice out on the lawn. His usual directives aimed at their wrestling techniques were words of encouragement, but today matters were obviously much more serious, and Aurelia stepped out into the garden so she could hear what he was saying.

Simon's voice was calm. "You must understand that I am telling you this because I am concerned about your safety. If you continue to go to these meetings with your mother, you will get in trouble. It's dangerous. People who practice this strange new religion are put to death or imprisoned. I have warned your mother about this. She is fully aware of the danger, and yet she keeps going to these rituals and insists on taking you with her."

Alexander spoke up and stroked his father's arm. "But Father, you don't understand. We sing songs, recite the same psalms you like to recite, and we have a meal together. Someone usually tells us wonderful stories about Yeshua. Nothing is dangerous. Why are you against that?"

"Because people who follow this cult are being put to death. It is a new version of our Jewish faith, but it has been distorted to make false claims that are more like magic."

Rufus lifted his shoulders with indignation. "We do nothing wrong. In fact, the last time, we spent the whole afternoon helping sick people. And that is what you do every day. Yeshua went about healing people. You would like his teaching if you got to know him."

Alexander spoke up with excitement. "At one meeting, a preacher named Marcus told us a wonderful story about a shepherd who had one hundred sheep. He took care of every single one of them. But one day, one of them got lost, and the shepherd looked everywhere and didn't give up until he finally found him and saved him. Yeshua said God is like that. He loves all of us. And God will take care of us when we get lost."

Rufus interrupted. "Father, the main thing I see is that you are like Yeshua."

When Simon reacted and reared back, shaking his head, Rufus quickly added, "Yes, you are! When you are late for supper and Mother gets worried and upset, it's usually because a sick beggar is lying on the Museion steps, and you stop to take care of him. You are doing exactly what Yeshua did. What Yeshua told us to do. You help people. You heal the sick."

Simon looked at his sons in surprise. "In your innocence, you only see the positive things your mother has emphasized with you. But you must be careful. Did you know that a crowd in Jerusalem stoned a man because he professed this new religion? Do you want that to happen to you?"

They shook their heads, and Alexander looked flustered. Rufus said, "There must be a lot more to that story than that. What did the man do that the crowd got mad enough to stone him?"

"I wasn't there, but I heard he was a great speaker and was followed by many. But some claimed he spoke against the temple, the very sacred place your Uncle Valerius risked his life to protect. You should ask Agrippa about that when we see him. I was very upset when I heard about it. But the fact that someone was killed just for proclaiming this new cult terrifies me. I want to protect you. I want to keep you out of danger."

Rufus said, "We don't control how other people react. Does the fact that he was killed prove that our beliefs are wrong? Althea keeps saying how dangerous it is to be a Jew. Does our safety depend on which god we believe in?"

Simon looked at his son with a new appreciation. "Perhaps it does. Valerius got a message just yesterday from Jerusalem about unrest there. That's why he is accompanying us to Jerusalem tomorrow. It seems that the Sanhedrin plans to prosecute and even persecute those who go astray and follow your Yeshua."

Alexander stomped his foot and stood up. "Matthaios told me that yesterday before the banquet. He said it was so unfair."

Rufus asked, "Does the Sanhedrin have the right to do that?"

Simon sighed. "I don't know. I want to keep you from harm."

"Is it like the time Yeshua was condemned to death? You were there. What do you think?"

Simon shook his head. "I wasn't there when they condemned him to death. When I saw Yeshua, he was carrying the crossbeam and fell. I learned later that there were two trials—one before the High Priest and one before Pilatus. Neither seemed very convincing from what I heard from Sedek. But the mob that wanted to crucify him was convincing."

Alexander said, "I think it's amazing that you were there to help him."

"Well, don't! It was sheer coincidence that I was in Jerusalem at the time and walking on that street when he fell. I almost refused to help when a Roman soldier forced me. But of course, I couldn't leave someone in trouble. I guess, I do tend to help people. It's part of my mission as a physician."

"Exactly!" Alexander sat back down and nestled against his father.

Simon was pleased because his son hadn't done that often since he had been a toddler. He looked over at Aurelia and smiled. She thought he hadn't noticed she was there and realized a lot of what he was saying was for her benefit.

"Exactly what?" Simon asked.

"You are like Yeshua. Marcus told a story about a poor fellow who was robbed and beaten and was calling for help at the side of the road. People simply walked by and didn't look at him, but a man from Samaria stopped and helped. He told us that Yeshua said we should be like the Samaritan, always willing to help. Like you. So how could that be dangerous? How could that be wrong?"

Simon shook his head. "You are full of nice stories that seem harmless enough. But what you don't understand is that this seemingly mild-mannered Yeshua is really a revolutionary. He wants to destroy our whole system and create a new one, and the priests are warning us. All I want to do is to keep you safe."

Alexander was indignant. "I think the priests are wrong."

"Be careful what you say. The priests have power."

Relieved that Simon was so much calmer than last night, Aurelia stepped into the garden to join them. She felt the boys had made valid arguments, and she wanted to support them. She sat down on the bench beside him and clasped his hand. "Simon, I know you want to protect us. We are grateful for your love and protection. Do you really think it's going to be that bad?"

"I wish I knew."

✦

A VISIT WITH AGRIPPA

Valerius provided a horse-drawn carriage for Aurelia and the children, offered Simon one of his stallions, and brought ten equestrian knights along with Quintus to provide protection for their journey. Their first stop was Sidon along the coast. During the months since he had left Palestine, Valerius assumed Sosias and Nicanor would be well on their way toward completing the bronze door for the temple, and he was eager to see it.

When they arrived in Sidon, the foundry was in the middle of an exciting moment of suspense as the first piece of mold was removed to uncover the bronze beneath. Valerius was disappointed to learn that Nicanor called it merely a practice piece to test the strength and consistency and formula for the mixture, but the first glimpse of the metal surface elicited gasps of wonder, for even before cleansing, chasing, and burnishing, the surface glowed like bright gold, and the relief that appeared was a splendid tree of life.

Simon, who had been observing without comment, was suddenly intrigued by the process and wanted to know all the details. "It looks like gold, only brighter. How can that be?"

He turned to Nicanor, who explained, "It is a secret formula most sculptors will not reveal. It is called Corinthian gold. Different sculptors have different formulas for the mixture."

"But it has gold in it?"

"It is a combination of bronze plus gold and silver. The proportions make it so bright. My formula was developed at my foundry in Alexandria."

Simon called Aurelia into the foundry along with the children so they could see. "I want you to participate in this historic moment. This beautiful tree of life will become part of a magnificent work of art to adorn our temple in Jerusalem." He looked sternly at Rufus and Alexander as he spoke. "It will glorify the Most High in our holy temple. And we owe it all to your Uncle Valerius here that the temple has remained undefiled."

The workers at the foundry who had gathered for the unmolding applauded and cheered. Rufus and Alexander did as well. Even Antonia, in her mother's arms, clapped her hands without understanding what it was all about. Aurelia studied her husband's expression with amazement. She had seldom heard him speak with such emotion and wondered if her confession of her new faith had brought about his defense of the old.

Valerius thought Simon might be offering an oblique apology for their strong disagreements. "Simon, you do me great honor, but you should know there were two whole legions of Roman soldiers who stood by me, and I owe much to Manius Cornelius, the top legate and centurion who gave his full support throughout the long ordeal. But today the heroes in front of us are Nicanor and Sosias."

Nicanor and Sosias were too busy to listen to speeches and kept working at liberating the golden bronze without comment.

Aurelia observed Sosias and was troubled. He looked tired

and distant. He had not greeted her and the children with his usual exuberance. With all the smells and noise of the foundry around them, she knew it would be impossible to talk, and there was so much she wanted to know. Still holding Antonia, she decided to use her as an excuse to ask Sosias to accompany them to the latrine. Sosias showed the way through the maze of halls and warned her that they would have to get away from the building to avoid the fumes as he led little Antonia to a latrine near the tavern. Afterward, Aurelia insisted on stopping at the tavern and buying bread dipped in olive oil and a cup of mint-flavored water. As Sosias sipped his drink, she asked him how things were going. She was alarmed when he refused to answer.

She took a bite of bread and said, "I went to see Rhoda just before we left. She is very unhappy."

Sosias sighed. "There is nothing I can do about it."

"Are you sure?"

"At least Rhoda will be taken care of. Nicanor will be able to grant her and her family every wish."

"Not every wish. She loves *you*."

"I was foolish. I thought doing this work for the temple would inspire her family to accept my commitment to Rhoda and to their heritage. It would prove that I have fully accepted the Jewish faith. But that is nothing compared to Nicanor, who is the star of this enterprise. Also, he is from an old Jewish family. There is no competition."

"Without you, he wouldn't have even competed for the door."

"It is already known as the Nicanor door."

"You could change that."

Sosias made a funny little snort. "That part doesn't bother me. What worries me is that Nicanor wants to build it his way, and it won't work."

"Tell me why."

"He is a magnificent artist, and the molds for his ornamental reliefs will be amazing. But he ignores the technical aspects of the door—the weight, the requirements for the frame, the way it should be hung."

"Have you told Alexander Lysimachos? After all, he is paying for it."

Sosias shook his head. "Nicanor managed to get him on his side."

"Isn't Agrippa making major renovations at the temple? He should know about your concerns."

"How would I get to tell him?"

"I'm sure we can figure out a way."

As they reentered the foundry, Antonia danced ahead and scurried off through a dark corridor. Sosias ran after her to stop her before she got hurt and caught her just as she was about to bump into a gigantic soldier, who loomed over her in shiny military dress. When Aurelia caught up with them, she screamed, because piercing eyes caught the light and glared down at her. Then she noticed that the huge soldier had neither arms nor legs. Antonia started crying and grabbed onto Aurelia's clothes. Aurelia turned to Sosias and mouthed a name. He told her the statue was almost ready for transport to Jerusalem when the news came that Caligula was dead. "Now they are taking him apart and melting him piece by piece to salvage precious metals."

Sosias was comforting little Antonia and guided her finger to touch the bronze surface. "See! He's not real."

Still shaken, Aurelia said, "His threats were real enough." She glared at the huge torso and the elaborate detail of the muscle cuirass and then up at his bronze face that stared at her with cold aloofness. She was stunned. This imperial clump of metal was the cause of more than two years of deep anguish and could have set off a monstrous bloodbath that would eclipse the horror of the massacre in Alexandria. She imagined what it would look like to see his features run together and melt in the raging foundry fires. Then she made a face at the statue and said, "It would be very satisfying to watch him dissolve. Piece by piece."

Sosias shook his head. "Let's get out of here. You have better things to do."

He lifted Antonia in his arms, and they rejoined the group that was admiring the full ornamental panel of the tree of life. Nicanor was pointing out intricate details in the veins of a leaf and bragging about their perfection.

The next day, Rufus and Alexander were excited that Sosias was traveling with them to Jerusalem and made room for him in the carriage. Aurelia took Antonia on her lap and discussed strategy with Sosias. "You are an equal partner in this enterprise. You won the honor of creating the door together. I am confident Agrippa will listen to your concerns. He is very involved with the renovations at the temple. He wants everything to be done right."

"I hope you are right."

"He's an old friend. He will listen to you. What are your dreams for the future after the door is in place in the temple?"

Sosias frowned. "My dream was to marry Rhoda."

"An excellent dream you should not give up. But beyond that? Every now and then you say something that tells me you are working on a special project. Rhoda called it a village of peace."

When Sosias didn't explain further, Aurelia sensed that she had touched on a subject that was very painful to him because he was watching his dream fall apart without Rhoda at his side. She was frustrated for him and wished there was something she could do.

Later, at a roadside inn, Sosias sought out Valerius's company. Valerius welcomed him with delight and shared a light supper that had been delivered to his room. For a while, they enjoyed their food in silence. Valerius said, "Your advice about Manius was very helpful. Thanks to your insights, we became good friends. I also learned a great deal from you, and I think you are a wise man. But right now, I sense you are troubled."

Sosias did not respond.

Valerius took a sip of wine and waited. After a moment, he said, "You once told me that you learn a great deal from what people do not say." He smiled. "Right now, I have learned that your thoughts may be too deep to share. I often feel that way. Lately, I have been reflecting on the fact that I fully expected to be dead by now. There was no way out of the dilemma Caligula created. At least not an acceptable one. But sometimes fate or the gods surprise us.

"It is strange, is it not? I often feel guilty because I have been the beneficiary of good fortune. My father did not enjoy that good fortune. He died for no good reason. People die every day who are innocent and good and deserve to live. Always there is the question of what makes a life meaningful, beautiful even. And that's when I discover the true and essential power of love. Without my love for Rachel, I am a hollow, meaningless shell. On my earlier visit to Sidon, I watched Nicanor place his hands in the moist clay and produce a thing of great beauty. Love is like the touch of a sculptor's hands. It molds us, transforms us, makes us greater than we were. And regardless of what happens that is evil or devastating or cruel or simply mean, Rachel will remain the light of my life."

Valerius raised his wine cup in a gesture of salute to Sosias and smiled. There were tears in Sosias's eyes. The lamp on the table sputtered and went out. They sat across from each other in the dark. Neither spoke. They didn't need to.

As Sosias rose to go to his room, he said, "I came to you tonight to ask you a question I did not know how to ask. And you gave me my answer. Rhoda is the light of my life."

✦

In Jerusalem, Agrippa welcomed Simon and Aurelia to the Herodian palace with open arms and acted like it had been just yesterday that they had been together. Aurelia thought he had not changed since she had seen him in Alexandria. He was slightly more rotund, if anything more jovial than before, always emotional and exuberant, and as excited as a child with a new toy to show them a model of the temple renovations. "Have you been there?" was his first question.

"Not today," Simon admitted. "But Valerius is there now looking around with Sosias, the young man who won the competition for the bronze door with Nicanor. Valerius wanted to walk around it on the temple mount to see the structure he risked his life to save even though he is not allowed to go in. Sosias is concerned about hanging the door."

"Ah! The door. I want to hear all about it. Is it finished?" He rubbed his hands together in anticipation and frowned when Aurelia said there was a lot more work to do before it would be on the way to Jerusalem.

The disappointed look on his face did not last because he immediately launched into his elaborate plans for the installation ceremony for the door. "I'm already working on a list of people to invite—kings and governors from neighboring lands, the alabarch of Alexandria of course, and Philo and his nephew Tiberius Alexander, and special envoys from Rome."

Simon and Aurelia looked at each other and remained silent while he went on with his list. When he stopped, Simon informed Agrippa that urgent issues needed his attention. "Nothing has been settled since the massacre in Alexandria that you witnessed. We desperately need your help. We need you to make our case to Claudius. The main issue is to regain our citizenship rights."

Aurelia held her breath as they waited for Agrippa's response. She thought Simon should have waited to discuss his agenda, for she could tell Agrippa wanted to control the conversation and was irritated. She remembered how proud Agrippa was of his special relationship with the powerful in Rome and said, "Do you think you are in a position to persuade the emperor?

We know how close you are to the imperial family."

Agrippa's face lit up. "Indeed. We all grew up together in the imperial household. A bunch of rowdy boys. Tiberius would return from some battle or other and challenge us all to mock sword fights. Germanicus was four years older and usually won. Claudius—" Agrippa chuckled at the memory. "He would try so hard. He was clumsy and limped and sometimes I let him win. It was natural that Tiberius favored his son Drusus. But when Drusus died—" Agrippa stopped and went over to the window that looked east toward the temple. "That was a very difficult time for Tiberius, but I think I made a difference."

Agrippa walked back toward them, his face now solemn. "Grief changes you. Most people do not know that I also had a son named Drusus who died young." For a moment he stood still and held his hands out as though he were cradling a child. When he looked up, there were tears in his eyes. He placed a hand on Simon's shoulder. "If you had been there, perhaps he would not have died." He pinched the bridge of his nose and returned to the window. "Tiberius and I had that common bond. After my Drusus died, we sat together for a long time and shared the scars of our loss. I think that is why Tiberius wanted me to tutor Caligula for the succession. An impossible task, as you know. But I did manage to stop a few calamities. Caligula was also affected by grief. Grief for Drusilla drove him mad, and I could not reach him. But you ask about Claudius. When the praetorians saw that Caligula had squandered the whole military budget, they stepped in and assassinated him. As soon as I heard, I went straight to Claudius, who was hiding in the palace, for fear that he was next on their list. I encouraged Claudius to speak to the senate and went to see the praetorians and argued that Claudius was capable; that Rome would fall into chaos if they refused to support him."

Just as Agrippa was about to continue, Simon spoke up. "It is our hope that you can be persuasive with Claudius and bring peace to Alexandria. The council in Alexandria has pre-pared requests to present to the emperor and asks for your advice and support."

Agrippa said, "One thing I can promise you. Claudius is not insane. In fact, he is quite level-headed and intelligent. We'll discuss this tomorrow. For now, let's have supper." He ushered them into the family dining room where he intro-duced his wife Cypros and his three daughters. "My son stays in Rome and thinks Jerusalem is dull and has too many priests and not enough circuses."

Berenice, Agrippa's oldest daughter, smiled and said, "My brother is not interested in politics, but I am."

Cypros rose to welcome them to their meal just as Valerius arrived with Sosias. After Agrippa made an elaborate toast to Valerius, whom he addressed as "our most distinguished gov-ernor of Syria who saved the temple," Cypros served supper herself. It consisted of salad greens, dried fish, and bread with a dish of seasoned beans and lentils mixed with chopped olives and sesame oil. It was tasty and plentiful and washed down with local wine.

Aurelia was impressed with Cypros's down-to-earth sim-plicity and admired her casual grace. She thanked her for receiving them and mentioned how impressed she had been by Berenice at her engagement party to Marcus. She turned to Berenice. "How gorgeous you looked in your purple gown." Cypros seemed pleased and bragged that she had done the gold embroidery on her daughter's dress.

Before long, Agrippa turned the conversation to the tem-ple and his favorite subject of the moment—the bronze door. Agrippa asked Sosias technical questions that showed he possessed an impressive understanding of the difficulties of mounting two heavy bronze slabs at the proposed site. He was obviously pleased with Sosias's answers until he asked when the door would be delivered. Sosias could not give him a date and explained that the level of artistry Nicanor was putting into each panel was both amazing and time-consuming.

Agrippa was not pleased. His face flushed red with anger, and Sosias became the immediate target of his wrath. "Surely, the original agreement you made with Alexander Lysimachos indicates a date of completion."

When Sosias explained there was no fixed date for completion, he ordered him to speak to Nicanor to hurry it up. Agrippa grumbled that he might have to go see what was happening in Sidon himself.

Sosias welcomed his intervention and said, "I want to have everything ready here for when the door is finished. I need your certification of me as your designated engineer to oversee the work properly."

Agrippa answered, "That is not a problem. I will draw up a document tomorrow."

"It could be a problem. I have no proof of Jewish ancestry, and I need full access to the temple for structural reasons."

Aurelia held her breath and wondered how Agrippa would respond. To her surprise, Agrippa erupted in laughter. When he recovered a bit, he said, "Ah, the question of Jewish ancestry."

Sosias didn't know what to think and glanced over at Aurelia with concern.

Agrippa looked down at his wine and said, "It's a long story."

At that moment, an aide came in and asked to speak privately with Agrippa. After Agrippa left the room with his aide, Aurelia asked Cypros what she thought about the renovations at the temple.

Cypros lifted her shoulders in a feeble shrug. "I've only been there once. But contrary to what I expected, the temple is not a place of peace. It is full of separate groups giving speeches and making all kinds of claims. People were even yelling at each other. Then there's the slaughter of animals for the sacrifice in the next hall. You can see and smell it from the women's court. There are two columns between the two courts. I think it would be nice to have the new door. Perhaps I was there on the wrong day, but I have no desire to go back."

Aurelia gazed at her brother, who had spent more than two years of his life in peril, struggling against all odds to keep the temple from being desecrated by Caligula's statue.

Cypros no doubt noted her surprise and said, "As you are surely aware, women do not play much of a role in religious festivals here. We make our home in Caesarea, a modern city with an airy palace by the sea. We don't live here in Jerusalem and only visit when Agrippa has to be here for political reasons."

Berenice rose to help her mother serve dessert—ripe apricots covered in rich cream. Aurelia saw Berenice serve Simon and lean down by his ear to say something that made Simon smile. The way she smiled back at him made her think Berenice was flirting with him.

When Agrippa returned, waving his fists in the air, he exclaimed, "No one can govern Judea! Enough is enough!"

Valerius asked what happened.

Agrippa picked up his wine and slammed the goblet down on the table without drinking. "These religious fanatics are at it again. They preach to larger and larger crowds and have the audacity to do it in the temple or near it. They're causing riots."

"Religious fanatics? They are Jews?" Simon asked.

"Of course, they are Jews. Troublemakers who believe that Galilean who was crucified was the Messiah."

Simon looked over at Aurelia, and she felt the accusation in his gaze. Then he said with some vehemence, "It is wrong when Jews fight against Jews. In Alexandria, Jews are fighting for their very existence; for their right to survive. And here they are fighting each other."

Calmly, Valerius asked what Agrippa proposed to do about it.

"I've commanded that their leaders be flogged and thrown into prison."

Valerius asked, "What laws have they broken? What are the charges?"

Agrippa dismissed the question with a derogatory hand gesture. "That's not my domain. The Sanhedrin will always come up with something." He snorted a sharp laugh, a mocking laugh without mirth. "They're good at that sort of thing."

Valerius said, "Are they speaking against Rome? Against your rule? Against the temple? Against the political power of the Sanhedrin?"

Agrippa shrugged. "These rabble-rousers are disturbing the peace. And I have discovered that it is wise to listen to what the Sanhedrin wants me to do."

After an uncomfortable silence, Aurelia hoped to change the subject back to Sosias and his request. "You were about to tell us a long story when you were interrupted." When Agrippa frowned, she prompted, "About Jewish ancestry."

"Ah, yes. It's no secret. I am not Jewish by blood, and yet I am king of the Jews." Agrippa cleared his throat, took a sip of wine, and held up his hand for attention. "First, a little history lesson. You have probably heard about my grandfather Herod the Great. His father was Idumaean and his mother Nabatean. Neither one a Jew. Their ancestors converted to Judaism, and they were raised as Jews. Rome didn't care about Jewish ancestry and appointed him king of the Jews. He was a cruel man. When I was four, he had his own son killed who was my father. I have no memory of my father. I was sent to Rome to grow up in the household of Tiberius. Tiberius was like a father to me. I don't even know why Tiberius took me in. I have always assumed it was because of my name. My name is Marcus Julius Agrippa. Marcus to honor Marcus Antonius. Julius to honor Caesar. Agrippa to honor the Roman general and victor of Actium who won the victory for Octavianus, future emperor Augustus. In naming me, my family was shamelessly seeking special favors from the most powerful in Rome. When Caligula made me king of the Jews, I was obviously acceptable to Romans. But how did the Jews feel about me? That was my big question. I was worried and anxious to find out. On the first day of Sukkot, I stood up in the temple to read from Deuteronomy. It states: 'You may not put a foreigner over you.' When I read the words, I wept, but the High Priest and the people hailed me as their brother."

For a moment, Agrippa was lost in thought. "I am proud to be part of both worlds. I am Roman to the Romans. I am a Jew to the Jews. As long as I am useful to both sides, all is well." He turned to Sosias. "Now, Sosias, tomorrow we will draw up papers for you so that no one will be able to question your authority when you supervise the installation of the new door."

As Aurelia and Simon made ready for bed, she expected an explosion of anger from him, but he said nothing. After checking on the children, she thought he was asleep.

But in the dark, he said, "You put our children and our whole family at risk by what you do. You see how Agrippa deals with fanatics. The next step is that he will likely put their leaders to death. I don't agree with what Agrippa is doing, and it was obvious tonight that Valerius is troubled by it. But what you learned tonight should make you turn away from your fanatic friends who will surely get you and our sons in trouble."

THE DESERT IS UNFORGIVING

THE JOURNEY FROM JERUSALEM TO ALEXANDRIA WAS more arduous than Aurelia remembered. Without Valerius and his men watching over them, she felt vulnerable and exposed. She rode with the children in a cart pulled by a donkey. Every step jolted through her spine and hurt. Uneven stones went by her lowered gaze in patterns that flowed together in dizzying monotony. Antonia cried and climbed on top of her, and the boys looked as uncomfortable as she felt. She tried to distract them with stories, but when they joined the desert caravan south of Jerusalem to cross the wilderness, speech became impossible.

Simon had to exchange his horse for a smelly camel that frightened Antonia. All Aurelia could hear was the ceaseless jangle of the camels' and donkeys' bells and the occasional hoarse calls of their drivers. Sand flew into their faces and clothes. Gritty particles blistered skin and tissue and left their throats parched, their eyes swollen, and their lungs burning. When Antonia whimpered in discomfort, Aurelia soothed her with a damp cloth over her face. Once, when she used an entire skin of water to bathe Antonia, Simon came up from behind and watched her. Only his eyes were visible between the folds of his keffiyeh, but they were glaring at her in anger. "You spoil my daughter as much as you have spoiled my sons. The water we carry must be reserved for drinking."

At the next stop, a cool breeze whispered over the sand. Aurelia stretched her face into it with pleasure, closing her eyes. When she opened them again, she saw Haman, the guide, exchange knowing glances with the drivers and heard them confer anxiously in a guttural language she didn't understand. Simon had told her that Haman's unerring sense of direction was based on the position of the sun. Only at midday and at dusk did he lose his certainty when the shadows thrown by his body were no longer of assistance. But now the sun was hidden by a strange haze.

It was late afternoon when Aurelia noticed that the surface of the desert was eerily transformed. Puffs of sand spurted like bubbles rising from a boiling kettle. Scurrying eddies whipped higher and higher in the wind, and it was getting dark too early. She gathered Antonia closer to her breast and tried to yell out to the drivers and Simon in front of her, but her voice was snatched away by the wind.

Suddenly, the light disappeared, and the caravan halted. Instinctively, the animals huddled in a half-circle, placing their backs to the prevailing winds. Simon pulled pitch-coated tenting over the cart for Rufus and Alexander and warned them to stay put. Next, he pulled another canvas down over the other wagon and yelled for Aurelia and Antonia to crawl under. The cloth whipped around and slapped into Aurelia's face, knocking her off balance. She fell, twisting so that she could cushion Antonia's fall with her body. As they struggled to get up, Antonia pulled away from her mother's grasp. Aurelia yelled for her but was blinded by the ferociously swirling sand. Holding onto the wagon, she groped in the darkness, while the sand stung her hands and face. She called out, but no one answered.

In a panic, she let go of the wagon and took a few steps into the wind. She flailed her arms about in all directions, telling herself that she must regain her wits and start a systematic search. If she could make it back to the wagon, maybe she could find Simon for help. By now, though, she was so turned around and disoriented she was not sure she was headed in the right direction. Surely, if she crawled against the wind, she would get back to the safety of the wagon, but the wind kept changing direction, and her hands touched only a thousand needles of sand.

She changed direction, circling wider. She was blinded by sand that pierced her skin. Each time she moved forward, all she found was more sand. She had heard the horror stories from the caravan drivers about people found buried under the sand within a stone's throw of shelter. Obstinately, relentlessly, she crept onward, vowing she would never again cross the desert. A vision of Antonia covered with sand haunted her each time she tried to catch her breath, and she began to pray in ragged syllables until she fell—completely spent—her *bournous* billowing out above her like a torn mainsail in the wind.

When the winds finally died down, the sun had already set, leaving a strange glow on the horizon. The caravan became a tiny bump in the vast sand-covered landscape. All the contours of the animals, tents, and carts were smoothed over by undulating dunes that sifted and shifted now as they dug themselves out and worked enough saliva to their mouths to be able to spit.

Simon did not yet know that his wife and daughter were not under the tenting he thought he had secured. He lit a lantern to check on Rufus and Alexander, shook them free, and gave them water to wash their burning mouths. It was only then that he noticed that the tent where he had led Aurelia and Antonia was flapping loose and hid nothing but sand underneath. Frantically, he called and ran his arms deep into piles of sand near the cart, but they were not there.

In a daze, he gathered the drivers and slaves for a systematic search. Their lanterns were lit, but all they could see in the small orbs of light was sand. When a quarter moon appeared over the horizon, the camel driver squinted toward the east and pointed. They all ran for the spot where a tattered cape fluttered forlornly above the sand.

Simon did not wait for a shovel but dug down furiously with his hands and found Aurelia. He picked up her limp body and whirled the sand from her and bent her forward to clear her nose and mouth. In an act of desperation, he pressed his lips against hers and sucked sand from her mouth and spit it out. Then he blew into her lungs. He pressed down on her chest and tried again. He felt her exhale, so he blew again and fumbled for her wrist, where he felt a thready pulse. He willed her to breathe again by blowing his own breath into her, and when she heaved on her own and coughed and sputtered, he made her gargle with water and spit and drink some more. He propped her up so she could breathe easier and washed her bleeding face, calling her name. He didn't notice that the camel drivers had pulled back in awe and were looking at him as though he had supernatural powers.

Aurelia looked up into Simon's burning eyes and tried to speak. She sputtered and gasped for breath and finally mouthed the syllables she had no voice for, and Simon understood. "We haven't found Antonia." Simon peered into the darkness and knew that the chances of finding her alive were slim indeed.

It was toward morning when Haman found a doll almost completely buried in the sand. They began to dig around and beneath it and found Antonia. From the looks of her almost-unblemished skin, she had been buried almost immediately by the unrelenting waves of sand. When Simon clutched her limp body to his chest, Haman said, "Now you breathe into her also and make her live again."

Simon cradled his dead daughter in his arms and keened

like a woman, for he had no moisture for tears.

The next day, the beleaguered caravan limped into an Egyptian village on the border of the desert. It was urgent to prepare Antonia for burial, and Simon thought it best to follow Egyptian customs. Aurelia was wheezing and feverish and overwhelmed with guilt, for she felt it was her fault Antonia had died. Simon never said a word of reproach, but his stony silence as they mourned their common loss created yet another gulf between them.

In the evening, while they waited for the embalmer's task to be done, the caravan drivers pulled out their kitharas, blew the sand out of them, and played lively dances for the villagers. Aurelia allowed Rufus and Alexander to sit by the campfire and watch the dances while she lay in the cart that had become her bed. She felt as though she were in another world, a world where laughter and music could never be heard again without pain—a world without joy. She leaned her head back against the rough wood of the cart and looked up at the brilliant panorama of stars. Valerius had taught her to gaze up at the stars and marvel at their beauty, but all she could feel now was the piercing agony of her aching heart.

She wondered where Simon was. In the last two days, he had wrapped himself up in his own cocoon of suffering as though he too were being embalmed. He checked on her welfare as though she were one of the many patients at the Museion whom he hardly knew. His laconic questions always dealt with her body, but it was her heart that was shattered into a thousand pieces.

If only she could have a long talk with him, she could perhaps face the next few days without total despair. Still shaky, she pulled herself up on the boards of the cart and lowered herself to the ground. With a lantern, she trudged around the wagon and animals and set out in the opposite direction to the music. Simon would not be participating in their festivities.

She saw him—an elusive pinpoint of light on the horizon.

She was not sure she would have the strength to get to him, but she would try. It was a slow process, and the distance seemed to be growing rather than shrinking. Finally, the lantern came closer. She called out, and he heard.

He came running then, kicking up clouds of sand as he came. She had collapsed in an exhausted heap. He picked her up, and she clasped her hands around his neck and clung to him as though she were drowning.

"What's wrong?"

Everything was wrong!

"Are Rufus and Alexander all right?"

She nodded.

"Why did you come to get me?"

"I—needed—you." She buried her head against his neck.

Simon frowned. "What a foolish thing to do! Have you no sense? You don't start wandering around in the desert. Ever! Don't you know by now that the desert is unforgiving? You don't know how to take care of yourself." He glared at her. "Or others for that matter."

She had no breath in her lungs to explain her anguish, nor did Simon have the will to hear it. He placed her in the cart and pulled the covers over her as though she were a naughty child who had to be punished. Then he walked away, heedless of her hoarse whispers begging him to stay at her side.

The desert was not the only thing that was unforgiving.

When the embalmer had finished his task and Simon had paid for linen, cedar oil, wax, tar, and spices, the village children gathered around the caravan to bid them goodbye. Aurelia watched numbly as Simon carried their linen-wrapped daughter and laid her gently in their cart. He had refused the traditional Egyptian mask over the head, and the white linen contours of her daughter's face stared up at her in featureless emptiness.

She wanted to hold her in her arms, but Simon wouldn't let her. She sank, weeping, to her knees in the sand.

As she wept piteously, a little hand reached out to touch her. A young girl was standing beside her, looking at her with dark liquid eyes that seemed to share her unspeakable grief. Aurelia patted her hand and was about to climb into the wagon when she noticed something strange about the little girl's face. She blinked her tears away and saw that her face was pulled toward her ear, and a fold in her cheek looped under her right eye.

Aurelia stooped to examine the girl and asked her name. Dark eyes merely stared at her, so Aurelia took her by the hand and walked over to the group of children, shielding her eyes against the sun. "Do you know who she is?"

The children stared up at her with wide eyes in dirty faces. No one answered. "Do you know where she lives?"

One boy pointed vaguely to a row of mudbrick houses behind them and scratched the back of one bronzed leg with the foot of the other. All the children stood barefoot and mute in the hot sand while Aurelia looked over to the houses, irresolute and frowning.

The caravan was ready to leave, and Simon was calling out for her to get into the wagon. He was impatient to get back to Alexandria. His fears about looting and violence in Alexandria had already been confirmed by one caravan that had stopped at the village on its way east. When Aurelia did not move at his bidding, he strode over to get her, angry now at the delay. Grabbing her arm, he jerked her forward. "We must go."

Aurelia let go of the little girl's hand and looked up at Simon as though dazed. "Not yet."

Simon pulled her back toward the caravan. She twisted around in his grasp to look back at the little girl. Large, solemn eyes stared up at her. As Simon helped her into the wagon, she shook her head. "That little girl is—"

"That little girl is not Antonia. Antonia is dead. Do you hear?" Simon's voice was bitter and impatient at the same time.

Aurelia felt the tears rush to her eyes. "I know that, but did you see her face? She—"

Simon gave a sharp command for the caravan to get started, mounted the camel he'd been riding, loped forward to the front, and did not heed Aurelia's frantic calls and frustrated gestures.

✦

When they arrived back in Alexandria, Althea stood at the door, smiling and eager to clasp the vivacious Antonia in her arms. Twice Aurelia tried to tell her. Then Simon strode up, carrying Antonia in his arms, and Althea fell to her knees, crying, "No!" While Aurelia and Althea huddled together in the kitchen, Simon set Antonia on the kitchen table and went to usher the boys to bed. Aurelia clasped her daughter in her arms and cooed endearments to the stiff fabric. Dazed, Althea held them both and gently swept Aurelia's tangled hair out of her eyes. The funeral and mourning period for Antonia were subdued, and the house drifted into smothered grieving.

Tiberius Alexander came to greet them with grim news of rebellion and bloodshed and warned them that new gangs were spreading violence and looting. When he noted the expression on Aurelia's face, he asked her what had happened and learned of Antonia's death. In a spontaneous gesture of sympathy, he reached for her hand to express his shock and sorrow. She thanked him with a quivering smile and felt Simon tense at her side.

Simon spent his days at meetings with Jewish leaders and his evenings debating strategy with Philo, who suggested a moderate approach and another delegation to Caesar to plead for the restoration of Jewish rights. Another more radical group had begun to win back formerly Jewish sectors with fists and stones and riots in the streets.

Simon supported appeals to Caesar based on Agrippa's firm belief that Claudius would be fair. He did not, however, agree with Philo that concessions must be made to regain their property, and backed an alternate delegation to Rome headed by Agrippa that would be far more demanding and aggressive about their rights as citizens of Alexandria. Lucius Aemilius Rectus, the new prefect of Egypt, supported Philo's more moderate approach.

In dealing with her loss, Aurelia longed for the support and solace of her Christian friends but had neither the courage nor the energy to thwart Simon's decree that she should stay away from their teachings and concentrate her efforts within the household. When the day came when she had to face putting Antonia's things away, even that small task overwhelmed her. Althea started to help her, but Aurelia shook her head. "I have to do this myself."

Afterward, Aurelia asked, "Do you ever stop grieving?"

"You don't," Althea said simply. Having lost her son and her husband, Althea knew she should tell her the truth. "On the day our son Yosef died trying to save the Torah in the burning synagogue, Sosias appeared in the bucket brigade beside Shemuel to help put out the flames. That very day, Shemuel brought Sosias home to supper with him. Sosias was a dirty, hungry, unkempt thirteen-year-old orphan who didn't have a decent piece of clothing to his name. Simon had rescued him but didn't know how to take care of him. Shemuel, the dreamer, called him an angel sent from heaven. I was furious with Shemuel. I was grief-stricken over our son. But I fed Sosias. I bathed him. I clothed him in Yosef's things I quickly altered to fit. My daughters came to help me prepare Yosef for burial. We all grieved together." Althea clasped Aurelia's hand. "We grieved together. Together! You and Simon must share the burden. It is as though you and Simon are grieving in separate houses. You walk by each other like strangers. You hardly pay attention to your sons. They, too, are grieving."

Aurelia grimaced. "I know." She shook her head. "I don't know what to do."

"Rufus and Alexander will be fine. But Simon? Simon grieves as much as you do. It's harder for him. He almost broke down when he placed Antonia on the table. He was quick to go take care of the boys, a task he would normally leave to me. Did you notice? He needs you."

"I didn't notice."

"You need to meet Simon more than halfway and grieve with him."

"He will push me away. He blames me."

"He knows better. You know that too." Althea cradled her head against her breast.

"You, Althea, are a better person than I. I would not have welcomed Sosias the way you did."

"I disagree. You would have and you did. You loved Sosias from the beginning."

Aurelia gulped down a sob but looked dubious. Then she smiled. "I can just see Shemuel showing up at your door with a grimy vagabond and calling him an angel from heaven."

"Our dear Shemuel."

"And our dear Sosias." Aurelia's face became animated. "Sosias! We must visit Rhoda and see what we can do." She jumped to her feet and said, "We need to make a plan."

ANNA

ON THEIR WAY TO SEE RHODA, AURELIA TOLD ALTHEA about the little girl in the desert who was eager to console her. "I must tell Rhoda about her. I believe it was Anna." At Rhoda's house, Rhoda stepped outside and walked away from the house, afraid of a confrontation with her family. She appeared defeated but was eager to hear about their visits to Sidon and Jerusalem. When she learned about Antonia's death, the three of them grieved together in each other's arms. Later, Rhoda shared her letter from Sosias, and they learned that Agrippa had ordered Nicanor to finish the door by Passover, but Nicanor balked and said an artist could not be hurried. Sosias was in Jerusalem, building the frame for the door and heavy hoisting equipment, pulleys, lifts, and cranes. At the end of the letter, Sosias wrote that he would not be surprised if Nicanor missed Agrippa's deadline. Althea asked if she had heard from Nicanor. When she shook her head, Aurelia was indignant. "Is your family still adamant about Nicanor and opposed to Sosias, who genuinely loves you?"

"They have decided."

"Do they not care about your feelings?"

"My mother makes the rules. She decided to sell Anna into slavery and could not be dissuaded. I have no idea where she is." For a moment she could not speak. "I don't even know if she's still alive."

Aurelia shook her head in exasperation. "How could she treat an innocent child in this way?"

"She sees her as God's punishment for my sister's sin. When Shira died giving birth to Anna, my mother claimed she had brought dishonor to the family. When Anna's tumor started to grow, it confirmed everything she believed. Shira lived in sin. Her child was the result of sin."

Aurelia told her then about the little girl in the desert, and Rhoda was excited and anxious to find out more. Aurelia worried that she might be wrong about the child she had seen in the desert and may have given her false hope.

It was Althea who warned Rhoda that if she found Anna again, it might cause a very painful confrontation with her mother.

Aurelia turned to Rhoda. "Do you think your mother would reject her a second time? What would you do if she did? Would that be worse than leaving her where she is?" Aurelia also wondered if she would be able to buy her back. Would they even be able to find her? What kind of person would have bought her and for what purpose? As these questions raced through Aurelia's mind, she reached for Rhoda's hand to convey sympathy and encouragement.

Rhoda said, "I don't think Anna will remember me. She was only three when my mother sold her. Almost three years ago."

Aurelia hired a driver who regularly traveled through the desert with two donkeys and a cart and told Simon she was planning an outing with their sons and Althea and would be back around nightfall. Preoccupied, Simon hardly listened and left to meet with members of the Jewish council. Aurelia piled cushions in the cart, took enough water and food for a week for their short journey, and steeled herself to face the desert again. Rufus and Alexander declared they remembered the little village where they had stayed several days while Antonia was being embalmed. They even knew the names of some children they had played with, and Rufus described the little girl who had reached out toward Aurelia as the girl with a strange face. On their way, they stopped at Amaria to pick up Rhoda.

The village on the edge of the desert was easy to find, but during the heat of the day, no one was outside. After they stopped under a few trees near a watering hole, Aurelia sent the boys to clusters of mudbrick huts in search of Anna. It didn't take long for her sons to round up the children and explain they were looking for a special little girl. Alexander demonstrated by pulling his cheek up close to his right eye. One boy pointed toward a small square hut at the edge of the village. Alexander knocked on a low wooden door, and a woman pointed to the next hut. Alexander soon came around the corner holding a young girl by the hand. Aurelia squinted against the light but could not see her face.

Rhoda hesitated a moment, walked toward them, knelt in the sand to be at eye level, and held out her arms. Anna looked toward her, and a sudden burst of joy lit up her face. She made no sound but flung her arms wide and rushed into Rhoda's arms. As young as she was when Rhoda's mother sold her into slavery, she still recognized the person who had loved and protected her.

Aurelia watched the emotional reunion with relief and a lump in her throat but was troubled to see that Anna's face looked bruised and smeared with dirt. She had outgrown a tattered shift. Her hands were sticky with fresh mud she had already spread on Rhoda's face. Alexander explained that she was behind the house filling forms with mud to make bricks.

A furious, middle-aged man came running and shouting that she belonged to him and snatched her out of Rhoda's arms. Aurelia yelled for her driver to rescue Anna, who was screaming. While villagers assembled to see what was happening, an elder of the village arrived holding a large, carved pole he pounded on a stone for silence. In a deep voice, he ordered the man who claimed to be Anna's owner to place the child in the largest hut on the mud-baked floor and made everyone sit in a circle around her. A young woman entered with a ceramic jar, poured liquid into small cups, and handed them around. Aurelia knew it would offend not to drink and picked up the cup and drank and smiled and urged her fellow travelers to follow her example. The wild sumac tea burst over her tongue with the invigorating tang of strong citrus. Aurelia asked her driver to bring in most of the food and waterskins she had brought and placed them like an offering at the elder's feet. When she started to speak, the elder pounded his stone for silence. The ancient custom of sharing food and drink was not to be tainted by conflict.

Aurelia studied Anna's owner, who wore a dark brown thoab with a blue keffiyeh on his head held in place by a circle of braided rope. He looked vicious, and Aurelia realized they would need more protection than her driver could give them.

When the elder tapped his pole again for discussion to begin, the men started arguing back and forth, and Anna crawled back into Rhoda's arms and sobbed against her breast. The elder gestured for Rhoda to place her back in the middle. Rhoda ignored him and said quietly, "No one should separate a child from her mother."

When the man who claimed Anna was his slave yelled that he paid good money for her, a wiry, gap-toothed old woman spoke up and challenged him to show his document of ownership. It was soon discovered he had none. He insisted he had paid the price of two goats for her, but the old woman pointed a finger at him and said she doubted he paid that much for a child who was deformed. Questions and answers flew back and forth in a dialect Aurelia did not understand. The old woman turned to the village elder and obviously succeeded in convincing the elder and came over to Rhoda and raised her arms in triumph. Aurelia was not quite sure if the hearing was over or not, but the elder and villagers started to file out into the bright sunlight and disappeared. Aurelia helped Rhoda to her feet. Anna still clung to her and would not let go to walk on her own.

On the way back to Alexandria, Rhoda opened a skin of water to wash Anna's face. The bruises near her lips were raw and looked recent.

Rhoda looked bewildered. "What do I tell my mother?"

Aurelia smoothed Anna's hair back out of her eyes. "What do you think you should tell her?"

"I don't know. My mother will be angry. Very angry."

"We'll know soon."

"Whatever happens, I need to protect Anna."

When they arrived at the house, Rhoda took Anna by the hand. Aurelia and Althea suggested she should simply assume her mother should be pleased that she had found Anna.

But the minute Rhoda's mother opened the door, she took one look at Anna and then at Rhoda and yelled, "What have you done?"

Rhoda turned Anna so she could see her face. "Look at Anna's face! See how beautiful she is." It was not clear from Anna's expression whether she recognized her grandmother or not, but she turned away and buried her face against Rhoda's side.

Rhoda ignored the scowl on her mother's face and said, "Thanks to Aurelia, we were able to find her and rescue her."

Rhoda's mother gave Aurelia a withering look. "You have no right to interfere with my family."

Aurelia was undaunted. "Surely, you are pleased to see that your dear granddaughter is healthy."

Rhoda approached her mother and said, "I'll take care of her. Please, Mother. She will be no trouble."

Her mother raised both hands in anger and shook them in her face. "She is not welcome in my house." She cursed her.

Aurelia could stand it no longer. "How can you reject your own granddaughter?"

Rhoda's mother said, "Go away! All of you. This child's mother brought dishonor to my house. To my family. She must go! Take her back where you found her." She spat in Aurelia's face, but Aurelia dodged the ugly insult.

Rhoda sank, weeping, to her knees. Anna started to cry.

It was Rufus who sprang into action and stepped forward to take Anna to the wagon and get her settled, while Althea tried to shield Rhoda from the onslaught of vitriol her mother launched against her.

Slowly, Althea steered Rhoda back to the wagon. When she was about to climb in, her mother called out. "Rhoda!"

She turned back and took a few steps toward her. "Yes, Mother?" Rhoda's voice was both hopeful and sad.

"You are not my daughter. Not anymore."

Stunned, Rhoda stood speechless. Aurelia was afraid Rhoda would collapse, but Althea took her arm and guided her back to the wagon where Anna climbed on her lap.

All the way back to Alexandria, no one said a word. Overwhelmed, Rhoda started to sob—long, shuddering sobs that shook her body and made her gasp every now and then as though she were coming up for air out of deep water. Anna kept stroking her face, trying to comfort her.

As they entered the busy streets of Alexandria, Rhoda finally stopped crying. Althea poured water on a cloth and handed it to Rhoda to soothe her flushed face. "Dear Rhoda," she said, "you cannot go home again until you have adopted her, or your mother will take her away from you."

Rhoda was confused. "I could adopt her?"

Althea said, "A legal adoption will save her from being sold again, or worse. I should have adopted Sosias years ago. The

Romans do it all the time to establish or preserve a family legacy. You will do it to save Anna's life, and your mother will be unable to interfere."

Suddenly, Rhoda frowned. "But I cannot go home. I don't know what to do."

Aurelia reassured her. "You will live with us until you and Sosias get married. Everything is happening at once, but you and Anna are safe now and you can get to know each other again. Right now, Anna needs you."

Anna lifted her hand toward Rhoda to caress her face. Anna's long-lashed eyes the color of black onyx were so expressive and trusting that it was hard to conceive of someone wishing her harm.

Back in Alexandria, Althea gathered fresh clothing for Anna. When she was clean and dressed, they brought her to the atrium, where Alexander exclaimed that Anna had been transformed into a princess like Atalanta. He took her hands and danced around the room with her, while Anna giggled with delight. Rufus wondered why Anna had yet to say one word. Rhoda was suddenly defensive and said, "You would be silent too if you had just been through what she's been through."

When Rufus banged a spoon against a pot behind Anna, Anna kept twirling around with Alexander to her own inner music. Everyone looked at Anna with new understanding, and Rhoda scooped her up in her arms and held her close.

Later that evening, when Simon came home, Aurelia led him to the atrium to see Anna. Though she did not say her name, she looked eagerly at Simon, expecting him to notice what his innovative treatment had accomplished. He interrupted her excitement and announced he had important news from Rome.

"But we have more important news for you right here." Aurelia's voice was intense. "This is Anna. Do you remember her? She once had a tumor bigger than a melon on her face."

Simon bent down and gently touched Anna's face. "I

remember. I clamped off some of the blood to her tumor. I thought the growth was shrinking, but then suddenly she disappeared. This is amazing! How did you find her?"

"She is the little girl I found in the desert. We went there to fetch her today and brought her back."

"I thought—" Simon looked at Aurelia in amazement. "I thought you were trying to—"

Aurelia interrupted. "I know. Rhoda is going to adopt her. Now you can write it up for the records at the Museion."

"As I recall, you gave me the idea when you told me about your gardening. Maybe you should write about this treatment for the Museion." He examined Anna again and said, "This could mean a whole new way to treat some patients."

Simon took Aurelia's hand and squeezed it. There was a welcome tenderness in his gesture, and Aurelia knew that the appeal in his eyes was deeper than a plea for forgiveness.

The miracle of Anna eclipsed for a moment Simon's news from Rome, but he did not wait long to announce that Philo had received an important letter from the emperor. Simon raised both arms to emphasize the importance of his news. "Claudius has restored the rights and citizenship of all Jews in Alexandria."

In the middle of their jubilant celebration, Philo arrived with the letter, waving it like a banner of triumph in the air. "This is a great day for Alexandria," he said. "It is a big step toward peace. Neither side got everything they wanted, a fact that proves Claudius has been evenhanded and fair."

Simon cautioned that the Alexandrians who had appropriated Jewish properties would not give them up without a fight.

Philo frowned at Simon and said, "You are right. There will be problems ahead. But this is the best news Alexandria has received from Rome in four years." His face was flushed with excitement as he thrust the letter into Aurelia's hands and said, "There is more. Aurelia, please read this passage out loud for all of us to hear." He pointed to a section in the letter,

Aurelia cleared her throat and read: "I, Claudius, do not wish to be offensive to my contemporaries, and my opinion is that temples and such forms of honor have by all ages been granted as a prerogative to the gods alone."

"To the gods alone." Philo repeated the phrase with sharp emphasis.

"An emperor who realizes he is not a god!" said Simon.

Everyone joined in a spontaneous celebration. Unaware of the drama surrounding Anna, Philo tweaked her cheek and exclaimed over the lovely little girl with dancing eyes. As he left, he said, "Let us hope we will have a few years of peace."

THE DEATH OF A KING

ANTICIPATION AND EXCITEMENT WERE IN THE AIR when word came after a three-year delay that the new temple door would be installed and dedicated at Shavuot, the feast that honored both the Torah and the harvest of wheat. Agrippa relished festivals and celebrations and had personally made intricate plans for a festival that would begin at sunrise to the fanfare of trumpets for the unveiling of the new bronze door.

Alexander Lysimachos, the alabarch of Alexandria who financed the door, acquired an entire ship for his family and friends to sail to Caesarea from Alexandria to become part of a procession to Jerusalem. Stories were already circulating that it was the most beautiful door in the empire and as luminous as the sun. Simon and Aurelia prepared to take their whole family along with Althea, Rhoda, and Anna. The alabarch had also invited all the members of the Nicanor family.

A month before departure, a frantic messenger knocked on Simon's door with summons for Simon to come to Caesarea at once. Simon started to argue with him about departure dates when the messenger grabbed Simon's hands and pleaded, "Agrippa is dying. We have fresh horses at every imperial post stop along the way. You must leave now!"

Even with a fresh horse at every station and little sleep, Simon arrived too late. He looked down at the ashen face on the royal bed in horror. He turned to the attendants who were mourning noisily in the corner of the bedroom. "When?"

"During the night."

Agrippa's physicians asserted that everything had been done that was humanly possible. Simon insisted on examining the body before attendants arrived with myrrh, aloes, and spices to wrap him in seamless linen.

The family told Simon he had suffered excruciating pain. Underneath the pallor of death, the skin was flaccid and cyanotic.

Cypros, Agrippa's loyal wife, sat on the floor and rocked back and forth, her eyes red with weeping. Their only son was in Rome and too young to be appointed an immediate successor. Their three daughters, Berenice, Mariamne, and Drusilla mourned nearby. Berenice greeted Simon with a solemn accusation. "Had you been here, I'm certain we would have been spared this grievous sorrow."

Simon bowed to her. "I've lost a dear friend, and Israel has lost a great king. I appreciate your confidence in me, but I doubt that I could have saved him. I assume this illness hit with great suddenness?"

Cypros nodded. "During the games in honor of emperor Claudius. Agrippa stood majestic in his silver robe. We were all celebrating when he suddenly doubled over in pain. I ran to him. That's when he ordered couriers to fetch you. The fever ravaged and shook him. The pain in his side was unbearable. He wept bitter tears for all he had yet to accomplish. He was looking forward to the huge ceremony he had planned for the dedication of the temple door."

Berenice said they could still have a ceremony.

Cypros shook her head. "It won't be the same without him. He was so excited about it."

Later that evening, as Simon walked out along the stone benches of the empty amphitheater, he thought back on all the times Agrippa had come to the rescue of his people. Thanks to Agrippa's friendship with Caligula as his tutor, Agrippa had been able to warn the Jews of Caligula's intention of desecrating the temple, and the Jews had been able to prepare their passive resistance. Repeatedly, Agrippa made Caligula back down in his confrontation with the Jews. Why was it so costly to be a Jew?

He felt very alone and wondered what Aurelia was doing. Why had she persisted in following the new sect that opened its doors to Greeks, Syrians, Romans, and Egyptians and distorted Jewish principles into new and preposterous beliefs? Agrippa had persecuted the sect outright and had imprisoned some and executed others. When confronted with that reality, Aurelia had merely said that even enlightened rulers made mistakes.

He refused to have maids spy on her in their home, but he knew without asking that she continued to participate in the new sect. After forbidding her to take Rufus and Alexander to their meetings, he discovered that his sons longed for them even more and played games with the servants where they would carry votive lights to a makeshift altar. Alexander would stand up in front of their servant "congregation" and preach. Simon exploded with fury and ordered the boys to their room without supper.

Aurelia's tearful intercession had no effect. After three days, Simon summoned the boys to the atrium, believing calm reasoning would eradicate the disease, but his sons stood proud like martyrs and eyed him with pity and affection. He quickly realized that they had adopted a stance of calm tolerance, while his face was hot with impatience, his voice hoarse with anger, and his fists clenched in frustration. He lashed out then and struck them both across the face. As the blows echoed through the room, he could hear his father's bellowing voice in his ears, not realizing it was his own. Aurelia stood to one side, her eyes flashing with anger as she watched him strike their sons.

Simon felt a lump form in his throat as he recalled Aurelia's stricken face when she ran from the room. It was not the first time they had had such a strong disagreement between them, but that very night he had been summoned to Agrippa's bedside.

Simon sighed. Had it not been for Agrippa, he might never have gone to Rome to marry Aurelia. A smile stole across his face as he remembered that afternoon in Antonia's house when Aurelia had so adamantly declared that she was not going to marry Agrippa or anyone else, and he had stepped forward and swept her into his arms. Dear old Antonia! She, too, was gone. When her grandson Caligula killed Gemellus—also her grandson—and declared himself a god, she committed suicide. Now her son Claudius ruled in his stead. Was it better to die at the height of one's power like Agrippa, or live so long that the changes in the world were no longer bearable? Then what about an innocent child like his little Antonia, who hadn't even had a chance?

He sat down in the empty theater. The sun was going down over the sea, strewing a brilliant path of gold, ruby, and amethyst across the water. What would happen to the province the Romans called Palestine now that Agrippa was dead? Simon tried to blot out the most ominous scenarios from his consciousness and shook his head.

At that moment, a voice from behind startled him. "You are distraught. Is there something the family should know?"

Simon turned to see Berenice in elegant silhouette against the lavender sky. She had come soundlessly and seemed almost ethereal and serenely beautiful. Simon cleared his throat but said nothing.

Berenice stepped lightly over the stone seat and sat down beside him. "You seem to have your own opinion as to why my father died. Tell me!"

"The reason for his death was a part of the bowel that burst open like an overripe fruit. It is not uncommon and can strike suddenly. Even if I had arrived yesterday, I could not have saved him." He did not tell her that even if he had been there when it happened, he could not have saved him.

For a long time, Berenice and Simon sat in silence. Finally, she said, "This is my favorite place to watch the sunset. I like to look out over the sea and wonder at all the things going on in the empire. Children are being born. Great men are dying. I wonder if there really is a supreme being in charge of it all. What do you think?"

Her direct question troubled Simon. After a while, he said, "We've lost our best hope for peace in Judea and beyond, and I am afraid Claudius will not trust your brother to take up the reins of government. That means we return to procurators and prefects appointed by Rome. They could be like Pilatus and ravage the land and murder thousands."

"Claudius could appoint good people like your brother-in-law, Publius Petronius."

"I have no way of knowing what he might do."

Berenice laughed. "Of course, you do. Don't tell me you don't know what circles your wife's family moves in. Valerius's father-in-law is Lucius Vitellius. He runs the senate. He is almost equal to the emperor. You know that." Berenice watched Simon's frowning denial and smiled. "You and Aurelia don't talk much about politics, do you?"

When Simon remained stubbornly silent, Berenice continued. "While Claudius was in Britannia, Vitellia's father ran the empire. He's been made consul three times now. Even Sejanus didn't have as much power, and they say Claudius, unlike Tiberius, is loyal to his friends."

Simon shrugged. "You know more than I about all this. I have no influence. For that matter, I don't know whether Valerius has any influence either now that Marsus will soon become the new governor of Syria. He told me he recommended his second in command, Manius Cornelius, to succeed him."

Berenice said she would continue with her father's plans to fortify Jerusalem and would govern Palestine better than any Roman if she were queen.

Simon regarded her with surprise. "You are ambitious to rule your father's kingdom?"

"I am! I see no reason why succession should be seen as a masculine affair. My brother lives a life of idleness in Rome. He has neither the skill nor the ambition to follow in our father's footsteps. You could get your brother-in-law to intercede for me with Claudius." She placed her hand on his thigh, and the fragrance of her perfume invaded his senses.

Simon felt her magnetic charm and realized suddenly how hard it would be to refuse her anything. "I doubt Valerius has that kind of influence."

Berenice laughed then and deliberately brushed against his arm so that he could feel the twin contours of her breasts. "You amuse me. You cannot make me believe that you are that naive. Every child in the empire knows that favors from the emperor are bought through influence. Besides, Valerius is in the enviable position of having other avenues of influence as well."

"What do you mean?"

"First his father-in-law. Then, your wife's famous uncle. Have you forgotten Aulus Plautius?"

"He's neither her uncle nor in Rome. He's the brother of her uncle's wife."

"But he has just accomplished the most glorious victory for the empire." She leaned against him again. "That island that lies like a sensuous woman along the coast of Gallia now belongs to Rome because of him! Don't you think the conquest of Britannia deserves a reward? Should Valerius approach his uncle for a favor—"

"Berenice!" Simon interrupted with vehemence and pulled away. "You can make your own requests directly. You do not need me as an intermediary. Besides, you should know that these decisions are made based on political debts and have little to do with competence and leadership."

"All the more reason why Claudius should be reminded of the debt Rome owes to the family of Herod Agrippa for peace and prosperity in the region, and you can do that for me. You could even ask Philo to write. Everybody thinks the old scholar is wise. Once before, a great eastern queen sided with Rome and became wife to Caesar. Like Cleopatra, I bring intelligent leadership and cunning. Above all, peace."

"And what does your husband think of all this?"

"My husband?" Berenice laughed, a deep, throaty sound. "Pure politics. My father tried to consolidate lands by marrying me off to his brother. After Marcus died so young—" Her voice caught.

"You still grieve for Marcus."

"He was gentle. But he lacked ambition, rather unlike his older brother, Tiberius Alexander. Why did Marcus have to die?" Berenice repressed the sob rising in her throat and blinked back tears. Then she pulled herself together. "It does no good to bemoan the dead. Life must go on."

For a while they stayed silent, gazing out to sea.

Berenice studied Simon's grim profile. "How is Aurelia?"

"Why do you ask?"

Berenice laughed hollowly. "She didn't look happy when she was at our place in Jerusalem."

"She's fine."

"It's already been six years since the massacre. Do you remember?"

"How could I forget?"

"I was there in the middle of it. Aurelia was magnificent. I dare say she did more to help the wounded and suffering than you did."

"How so?"

"Aurelia was incredible. You didn't see everything that happened. I yelled at her in fury because she tore up my dowry linens to bandage the wounded. I wonder if Aurelia will ever forgive me. I was stupid and selfish. When I yelled at her, she just said she didn't have time to argue and ran right into Tiberius Alexander. Did she tell you about that?"

"I don't think so."

"She tore into him for not caring for his own people, and he said that any Roman who married a Jew was degrading herself. You should have heard her then. She said he was not worthy to untie the sandals on your feet! It was one of the few times I saw Tiberius Alexander grope for words. He was stung." Berenice threw a mischievous smile at Simon. "You do know that he is quite smitten with Aurelia?"

"That cannot be. She hates him."

"That may be true. But he does not hate her. Do you know what Tiberius Alexander told me the next day when I teased him about Aurelia?"

"Of course not."

"He said, 'The Petronia has spunk and mettle. I want to take her to my bed and see what she's really like!'"

The blood rose in Simon's face. "The bastard!" he muttered. Then he turned a piercing gaze on Berenice. "How dare he even think such a thing?"

Berenice laughed. "Men think about that all the time. They're all alike. They want the challenge of conquest. Then they want to gloat over the spoils of their victory." She clasped his arm and gazed into his eyes. "You are no different!"

Simon pulled his arm away, and Berenice moved against him and studied the look on his face. She smiled seductively. "You needn't fear the wrath of my husband. He's in Chalcis, and at his age— Well, let me just say that he's not vigorous and manly like you. And Aurelia need never know."

The night air whipped up a cold wind, and Berenice drew

her shawl around her and shivered against him.

Simon rose quickly and felt like a hapless insect caught in the sticky web of a spider.

There was no gallant way to avoid her company along the path to the palace as she pressed against him in the dark. At the entrance to the Herodian palace, she turned to him and smiled. "I'll see you in a little while. Follow Hyrcana."

Simon said nothing and watched her slender form disappear in the maze of hallways. Hyrcana led him to his door and showed him the bath chamber, where a tub of hot, perfumed water stood ready for him with a stack of fresh towels. When he was dry and dressed in a clean linen tunic, Hyrcana beckoned for him to follow her. Simon pressed a coin into her palm. "Tell your mistress I am too tired from my journey and wish her sweet dreams."

Hyrcana shrugged and said she would wait for him at his door.

Simon fell across his bed and wondered what Berenice truly wanted. He realized he was not indifferent to her charms but was troubled by her intent. Her proposal within hours of the death of her father shocked him, but he was too tired to analyze her motives and even too tired to be able to sleep. Before dawn, he raced to the royal stables, picked their swiftest horse, and galloped through the gate and up the hill on the road to Jerusalem, where he could join a caravan for home. Agrippa's widow would be dismayed at the sudden departure of her guest, but he did not stop to ponder what she might think. He was far more concerned about what Aurelia was thinking at that moment.

What he had heard chased the image of the dead Agrippa from his mind. All these years while they lived in neighboring houses on Philo's estate, Tiberius Alexander had been there, a constant thorn in his side, a constant threat to his tranquility, a constant advocate of Rome versus the Jews. Was Berenice right about him? More important, how did Aurelia feel about him?

Sudden anguish stabbed through Simon's heart. He had left her under a cloud of angry accusations. Why was she so reluctant to obey his wishes? Why was she being so obstinate when he knew what was best for her?

292

✦

DIVERGING PATHS

AGRIPPA'S SUDDEN DEATH BROUGHT UNREST AND uncertainty to Judea. Sensible Jews were grateful for the years of relative peace that Agrippa had ushered in, recognized his role as intermediary between Rome and Jerusalem, and mourned his premature death. Others scrambled to jump into the power vacuum created by his death and openly lobbied for control by rousing dissidents among the population, sometimes while courting Rome at the same time. The High Priest proclaimed he should be the authority over both religious and political matters and fomented unrest and spoke openly against Roman rule. What he and many Jews failed to recognize was that Agrippa's standing with Rome had kept Rome from crushing them.

It was not the most auspicious moment for the celebration of the new temple door, but since the invitations had already been sent out, Berenice insisted that the dedication be held as scheduled on Shavuot and transformed some of the events into a memorial for her father. Shavuot commemorated the giving of the Torah to Moses on Mount Sinai and the harvest of wheat. The deeply spiritual aspect of the Torah was often overshadowed by the festive celebration of the first harvest and initiated several days of feasting not limited to bread. After weeks of mourning, Berenice gave speeches near the temple that honored her father's vision for the temple but were also meant to exhibit her leadership skills and her love for Judea.

In Antioch, Valerius met with his loyal legions in a ceremony of farewell and introduced Gaius Vibius Marsus, the new governor of Syria, who had just arrived from Rome. Given the uncertainties of leadership in Palestine, Marsus asked Valerius to represent Rome at the installation of the new door in Jerusalem. It would be the last official role for Valerius as governor of Syria, and Valerius thought it would be both personally gratifying and politically wise to emphasize Rome's beneficent efforts to protect the sanctity of the temple.

After seeing his wife and son off to Italy, Valerius spent his last day in Antioch with Sedek, Rachel, and their two sons. Rachel served a festive meal in the peristyle, where they discussed the priorities of Emperor Claudius, the hopes for the new governor of Syria, the fate of Palestine, and the changes Valerius would fight for in the Roman senate. At fourteen, Matthaios was quite versed in regional and imperial issues and participated in the discussions while being a watchful and patient big brother to Yohanan, who already exhibited a fiery temperament.

When Valerius asked about their travel plans to the festival in Jerusalem, Sedek said that he had hired a carriage for their travels and offered Valerius a seat, but Valerius explained that his military escort would convey a message of Roman power while remaining non-threatening by their modest number.

Sedek frowned but made no comment.

When Valerius rose to say goodbye late that afternoon, Rachel accompanied him to the stable and reached out to clasp his arm just as he placed his hand on Rex's neck. When he turned to face her, she looked into his eyes and said, "I am not going to Jerusalem with Sedek. Our Yohanan needs constant supervision. He's still too young to travel."

"I was afraid you might not want to go. So, this is—"

She nodded. She still held his arm. He turned toward her and pulled her close as he bent to kiss her lips. It was a soft and tender kiss. Then they looked at each other, realizing it would be the last time they would see each other. He sighed deeply, and the torture of that thought brought tears to his eyes. The sheer agony of leaving her overwhelmed him as he clutched her tighter against his chest and covered her mouth. His second kiss was urgent, almost frantic, as they both felt the agony of loss along with the need to impress this moment forever on their memory to sustain them in the lonely years ahead. When he pulled back to gaze into her eyes, he read her full devotion, her longing for more, her full surrender to the passion they shared, the depth of their mutual love. They hugged each other, wishing they would never have to let go.

"Rachel," he whispered. "I will always love you. No matter what happens, I will come to you if you need me. You need only write to me, and I will come. I can also count on Marsus to check on you and Sedek. I have already told him that he should look out for you and Sedek and be certain you are safe in case of upheavals, unrest, or—the gods forbid—more earthquakes. He understands that we are family, since my sister married your brother. He has promised to watch out for both you and Sedek. Promise me to write to me to tell me how you are."

She closed her eyes and rested her head against his shoulder, holding him tight as though she had the power to change their fates and keep him from leaving. For a long time, they clung to each other.

Behind him, soft grunts and whinnies made it apparent that Rex had decided he was not about to trot out of the stable any time soon. Rex's snuffling and chomping set a measured pace as Valerius stroked Rachel's hair and savored the feel of her in his arms. Closing his eyes, Valerius focused all his attention on this moment that he would treasure forever. Their bond was stronger than tradition, religion, or law. Loving her felt right. Noble.

She reached up to trail her fingers gently through his hair, then along the contours of his cheek and over his lips. She placed her thumb gently near his mouth and murmured, "Once, long ago, you rubbed your thumb at the corner of my mouth like this."

"We were very young then and had no idea what awaited us."

"You shared the wine I brought you. That day in the courtyard of our house in Cyrene. I didn't know then how much sorrow we faced. But I loved you even then." Her eyes reminded him of another time in Galilee. "And now? We may never see each other again." Her thumb drew tender circles over his lips, and he caught her hand and kissed her palm.

When she raised her hands to caress his short-cropped hair, he brushed his lips over her eyelids, cheeks, and mouth, and placed another kiss at the hollow of her neck. When she took a deep quivering breath that was more like a sob, their kisses became hungry and desperate and ardent. She leaned against him, pushing him back against the wooden wall of Rex's stall so that he took a step back, pulling her with him, and tripped on a feed bucket that rolled toward his horse and caused Rex to protest, as they both fell backward into a pile of hay. Rex whinnied again.

They were laughing when Matthaios came running to check on Rex. Matthaios helped his mother up and led the horse out of the stall for Valerius. After they plucked straw from their clothes, Valerius bent to kiss her goodbye, clasped her hand to his heart, and said, "Pray to the god you profess that someday we will be together!"

✦

All the way back to Alexandria, Simon did not think about the fate of Palestine but stewed about how he would confront Aurelia. She had to listen to reason about this sect that put their lives in danger. But this deep worry was not the issue that caused him heart-stabbing anxiety. Had the last years of turmoil created lasting cracks in their relationship? Did she seek solace elsewhere when he was away? What were her feelings for Tiberius Alexander? He pictured her in his arms and felt rising nausea in his throat. The long journey home did not calm his fears. At the last station, he retrieved his own horse, who trotted homeward without commands. With each step closer to Alexandria, his frustrations mounted, and he was about to erupt when he led his horse through the gate to the stables.

He stormed into the house and called Aurelia's name. There was no answer. He wandered from room to room, but no one was home. He realized Aurelia would not have expected him to return so soon and looked over to the alabarch's house. Could she be there? Would he find her in his arms? He rushed out the door and stumbled into Althea, who was weeding the herb garden.

She jumped up, smiling in surprise until she saw his face. "What's the matter?"

"Where is everybody? Where's Aurelia?"

"She went out with the boys. What happened in Jerusalem?"

"Agrippa died before I got there."

Althea made Simon sit down on the garden bench and asked him about the details of his journey. Simon simply said he had arrived too late to save Agrippa, and Althea warned him that it might be too late for him to make peace in his family.

Simon rose in anger and said, "Why? Has she run off with Tiberius Alexander?"

Althea was struck speechless and decided his question did not deserve an answer.

Simon interpreted her silence to mean he had guessed right and spoke in fury. "I will go over there and confront them right now. I want to get to the bottom of this."

Althea blocked his way. "Stop! You have to listen to reason. The role of a blustering, jealous husband does not become you. Tiberius Alexander is not here. Months ago, Claudius appointed him magistrate in southern Egypt to intervene with warring tribes in Thebes."

"So, where is Aurelia? My sons? I demand to know where they are!"

"They should be back soon."

"This new sect?"

"I think so."

"Where do they meet? I'll go get her and bring them home."

Althea studied his face. "That would be most unwise."

"What she does is dangerous. I'll go talk some sense into her."

Althea glared at him. "I need to talk some sense into *you*! The day you left in a hurry for Caesarea, I heard everything you said to her and your dear sons. I heard you yelling at your innocent sons like a madman. Then you slapped them. You stormed around like a raging bull. Aurelia escaped then, and I saw the expression of horror on her face."

For once, Simon had no comment.

"When she returns, you should beg her and your sons for forgiveness." Althea walked to the house but turned back and said, "How would you feel if she told you what you should and should not believe?"

Simon's voice was raw, almost pleading. "You, Althea, have to agree that what she believes is dangerous."

"How soon you seem to forget. I lost a husband and a son because Jew-haters set fire to the synagogue. Not once, but twice. And you? Have you forgotten the massacre? Think about the high price we pay for what we are. Just because we are Jews."

Stunned by the obvious truth of what she said, Simon had no answer.

Althea had not finished. "You and Aurelia need to talk. Let her explain how she feels." When she looked up, she saw Aurelia standing at the door. Althea wondered how much Aurelia had heard. Althea turned back to Simon and sighed. She felt he didn't grasp the seriousness of what she was saying. Trying to reason with him was not achieving anything. In desperation, she said, "If Aurelia were deathly ill, you would try to save her. You would do everything to make her well again. Is that not true?"

"Of course. Is she unwell? Tell me!"

"She is suffering. You have broken her heart. She grieves for the way you treat your sons. In that sense, she is unwell."

"But she is responsible for that. She led them astray. I am trying to keep them safe."

"She grieves for Antonia."

"Does she think I don't? Every day I wake up and feel a heavy stone in my heart that doesn't go away. I miss Antonia so much. But Aurelia didn't keep her safe either."

Althea frowned and looked over at Aurelia. Simon followed her gaze. From the expression on Aurelia's face, he knew that she had heard what he said.

At that moment, Rufus and Alexander burst through the door into the garden and ran up to their father to greet him.

Alexander ran to hug him. "Did you save the king?"

Simon sank to the bench and gravely shook his head. "No, I could not save the king."

Althea rushed to Aurelia to comfort her, but Aurelia remained at the door, holding herself rigid against the frame, her gaze firmly fixed on Simon's face. Her eyes misted, but she did not cry. Rufus and Alexander sensed the tension between them and quietly followed Althea's cue into the house.

✦

It was a grim homecoming. Simon knew that their first words would determine how things stood between them, and he didn't know what to say. He realized he had already said too much. He tried to think of excuses for revealing his resentment at such an awkward moment and fell back on his conviction that Aurelia would have to own up to the reality that she was at fault for letting go of Antonia's hand. For months he had tried to hide his bitterness over Antonia's death, but it had erupted and become part of his frustration and added to his accusation that she did not keep their family safe from harm. Althea often helped smooth things over, but right now she had made things worse with her comments. He looked away from Aurelia's tortured face and studied the way his right hand clasped the bench and tensed and unclenched in a rhythm he was unable to control or stop. He wanted to weep.

He held up his left hand and made a fist, grimacing as he felt the throbbing twinge of the old wound Meidias had left behind. He raised his fist to God in despair and shook it at the sky.

Aurelia remembered other times when he complained that his hoarse cries to God remained unanswered. Slowly, she moved closer to hear what he might say, but he didn't speak. Tears started down his cheek. His exhaustion was tangible in the way his whole frame was shivering, though it was not cold.

As hurt as she felt, to see him in such distress was almost unbearable. She realized that his usual strength had drained out of him, and he needed comforting as much as she. Softly, she said, "Let's get you to bed. I don't think you have slept since you left. Come." She let him lean on her as they walked up the steps to their room, and all she could do was pull his boots off before he collapsed on the bed. She stroked his forehead in the way a mother would tend to a sick child and offered him a cup of water, which he gulped down. He was asleep before he could ask for more, and the cup fell to the floor.

The next morning, he turned to her and watched her sleep.

She must have felt his gaze, for she awoke and noted that his eyes were still bloodshot and set in deep shadows. "Simon?"

He reached for her hand and held it over his heart. "Aurelia, I should not blame you. I miss Antonia so much."

"We all do." Then she thought about the fact that he could never blame her as much as she already blamed herself.

✦

CELEBRATION

TWO WEEKS LATER, THE SHIP THE ALABARCH HIRED backed slowly out of the harbor of Alexandria, turned north into the open sea, and headed for the port of Caesarea. Onboard were many prominent Jews of Alexandria along with their families. Simon had not fully recovered and was reluctant to return to Jerusalem so soon, but Aurelia knew they owed this journey to Sosias, who, from the time of his rescue in childhood, had been a member of the family. Their extended family now included Rhoda, Anna, and Althea. The big shadow that hung over the festive voyage was the death of Agrippa, but most felt the celebration of the temple was a fitting tribute to the king who had done so much toward the temple's restoration to its former glory. Aurelia was relieved that she didn't have to cross the desert again. Rhoda anticipated a reunion with Sosias and Nicanor with more dread than joy.

In Jerusalem, Rhoda wanted to go find Sosias immediately, but Simon warned her that it would be wise for her to wait until he went to the temple to check on him first. With the coming festival, the temple mount would be crowded, and she would not be able to go beyond the court of women. When he came back, he told her it would be easy to see Nicanor, because he was walking around the temple mount after finishing his part of the door, and it was now entirely up to Sosias and his crew of fifty men to secure both sides of the door in place. He did not tell her that he had found Sosias high up on the top of a wall, leaning precariously over the ledge while working on structures that would hold the door in place and allow the door to swing open and close. One of the crew members told him they hoped it would swing. The grinding of metal against metal required great precision and lubricating oil. The heavy pounding of steel bars deep into the earth had yet to be accomplished, and many worried they might not finish in time. Simon was concerned about Sosias. He told Althea he looked haggard and exhausted. Rhoda wanted to know if Simon had been able to see the door, but he explained that the door was still tightly wrapped in the wool cloth that had protected it on its journey south from Sidon.

Alexander Lysimachos, Tiberius Alexander, and Philo hosted the banquet that evening, eulogized Agrippa's legacy, and lavished praise on Nicanor, who sat at the head table with all the dignitaries: kings, princes, governors, the High Priest, members of the Sanhedrin, and Agrippa's family. Princess Berenice gave a moving tribute to her father and made an impassioned plea for Roman support during the period of transition.

After the banquet was over, Nicanor found Rhoda and explained that they would live in Jerusalem. "Since I am already famous for the door, I will get commissions. How many artists will have a part of the temple named for them? Do you know of any other?" He did not stop to ask her opinion, not even to discover her reaction to his plans.

When Rhoda noticed Aurelia and Althea were about to leave, she told him she must leave with them because they were her family now. He nodded and turned in their direction but paid no attention to her revealing remark.

Early the next morning, Simon escorted all of them to

the temple. It was still dark. The door was to be unveiled at sunrise. The hoisting machines, cranes and pulleys, lifts, and counterweights had been removed. The whole temple mount had been swept clean of debris. In front of the gate called Beautiful, a wide walkway was roped off, and behind the new door, Sosias and his crew clasped the ropes to pull off the cloth that kept it protected. One solitary shofar blast announced the first sighting of the sunrise from the Antonian Tower. The crowd stilled in expectation.

At a full blast of trumpets, the new bronze door was unveiled. As the cloth dropped and the bronze door mirrored the sun, the crowd remained still, caught up in the moment.

Suddenly, the spell was broken when a lively trumpet march accompanied a cortège of richly clad officials who arrived to the cheers of the crowd and ascended a platform that had been erected on the temple mount. Guards in the wine-colored livery of the late king with golden crowns of wheat on their chests channeled the crowd in double file through the cleared passageway up to the outer gate so all could see the new door on the other side of the women's court, glistening bright in the early morning sun.

During the High Priest's long speech that he delivered in Aramaic and then Greek, the crowd in front of the gate had thinned, and Aurelia could catch a glimpse of the door. She looked across the women's court and caught her breath. It was so much taller and grander than she had pictured it and shimmered bright gold in the morning light. Four half-circle steps led up to the door, and she could well imagine the adoration people felt as they stepped across the threshold into the holiest areas of the temple, open only to Jewish men. The deep reverence the Jews felt for the holy was something she had learned to appreciate thanks to Simon, and her first experience of the temple in Jerusalem gave her a sense of awe that she had never experienced before.

At that moment, Philo rose to speak, and Aurelia moved

closer to the rostrum so she could hear. Philo started with a story about a man of great courage who had dared defy an emperor because he believed in justice and righteousness and who, at personal peril, had protected the sanctity of the temple. He painted a picture of defiance, steadfastness, integrity, and courage. Then—rather dramatically—he turned and pointed toward Valerius and said, "The man of such valor is here: Publius Petronius, governor of Syria. He is the hero of my story." Philo urged Valerius to his feet and held his arm aloft as thunderous applause erupted in the crowd.

When the cheers faded, Philo turned back to the crowd. His voice was deeper now, more intense. "Publius Petronius did not accomplish this alone. The Most High was with him. The Lord reached out and stilled the Roman weapons. The Lord was with us all."

Philo embraced Valerius as the crowd erupted in cheers, chanting his name.

Aurelia saw that her brother was embarrassed and had not expected to be the center of such an accolade.

Valerius waited for the chants to die down and said, "My friends, as governor of Syria, I bring you a solemn promise from Emperor Claudius to assure you that Rome wants to live in peace."

A man in the crowd yelled out. "How can you promise peace when Rome stands on our necks?" The heckler raised his fist, and several around him chimed in to support him. Aurelia surmised he was one of the zealots who had recently stirred up trouble near Galilee and wondered if Valerius would respond.

Valerius studied the young man, waited until his tirade faltered, then spoke calmly, "For more than two years, twenty thousand Roman soldiers under my command never lifted their swords against you. Every Roman soldier kept his sword sheathed and never harmed you."

The heckler fell silent as the crowd cheered.

"Philo called me the hero of the story, but there are many heroes of this story. All the Roman soldiers who helped keep the peace are heroes of this story. And all of you, the people of Judea, are heroes as well. I am very moved by your devotion to your holy temple. Thanks to all of you, we can celebrate today in peace. Shalom!"

Valerius sat down to roaring applause. It took some time for the High Priest to gain enough silence to intone a chanted prayer. At the end of his prayer, he descended the rostrum and walked through the gate, giving the signal for the trumpeters to play. This was the cue for the Levites to unlatch the door and swing it open.

Nothing happened.

There was a moment of panic. The priests pushed harder against the bronze, and Sosias gestured for a few more Levites to join in, and, after considerable effort, they managed to swing the door open. The stunning reliefs were beautifully detailed on the other side, and the panels reflected the sun in golden splendor.

The first to cross the threshold into the inner court were two priests who carried two large loaves of bread and sheaves of wheat tied together with colorful ribbons to place on the altar. All the priests lifted their voices in a traditional psalm praising the Lord for the harvest.

✦

Suddenly, there was music everywhere, and Aurelia realized that the solemn part of the celebration was over, and the fun was about to begin. Children started playing hide and seek in the porticoes; young people pranced through traditional dances; mimes performed, and gymnasts set up impressive pyramids while acrobats cartwheeled through the temple mount. Dancers circled in iridescent skirts; jugglers and clowns entertained the crowds; food vendors and merchants shouted above the noise to hawk their wares. The temple mount turned into a swirling bazaar. The usual beggars who solicited in the shadow of the temple were already hard at work. For the rest of the day, the festival exploded into a joyful party.

Rhoda took Anna by the hand and told Aurelia she was going in search of Sosias. Aurelia insisted on going with her until Simon shook his head. "Festival or no festival, the temple itself is still restricted to Jews."

Aurelia stayed outside and watched the rest of her family enter.

✦

It didn't take long for Rhoda to notice Nicanor, who was surrounded by a group of admirers asking questions about the process of creating the door. With Anna at her side, Rhoda made her way up to the steps to look for Sosias and finally saw him threading his way through the crowd. She was shocked to see how tired and worn he looked. But his face lit up with surprise and joy when he saw her. Sweaty and grimy and dressed in a torn and dirty tunic, he started to apologize when she cut him off and said, "I've missed you so much. Here is Anna. I wrote to you about her rescue."

Sosias stooped to greet Anna, but Rhoda had to remind him that Anna was deaf.

At that moment, Nicanor arrived, grasped her arm possessively, and took over the conversation. Althea felt the tension rise between them and took Anna aside to wait.

Nicanor said, "Now that the ceremony is over, we can go celebrate. Of course, I'll have to stop now and then and greet people who are excited to meet me."

Rhoda looked from Sosias to Nicanor and said, "You go ahead and celebrate. I want to talk to Sosias."

"Of course. He had the gritty part of the job. I'm sure he's glad it's done."

Rhoda looked straight at Sosias and smiled. "He did a magnificent job. I don't see how you managed to lift such a huge door—"

Nicanor interrupted, "You should know that I've arranged for us to meet with the High Priest later this afternoon. He promised to give us his blessing. Last night when I saw you were here, I thought we should go ahead with the wedding. And what better place than here in Jerusalem at the temple? Your mother will be delighted."

Stunned, Rhoda asked, "What wedding?"

"Our wedding."

"I have not agreed to a wedding."

"It was arranged some time ago." Nicanor fumbled through the folds of his robe and pulled out a document. "Here is the marriage contract signed by your uncle and your mother, and by both of us. See!" He held it out to prove it.

Rhoda shook her head vigorously. "That was my mother's doing. You have been away for more than four years. It is no longer valid."

"It's a binding legal contract."

"Not anymore. My mother disowned me. She can no longer sign for me." She gestured for Althea to join her. "She was there and witnessed it all."

Althea nodded. "It is true what she says. Her mother has disowned her. She has no authority over her."

For the first time, Nicanor seemed to hesitate. He confronted Sosias. "This is your doing." When Sosias didn't respond to his accusation, he turned back to Rhoda and demanded to know why she hadn't told him last night when they talked. He shook the contract in her face.

She stepped back and said simply, "You talked. All I did was listen." She took Anna's hand. "Last night I wanted to tell you about Anna, but you didn't give me the chance. This is Anna." She gently swept the hair out of Anna's eyes and smiled down at her. "She is my daughter."

Speechless, Nicanor kept looking from Rhoda to Sosias, then down at Anna. Finally, he glared at Sosias. "You didn't tell me you had a daughter."

Sosias smiled at Rhoda but said nothing.

Furious now, Nicanor tore the marriage contract in two, threw it at her feet, and stormed away without greeting the people who were eager to meet the famous artist of the door.

Trembling with relief, Rhoda rushed into Sosias's arms. He tried to warn her that he was dirty, and she would get messy. But she did not care.

+

Aurelia was getting tired of waiting for her family to emerge from the temple and peeked through the gate to see if she could see Althea and Rhoda. Suddenly, Tiberius Alexander grabbed her arm and asked for Simon. Aurelia started for the gate, but Tiberius Alexander held her back. "You can't go in there. I'll go find him. Philo collapsed from the heat. We need Simon."

Feeling helpless, Aurelia looked over to the platform where Philo had been sitting in the sun during the heat of the day. She felt faint and dizzy herself and sat down on the steps and worried about Philo. She wanted to defy the rules and simply walk into the women's court as though she belonged there.

+

When the official ceremony was over, the family gathered for a quiet meal in the rooftop garden of Sedek's house. The boys kept running to the parapet to look down the street to see if Simon was coming because Sedek refused to eat until they had news of Philo. Alexander started climbing the trellis to pick clusters of grapes, but Aurelia warned that they were not ripe yet. When Simon finally arrived and reassured every-one that Philo was recovering, Rufus and Alexander rushed to the table, but Sedek insisted on long prayers of thanksgiving before anyone could eat.

At dinner, Simon spoke about the first time he had come into Sedek's house and was reunited with his sister after his long and desperate search for Rachel. The children were fascinated and wanted to know more about how Sedek had met their Aunt Rachel. Sedek told how he had found Rachel at the slave auction in Alexandria, and Valerius was so affected by his account that he got up and went over to the parapet to look out toward the temple, where the music and dancing continued, muted now and therefore more pleasant. Aurelia guessed Valerius had tears in his eyes, remembering how close they had all come to losing Rachel. She went to stand quietly beside Valerius and clasped his arm to feel his comforting presence and to comfort.

She asked him quietly if he had been able to make peace with Simon. "You used to be such close friends. Like brothers."

"Indeed. And like brothers we fight."

Aurelia persisted. "Is there a way you could find your way back to friendship? Simon is too stubborn and too proud to make the first move."

"Simon is as hard as flint. There is fire if you rub him the wrong way."

"True. He misses your friendship and mourns."

"I already feel how much I'll miss you. I leave tomorrow for Rome. Vitellia and Lucius are already there, waiting for me. I have my own obligations to tend to."

"All the more reason to revive your friendship with Simon. You may never see each other again. Ever since Agrippa's sudden death, I am keenly aware of how short our lives are. On a day like this when we all are supposed to celebrate, I think a renewed friendship between you and Simon would be beneficial for both of you. For all of us."

When Valerius remained silent, Aurelia said, "The man with the most courage makes the first move. You are more flexible, less stubborn. What does it really cost you?" A sob rose in her throat, and her voice trembled. "If you cannot do this for him, do it for me. Please!"

Valerius smiled. "For your sake, I will seek Simon out before I leave and see what I can do. I have great respect for Simon. His devotion to saving lives was a daily inspiration as I spent more than two years trying to keep peace."

"Why not tell him that? I know he suffers when he thinks your friendship is broken. He still loves you. He is a man who loves deeply."

"I'm not sure he will listen. In the meantime, there is a far more urgent matter that you need to tend to." He searched her eyes to assess if she understood his meaning.

She averted her eyes.

Valerius persisted. "Since you expect me to take the first step, maybe you need to make the first step with Simon as well. He is afraid for you. He genuinely believes that you are courting disaster with this new religion. I have heard that some followers of Yeshua have been imprisoned, some put to death by stoning, and some executed. And Rome will not be on your side. There is even the possibility that Rome will start persecutions. You should be cautious. Right now, we seem to have a sensible emperor. That can change in an instant. An emperor could come along who is worse than Caligula."

She shuddered in his arms as he clasped her close and kissed her on both cheeks. "I will miss you, little sister."

✦

When Sosias arrived with Rhoda at his side and Anna in his arms, everyone erupted in spontaneous applause. Sosias wore a splendid white tunic trimmed with royal blue and looked boyish and dashing with his freshly trimmed beard and unruly blond hair. All three had big smiles on their faces. Althea beamed with maternal pride.

Simon proposed a toast to the couple. After an enthusiastic salute all around, Simon turned to Sosias and expressed his sympathy that Nicanor had received all the glory and Sosias had hardly been mentioned.

Sosias was quick to respond. "It's as it should be. The artist should be celebrated. The engineer works behind the scenes to make everything function properly, so you don't have to think about the way the door is hung and whether it's secure. Besides," he looked over at Rhoda, "I won the grand prize."

Valerius cheered him with his wine. "How did you convince Nicanor? When I saw him, he was very determined and would tolerate no rival. Least of all you."

"I didn't say a word."

"That's true." Rhoda was happy to fill in the details and confessed that she had no idea Nicanor would jump to the conclusions he did. "It all worked out in our favor."

Valerius asked, "Is Anna now legally your daughter by adoption?"

"Not quite. The final judgment is pending."

Valerius warned them to be cautious. "Be sure to get all the proper forms signed and stamped. Otherwise, your mother could sell her into slavery again and you would have no legal recourse. I suggest you get a Roman administrator to sign your documents."

At the mention of slavery, Simon launched into an earnest discussion about the slave trade and the abduction of Jewish children who had no protection from the Roman legal system and raised his wine goblet to Valerius in a challenge. "When you argue for justice in the senate, don't forget the slaves."

Valerius lifted his wine in response. "I share your concern and will try to get laws through the senate. But the power of the senate is limited. The power of one senator? Negligible. Unfortunately, we were not able to find Hallas and stop his illegal slave trade along the coast."

Sosias made a sweeping gesture with both hands. "Ah!

There's where engineering can change everything! We need to make better machines to do the labor slaves do. My dream is to create a village where we build labor-saving devices to do the work. We will all have to work together, but in my village, there will be no slaves."

"You would have to invent a lot of new devices to do that." Rhoda was worried that it would be an impossible task.

Sosias pointed out that Heron of Alexandria had already invented many of the machines he was thinking of. He had just not seen how practical they could be.

Rufus applauded. "A most noble dream."

Simon shook his head. "But just a dream. Today, we should focus on the magnificent new door!" He lifted his goblet in a toast. "To the new bronze door!"

They echoed his toast in unison.

Simon was in a reflective mood. "A door represents an entrance into something different, a new beginning. In the case of the temple, an entrance onto hallowed ground, into a sacred place. It is a transition from our everyday life into a totally different experience. The door provides a threshold, a boundary where two realities meet. It provides a point of passage into another world."

Aurelia was impressed that he had given it so much thought but knew he had not considered the way she felt about the door. "The door also functions to shut others out. I can look through the iron grill of the Beautiful Gate, but I cannot even step into the court of women. And the new bronze door stops all but men. And they must all be Jews. And beyond that, yet more exclusions. What about believing in a God who welcomes all within the fold, who opens wide all doors rather than shuts people out?"

Valerius nodded approval of his sister's remarks.

It was Rufus who spoke up with an eloquence that was unusual for his young age. "Today, for the first time, I walked through the gate and toward the door that was now open, and

I could see the altar and, in the background, the sacred curtain that shields the holy of holies, and I felt wonder. I felt, as Father says, that I was walking into another world when I crossed the threshold, a world where everything beyond the door was mysterious. But then I looked back through the gate and saw the temple guard. How can they exclude my mother?"

Simon was about to say that his son was too young to understand, but one look at Aurelia's face stopped him. It was not the time or place to discuss their differences.

Aurelia sensed Simon might turn the focus of their discussion away from the essence of the new door and turned to Sedek. "Sedek, you are the visionary among us, our guide to the deeper meaning of what we have witnessed. What do you think?"

Sedek cleared his throat and lifted his eyes to the heavens. "Today is the moment to proclaim that all of creation should sing praises to the Most High. We see it in the splendor of the sunrise which needs no gold to reflect the glory of the Lord. We see it in the smallest seed that explodes with life more powerful than the strongest bronze. We see it in the movements of the stars that chart infinite pathways through the doors of the heavens."

✦

THE TEMPLE

As Aurelia started downstairs, she heard Simon's voice raised in anger. She caught snatches of old arguments and realized that both Alexander and Rufus were upset that their mother was not allowed to get close to the new door. She fled back to the terrace. As the skies darkened, the Levites were beginning to circle around the temple to light huge torches. As she watched, the temple emerged white and glowing with a magical brilliance all its own. From the perspective of Sedek's terrace, the temple appeared grander, more mysterious, and somehow untethered from the earth. She could see the lofty columns that enclosed the Portico of Solomon and could easily imagine Yeshua with his disciples there. She was deeply moved to see places where Yeshua had proclaimed his teaching. She wondered if she would find the right words to convey the message she treasured in her heart.

Could she explain her feelings without making Simon angry again? The distance between them had grown, and though it was mostly about her allegiance to the new faith, it was deeper and more troubling. Rufus's words echoed in her mind. She didn't really care about entering the women's court, but she cared deeply that religion was splitting their family apart. She longed for the eloquence and wisdom of Sedek to explain the depth of her resolve.

She heard footsteps behind her. Simon came up to the terrace and gazed out at the temple.

After a long silence, he said, "To be here in Jerusalem—the holy city—to feel the awe. And this view of the temple. Is it not magnificent?" He turned to study his wife's face in the dim light. "Now that you have witnessed this festival, how do you feel?"

"I agree with you. The temple is magnificent. It is a holy place."

Simon looked relieved and smiled. He clasped her hand in his and gently nudged her chin around to face him. "My love, I'm so glad you feel that way."

She stroked his hand as pleased by his conciliatory tone as by his endearment. "You heard what Rufus said tonight. He is awed by the experience of the temple. You saw that. He is not rejecting what you stand for. Rather he wants to share the experience with me and with others."

Simon sighed. He tried to keep his voice even, but Aurelia could tell right away that he was dismayed. "If you and Rufus made all the rules, you would open the temple up to everyone. You would even let Roman soldiers walk on holy ground!"

"A Roman general you know and two legions risked their lives to save the temple from Caligula. How can you forget that?"

"But—"

"Have you spoken to my brother?"

"Not yet."

"You are so terribly wrong not to acknowledge what Valerius did. He spent more than two years opposing Caligula at the risk of his life. To save your temple. To save your people."

When Simon did not acknowledge that fact, she put her fist against his chest and pushed against him, emphasizing her words. "You owe so much to Valerius. Have you ever told him that? From what I know, you quarreled with him over Rachel. You never showed gratitude for what he did. Philo did this morning. Publicly. But not you!" She felt tears threaten and didn't want him to clasp her in his arms and focus on consoling her. Instead, she cleared her throat to steady her voice to speak with conviction and strength. "Your best friend! My brother risked his life for you and for your people! And you haven't spoken a kind word to him to thank him for the sacrifices he made to save your temple."

She pulled her hand away.

"Aurelia, I'll talk to him. But remember there is a fundamental difference between us. I had to take the position that we must strive to save our people. The greater good requires saving as many lives as possible. That sometimes means one person is sacrificed to save many. In this case it meant Valerius. It is a terrible choice. In a choice between two evils, you choose the lesser evil. Fortunately, it didn't come to that."

"Your arguments sound logical to you, but they are heartless."

"I'm sorry, Aurelia."

"I'm sorry as well."

"I came back up here to tell you how much I admire you, how much I love you. I even came up here to make a suggestion that you will probably reject without giving it a thought."

"You speak in riddles. I cannot reject or accept something without knowing what you are talking about."

"Aurelia," he took her hand again, "you could be accepted as a Jew if you wish and become one of us, then you could enter the women's court and you would not feel excluded."

Surprised by his unexpected offer, she asked, "You believe I must become a Jew to be loved by God?"

"I thought you would want to belong."

"I agree with Rufus. If God is the creator of all, why should anyone be excluded?

"There are traditions."

"Traditions imposed by men or by God?"

"Teachings from the Torah we uphold as sacred."

"It seems to me that for ages men have dictated what our conception of God should be. And then came a rabbi who dared to say that God is not limited to one group alone." She saw him stiffen, and added, "Surely, the way to God is not through laws that keep people out. The door should be wide open to welcome people. Don't you agree?"

"I accept what the High Priest and the scriptures say."

"Ah, Simon, you did not answer my question. Is God not great enough to include all of his creation?"

"I don't know."

"Do you think God is limited to one place?"

He did not answer.

"Let me ask my question another way. Is there a God just for Jews and another God for all the rest of us?"

"There is only one God. You've heard the Shema: "Hear, O Israel: the Lord is our God, the Lord is one."

"It's a beautiful prayer but why is it addressed to Israel and not to the whole world?"

"I don't know. Most likely God thought Israel was not listening enough. Either that or God believes that Israel was the only one willing to listen."

"But surely God cares about more than just Israel?"

"But the heart of Israel is right here. Right in front of us. In Jerusalem."

"Only in Jerusalem? Surely, God is far greater than the temple? Sedek believes in Yeshua and is a fervent Jew. He sees no contradiction in that."

"Sedek is a visionary, a mystic."

Aurelia smiled. "You are as well. You seek to understand the mysteries of the human body. Thanks to you, I have learned so much about what you believe and treasure. It is from you that I have learned that God is far greater than the temple.

Remember your deep conversation with Gamaliel? The awe Rufus talked about tonight. I know you believe that too."

"I do."

"That's why I was so moved to find a group of people in Alexandria who believe in a loving God who welcomes all people, not just Jews. The healing message that Yeshua preached right there in Solomon's Portico does not diminish the power of God but expands it to embrace everyone, including me."

"I fear for you. For our sons. Just today the High Priest warned me. He said tensions are high between the two groups. The Sanhedrin threatens persecutions."

"Why? What are they so afraid of?"

"I don't think they are afraid. But they must uphold the sacred laws."

"Isn't it just as dangerous to be a Jew? Have you forgotten the fire and the horrible massacre in Alexandria? Have you forgotten Meidias and those who followed him in his war on Jews?"

Simon looked at her sharply. "I can never forget what Meidias did. You know that."

"The message I heard from Yeshua's followers is that we must learn to forgive. If we don't, the burden we carry becomes too heavy. You still carry a heavy burden."

Simon drew a deep, quivering breath and did not answer.

Aurelia realized anew how deeply wounded he was. He was still fighting for his people. He was still seeing any change as a threat, even a betrayal. What she experienced as liberating, he found ominous, dangerous, and threatening.

Finally, he said, "You are leading our sons into danger. I am afraid."

Stunned, Aurelia turned and looked at him sharply. Simon's features were in shadow, but she heard the anguish in his voice, the raw suffering, and she felt the need to comfort. She said, "We can be strong together."

"You are taking the wrong path."

"How can a faith that preaches love be wrong?"

He drew her closer and cradled her in his arms. She felt the comforting warmth of his arms around her, the gentle caresses of his fingers through her hair and along her cheek, the welcome tickle of his beard on her neck as he placed a possessive kiss on her lips. She wanted him, longed for his passionate embrace, but she also felt he should ponder the message of love she found in her new faith. "You did not answer my question."

"You spoke of love. I'm just agreeing with you."

"Do you remember our wedding night? You taught me the love poem from the *Song of Solomon*. You opened my mind to a different concept of love that makes Venus look like a failed goddess who demotes love into a game of lust and conquest. The message I hear in Yeshua's teaching is a message of a deeper kind of love."

"I don't understand how your Yeshua, a Jew, can reject what Jews stand for."

"Did he?"

"Did he what?"

"Did he reject them, or did they reject him?"

"I don't know."

"I think you know. More than anyone, you know the truth. You witnessed his rejection. You saw him crucified. You wanted to save him. You were upset. You are still upset about it because you honor life. God-given life. I think you would like what Yeshua teaches."

"How can you say that?"

"Like you, Yeshua devoted his life to the sick and the weak. You live his message."

Simon flinched. "His message creates discord. You refuse to understand how dangerous it is." He grabbed her shoulders and shook her to emphasize his concern. "I want to keep you and the boys safe."

She shrugged away from his grasp and realized she had

only managed to frustrate him not convince him. "I know you want to protect us. I am grateful for your love and protection. Does our safety depend on which god we believe in?"

"Perhaps it does. The Sanhedrin wants to persecute those who go astray and follow your Yeshua. Life is precious. I have sworn a sacred oath to do no harm. To heal. To save lives. Killing in the name of God is wrong."

"We agree, Simon. So why do you oppose us?" Aurelia clasped his arm.

"I fear the destruction that will be unleashed in the name of Yeshua."

"Do you really believe that could happen? No one should kill another because of what they believe."

"I don't agree with them, but I cannot stop them. I want to keep you from harm. I fear for our sons."

"When you seek to heal patients, do you stop and ask if they are Jews or what they believe or where they come from? You know you don't because you honor the higher calling of your profession. In the same way, Yeshua proclaimed that his message is open to all. Come with me to hear the message before you push me and your sons away from you."

"The last thing I want to do is push you away." He reached out to hold her closer to his chest and spoke in a pleading tone, "What do you want me to do?"

She stepped away from him and looked toward the temple. For a moment she was silent, and he waited. When she turned to look at him, he looked stricken like one of their sons when he was about to be punished. "You must forget all the hate you endured and focus on your family who loves you. Be open with our sons and let them find their own way. Promise me to make peace with our sons." She reached for his hands. "Will you promise me that?"

"I want peace between us."

"Talk to them. Listen to them. They love you deeply. Do you even know what they want to be when they grow up?"

"They are too young to know."

"That may be true. But you knew when you were younger than they are. Rufus wants to be a healer."

"Like Yeshua?"

"No. Like you."

"How do you know this? He hasn't told me." Simon turned to her, and she saw both wonder and pleasure brighten his face.

"He told you many times, but you didn't hear him. What kind of questions does he ask at the table on the nights when you come home in time for dinner? Where does he go on the days you are in the operating room? Do you even know he is there? Cydias tells me that he often discusses symptoms with him, and that some day he will be a fine physician. He wants to follow in your footsteps."

Simon's gaze was already far away. He looked beyond the temple to a distant horizon where he could see his son becoming the head physician at the Museion. He smiled.

Aurelia decided it was not the moment to tell him that Alexander practiced rhetoric and oratory and hoped to be a persuasive preacher of a new message of hope.

A SIMPLE LESSON

AT NIGHT, SEDEK IGNORED THE USUAL COMMOTION in his household and escaped to a small balcony above the terrace where he often spent the night lying on cushions so he could gaze at the firmament and follow the journeys of the planets. It had been a long day, and he was afraid he would nod off before he finished his prayers. Somewhere in the hills, someone started playing a flute. The plaintive sound was both sweet and haunting. A solitary prayer lifted to the heavens. Sedek closed his eyes and whispered a blessing for the holy city. Jerusalem meant the city of peace. Yet, during the long celebration of Shavuot, he had spoken to the High Priest and members of the Sanhedrin and the great scholars of the Torah and learned that conflict was about to engulf Jerusalem and become violent. In vain, he tried to persuade them that Jews and the new sect could worship the same God in harmony and peace. Zealots were also roaming the hills around Jerusalem, preaching violence and sedition. Sedek prayed fervently for peace.

Sedek heard footsteps and opened his eyes to see Rufus standing at the edge of the steps.

"Rufus, you should be asleep."

"I know. I couldn't sleep. I have too many questions to be able to sleep."

"Come. Lie down beside me and look up into the sky. Maybe you will find some answers when you do."

"Really? Is that what you do?"

"Looking up always gives me new perspective. What are your questions?"

"Does God need a temple or do we?"

"That's a very good question. What do you think?"

"Mother says you are the wisest man she knows."

"Rufus, let me tell you a secret. Most of the answers that are meaningful we find within ourselves. I cannot tell you what to think."

After a moment of silence, Rufus said, "I don't think God needs the temple. He created the whole world and the heavens. Maybe *we* need the temple."

"That's a valid answer." There was a long silence between them. "Do you have more questions?"

"Are things holy in themselves? Or do we make them holy?"

"I think we make things holy by how we give meaning to them."

"So, something could be holy to one person and not necessarily to another?"

"I believe so."

"So, a Roman sees Jupiter as all-powerful, but we don't."

"You could say that. That can be true for some Romans."

"And my mother can see Yeshua differently than my father?"

"True." Sedek clutched Rufus's hand to his chest.

Rufus said, "Who is right?"

"Ah, Rufus. Perhaps they are both right."

"How could both be right?"

"Both Yeshua and the Torah agree about a simple lesson: 'We must love the Lord our God with all our hearts and with all our souls and with all our might. These words must be written on our hearts.'"

Rufus looked puzzled. Then he said, "I am not sure what that means."

Sedek smiled and let him think about it for a while before he asked, "Did Yeshua show us ways to love God?"

Rufus said, "Maybe loving God means to be like the good Samaritan who helped the poor wounded fellow by the side of the road."

"Right. We must all find our own way to love God."

"But I don't find that so simple."

"True. Loving God cannot be defined by one answer. There are many ways to love God."

"I heard them argue tonight. Mother and Father don't agree."

"And this upsets you?"

"Yes. Because Father believes it is dangerous to believe what Yeshua preaches, and that makes no sense to me."

"Not long ago, thousands were murdered in Alexandria just because they were Jews. Some day, it is quite possible, that thousands will be murdered because they are Christians."

"That's very scary. Is that what God wants?"

"No. God wants us to live in peace and love one another. Remember Jews and Christians believe a lot of the same things. Yeshua did not renounce his heritage. He showed us aspects about God that we often forget. God's love is infinite. God wants our hearts, not rigid rules that separate us, but love and kindness that bring us together."

Rufus sighed. "Do you think we will come together in peace?"

"I don't know, Rufus. We may have to be brave."

"Brave like my Uncle Valerius?"

"Maybe. I don't know."

They gazed heavenward for a while. Then Rufus asked, "Why are there so many stars? What are they doing up there?"

"I don't know. I think that is God's secret."

"They are high in the sky, even higher than the tallest mountain."

"You are right, Rufus. They are far, far away. We cannot touch them, yet we can see them with our eyes. But it is what we cannot see that is the greatest mystery of all."

Sedek squeezed Rufus's hand. "You should go get some sleep. It's been a very long day."

THE GREEN SAPLING

AS HE PACKED HIS THINGS, VALERIUS WONDERED
when he would see his sister again and worried about her.
He knew Aurelia was strong, but underneath her determination and courage, he sensed a certain fatigue, maybe even vul-
nerability. She was an amazing mother. He smiled when he
thought about his nephews Rufus and Alexander and already
missed their intelligent questions and their interest in what he
was going to do in Rome. He didn't know how he felt about his
new duties in the senate. He would miss the soldiers and their
light-hearted camaraderie, their love of games and jokes, and
their gruff respect for their officers. He would not miss long
treks in the heat on horseback when every muscle in his body
ached and his feet were too swollen to take his boots off.

He had promised Aurelia he would talk to Simon. Could he
say goodbye to his old friend without making things worse?
He thought back to their school days together and relived
moments when their bond was as solid as the bronze in the
new door. They used to wrestle each other with fierce determination to win, but as soon as a third person threatened,
they were loyal in their defense of each other. No, he decided,

their friendship was not so much like bronze, but more fragile, like a tree that needed watering and tending if it were to survive. His experience with trees was that no matter how gnarled and dead it looked, you could always hope to revive the green sapling within. Had they both been unwilling to do that? Had the years of conflict caused by Caligula uprooted their ability to nurture their friendship?

He would have to focus on Simon's good traits and forget how he had treated Rachel. He asked his nephew where Simon was, and Rufus showed him to Sedek's large sitting room and innocently provided the information that Sedek had married Rachel in this very room. Since Rufus was very fond of his Aunt Rachel, he thought Valerius would be pleased to know that.

Valerius stood at the door and took a deep breath. "How is Philo?"

Simon looked up, startled. "Recovering. I'll go check on him in a moment. When I left, he was already dictating letters. He's one of my most difficult patients. He thinks he's personally responsible for all Jews across Egypt and Judea and beyond."

"You are equally obsessed with saving Jews, even if it means you demean your sister."

"It was for a great cause. And it worked. You retreated. I succeeded."

"Not true." Valerius entered the room and shut the door. "You succeeded in humiliating her. She didn't deserve that. Nobody does."

"You pulled your troops back right after we left."

"I withdrew the troops because the Jews refused to finish the fall harvest. Winter was coming. The Jews and my army would have starved. It had nothing to do with Rachel."

Simon stood up. "I don't believe that." His stance seemed belligerent.

Valerius took a step back and said, "It makes no difference

to me what you believe. But how you treat your sister makes a difference to me. Rachel deserves better, and you know it. I miss the days when we were best friends; when we wrestled each other and genuinely hoped that we would never do each other harm. I grieve for the love we once had for each other."

Simon stood stolid and remained silent.

Valerius hesitated a moment, hoping their friendship wouldn't end on such a sour note. Slowly, he turned to go and reached the door before Simon spoke.

"Is this how you want our friendship to end? We are still family."

Valerius asked, "Are we? I was not going to bring up Aurelia, but I know enough to ask if you are truly willing to lose Aurelia and your sons."

"No. Losing your friendship is more than enough."

"Then do something about it."

Simon's combative posture of a moment ago seemed to dissolve, leaving him limp and uncertain. He looked around the room, examined the design in Sedek's fine carpet, and cleared his throat. Finally, he asked, "Are you headed back to Antioch?"

"No. Tomorrow, I leave for Ptolemais. From there I sail to Rome."

There was a sharp knock on the door.

"That's my reminder to go check on Philo." Simon approached Valerius and held out his hand. *"Ave et vale."*

Valerius took his hand and then clasped him by the shoulders. "You may have the most noble intentions, but you hurt the people who love you most." He turned to open the door as Sedek's guard was just about to knock again.

The guard held out a sealed note to Valerius. "Quintus was just here and insisted you get this right away."

"Quintus? Is he still here?" Valerius was poised to run after him.

"No. He was in a hurry. But he said the message is urgent."

Valerius ripped the message open and froze. His face went chalk-white before he found his voice. "Jamnia!" He clutched the door frame.

"What is it?" Simon looked at him in alarm. He took his arm. "Let's go sit down." He led Valerius to a chair.

Valerius was jolted by a sudden stab of fear. His heart was racing. He felt dizzy. "I—I forgot that Jamnia is so close to Jerusalem."

Simon poured some water for him and waited.

Valerius stared down at the water. His hand was unsteady. "I should have been more alert to the danger. I didn't even think—"

"What danger?"

"He wants revenge."

"Who?"

"Herennius Capito." Valerius rubbed his hand over his eyes as though he was just awakening. "I was a fool," he mumbled. "I should have listened to Manius."

Simon encouraged him to continue. "Herennius Capito?"

Valerius swallowed a sip of water. "He's the commander of the Roman garrison at Jamnia and the most powerful and fervent Jew-hater I know. Worse than Meidias. Because he has power. Roman power. He is the reason why I spent two years on the road with two legions trying to keep peace all the way from Antioch to Galilee. He incited rebels and hoodlums to desecrate an altar in Jamnia dedicated to the emperor, blamed it all on the Jews, and wrote fiery descriptions to Caligula to inflame revenge against Jews. The idea of a statue in the temple was born."

Simon was speechless.

Valerius said, "Of course, the incident in Jamnia was the official reason. Caligula also had a personal vendetta against you and Aurelia."

"Aurelia! I know Caligula blamed me for keeping Tiberius alive. But Aurelia?"

Valerius had not anticipated that Simon did not know and

was caught off guard. It was too late to take back what he had said. His throat tightened when he suddenly understood why Aurelia would not have told him. Still, he had no choice. He would have to explain. "Caligula tried to molest her. By chance, Tiberius intervened. Aurelia told me. Caligula never forgot her forceful rejection. He was furious."

Simon rose and stormed through the room. "She never told me."

"Aurelia is wise. And brave. What would you have done if you had known then?"

Simon was beginning to grasp the extent of evil that had surrounded them. "And he appointed you governor of Syria to carry out the mission because you are her brother!"

"Agrippa thought so. He said Caligula was out to get all three of us. Ha! He said Agrippa called us the three boars he would catch in his net. I'm just glad it's over."

"Except, it's not over."

"Right. Herennius Capito is trying to find me. Capito claimed he had direct orders from Caligula to take over the legions and march on Jerusalem. I ordered his arrest. They couldn't find him. That night, he tried to murder me while I slept. I locked him up and stupidly allowed him to return with his troops to Jamnia under the threat that any report of misdeeds would deprive him of office for life."

"You should have locked him up and put him on trial for attempted murder."

"I agree. But he had already spread lies among my troops that he had direct orders from Caligula to take over the legions and get the statue to Jerusalem. He was about to get the troops all riled up to march on Jerusalem—the very thing I had been trying to avoid. I wanted to get him out of there before he did more damage. Manius warned me. He told me that Capito would never forget that I humiliated him in front of his men by demoting him and ordering him back to Jamnia. I should have listened to Manius." Valerius grimaced. "I doubt you have true understanding of how hard it is to keep two legions from fighting when that is exactly what they've been trained to do. And here I was holding them back. I couldn't let Capito's rage take over and lead us to disaster. Not after all the effort and energy I'd used up to keep that from happening. I let him go." Valerius paced around the room, picked up an elegant ceramic vase and plopped it back on the table.

Simon gazed uneasily as the vase rocked back and forth and finally righted itself.

Valerius circled back to stand right in front of Simon. "Quintus was there. He agreed with Manius. I have already dismissed my military escort. They left for Antioch this afternoon. Only Quintus is traveling with me. So, my failure to deal with Capito has put him in danger too. We could easily become victims of an ambush on the road. In some ways, Capito is more devious than Caligula was. I need to go take care of this."

Simon grabbed his arm. "What are you planning to do? If you appear on the street, everybody will know who you are. You, in your Roman military outfit! Everybody saw you this morning at the ceremony. And Capito is looking for you."

"True."

"Don't go out on the streets. Unless—"

"Unless what?"

"Unless you dress like a Jew."

Valerius laughed and recognized Simon's boyish grin he remembered from years ago.

Simon studied him critically. "You laugh, but it's not such a bad idea. The problem is you would still walk and act like a Roman."

"What do you mean?"

"You have that Roman swagger, a certain way to walk that shows your—your cockiness."

"I do not!"

"But you do. You always did. Even when you were seventeen."

They both burst out laughing, but Valerius sobered quickly.

Simon warned, "You'll be recognized immediately. I need to go check on Philo. Is there anything I can do to help? I could talk to Agrippa's men."

"You could ask Tiberius Alexander. He might be able to help. Ask him if he has any news about Herennius Capito."

Simon made a wry face.

"I know you and Tiberius Alexander have had your differences."

"How can he help? He has authority in Egypt. Not here."

"It hasn't been announced yet, but Claudius has just appointed him prefect of Palestine. He'll be reporting to the governor of Syria—my successor."

Simon looked like he had just swallowed vinegar when he expected wine. "Tiberius Alexander! Are you sure?"

"As governor, I get appointment information directly from the emperor. I've talked with Tiberius Alexander about it. I'm sure."

"Why didn't they announce it at the ceremony today?"

"Because Berenice wants to succeed her father. She is forcing Tiberius Alexander to wait until she gets an answer from Claudius about her petition to become queen."

"Does she have a chance?"

"Probably not. But she sees herself as the next Cleopatra. Tiberius Alexander tells me that she makes quite a case for herself. But I think he will be the one forced to deal with Herennius Capito. In any event, I would think this is good news for the Jews."

Simon clasped his arm. "In the end, *you* were good news for the Jews."

Valerius studied Simon's face. "I hoped you would be pleased about the appointment. I think Claudius is trying to be sensitive to Jewish concerns. That's why he appointed Tiberius Alexander."

At the door, Simon picked up his medical bag. "I do not like him much. I don't trust Tiberius Alexander. It's personal."

"I know."

"I'll talk to him. Are you at least armed? Capito and his goons are out looking for you. Why don't you stay here until we know more." He was out the door before Valerius could protest.

"Is Simon in danger?" Aurelia stood on the bottom step and studied her brother's face for reassurance and found none.

"No, I am." Valerius started up the stairs. "Come with me. I'll explain while I put on my armor."

PHILO

SIMON SET OUT FOR THE HERODIAN PALACE AND made a wide circle around drunks and diners who populated the taverns along the street of goldsmiths and jewelers. He was on the lookout for Roman soldiers, but they usually gathered in the lower parts of the city where the beer and the women were cheaper. He wondered how many of Capito's soldiers had been sent out on a mission to ferret out Valerius's whereabouts and felt relieved when he saw no soldiers about. He was afraid that any visit with Tiberius Alexander would be confrontational, and he realized he had to keep calm and focus on Valerius's safety and not let personal feelings get in the way. His stubborn fearlessness in the face of threats and conflicts had usually stood him in good stead, but that very strength could cause trouble in his search for help.

Would Tiberius Alexander be their ally or their enemy? Was it true the fate of the Jewish homeland would now fall into his hands? How could a man like Tiberius Alexander be a wise leader when the sword he wore was destined to defend Rome?

Simon hoped his head could stay in control but knew his

heart was in rebellion. He had wanted to warn Valerius that what he thought was good news was going to lead to disaster. But Valerius's safety had to overrule any scruples he had about begging Tiberius Alexander for help. He tried to steel himself for what lay ahead. Would Tiberius Alexander even listen to him? Would he believe him? Without Agrippa looking out for Israel, who would have the power to save such a fragile strip of land from the Roman boots that were poised to stomp down and crush it? Claudius, no doubt, thought he was being kind in appointing a Jew to oversee Judea and believed it to be a concession to peace and cooperation. Simon thought that was the cruelest kindness of all.

He wondered about Berenice. Would he meet up with her again in the cavernous maze of the Herodian Palace? How would she react to his earlier rebuff in Caesarea and his precipitous departure? He couldn't shake the memory of his visit when he was called to minister to Agrippa and arrived to look down on a corpse. Would Berenice have a chance to become queen? She knew a lot more about Judea than Tiberius Alexander. She also knew how delicately Agrippa balanced his policies between satisfying Rome and protecting Jerusalem. He thought she would make a good queen. He would tell her that if he got a chance.

After the guards let him in, Simon was led into Philo's room where an attendant was hovering over Philo and spooning water into his mouth. Simon laid his hand gently on the old man's forehead. His fever was flaring. Philo seemed annoyed and was still dictating a letter to a scribe who sat in the corner. Simon placed himself between Philo and the scribe and warned, "You cannot go on working and expect to recover. You need rest. Sleep." Long ago, it had become obvious to Simon that Philo would not stop until he exhaled his last breath. He just hoped he could push that moment far into the future.

Philo slapped the spoon away and continued to dictate without pausing for breath and testily ignored Simon who checked his heart rate, his lungs, and his body for lingering effects from his sunstroke.

Simon looked over at the scribe when he noticed Philo was repeating the same sentences that made no sense. "How long has he been like this? He was coherent this afternoon."

The attendant explained that Philo had become confused, dizzy, and nauseous toward evening.

Simon ordered the attendant to place damp cloths on his face, neck, and wrists. Then he mixed a drink of lemon balm, valerian root, and lavender, and sent the scribe to fetch Tiberius Alexander.

When Tiberius Alexander entered, he gazed at Philo and frowned, then looked at Simon with accusing eyes. "Why is he not better? You claimed he was recovering."

"He was. But his stroke has left him confused. He needs to drink more. We need to bring his fever down. Above all, he needs to stop working. Maybe you can get that message through to him."

Tiberius Alexander felt Philo's forehead. "See that you get him well enough to travel tomorrow." Tiberius Alexander's voice was low in deference to the patient yet challenged with intensity.

"I cannot promise you that he'll be able to travel tomorrow."

"You need to do better than that. Everyone claims you are an amazing physician. Prove it!"

Bile rose in Simon's throat, and he swallowed hard, aware that he could not win this battle with Tiberius Alexander, nor did he have time to. There were other things far more pressing, and there was too much at stake. He gestured toward the door and asked to speak to him in private in the hallway.

Alarmed by Simon's solemn manner, Tiberius Alexander obeyed.

Simon worried it might be impossible to explain the urgency of Valerius's plight. One look at the expression on Tiberius Alexander's face stirred a gruesome memory of his fight with Meidias. Just for a moment, he was no longer in Jerusalem but in Alexandria, facing Tiberius Alexander who intervened in his struggle with Meidias and robbed him of his victory. Tiberius Alexander had haughtily retrieved Meidias's sword after Simon had kicked it out of Meidias's hand. Then, Tiberius Alexander challenged him for proof he was in the right. Now, he had to accuse a Roman officer Tiberius Alexander would want to protect.

Simon was so engrossed in his memory that he failed to notice that Berenice had come through the corridor behind them and stood now at Philo's door, listening.

Simon's voice was low but insistent. "I asked to speak to you because Valerius is in danger, and we need your help."

"What kind of danger?"

"Do you know Herennius Capito?"

"He's on the list of Roman officers in Judea."

"Correct. He's in charge of the garrison at Jamnia. When Valerius was with his legions in Ptolemais, Capito wanted to take over the legions and push straight through to Jerusalem. When Valerius kicked him out of his office, Capito tried to murder Valerius in his sleep. Instead of putting him on trial, Valerius stripped him of his rank and let him go with a warning. Since then, Capito has worked his way up to command again."

The expression on Tiberius Alexander's face was unreadable. Simon had no clue as to how he might respond to a complaint about a Roman officer.

"Why did Valerius wait to deal with this now?"

"I believe Valerius forgot that Jamnia is so close to Jerusalem. After Caligula was murdered, Valerius wanted to put the whole unpleasant incident behind him, and he forgot about the danger Capito represented until he learned that he and his men were looking for him, I begged him not to go out. After this morning's ceremony, everyone knows who he is."

Tiberius Alexander shook his head. "Valerius should have

prosecuted him while he had all the incriminating evidence at hand."

"Agreed." Simon lifted his shoulders in a shrug that conveyed the message that his observation was not helpful. "As prefect of Palestine, you are, I would think, under obligation to provide protection for Romans in this province. Especially when he happens to be the governor of Syria."

Tiberius Alexander said, "Apparently, Valerius told you I am to be appointed prefect of Palestine. We need more information before I can order an arrest. I did not expect to deal with such thorny issues before I take on official duties."

"I don't think this can wait. Maybe this case is not so much an official duty but a favor for a friend."

Tiberius Alexander raised a quizzical eyebrow, and his lips curled into a quirky smile. "I suppose I should feel honored that you suddenly consider me a friend."

Simon caught the sarcasm in his tone and chose to ignore it. "I am a close friend to your uncle. Not just because I am his physician. I care for him deeply."

The sincerity in Simon's voice soothed some of Tiberius Alexander's earlier rancor. He said, "I expect you to focus all your energy on him."

"I'll stay by his side and hope he quiets down enough so he can get some sleep. I am worried about him, and I promise I'll do everything I can to help him recover. But he is seventy years old. Today was too much for him." Simon turned toward the door and almost bumped into Berenice.

She gave a little nod and asked, "How is he?"

Somewhat disconcerted, Simon bowed to acknowledge her presence and gestured toward the room, but Tiberius Alexander stepped in front of his sister-in-law, pushed the door open, and gallantly ushered her into the room. After placing his hand lightly over Philo's forehead, Tiberius Alexander said, "I think he may be less feverish. Your potions may be working." At the door, he turned and said, "I'll see what I can find out."

Simon realized that Tiberius Alexander acted more helpful in front of Berenice and wondered how long that would last.

After Tiberius Alexander left the room, Simon and Berenice looked at each other, but neither spoke as they turned toward Philo.

Simon left one lantern near the door, quenched the other lights in Philo's room, gestured for the scribe to leave, and asked the attendant to refresh the damp cloths and leave. Berenice hovered in the room and did not speak. Simon offered her a chair, but she refused.

He sat down at Philo's bed and held his frail hand in his. His pulse felt normal. His forehead and hand were no longer quite as hot with fever. His eyes were closed, and he was breathing deeply. Simon hoped he would soon drift off. Sleep was the physician's most effective remedy compared to the concoctions he could conjure up from his medical bag.

He sensed Berenice's presence behind him and wondered how much she had heard of his conversation with Tiberius Alexander. Then he felt her hand on his shoulder. She whispered, "Will he be all right?"

Simon nodded. "I will do everything I can."

She spoke softly. "I trust you will. You should know that I have a whole file on Herennius Marcus Capito. My father and I have documentation of his mismanagement, theft, and information Valerius forwarded to Jerusalem from Ptolemais."

Simon acknowledged what she said with a nod. He was reassured to sense that their relationship had changed since their last awkward encounter in the amphitheater at Caesarea and was relieved.

She squeezed his shoulder. "You should know that I have petitioned Claudius to become queen as my father's rightful heir."

He bowed and smiled. "You would be an excellent queen during this challenging time."

"Thank you, Simon. It would be nice if you could convince my brother-in-law."

She left as quietly as she had come. There was a little flutter of curtain at the window, a door softly shut, and Simon knew he was alone with his patient. He gazed down at Philo and was surprised to note that Philo's eyes were wide open, and he was looking at him.

"Where are we?"

"In Jerusalem."

"Did they get it up?

"The Bronze Door is in place at the temple. It is beautiful."

"I haven't seen it."

"You will after you get well. I will take you there."

"You are very kind. It is important to be kind, for everyone is fighting a great battle."

"Your battle right now is to regain your strength. You must sleep."

"So you say. What battles are you facing?"

"My wife and sons have turned to the Christos. It is a difficult battle."

"We cannot understand the mind of God. He is the architect with the blueprint. He created the world. But we see only a very small part of the blueprint."

"What should I do about it?"

"I cannot tell you what to do. But you must remember that God is the charioteer holding the reins. He is the helmsman at the rudder. No matter what you do, you cannot change that. In time, perhaps, you will accept that and find peace."

"You have spent your life interpreting the scriptures."

"And people who come after me will see things differently. That is good. In this day and age, I already see things differently than when I was thirty and thought I understood all."

Simon smiled. "What has changed?"

"I used to see things literally from my limited human perspective. Then I began to see the power of allegory. We cannot explain God. We cannot begin to understand the miracle of creation. It is a sign of great simplicity to believe the world should have been created in six days. God is not limited by time. We interpret our lives in terms of time. God is eternity."

Simon stroked his hand, hoping he would soon settle down to sleep and pondered the fact that he did not have Philo's grasp of philosophy but possessed the same passion to learn about the mysteries of creation.

Philo closed his eyes. Gradually, the grip of his hand relaxed. He was asleep.

TENTACLES OF EVIL

AURELIA WAS STUNNED TO LEARN THAT VALERIUS could be in danger because of events that took place while Caligula was still alive. Like circles that ripple through water from a dropped pebble, the havoc wreaked by Caligula spread in ever-widening waves to threaten their lives. It was hard to believe that a minor Roman official could emerge as the main instigator of the tragic drama that had threatened their security for so long. The frightening effects of Caligula's power were staggering. Aurelia was beginning to understand that tentacles of evil can reach out across time and across the empire and entrap them still.

During the long ordeal when Valerius and his army were trying to avoid bloodshed, Aurelia had tried to be the very definition of calm and hope for the future. But after today's ceremony along with the celebration of Valerius's good leadership and the promise of closure, she could not swallow her rage and accept that another menace was already knocking on their door. One they could not control. One that even the cautious Valerius had not foreseen.

Exasperated, she exclaimed, "Even the death of a vicious

tyrant does not free us from the evil he left behind."

Valerius agreed. "Don't forget the consequences of Tiberius's actions and inaction and how they affected our family forever."

"Do you think Claudius is any better?"

"It's hard to know. Absolute power corrupts the best of men."

"It's just not fair that you should be subjected to this threat now after all that you've been through." Aurelia looked around his room and saw that he had already packed and was ready to leave. She sat down on his bed and kept her eyes set on his sword and watched him sharpen it. She knew by the way he tested its edge that he was anxious, indecisive, and still weighing his options. Then he picked up his wide dagger to sharpen and hid it in a leather pocket that would loop on his belt.

Aurelia wanted to weep and could not speak without betraying her anguish, so she watched the way he tied on his cuirass and wondered how many times she had knelt in prayer to Mars and to Neptune to keep him safe. Lately, she had switched to asking Yeshua for assistance. Yeshua had preached a message of peace. But there was no peace. Oh, God! she thought, how do you fight such insane evil? Finally, she trusted her voice enough to ask, "Did Simon agree to get help from Tiberius Alexander?"

"He did."

"I'm relieved."

Valerius looked at her in surprise.

Aurelia quickly added, "I mean, I'm glad Simon felt so protective. That means you must be friends again. You have given me a gift beyond measure."

Valerius shook his head. "I think it's the other way around. Simon is giving this gift to you. It was a gratifying moment when I realized he cared."

"He always has, even when you thought he did not."

"I think Simon is genuinely afraid for my safety since this morning's accolade made me stand out from the crowd. He thinks I am now an obvious target for Capito and wants me to wear his cloak and look like a Jew."

"That's a clever idea. It shows how much he truly cares for you."

Valerius strapped on his belt and placed his sword in the scabbard. "Since Quintus alerted me that Capito was looking for me, I've known what I must do. I know I must take full responsibility for my mistake. I was warned not to turn Capito loose, and I didn't listen."

"Where are you going?"

"The Antonia Fortress."

"Why?"

"Quintus is there. I don't want him to get caught up in this mess. In Ptolemais, Quintus came to help me as soon as he heard I had almost been choked to death. He was there when I demoted Capito in front of his troops. Quintus is in danger because of me. He could be in trouble as we speak. He may have risked his life to come and warn me."

Aurelia jumped up. "You could go to the Herodian Palace first and get help. When I was a guest there, Agrippa's bodyguard was quite intimidating, and I'm sure they are now as loyal to Berenice as they were once to Agrippa."

"How do we know Berenice would be on my side? She doesn't know me."

"Trust me. She likes you. I could tell by the way she looked at you at the banquet. She was trying to flirt with you, but you didn't respond."

Valerius looked at her as though he hadn't heard. "Do you know what the hardest part of this whole ordeal has been?"

"I can imagine many days when you were in despair."

"That, too. But the hardest part was the waiting. Endless months of waiting. Strategic delays, stalling, inaction. Odd military tactics for a Roman general. I remember how brash I was when I first met Lucius Vitellius. I made a bold speech that avoiding a fight was preferable to engaging in battle and quoted Julius Caesar."

"Such good advice, and you refuse to take it now."

"What do you mean?"

"As you just said, waiting is a wise tactic. Why seek out a confrontation when you would be safer here?"

She wasn't certain she was right. Were they truly safe in Sedek's house? It had not been designed like a fortress. A clever athlete could scale the walls in the back and come in over the terrace. She shivered at the thought and realized she would have to be vigilant for the sake of the children. And how much protection could Sedek offer? His litter bearers and one guard at the door were no match for Roman-trained soldiers. She made one last attempt to stop him. "Let me get Sedek's litter bearers ready for you, and you could at least have their protection." She started toward the door.

Valerius clasped his sister's shoulders and stopped her.

Aurelia felt both anxious and angry. "You are the governor of Syria. You could call on a whole legion to guard you, and yet you set out alone when you know he's out there ready to pounce. Don't be foolish. You owe it to your wife and little Lucius to survive and not be murdered by hooligans who don't deserve to have their daggers stained with your blood. You owe it to the memory of our father to continue to work for the public good in the senate."

Valerius was already halfway down the steps when he said, "After I find Quintus, I'll come get my things, and he and I will ride out together before sunrise."

"Please, Valerius. Be careful!" What else could she say?

✦

Aurelia went back up to the terrace and tried to pray. Too many images flashed through her mind for her to be able to settle down enough to pray. The view of the temple was no longer comforting. All the torches at the temple had burned out except one, and everything was dark and quiet. She felt very alone as she thought about all the dangers they still faced. Valerius had not been gone for long, but it already seemed like an eternity. She tried to imagine what might be happening and could not.

Simon should be home by now. She kept expecting to see him coming up the terrace steps and imagined him taking her into his arms and having a quiet talk about all the things they had been through this day. He would reassure her. He would tell her Philo would be all right. And she would tell him how happy she was that he and Valerius were friends again. She would not spoil the end of their day by having a discussion where they would likely disagree but would embrace him with relief, secure in their love for each other.

Just moments ago, she was so sure she was right, and Simon was wrong. But now she regretted arguing with him. Suppose he, too, was in danger?

Simon should have been home hours ago.

Unless Philo was gravely ill—?

She felt guilty. She should be praying for Philo's recovery. What would they do without him? She remembered every word he said about Valerius. She was so proud of her brother. Philo's speech of this morning now felt like it happened a lifetime ago.

She had to stay hopeful and believe that everything would be fine again. Philo would recover, and they would board ship at Caesarea and sail back to Alexandria. Surely, Tiberius Alexander would have the power to arrest Herennius Capito and his gang of Jew-haters who had brought so much evil down on their heads. Their hatred was powerful. To die just because you were a Jew is a terrible thing.

But now, Simon claimed people will die because they are Christians. How could Yeshua's teaching be construed against them? She balled her hands into fists and started to sob. She felt as if she were spiraling down into such a deep hole of darkness that she would never manage to climb out. What was happening with Valerius? Would Tiberius Alexander let her know if something had happened to him?

She knew there was one place she could find comfort. She would go watch the boys while they slept. It had been a long and emotional day for them, too. What kind of future did they face? If what Simon feared was right, had she led them down a dangerous path?

$\textbf{+}$

ENDGAME

The Antonia Fortress was built right up against
the north wall that surrounded the temple mount. All Valerius
had to do was turn right after Sedek's house and then left
along the wall and keep the wall at his side as he made his way
north to the Fortress where Quintus was lodging. It gave him
a chill to realize how close Sedek's house was to the barracks
where he believed Capito and his thugs were staying. Every
now and then, there was a niche in the wall where an assassin
could lurk in the shadows. He tried to tread softly and decided
he certainly didn't have a Roman swagger right now.

His eyes adjusted to the dark. Outlines of buildings emerged
on his left, then doorways, windowsills, flickering lights coming from a few high windows. Alert to every sound, he heard
muted voices and kitchen noises in the next building. He noted
the difference between the rustle of leaves in a tree on the
temple mount and the swish of long robes of pedestrians coming toward him, their sandals skimming over cobbled stone.
The scuff of military boots caused him to duck into a doorway
until the sound faded down the street. He was more afraid of
an ambush than a fight.

The Fortress was built by King Herod and named Antonia in honor of Marcus Antonius, King Herod's Roman patron. Its official purpose was to protect the temple, but to the Jews of Jerusalem it was a huge eyesore and a constant reminder of their subservience to Rome. It was also an insult that its vast footprint was larger than the temple. Thousands could be housed inside its walls made of massive stones. Only about one hundred soldiers were stationed there on a regular basis. He surmised you could get lost in the vast rooms and towers and hide out there for weeks if you were on the run, a thought that made him determined to find out what the soldiers who lived there knew about its secrets.

Valerius wondered how many men Capito brought with him from Jamnia for he realized that Capito could not have regained command of the garrison if he had not acquired a loyal following among his troops as well as some Roman support. He had underestimated Capito's cunning. Hate can be a great motivator.

He reached the south gate of the Antonia Fortress, took a deep breath, checked the bulge of his sword at his hip, and entered in the authoritative manner he assumed naturally as the Governor of Syria.

The guard at the gate was slumped over and half asleep. Valerius tapped on his shoulder, and he jumped up and was instantly awake enough to salute. Valerius asked to see Quintus, and the flustered guard called an orderly to go get him. Valerius entered the mess hall to see about twenty soldiers at table drinking beer or playing games of chance. Many didn't look up because they were already drunk or quibbling over bets and loaded dice.

"*Milites romani,*" Valerius's strong voice echoed through the hall, "Roman soldiers, I come to ask for your assistance." Several legionaries leapt to their feet and hailed him with cheers that woke the others up. His high military rank was obvious from his muscled cuirass even though he had chosen not to wear his ornate helmet. "I seek Herennius Marcus Capito whom you may know as the commander of the garrison at Jamnia."

At the mention of Capito's name there was a collective groan, and one brave soldier yelled out, "If you find him, wring his neck. He owes me twenty shekels. He's a cheater." Several stomped their feet in agreement.

Valerius said, "If you know where he is, tell him the governor of Syria wants to see him." Valerius looked around the hall and saw two soldiers who had not participated in the common outrage. They were looking at each other with conniving expressions on their faces. Neither looked drunk. He wondered if they were part of Capito's garrison he had confronted in Ptolemais. They looked vaguely familiar.

Valerius ordered the soldiers to sit down again and walked among them, asking their names, their hometowns, where they had been stationed before Jerusalem, and any battles they had fought for Rome. One soldier proudly hopped up with another salute and exclaimed he had valiantly served in Parthia under him. Valerius sat down beside him and listened to his story. It wasn't quite the way Valerius remembered it, but he slapped him on the back like an old comrade, and others joined eagerly in the discussion. As Valerius neared the two soldiers who acted aloof, he noted their edgy posture as though they were about to flee. When Quintus joined him and gave a formal salute to his general, Valerius watched his two suspects sneak away. Valerius squeezed Quintus arm and nodded in their direction and whispered, "I think we have the bait to catch the bigger fish."

Quintus said only one word: "Ptolemais."

Valerius nodded and noticed that Quintus had come fully armed, a precaution a good Roman soldier takes when his general summons.

One bold recruit asked Valerius to tell about one of his

adventures, and Valerius obliged with his story of the time he was almost forced to marry a Parthian princess. He kept the soldiers spell bound as he described the queen. Then he portrayed the princess in detail—her sapphire blue eyes, the jewels around her graceful neck, the way the soft fabric of her dress molded around the curves of her body, leaving little to the imagination. From the expressions on the faces in front of him, Valerius knew they were deeply preoccupied with erotic images when, out of the corner of his eye, he noted Capito enter with the two suspected accomplices on either side.

Abruptly, Valerius and Quintus were on their feet to confront them. A table stood between them in their way.

Valerius announced, "Herennius Marcus Capito, in the name of Emperor Claudius, you are under arrest for the attempted murder of an imperial officer."

Capito and his goons went for their swords.

Quintus knocked the table over in front of them which stopped their advance long enough for the rest of the soldiers to take in what was happening. One yelled, "Three against two ain't fair!" and raised his weapon to join them. Valerius waved him away, drew his sword, and prepared to counter Capito's first blow. The soldiers in the hall cheered. The up-ended table between them hindered the fight.

One of Capito's men jumped over the table with his sword drawn, but Quintus knocked him off balance. As he fell, his feet tangled with the table legs and his sword flew out from under him and slid across the floor. A soldier in the back grabbed it and held it up like a trophy.

At the same time, Capito and the other accomplice pressed in on Valerius.

Valerius backed away from the double attack and chose to dodge their wild swings as he distanced himself from the table. "I warn you. Initiating a fight against an officer of the empire is a grave offense. I don't want to fight you. Lay down your weapons!"

Capito screamed, "Ha! You are the same old coward who refused to fight in Ptolemais."

Both assailants curved around the upturned table in eager pursuit. Intent on their prey, they failed to prepare for Quintus who struck Capito's partner from the side. His blade clashed ringing against his sword and bent his arm back, a tactic that allowed Quintus to force his assailant to turn away from his fight with Valerius. They circled each other, exchanging blow for blow, as Quintus slowly backed his opponent toward the wall.

Capito growled like a wild animal as he strutted forward to attack. His swings against Valerius were blustering, energetic, and fierce, more random than purposeful, powered by hatred and revenge. Valerius blocked or dodged and wasted little energy on pushing back with his weapon. This strategy elicited malicious grins from Capito who erupted in vile taunts, accusing Valerius of panic, weakness, cowardice, spinelessness... His litany of invectives ended in sputtering. Capito thrust his sword straight at Valerius's neck, the most vulnerable spot above the cuirass, a strike with the intent to kill.

Valerius waited until the last instant to dip out of range, and Capito almost lost his balance. It was a ploy Valerius had often used in wrestling—an unusual ruse in sword fighting, but it sent Capito almost to his knees. Gasping for breath, Capito's staggered forward and twisted toward Valerius who parried his next lunge with ease.

The metallic clang of swords against swords intensified and reverberated through the hall. The four weapons caught the light from the lanterns on the wall and created a spectacle of lightning-like glints of steel. Valerius countered vigorous swings with defensive blocks which shielded rather than attacked, waiting for Capito's arm to tire, while Quintus moved in from the side and caught the accomplice's blade at an angle that wrenched his wrist backward. He stepped back in pain and almost dropped his weapon. His lowered arm opened his chest to Quintus's masterful blow that hit home. He fell, wounded.

Capito stepped forward, his blade steady now, poised for any opening. Valerius never took his eyes off the angle of Capito's arm and the tip of his sword.

Capito veered to a low thrust to the groin. Valerius lowered his blade to counter.

Capito jabbed higher toward the throat. Valerius deflected his sword high in a ringing collision of steel against steel.

A deadly dance in mirrored symmetry.

Sweat poured down Capito's face and into his eyes. He was squinting to see, and his next blow went wide, leaving him open to Valerius's stabbing blow against his arm that sent his sword sailing. He stumbled and fell, clutching his arm.

Raucous chants filled the hall as Valerius called for soldiers to hold him down and tie both of them up.

Amid the confusion of cheers and Valerius's calls for a medic, the third accomplice disappeared into the bowels of the Fortress.

There was not much glory in triumph but there was some satisfaction for Valerius to stand over Capito and say, "You will live to stand trial."

Still defiant, Capito said, "What charges dare you bring against an officer of Rome?"

Valerius said, "You are under arrest for the attempted murder of an imperial officer, for embezzlement, conspiracy, violation of military law, instigation of violence, mismanagement of your office, theft of tax revenues, defamation of an altar to Caesar, and now a second attempt to kill your superior officer."

"All lies!" he called as they tied him up.

After examining the soldier with the chest wound, the medic shook his head and was doubtful about recovery. When he started to wrap the arm wound, Capito was still cursing and crying for justice.

Valerius turned to the soldiers. "Anyone here who believes he can make a legitimate claim against Herennius Marcus Capito should present that to the military court at the time of trial." Valerius looked around to be sure that everyone had heard and discovered that he had a larger audience than he thought.

Tiberius Alexander was standing there, grinning. In full Roman armor, accompanied by his bodyguards, he raised his arm in salute and proclaimed, "*Veni, vidi, sed tu vicisti—* I came, I saw, but you conquered!" He clasped Valerius's shoulder.

Valerius nodded. "*Ave!* Why didn't you help?"

"The last time I intervened, Simon never forgave me. But frankly, it would have saved a lot of trouble if you had just gone ahead and killed him."

"Because the trial will be under your governance."

"Right."

"There's a simple solution. Hand it off to Queen Berenice." Valerius studied Tiberius Alexander's face for a reaction.

"A woman!"

"Why not? She is the rightful heir to King Agrippa, is she not?"

While the medic was hard at work with the two wounded, Tiberius Alexander turned to the guard. "I assume the prison here at the Antonia is reasonably secure?"

Valerius said, "Berenice would know the answer to that question."

✦

Aurelia heard noises below and quietly shut the door to the children's bedroom. Thank God, Simon was back! Now they could wait together for news of Valerius. She was poised to run and embrace him.

Something was wrong. It didn't sound like Simon. There

were more people. Louder steps. More voices. Could it be Capito with his men? She shrank back into the shadows and looked around for something she might use as a weapon.

Then she heard Valerius's voice. Excited now, she hurried down the steps and ran straight into Tiberius Alexander at the foot of the stairs. Thank God he had come to Valerius's rescue. She hugged him with a joyful cry of thanks. Then she turned to Valerius to hug him and exclaimed how happy she was to see him safe and sound.

Valerius thought it was up to Tiberius Alexander to set the record straight, but Tiberius Alexander was relishing Aurelia's reaction and basking in his undeserved glory. Tiberius Alexander winked at Valerius but said nothing. Quintus stared at Valerius with a question in his eyes, but Valerius shrugged and said, "Later."

Aurelia wanted to know about Simon, and Tiberius Alexander explained he was staying with Philo for the night.

"How is Philo?"

"Philo was a little better when I left. Simon is staying as a precaution. We still hope to sail tomorrow afternoon."

Tiberius Alexander turned toward Valerius and Quintus and invited them to travel to Caesarea with them and board their chartered ship to Alexandria. "Instead of sailing from Ptolemais, you can sail from Caesarea and then depart from Alexandria to Rome. That will cut your travel time by almost a week. We also have a full escort of my men."

"Thank you, Tiberius Alexander! Thank you!" Aurelia assured him she would tell his father how grateful they all were that they would be able to travel together.

As Tiberius Alexander and his men were leaving, Tiberius Alexander enfolded Aurelia in his arms once more and held her a little longer than was proper. This time she pulled back and was about to scold when he said, "Ask Valerius what really happened at the Antonia Fortress."

✦

THE STATUE

IN ROME, VALERIUS MADE HIS WAY THROUGH crowded streets on his way to the senate. He found his morning walk to the senate pleasant with the sun at his back, and the downhill slant of the streets gave him a sense of momentum. The population of Rome had grown. Near the forum, cheap housing was surging upward into five-story buildings. The price of land within the city had tripled. Fortunately for Valerius, Lucius Vitellius had welcomed his family back to Rome by arranging the purchase of a fine house on the Esquiline Hill that looked west toward the center of the city. Valerius recognized that there were advantages to having a famous and powerful father-in-law.

Every time he entered the curia and sat down in his senate seat, he had to cross the marble floor where his father had fallen on his sword. There were days when he wondered what his father would think about his son serving in the same senate that had so ingloriously refused to defend the falsely accused. Sometimes, the sun coming through clerestory windows left a red glow in the very spot where his father's blood had gushed forth from his self-inflicted wound. Since then, how many more had fallen victim to imperial whims, commands, and indifference? How had he been able to escape the same fate? Philo and Sedek invoked the providence of an all-powerful God. Rachel believed in the power of prayer. Aurelia credited Valerius with a strategy of delaying tactics. Simon praised the power of organized Jewish resistance. Manius gave credit to Neptune, who had sent storms to delay the ominous letter from Caligula. Vitellia accepted his survival as the result of Roman valor and superiority. And her father, Lucius Vitellius, simply called him lucky.

Indeed, Valerius felt fortunate he had survived, but he also felt distressed to represent imperial Rome, for the grand and noble sentiments symbolized by the great altar to peace erected by Augustus made a mockery of peace, and every time he walked through the forum, the temple of Janus stood wide open, indicating that wars were being fought somewhere in the vast empire that still proclaimed the *pax romana*.

At least the long ordeal and stand-off with Caligula was over. So far, Claudius had shown restraint. No one knew how long that would last. At this point in his life, Valerius hoped he could be a voice of reason and fairness in the senate and decided he could do the most good by working diligently and quietly to that end. Perhaps his son would not have to grow up in an empire that was constantly at war. Five-year-old Lucius greeted him every evening at the door with wide grins and excitement. For the moment, his son could remain innocent and unaware of the evils in the world.

In the evening, as he made his way back up the hill to his house, he often reflected on his walks with Simon in Cyrene where, at the end of their climb from the agora, Rachel waited for them at Simon's house with a welcoming smile. Life seemed so uncomplicated then. Then, he believed his love for Rachel would conquer all obstacles. Rachel's reactions to his dreams had always been more realistic than his own. It was both easier and harder to be so far away from her. Easier because he was spared the torture of being with her while unable to show the ardor of his love. But harder now because all that remained for him were poignant memories: the blush in her cheeks every time they met, the message in her eyes she never put into words, the warmth of her embrace when he returned alive from his ordeal. He often wondered if Rachel even realized the power she held over him. The confession he had made to her in Galilee remained true. He still deferred to what he imagined her opinion would be when he made difficult decisions and sought to emulate the principles that guided her.

When Lucius jumped into his arms that evening, eager to tell his father about his exploits that day, Vitellia met him at the door, and something about her expression made him pause and place Lucius on his feet. Lucius tugged him forward to his playroom to show him his new set of toy soldiers all lined up for war. Valerius knew his son's fascination was inevitable but had hoped it would not come so soon; that he could harbor the illusion for a while longer that his son would not have to follow in his father's and grandfather's footsteps.

After Lucius demonstrated a fight between two soldiers holding Roman swords, Valerius turned to Vitellia. "What is it?"

"There is a message from the emperor." She held it up.

"Well? What does it say?"

"I don't know. I didn't dare open it. The last time you had a message from the emperor, it was a command for you to fall on your sword." He saw both concern and affection in her gaze.

Valerius sliced open the seal. "Let's hope Claudius is different." He glanced down at the message and said, "He wants me to come to see him."

"Does he say why?"

"No."

Vitellia gathered Lucius in her arms and fretted. "Maybe he wants you to take on a new post in the provinces." She sighed. "Just when we are getting settled in Rome."

"I doubt that." But Valerius remembered the dinner in Alexandria when everybody fell silent when they heard he had been summoned to Rome to see the emperor and felt a twinge of uneasiness. "Maybe he's read my report on Syria and wants to talk about it."

"How can you be sure he won't be like Caligula?"

"You are right to be cautious. But everything I know about Claudius so far makes me believe he is quite different. I will go tomorrow and see what he wants."

Meeting with the emperor meant crossing through a district he scarcely knew and a steeper climb up to the old palace of Augustus that was sprawled across the southern flanks of Palatine Hill. Compared to palaces of high-ranking potentates and kings on the eastern borders of the empire where Valerius had negotiated peace treaties, the old house of Augustus looked run-down and in need of repair. Tiberius was more interested in palaces far from Rome, and Caligula was too busy seeking prominence for his divine likenesses in temples. Claudius had grown up next door at his mother's old-fashioned house and didn't seem to care about palatial grandeur.

When Valerius was announced, Claudius rose from his desk to greet him and welcomed him cheerfully. "*Ave*, Publius Petronius, I'm delighted to meet the governor of Syria who avoided war with the Jews." He motioned toward a chair.

"With the help of loyal legions and leaders like Manius Cornelius." As Valerius sat down, he noticed Claudius's fingers were stained with ink. He also saw that he looked older than he expected. After seeing so many statues set up all over Rome, he realized that sculptors had chosen to be realistic about his protruding ears and small mouth but had omitted the deep grooves on his forehead, the puffy bags under his eyes, and his scrawny neck.

"I read your account of the expedition with great care. Your praise of Manius Cornelius is well noted. I'm amused you engaged in a wrestling match to entertain the troops."

Valerius laughed. He had not expected Claudius to take the trouble to read it.

"And what you and Vitellius achieved in Parthia is quite extraordinary."

After a pause, Valerius said, "I sent Servius back to Parthia to deal with the uprising there. Then I heard he was summoned to Rome. Do you know why?"

Claudius looked at Valerius in surprise. "Servius didn't keep you informed? Well, it was top secret at the beginning. Caligula was getting impatient for his apotheosis. He spent a fortune on a gold statue of himself and wanted Servius to take it by boat to Caesarea. Without fanfare. Without legions. Like a miracle, the statue would suddenly appear in the temple. It might have worked if the praetorians hadn't taken things into their own hands and killed him. I used the gold to start rebuilding the treasury Caligula had depleted."

"What happened to Servius?"

"It turns out Caligula promised him a seat in the senate. I felt sorry for him when he missed his golden opportunity—so to speak." Claudius laughed. "So, I appointed him to Hispania, where the silver mines are lucrative, so he can save up the funds for a senate seat."

Valerius frowned and didn't know what to say.

Claudius noticed. "I thought you would be pleased for him. Based on your glowing letter to Caligula on his exploits in Parthia, I assumed—"

Stunned, Valerius shifted uncomfortably in his seat. "I never sent such a letter."

Claudius stared at him in unnerving silence. For a moment, his eyes showed bewildered disbelief, then a flash of anger, followed by deep distress. Finally, he sighed, a deep sigh more like a moan. "In the old Republic, this amount of ambition mixed with dishonesty and lack of honor would lead to a trial."

Valerius felt the need to defend his former legate. "He was

a fine soldier and a good friend. Parthia was a most difficult assignment."

"I am sure you are right about that."

Valerius worried he shouldn't have revealed the truth.

Claudius picked up an elaborately crafted sword. "Servius sent amazing spoils of war—archery bows, fancy cataphract armor, this unusual Parthian sword. Too bad he wasted all that stuff on the wrong emperor." He sighed. "There is always trouble in Parthia. Their kings have too many wives. Then they have too many sons. And brothers fight against brothers for power. It's hard to keep them all straight. Ungovernable."

Valerius thought to change the subject. "I'm sorry we lost the stabilizing influence of Agrippa."

Claudius sighed. "A great loss to both Rome and Palestine. And to me. We were the same age. A boyhood friend." His neck jerked back, and Claudius made it look intentional by shaking his head. "How suddenly he was taken from us. A painful reminder of our mortality."

Over the last years, Valerius felt he had constant reminders of his mortality. "Berenice was hoping to be appointed queen."

"So, I heard. I would have gladly appointed Agrippa's son to be Agrippa II. But I have been advised against it. He lives here in Rome and is by nature impulsive and immature. Not fit for governance I hear. Hence my choice of Tiberius Alexander—a good administrator and a Jew."

Valerius was impressed with the thought Claudius had put into his choice and studied the paintings on the wall behind him.

Claudius glanced over his shoulder at them and smiled. "You note the paintings behind me? Augustus himself put those up. He was quite the art connoisseur. I'll tell you a funny story. He used to sell them to his friends. And when he held such an auction, he turned them all against the wall and made buyers select a painting without knowing the subject. He apparently got a thrill out of their surprise when they turned them around. I assume the buyer never dared show disappointment."

Valerius tried to imagine what it must have been like to grow up in the large household of Augustus, who took in children from relatives and kings or former kings from all over the empire even though he himself had no sons and only one daughter. Tiberius was his stepson.

Claudius leaned forward and said, "Tell me, what is your ambition for the senate?"

"First, to discover how the senate operates."

Claudius gave a sharp laugh. "If you ever figure that out, let me know." He scratched his shoulder through his sleeve and left a trace of ink on his tunic.

Valerius felt emboldened to ask, "Are you still writing your history of Rome?"

Claudius laughed. "Ah, you note the ink on my fingers. No, nothing as interesting as that. I write most of my letters myself. I want to be certain my letters say what I want to say."

"Very wise."

"Just cautious." Claudius gave him a wide grin.

"I hope you find the time to finish your history of Rome. We need your perspective."

"I've just finished the section on the ancient Etruscans."

"Etruscans? I know so little about them."

"We owe much to them for the stalwart Roman character. Amazing builders and engineers. They built the Servian wall around Rome. We even borrowed their alphabet. Have you ever thought about the fact that Roman letters are easier to chisel into stone than Greek? At least, a mason once told me that."

Valerius was struck by his scholarly interests. "Where do you find sources about them?"

"Ah, you probably don't know that I was married to a daughter of an Etruscan general for twenty-five years. I learned much from her and her family at a time when I was completely free to be a student of history. Now—I regret to say I have little time for my studies."

Valerius said in sympathy, "The onus of your office lies heavily on your shoulders."

"Indeed. That is why I asked you to come see me. I want your advice. You have demonstrated such wisdom in your dealings with the Jews. I must confess I am at my wit's end to know how to deal with them."

"New upheavals in Jerusalem?"

"No, in Rome."

Valerius raised his eyebrows in surprise.

Claudius gestured at a stack of documents on his desk. "Petition after petition."

"What do they want?"

"They want me to take sides. How did you manage to avoid bloodshed and war? I understand only now what an extraordinary feat you accomplished to keep peace, because no matter what I suggest, there is no peace between them. The Jews are being irascible, irritating, irresponsible, implacable." Claudius threw up his hands in frustration.

"What sides do they want you to take and why are they petitioning you?"

"They are divided into at least two factions and are at each other's throats. The violence and disruptions started in the synagogues in Subura, spread to the Trans Tiber, spilled over into the Field of Mars, erupted in the streets, and reached the forum. Almost daily, the police are called out. What do you suggest?"

"I would be very hesitant to judge a religious issue."

"You suggest I shouldn't take sides?"

"Agrippa took the side of the traditionalists in Jerusalem and ordered several leaders of the other side imprisoned or killed. It did not stop them. If anything, it made things worse."

"What options do we have to restore law and order?"

"You may have to be both firm and creative. Find a way to

affect both sides equally so you don't favor either position with imperial sanction."

"How do I do that?" Claudius shook his head and sighed. "Sometimes I think we should just banish all Jews from Rome whether they be traditionalists of the old school or these fervent revolutionaries who preach a new cult."

"That might work." Valerius smiled. "In fact, that might work very well. They will either follow your decree and leave Rome or remain here and stay out of public conflicts that disturb the peace lest they be banished."

Claudius nodded. "It would be easy to enforce. The city police must remind them of the new law and make them leave." Claudius heaved a deep sigh. "I sometimes feel like a father with unruly children, and I have to scold and send them all off to bed."

"In this case, you send them away and you don't have to harm, prosecute, or punish."

"Banishment for some will be punishment enough, especially if they have to abandon flourishing businesses." Claudius tapped the petitions on his desk. "But clever," he said as he rose from his chair. "I'll have to think about it. I'll let you know what I decide. Thank you for coming. I appreciate your service to the empire. *Ave!*"

Valerius had risen to bow and say goodbye.

At the door, Claudius called him back. "Whatever happened to the statue of Caligula?"

"It was melted down to make cooking pots."

Claudius chuckled. "I'm glad they found a good use for him."

✦

AUTHOR'S NOTE

The past is like an old mosaic where many pieces are missing, and some fragments don't seem to fit. The task of the historian and archeologist is to put the pieces together to give us as accurate a picture of the past as possible. In historical fiction, I get to put some missing tiles together with the mortar of imagination to discover what it could have been like to be a Roman general charged with placing a statue of the emperor in the temple in Jerusalem.

Travelers to Jerusalem today can see the religious site called the Western Wall which is the last remaining section of the ancient wall surrounding the temple mount. The bronze door became valuable booty for the Romans when the temple was destroyed in the Roman-Jewish war in 70 C.E. Research travel to the Middle East allowed me to imagine Jerusalem as it once was with its glorious temple.

It is my good fortune that both Philo and Josephus wrote about Publius Petronius, the protagonist of this story. Each writer tells the story from his point of view, and, in this case, they agree on the significant facts. Philo lived through the nail-biting anguish of not knowing what horror Caligula could dream up next. Josephus was born the year Tiberius died and was not an eyewitness of the conflict but provided our best source of information about the Jewish history of that time.

Philo was a philosopher and a theologian, but he interrupted his scholarly writing to lead a delegation to Rome where he begged Caligula for justice for the Alexandrian Jews and asked him to refrain from being worshiped in the temple in Jerusalem. Thirty years later, Josephus was a general in the Jewish army who fought against Rome. The Romans captured him, but they spared his life because he was a member of the Jewish elite. After the fall of Jerusalem, Josephus devoted his life to writing works in Greek about the history of the Jews.

We owe it to Josephus that we have a description of the bronze door: "The door was forty cubits: and adorned after a most costly manner; as having much richer and thicker plates of silver and gold upon them than the others." (War of the Jews: V) Since a cubit is 1.5 feet, Josephus claims the Nicanor Door was 60 feet tall! The existing bronze door on the Pantheon in Rome is 25 feet tall. The Nicanor Door's height is a possible exaggeration, but the temple structure itself was supposedly 151 feet tall, the size of a 15-story building. Josephus also claimed it took twenty men to open or close the door. Thanks to Josephus, we also know that Alexander Lysimachos, Philo's brother, financed the construction and installation of the bronze door and commissioned Nicanor, an Alexandrian artist, to create it.

In the early 1920s two large luxury ships built for Caligula were found almost intact at the bottom of Lake Nemi 24 km from Rome. The ships were hailed as great technological achievements that survived almost 2000 years. Mussolini planned a large museum to house them, but they were badly burnt during a bombing toward the end of WWII. The Italians recently built a new museum at the site to house what was found and show models of the boats. Advances in building techniques found in the boats are new anchor designs, piston pumps for cold and hot water, and the use of thrust ball bearings that held rotating statues that may have been powered by wheels turned by slaves below deck.

Six months after the death of Caligula, the Alexandrian question about Jewish citizenship and the losses from the massacre in 38 had yet to be resolved. One of the first things

Claudius did as the new emperor was to write an open letter to the Alexandrians in Greek in which he proclaimed that the Jews should be restored to their rightful citizenship and to all the privileges they used to enjoy. He refused to place blame on either side but encouraged all Alexandrians to live in peace. One sentence in the letter is a direct rebuke of his predecessor Caligula. "But," he wrote, "I refuse the appointment of a high priest to me and the building of temples, for I do not wish to be offensive to my contemporaries, and my opinion is that temples and such forms of honor have by all ages been granted as a prerogative to the gods alone."

It is an amazing fact that Claudius's letter has survived intact on the back of an ancient tax document and is stored in the Papyri Collection of the British Library (P. Lond. VI 1912v, or BL Papyrus 2248).

In the early days of Christianity, Jews and Christians caused strife that often became public disturbances. Claudius wanted to restore peace and banished the Jews from Rome. At this time, no official distinction was drawn between the two groups. That will happen later under Nero. Suetonius tells us: "Since the Jews constantly make disturbances at the instigation of Chrestus, he (Claudius) expelled them from Rome." (Suetonius: The Twelve Caesars); Penguin, p.202.) In the New Testament, the banishment of Jews from Rome by Claudius is also mentioned in Acts 18:2. For questions related to historical aspects of the novels, contact me at karin@ciholas.net or visit my Author Page.

✦

LIST OF HISTORICAL CHARACTERS

Agrippa I (Herod Agrippa; Marcus Julius) – king of Judea (37-44 C.E.), grandson of Herod the Great, son of Aristobulus and Berenice. Born in 10 B.C.E. and educated in Rome with the children of Antonia and Tiberius. Wife: Cypros. Children: Agrippa II, Berenice, Drusilla, and Mariamne. Tiberius assigned Agrippa to tutor Caligula. When Tiberius died, Caligula became emperor and appointed Agrippa king of the Jews.

Alexander Lysimachos – alabarch of Alexandria, father of Tiberius Alexander and Marcus Lysimachos, brother of Philo. According to Josephus, one of the richest men in the empire.

Alexander – son of Simon of Cyrene and brother of Rufus, mentioned in Mark 15:21. Both brothers appear in the apocryphal Acts of Peter.

Antonia (36 B.C.E. - 38 C.E.) – daughter of Marcus Antonius and Octavia, wife of the elder Drusus, mother of Livilla, Germanicus, and Claudius, grandmother of Caligula, and sister-in-law to Tiberius.

Aretas IV – king of the Nabataeans (9 B.C.E. - 40 C.E.). His daughter married Herod Antipas, who divorced her when Herod Antipas took a new wife called Herodias, mother of Salome. Salome asked for the beheading of John the Baptist. In retaliation for the divorce, Aretas invaded and defeated Herod Antipas's domain. Herod Antipas appealed to Tiberius, who sent Lucius Vitellius, Roman governor of Syria, to fight against Aretas. When Vitellius arrived with his troops in 37 C.E., he learned that Tiberius had just died. Vitellius stopped the war and went back to Antioch.

Aristobolus – grandson of Herod the Great, brother of Agrippa I. He was educated in Rome at court along with Agrippa, his brother.

Artabanus II (30-25 B.C.E. - 41 C.E.) – King of Kings of Parthia (12 – 38/41). He signed a treaty with Vitellius in 37 in which he gave up pretensions to Armenia. Deposed shortly thereafter as king of Parthia, he regained the throne of Parthia just before he died.

Augustus (Julius Caesar Octavianus, Gaius Octavius, Octavian) – first Roman emperor (27 B.C.E. to 14 C.E.).

Aulus Plautius (15 B.C.E. - 57 C.E.) – conqueror of Britannia in 43. First governor of Roman Britannia.

Berenice, Julia (born 28 C.E.) – daughter of Agrippa I, sister of Agrippa II. Married very young to Marcus Lysimachos, son of Alexander Lysimachos, the alabarch of Alexandria, nephew of Philo. During the Roman-Jewish war, she met and fell in love with Titus, future emperor. Their relationship lasted about seven years. When she joined him in Rome, the Roman court rejected her as future empress, and she returned alone to Palestine.

Caesar, Gaius Julius (100-44 B.C.E.) – energetic statesman who founded the Julio-Claudian line and consolidated or conquered large portions of the future empire.

Caligula, Gaius Julius Caesar Germanicus (12-41 C.E.) – emperor 37-41. He was probably both insane and physically ill. He aspired to be worshiped as a god. Inconsistent, cruel, and irresponsible, he was assassinated on January 24, 41 C.E. During his short time on the imperial throne, he squandered the surplus funds Tiberius left behind.

Capito, Marcus Herennius – procurator of Jamnia in Judea. He stole public funds, sought special recognition from Caligula for his persecution of Jews, and informed the emperor when an altar to Caligula had been torn down in Jamnia. He was eager to ingratiate himself with Caligula and lost his office under Claudius.

Cassius, Gaius Longinus – governor of Asia (40-41), nephew of one of Caesar's assassins, a jurist who wrote ten volumes of commentary on Roman law. A senator in the time of Nero, he called the law that allowed the state to execute a whole household of slaves when a single slave murdered his master unjust. Nero exiled him from Rome, and Vespasianus allowed him to return.

Claudius, Tiberius Claudius Drusus Nero Germanicus – Roman emperor (41-54). Son of Antonia and Drusus.

Crassus, Marcus Licinius (115-53 B.C.E.) – politician who formed the first triumvirate with Julius Caesar and Pompey to challenge the power of the senate. In 72-71, he put down a slave revolt by Spartacus. As governor of Syria in 54, Crassus attempted to gain military glory by embarking on an invasion of Parthia. He was defeated and killed at the Battle of Carrhae just south of Edessa. It was one of the biggest defeats of the Roman army. Without Crassus, the triumvirate became a civil war between Caesar and Pompey, leading to the republic's death and the birth of the empire.

Cydias – physician of the Alexandrian school mentioned by Erotianus, who wrote during the Neronian period. Other than the fact that he engaged in Hippocratic criticism, we know very little about his life.

Flaccus, Aulus Avillus – friend of Tiberius and Macro, prefect of Egypt (32-38 C.E.). Arrested by Caligula in 38, he was banished to Andros, then executed.

Gamaliel – distinguished teacher and Pharisee, member of the Sanhedrin, grandson of the famous Rabbi Hillel, and teacher of the Apostle Paul before his conversion to Christianity.

Gemellus Tiberius – grandson of Drusus and Antonia. Some favored his rise to the throne instead of Caligula.

Germanicus, Julius Caesar (15 B.C.E. - 19 C.E.) – oldest son of Antonia and Drusus, consul in 12 and 18, father of Agrippina the Younger and Caligula.

Gotarzes – brother of the Parthian king Artabanus II. He murdered his nephew to take the throne when Artabanus died.

Herod the Great (37-4 B.C.E.) – king of Judea. He cooperated fully with Rome but brought much misery to his own family. He started the rebuilding and enlargement of the temple, which was finished under Agrippa II.

Heron of Alexandria (10 B.C.E. - 70 C.E.) – mathematician and engineer. He built the first known steam engine and used it to power toys and mechanical devices and open temple doors. He invented the first known vending machine that provided a slot for a coin and dispensed holy water. His other inventions included a wind-wheel that powered a pipe organ, automatic theater props operated by cylindrical cogwheels, a force pump, a cart powered by weights, a self-filling wine bowl using a float valve, and mechanical toys.

Hippocrates (c. 460-370 B.C.E.) – best-known physician of antiquity, mainly because of his extant writings and the Hippocratic oath.

Jesus (Yeshua, Jesus of Nazareth, Christ, Christus, Christos, rabbi, master, Messiah) – his public ministry began during the twenties of our common era and ended with his trial and crucifixion at Passover under the procurator, Pontius Pilatus (Pilate). Christians believe he rose from the dead on the third day.

Marcellus – prefect of Judea under Vitellius. After Vitellius shipped Pilatus off to Rome for slaughtering Jews at Mount Gerizim, Vitellius appointed Marcellus prefect of Judea in his place.

Macro, Quintus Naevius Cordus Sutorius – successor to Sejanus as praetorian prefect; later appointed prefect of Egypt. Just as he embarked from Ostia for his journey to Egypt, Caligula required him to commit suicide because he was becoming too powerful.

Marcus Lysimachos – son of Alexander the alabarch of Alexandria, brother of Tiberius Alexander, and first husband to Berenice, daughter of Agrippa I. He died very young.

Mithridates (also known as Meherdates) – the younger brother of Artabanus II who occupied the throne of Armenia around 36 C.E. Lucius Vitellius, the governor of Syria, rescued his throne for him for a short period. He is best known for his role as a rival claimant to the Parthian throne during his brother's reign.

Musa (Mousa, Thea Musa) – ruling queen of the Parthian empire (2 B.C.E. - 4 C.E.) with her son, Phraates V. She was an Italian slave girl in the household of Augustus. The emperor sent her to Parthia as a gift in exchange for some Roman standards and Roman prisoners after the battle of Carrhea in 53 B.C.E. She was also a reward to Phraates IV for having switched loyalties from Marcus Antonius to Octavian, who became emperor Augustus. She became the favorite and most powerful wife of the king. After her son Phraates V came of age, she murdered her husband, Phraates IV.

Nicanor – Alexandrian artist who was commissioned by Alexander the alabarch to craft an elaborate bronze door for the temple in Jerusalem. The Nicanor Door at the temple was named for him, the only part of the temple that proclaimed the name of an artist or an architect. In 1902, archeologists found the burial tomb of Nicanor of Alexandria in Jerusalem on Mount Scopus. The inscription in Greek reads: "Bones of those (i.e. of the house or family) of Nikanor of Alexandria, he who made the doors. Nikanor Alexa."

Petronius, Publius (Valerius) – proconsul of Asia (31-39); appointed by Tiberius to replace his uncle, also named Publius Petronius, who was proconsul of Asia, subsequently governor of Syria under Caligula and Claudius (39-44) His sensitivity to the Jews and his respect for the sanctity of the temple in Jerusalem is well documented by Philo and by Josephus.

Philo of Alexandria (Philo Judaeus) – philosopher and writer who combined both Jewish piety and Greek ideals in his writings. He was a delegate to Rome to seek the restoration of Jewish rights under Caligula in 40 C.E., which he describes in *Legatio ad Gaium*. He is also one source for the story about the first pogrom in Alexandria, the indifference of Flaccus, and Flaccus's downfall. He personally planned an annual festival at the lighthouse to celebrate the translation of the Septuagint.

Pilatus, Pontius (Pilate) – governor of Judea (26-36 C.E.) appointed by Tiberius; played a role in condemning Jesus to death. His harshness and his cruel slaughter of Jews at Mount Gerizim caused Lucius Vitellius, governor of Syria, to remove him from office.

Phraates IV – King of Kings of Parthia. Fought the Roman Republic led by Marcus Antonius. Phraates IV initially supported Antonius but later switched sides to join forces with the Roman general Octavian, later known as Augustus. Augustus rewarded him with Musa, a beautiful Roman slave who became one of his wives. She became the mother of Phraates V. When her son came of age, she plotted with him to kill Phraates IV and ruled with her son as a powerful queen.

Phraates V – son of Musa and Phraates IV. He reigned with his mother (2 B.C.E. - 4 C.E.). Phraates V's reign was characterized by instability and political intrigue. He was eventually overthrown by a conspiracy led by his brothers, who installed their own candidate.

Ptolemaios II Philadelphos (309-246 B.C.E.) – pharaoh or king of Ptolemaic Egypt, son of Ptolemaios I, Macedonian Greek general of Alexander the Great. His kingdom went way beyond Egypt and included parts of Greece and countries along the Aegean. He expanded his kingdom and fostered learning and culture. He promoted the Museion and sponsored research and science. Under his reign, the Greek version of the Hebrew Bible (the Septuagint) was created in rooms housed in the famous lighthouse of Alexandria.

Ptolemaios, Gaius, Julius (13 B.C.E.? - 40 C.E.) – king of Mauretania, client king for Rome. As the grandson of Cleopatra and Marcus Antonius, his lineage was perceived by Caligula as a threat and Caligula had him assassinated when he was on a visit to Rome.

Rufus – son of Simon of Cyrene and Aurelia Petronia and brother of Alexander. Named in Mark 15:21. Both brothers appear in the apocryphal Acts of Peter.

Sejanus, Lucius Aelius – prefect of Rome 14-31 C.E.; encouraged distrust in the emperor's own family and hoped for a dynastic marriage with Livilla, the daughter of Antonia. He planned a conspiracy to wrest all power from Tiberius that Antonia uncovered and revealed to her brother-in-law. Tiberius sent a letter accusing him to the senate, and that same day Sejanus was condemned. The mob that had almost hailed him as Caesar in the morning tore his body apart that same evening.

Simon of Cyrene (Simon ben Toubias) – Matthew, Mark, and Luke reported that a Cyrenian named Simon was forced to carry Jesus' cross to Golgotha after Jesus fell under its weight. According to Mark 15:21, Simon had two sons—Rufus and Alexander.

Stephanos (Stephen) – considered the first Christian martyr. He was stoned to death for preaching his new faith. (Acts: chapters 6 and 7.)

Tiberius, Tiberius Claudius Nero (42 B.C.E. - 37 C.E.) – emperor 14-37 C.E. He was a competent general in his younger years but became a virtual recluse toward the end of his life. His treason trials of *maiestas* did away with many noble senators in Rome. He was harsh, frugal, learned, stoic, and bitter. Not keen to be emperor, he was unhappy in his private life. Augustus forced him to divorce Vipsania Agrippina and marry Augustus's daughter Julia for the sake of succession.

Tiberius Alexander (Tiberius Julius Alexander) – son of Alexander, the alabarch, nephew of Philo. Administrator in Alexandria with the prefect Licinius Rectus, procurator of Judea 45-48 C.E., appointed by Claudius, general in Armenia 63-66. In 66 he became prefect of Egypt.

Theophilus ben Ananus – High Priest in Jerusalem (37-41 C.E.). From Josephus we learn that he came from a very wealthy Jewish family and was highly respected. In fact, some scholars believe he is the one addressed at the beginning of the gospel of Luke. His son Matthias was the High Priest right before the fall of the temple in Jerusalem in 70 C.E.

Valerius – see Publius Petronius Valerius.

Vitellius, Lucius (10 B.C.E. - 51 C.E.) – Roman senator, served as governor of Syria, was consul three times. He was a master at diplomacy and managed to keep the peace in volatile regions. Through his close friendship with Antonia, sister-in-law of Tiberius, he gained access to the imperial family. When emperor Claudius left to conquer Britannia, Vitellius was in charge of the government in Rome. Aulus, one of his sons, became emperor in 69, the year of the four emperors.

ACKNOWLEDGMENTS

I owe a special debt of gratitude to Centre College, a jewel of an institution, set in the green splendor of Kentucky. The staff at the Centre College Library found hard-to-find research materials, and two sabbaticals gave me time off from teaching to explore. A professorship from the Van Winkle family and a professorship from the NEH gave me financial assistance for travel and books.

Ten volumes of Philo's writings and four volumes of Flavius Josephus have been my constant companions for years. I am deeply indebted to the scholars at Loeb Classical Library who published Philo's works and to William Whiston, professor of mathematics at Cambridge, who published the works of Josephus at Baker Book House in Grand Rapids, Michigan. Philo and Josephus provide us with intriguing details about their lives and the history of their times. I am also indebted to hundreds of scholars who devoted their life's work to elucidating the history and archeology of the first century. They drew the maps for me to travel back in time.

I am grateful to numerous colleagues and friends who provided encouragement and to my hardworking publishing team at Atmosphere Press. My special thanks to all the members of the Screnoa Book Club who give me the courage to send this book out into world. They are perceptive, and judicious readers. And very demanding critics.

My heart-felt thanks to my ever-patient and loving family who believed with me that there is a story to tell about Simon of Cyrene and his times.

THE CYRENIAN TRILOGY

THE LIGHTHOUSE

Simon is a gifted physician whose passion is saving lives, but he is no match for the cunning villain who terrorizes Jews across the Roman Empire. The search for his sister Rachel, who was abducted by the villain, leads him to Jerusalem where a Roman soldier forces him to carry a crossbeam for a stranger. He does not know that this moment will change the world forever. Boldly, he seeks justice for his family and his people and tries to stop the first pogrom in Alexandria. At stake, for him, is the survival of his people.

THE BRONZE DOOR

Caligula finds a vicious way to carry out his vendetta against Simon and his family. He appoints Publius Petronius Valerius, Aurelia's brother, to be governor of Syria and orders him to take his legions to Jerusalem to erect his statue in the temple. Valerius faces an excruciating choice: to obey Caligula will unleash the slaughter of thousands of Jews who are ready to die to save the sanctity of the temple. To disobey means death for Valerius and his family. Valerius finds strength in his deep love for Rachel as he tries desperately to defy a ruthless tyrant.

BEYOND THE HORIZON

In the third novel, we witness the devastating fire in Rome, the confrontation between Simon Peter and Simon Magus, the trial of the Apostle Paul, and Nero's persecution of Christians. A new and deadlier massacre of Jews in Alexandria, the fall of the temple in Jerusalem during the Roman-Jewish war, and the adoption of unsound medical practices at the Museion bring Simon to his knees in despair. Shattered but not defeated, Simon continues to defy Rome, holds to the faith of his fathers, and carries on in his mission of healing.

ABOUT THE AUTHOR

KARIN CIHOLAS was born in Virginia and grew up in Switzerland where she studied classical languages. The study of Latin and Greek led to her fascination with the ancient world and its history. She earned advanced degrees in languages and comparative literature at UNC, Chapel Hill and enjoyed teaching modern languages and courses on the ancient world. She lives in Sarasota with her husband, author and theologian Paul Ciholas.

thecyreniantrilogy.com
tinyurl.com/Ciholas-FB-Author

Praise for *The Lighthouse*

"*The Lighthouse* is a fast, smart, and engaging historical novel that entertains hugely and invites readers to look forward to the next exciting adventure in the trilogy, a tale of one man's quest for justice for those he loves."
- **Christina Prescott**, *The Book Commentary*

"Ciholas creates a vivid, memorable story powered as much by strong characters as by the forces that influenced this world's decisions. Her descriptions are memorable and hard-hitting, embracing not just Simon's perspective, but the men and women who circle around him in various ways."
- **D. Donovan**, Senior Reviewer, *Midwest Book Review*

"If you love James Michener, you will love this book! It evokes his keen sense of history and his ability to bring long-ago characters and settings to life."
- **Margaret George**, author of *The Autobiography of Henry VIII*, *The Memoirs of Cleopatra, Mary Queen of Scotland and the Isles, Mary Magdalene, The Splendor before the Dark, A Novel of the Emperor Nero*

"*The Cyrenian Trilogy* is an extraordinary accomplishment as to the scope of material, the command of literature and the balance of judgment. It is also a vivid account of unrest. Readers gain insight into an era in which Jewish nationalism, nascent Christianity, Roman power and Hellenistic culture in the Mediterranean world converged, sometimes violently and tragically. Concentrating on Simon and his extended family, Ciholas adeptly and emphatically describes the tensions and polemics that arose when some family members adopted a new allegiance (Christianity) while others clung to the ancient paths (Judaism). At stake was nothing less than the self-definition of both Jews and Christians."
- **Beth Glazier**, author of *Malachi, The Divine Messenger: A Critical Reappraisal*

"*The Lighthouse* is a fascinating book. It was quite an experience to read a novel about people that are so familiar to me as objects of study."
- **Pieter W. van der Horst**, author of *Studies in Ancient Judaism and Early Christianity*; *Philo's Flaccus: The First Pogrom*

"The story allows the reader to follow Simon on his journey and we are overwhelmed and awed by what he faces and accomplishes. ...This novel is packed with so much true history intermixed with a wonderful storyline

that will thrill any reader. I love a wonderfully written page-turner that the reader does not want to put down. I'm sure that part two will be just as interesting and well-written and I am anxiously awaiting it."
- **Kathy Stickles**, *Feathered Quill*

"A beacon in the dark, *The Lighthouse* takes readers on a heartbreaking journey to first-century Egypt. ...I really grew to love Simon as a character. Ciholas's decision to make him so complex—kind, yet vengeful—always kept me engaged. ...*The Lighthouse* has got me hooked into this series. I'd gladly recommend it to those historical enthusiasts who are looking to dive deep into human history."
- **Jadidsa Perez**, *Independent Book Review*

"The author painstakingly documents the perilous situation of Jews under Roman governorship—not quite excluded from commercial or civic life but not entirely accepted either and often subjected to withering persecution. In addition, the romance that develops between Simon and Aurelia, the daughter of a prominent senator and the sister of his best friend, Valerius, is depicted with immense sensitivity and poignancy. ...Ciholas's portrayals of the time and its tumults and Simon's agonizing plight are captivating."
- ***Kirkus Reviews***

"The novel reveals an astonishing knowledge of the 1st century, including details of Jewish and Hippocratic medicine, the political intrigues and personalities of the Roman Senate and succession, a new vision of what Matthew Arnold called the Hellenic and Hebraic worldviews, the philosophical/ moral issues of the time such as mind-body and means-end relationships still with us today, and vivid details of the geography and everyday life in both the Jewish and Roman worlds in Cyrene, Alexandria, Jerusalem, and Rome. ...This is an amazing book."
- **Milton Reigelman**, author of *Hearts of Darkness: Melville, Conrad, and Narratives of Oppression*, 2010, *Secret Sharers: Melville, Conrad, and Narratives of the Real*, 2011.

"Richly researched and splendidly narrated, *The Lighthouse* follows Simon of Cyrene on a fascinating and fraught journey through the Roman Empire of the first century C.E. ...This unusual point of view on the rise of Christianity brings historical figures alive and provides crucial context to events that still reverberate through the world today. The first volume of a trilogy."
- **Elaine Fowler Palencia**, author of *Small Caucasian Women, Brier Country, On Rising Ground*

ABOUT ATMOSPHERE PRESS

Founded in 2015, Atmosphere Press was built on the principles of Honesty, Transparency, Professionalism, Kindness, and Making Your Book Awesome. As an ethical and author-friendly hybrid press, we stay true to that founding mission today.

If you're a reader, enter our giveaway for a free book here:

SCAN TO ENTER
BOOK GIVEAWAY

If you're a writer, submit your manuscript for consideration here:

SCAN TO SUBMIT
MANUSCRIPT

And always feel free to visit Atmosphere Press and our authors online at atmospherepress.com. See you there soon!